Destroyers of the Dawn:

Book 3 of the Dawn Saga

I0537083

ZACHARIAH WAHRER

Copyright © 2018 Zachariah Wahrer

All Rights Reserved. This book or any portion thereof may not be reproduced or used in any manner whatsoever without the express written permission of the publisher except for the use of brief quotations in a book review.

Second Print Edition

Wahrer of the Worlds Publishing
www.wahreroftheworlds.com
publishing@wahreroftheworlds.com

ISBN-13: 978-0-9983827-4-6

DEDICATION

For Sarah.
Your vision inspires me. Your persistence motivates me. You fill my heart with love. Thank you for making our life (and this book) possible.

CONTENTS

01 – Crasor......1

02 – Aza......6

03 – Wake......11

04 - Felar......15

05 – Gav......22

06 – Cazz-ak-tak......26

07 - Lothis......29

08 – Tremmilly......33

09 – Maxar......37

10 – Crasor......41

11 – Aza......46

12 – Wake......49

13 – Felar......54

14 – Gav......57

15 – Cazz-ak-tak......63

16 – Lothis......68

17 – Tremmilly......72

18 – Maxar......75

19 – Crasor......81

20 – Aza......88

21 – Wake...92

22 – Felar..97

23 – Gav..102

24 – Cazz-ak-tak...108

25 – Lothis..113

26 – Tremmilly...117

27 – Maxar..123

28 – Crasor...127

29 – Aza...131

30 – Wake..135

31 – Felar...142

32 – Gav..149

33 – Cazz-ak-tak...153

34 – Lothis..158

35 – Tremmilly...164

36 – Maxar..170

37 – Crasor...173

38 – Aza...183

39 – Wake..190

40 – Felar...193

41 – Gav..197

42 – Cazz-ak-tak...203

43 – Tremmilly...207

44 – Lothis...213

45 – Maxar...215

46 – Crasor..222

47 – Aza..227

48 – Cazz-ak-tak...232

49 – Wake..236

50 – Felar..241

51 – Gav...247

52 – Cazz-ak-tak...250

53 – Lothis...252

54 – Maxar...255

55 – Tremmilly...263

About the Author...267

ACKNOWLEDGEMENTS

I'd like to say thanks to Lois Rahal, Frank Frey, Shreve Fellars, Walter Scott, Helen Brookman, Patrick Wahrer, and Megan Rahal for their continuing help with this book and the Dawn Saga as a whole. It means a lot to me that you spend time critically reading my books. Thanks for sticking with me!

Barney Rahal, thank you for your continuing patronage and support. I love working with you on annual stories. You have a creative, inspiring mind.

And I have to send my biggest thank you of all to my wife, Sarah Wahrer. I couldn't do this without you. Your thoughts and criticisms transformed this book in amazing ways.

To all my readers: Thanks for supporting me by purchasing this book and giving me reviews and feedback. I wouldn't be doing any of this without you! Our symbiotic relationship means a lot and is what keeps me writing. I hope you enjoy this book!

May the fires of the black star be quenched in your life,
Zachariah Wahrer

"As you bind with the Dawn, know you are making an invaluable contribution to the preservation of our universe, one enabling all future life."
— Aris, Empress of the Accord

"To find truth—fundamental reality—one must be willing to transcend evolutionary caste. We must push forward, delving, even if it contradicts our perception of morality."
— The Ascended Pathway of See'dek

"The Founder, our great architect of love and progress, asks us to unite despite his sudden death, to forge the future in his image."
— Exalted Head of the Ashamine Holy Order, Founder's funeral

01 – CRASOR

Crasor's mind drank in the detailed display, voraciously feeding on the information. Since he and the Breakers had captured the ASN Founder's Justice, they'd become much more powerful. Yet, his tactical mind suppressed excitement. They were still at risk. Every Breaker, except the occupying forces in the Noor, Eishon, Qi, and Taggardt systems, was here, lending their mental force to him. *We gamble with millions of our credits in one place. A big potential payout, but an equally large risk as well.*

Time passed as Crasor continued watching the display. The Ashamine Forces had sent several transmissions to the Justice when it wormed into the Psinar system. Originally they acted surprised, then puzzled, and were now defensive. *Evidently, intel of the Justice's capture hasn't made it this far yet.* The few fighters and gunships that escaped him during the Eishon battle would have made it back to the Ashamine, notifying them of the Breaker threat. *But since I killed the Founder, they are task-saturated.* Crasor's face twisted in a wicked grin, remembering what it had been like to destroy the man he once idolized. The sensation of shoving his arm into the Founder's torso, questing for his heart, had been exquisite.

A small part of him wondered how he had come so far, how he had gone from obedient servant to assassinating the supreme human leader. *What is driving my ambitions?* Crasor wondered vaguely, feeling his body grow heavy.

No, not now, he told the Breaker mind, recognizing they were drawing him away.

"We must show you something," they boomed in his mind.

But the invasion!

"Is proceeding well. Karoth has everything under control. This will not take long."

**

"Come on, Cras," Emili Trayfis said, bouncing with enthusiasm. "We don't want to miss the tube." Crasor hated being in the under-levels of the Founder's City. In all his 15 years of life, he'd never gone down this far; and now he knew why. They were dirty. The smell of piss and refuse filled his nostrils with every breath. *Why am I doing this?* Crasor wondered, feeling disgusted. He followed Emili through the tube transport entrance and sat down next to her, back straight, inwardly cringing at what he was probably sitting in.

Emili smiled, a big toothy grin that made Crasor's heart beat faster. She was his first love, the only person he'd ever felt an attachment to. The girl was an indentured servant to the Tah Ahn family, had been for the past few months. When Crasor first saw her, something he didn't know existed bloomed within, causing him to do things he'd never expected. *Like going to this stupid party.*

"I'm so charged to see The Black Fire," she said, breaking into his thoughts. "I really hope they play Ascension. That song has the best drop ever!"

Crasor couldn't think of a response, so he just nodded and smiled. Music wasn't really something his parents did, so consequently, he'd had little exposure to it.

Emili kept talking about the Electro-Narco Party, which stims they would take for each act, and how much fun they were going to have. Crasor couldn't pay attention, though. Every second, he kept expecting one of the grungy passengers to attack or rob them. Crasor's clothes were likely worth more than any of these people made in a lifetime. Even Emili, a servant, dressed exponentially better.

Thankfully, everyone kept to themselves and Crasor and Emili arrived at their destination without incident. Crasor felt an ache in his hand and realized he'd had a death grip on the small flechette pistol in his pocket. *Calm down. If something does happen, you know how to handle yourself.*

"Is something wrong?" Emili asked, concern etched on her face.

"Uhhh," Crasor said, taking his hand from his pocket. "No. I'm fine."

"OK, good." She pulled out a small portable terminal and checked it. Crasor winced, looking around to see if anyone would notice and try to snatch it from her. "I think Electro is still a few k's from here. It's about to start. We need to hurry."

Emili grabbed his hand and began fast-walking out of the tube station. Crasor still didn't understand why he loved the girl so much or why he let her take him to these crazy places. Her appetite for exploration was insatiable.

"Can't we just take a ground transport?" Crasor asked.

"Sure, but that's a good way to get taken for ransom," Emili replied. He hadn't thought of that, and it upset him she had a better grasp of the situation than he did.

The pedestrian paths in this part of the under-city were wide and relatively well lit, which relieved Crasor. They allowed him to avoid the worst of the garbage and puddles of questionable liquids. Looking up was disconcerting. Instead of structures and the blue sky of Ashamine-2, there was only a ceiling. It hung high above, but was just a flat black surface, devoid of even an attempt at disguise or beauty.

When they'd covered half the distance to the festival, Crasor started to hear the rumble of bass. Emili tugged at his hand and began to jog. For a moment, he considered letting her go, but he didn't want to ruin this for her. Grumbling inwardly, he quickened his stride to keep pace.

Rounding a tall tenement building, they got their first view of the Electro-Narco Party. It was huge, spanning a space that multiple housing units would normally occupy. Crasor almost turned around, love of Emili or no. There were too many lights, sounds, and crowds for him to cope with. He looked into Emili's eyes, and his love was enough to override the revulsion. *Besides, maybe after tonight, she'll do me.* A smile crossed Crasor's face, and Emili returned it enthusiastically.

They passed through the entrance scanners. Crasor breathed easier when he confirmed his pistol was as undetectable as the dealer said it would be. There was no way in the fires of the dark star he would go into this situation without having a way to protect himself.

Emili found the tent for one of the musicians she was excited about, an artificial intelligence called Tym-Panic, and they went inside. Crasor stiffened as they plowed into the mass of people. The crowd jostled and bounced him around. He grasped Emili's hand tightly, trying to stay with her. Somehow, she easily wound her way through the dense mass, calm and at ease.

Emili stopped in a less congested space, pulling two bright green pills out of her jacket pocket. "Take this," she yelled into his ear, swallowing the other quickly. Crasor took the small sphere and stared into its acid green depths.

Just do it, part of him said. Still, he hesitated. Moments passed as he looked at the pill. The lights flashed, bass thumped, and the crowd gyrated. Emili said nothing, just smiled and waited. Finally, he popped the sphere in his mouth and swallowed.

For several moments, nothing happened. He still felt agitated by the crowd. Tym-Panic's music was awful, a jumble of screeches, beeps, whoops, and sub-sonic thuds. A weight settled on Crasor's shoulders and he looked around, wondering what was happening. The lights changed, seeming to synchronize in a pattern connected to the flow of the universe. The music made sense, entered his mind, coalescing into shapes that bound his heart and soul.

When he looked at Emili, Crasor gasped. She was the most beautiful thing he'd ever seen, entangled with the patterns of light and sound. He felt himself spiraling out, connecting to everyone around him. It was an exhilarating feeling; joyous, yet tinged with fear. The universe bound itself together, forming a colossal structure that dwarfed him. A deep tendency within Crasor revolted against the loss of control, screamed he had made the wrong choice. Then, his logic faded and Crasor lost himself in the lights, music, and most of all, Emili.

His sense of time disappeared, and he was content to follow Emili from tent to tent, taking a new pill at each. Orange, purple, blue, and another green. The festival lasted days, seconds, eternity, an instant. Nothing but sights, sounds, and sensations mattered anymore.

As they entered the tent of one of the human musicians, Crasor felt something shift. The music was different here, subtle, sensual. Emili gave him a purple pill, which he swallowed without thinking.

Flashes of passion followed: kisses, caresses, desperate need. "This is my first time," Crasor said in Emili's ear. She laughed, and he felt a similar sound come from his own throat.

"What are your orders, sir?"

Crasor felt confused. He opened his eyes, realizing where he was.

"Sir, we are nearing the effective range of the Ashamine ships," Karoth stated. "Have you decided our course of action?"

"Yes," he replied, struggling to clear fog from his mind. "Contact all enemy ships. Tell them if they don't completely power down, we will obliterate them. Once they comply, send the Descended-led boarding parties to convert or kill the inhabitants. I leave priorities and tactical maneuvers to you, Karoth."

The enemy fleet was large, but the Breakers controlled a Tarton class ship, as well as one of the best tactical minds in the Ashamine Forces. Karoth was an excellent commander, and with his conversion to Breaker, Crasor trusted his obedience. The former Ashamine Ascended began barking orders, and techs instantly followed them. Crasor sat back and focused on the large tactical display. He relished the power and control the Breakers had given him. It was what he'd been searching for, both knowingly and unknowingly, for his entire 33 standard years. His Descended, Karoth, and every single Breaker in the ships and occupying forces: all were obedient and under Crasor's control.

He tried to shut thoughts of Emili out of his mind. The Breakers were silent, not giving any follow-up or explanation of why they had immersed him in that particular memory. Something felt off about the recollection, but he couldn't explain what it was. The Party had been an incredible experience of sensations, yet now it felt faded, darker somehow. *Maybe that is because of the way things ended with Emili.* Crasor couldn't tell if it was his own thought or something insinuated by the Breakers.

Why does any of this matter? Crasor growled at himself. *It is history long passed. I don't want to think about it, don't need the distraction.* He expected a reply from the Breakers, an answer as to why they had brought it up. Their silence felt ominous.

Returning his attention to the surrounding room, Crasor forced everything but the Psinar invasion out of his mind. *Back to work.*

02 – AZA

"So," Professor Wulkland continued, "even though the masses use the term dark star as profanity, you can understand why it is a serious matter. Being damned to burn for infinity is not something to scoff at."

Aza took notes in her portable terminal, breathing in the professor's words. At only 13, this class was advanced for her, but she was doing well and had received high scores on all evaluations.

"Sister Kissawai," Wulkland prompted, making Aza wince. She didn't like it when people used her last name. "Who are those that inhabit the fires of the dark star?"

Easy, she thought. *Why does he still think I am not old enough?* "It is for those who forsake the Ashamine, who turn their backs on the Founder." Aza felt a stab of pain at the thought of the dead leader. It had been less than a week since his assassination. She had to fight hard not to start crying.

"Correct," Wulkland replied, his droopy face giving away no emotion. He turned, walking towards the front of the room. "Tonight, I want you all to meditate on the dark star, to imagine its black fire, writhing bodies, and screams of torment. For those who aspire to lead the Holy Ashamine Order, it would be well to remember there is a hotter, darker area reserved for those who deviate from the faith."

Aza took a few additional notes as Professor Wulkland made the sign of the Ashamine, left palm covering the top of his upraised right fist, and dismissed them. When she walked out into the corridor, the floor-to-ceiling windows overlooking the Founder's City almost took her breath away. Air transports sped to and from the Holy Order tower and the other surrounding colossal structures. The scale was so immense Aza had a hard time comprehending it. She paused for a moment, taking in the majesty of the view.

Being above the clouds of smog that veiled the lower city was still a novel experience. Each year, as a student advanced their studies, they also moved up in the tower. Only those high in the order had permission to enter its pinnacle. *Perhaps someday that will be me,* she thought, resuming her walk towards the next class.

Thinking about higher levels brought Aza's parents to mind. As ascended level administrators, they oversaw several new colony worlds. It wasn't as prestigious as an Ashamine-2 position, or even one of the other primary worlds such as Kii-la-ta or Exis-7, but it did afford them a comfortable, rewarding life.

"Wulkland is so boring," one of the older girls said to her friend. Aza mentally agreed, then immediately felt guilty.

"Does anyone actually believe in the dark star?" the friend replied.

"You mean you don't?" Aza blurted before she realized what she was doing.

One of the older girls snorted, and the other laughed. "When you get older, Kissawai, you'll see." Aza tensed, both from the use of her last name and the attention she was getting. "Kissawai, Kissawai, Kissawai. Do you actually do it?"

"Do what?" Aza replied, wanting to get away from this conversation, but knowing she couldn't. Both girls were in her next class.

"Kiss a way?"

Aza shook her head, feeling her cheeks redden.

"You're embarrassing her," the other girl said with a laugh. "The little kid is blushing."

"You know if you kiss boys you'll go to the dark star," the first said, a malicious smile on her face. "You'll burn forever, all for one little kiss. Not that any boy would ever want to kiss you, with such a plain face and stringy body."

Putting her head down, Aza walked faster, trying to reach the relative safety of the classroom. Both girls laughed at her retreat, a cackling sound Aza despised. *Forgive,* she thought, everything within her rebelling against the commandment.

The comments about her appearance dug at Aza. Somehow, the meanest girls always knew her weak spots. She normally didn't take much notice of the way she looked, but recently, her parents had noted she was going through a growth spurt. She had been self-conscious ever since. *At least my eyes are pretty.* Aza loved their deep green color, and how they sparkled, although she felt guilty admitting it.

Kissawai, she thought, replaying the way the girls mocked her. *Why couldn't they have changed our last name?* Kissawai was a unique surname within the Ashamine, and especially so within the Holy Order. As Aza had learned, being different was not a good thing. It was hard enough with her darker skin. Add to that an old, unpopular surname, and she felt like everything about her stood out. Her parents said it was a proud name, one with a millennia full of history, but Aza didn't care.

If only the Order had some rule about surnames. If it did, her parents would have switched for sure. They were devout, lifelong servants of the Ashamine faith, and despite their love of an odd last name, Aza wanted to be just like them.

How can you worry about a surname when the Ashamine is in such a state? A twinge of guilt pierced her gut, and Aza tried to refocus. *With the Founder assassinated and the Successor kidnapped or executed, how will we survive?* Despair threatened to overwhelm her. *The Classad will handle everything, just as they have done for the past week.*

Things were tough: for Aza, her family, and the entire Ashamine. For the first time in its thousand years of existence, it was without a Founder. Every day, additional bits of terrible news came out. It felt like the entire empire might collapse at any moment.

First, an unknown force had kidnapped the Founder's son and only heir, Lothis. Then Haak-ah-tar primary had gone supernova and destroyed millions of citizens. The Enthos had obliterated the Hammer, one of the Tarton class battle cruisers the Ashamine worked so hard to create. All this struck new fear into everyone.

The greatest blow of all had come next: the assassination of the Founder. The Internal Security forces rounded up several suspects, but none had been the person who'd killed their beloved leader. Aza bit her lip and calmed her breathing. *The Ashamine will survive, we always have.*

Aza thought back to the millennium of existence the Ashamine had faced, to what she'd learned in the class before Wulkland's. The stories of the first Founder overthrowing the corrupt Thousand Stars regime were magnificent. How the leaders of that administration had managed to sabotage the newly formed Ashamine government, even from their graves, astonished Aza. More exciting was how the successive Founders had fought back from the brink of human extinction, all culminating in the Entho war that was restoring humanity to its rightful position in the Akked. *But now we have lost our finest leader, the one who built the mightiest ships anyone has ever seen. Who will take us forward to the next glorious step of humanity?*

Walking into the next class, Aza felt conflicting emotions. It was a course about current events and their impact on the Order. It often gave her a positive perspective on the future, but lately it just seemed to magnify the hopelessness everyone felt. Today, the brightness of the room felt harsh, rather than cheery, and the even rows of plasti-glass desks felt too orderly. She sat in her assigned place, grateful the older girls she'd walked with sat in front of her. As they came in, neither looked in her direction. *Good,* she sighed.

"Have any of you heard about the ASN Founder's Justice?" the professor said, jumping directly in without introduction, the way she always did.

Everyone was silent. A few shook their heads. Aza felt her stomach clench.

"No one? Did I not assign you to watch the evening briefing?" She had, but Aza, bogged down in other assignments, had missed it. "Fine," the professor sighed, "we will waste valuable time going over what you should already know."

The professor walked up to the large terminal screen at the front of the room and selected several options. A vid of the previous night's briefing began to play.

"The Ashamine Forces released news that an enemy power has captured the Founder's Justice," an off-screen voice said, as video of a huge ship played. It was a massive vessel, capable of carrying hundreds of fighters and gunships. The ship, similar to the Hammer, had taken the Ashamine years to construct, consuming the valuable resources mined on captured Entho worlds.

"AF Command doesn't know who the perpetrators are, but based on the stories of escaped survivors, it appears to be some type of pirate organization. When we asked if this is connected to the death of the Founder or the kidnapping of Lothis, AF Command said they didn't believe so. Please be aware the following video contains scenes of violence."

A shaky scene replaced the hulking ship. Aza saw fire, chaos, and destruction. Screams and wails sounded in the background. "I'm here in the capital city of the Psinar system, which is being bombarded by Ashamine ships. The Founder's Justice is orbiting us. They have ordered we surrender and prepare for processing. We told them we are Ashamine citizens and demanded they treat us as such." An Ashamine atmospheric fighter screamed across the sky, and everyone in the video dove for cover. Explosions boomed all around, then the video cut off.

"So," the professor said, somber, "what are we to make of this situation?"

Silence, broken only by the sounds of sniffles and muffled sobs.

"Yes, it is sad," she continued, "but there is more to it."

Aza wanted to answer, but she felt overwhelmed.

The professor waited several moments longer, and when it became clear no one would speak, she sighed. "Look at the death, pain, and grief. This is what our order must always do. We comfort and mend. We promote unity and healing. The Psinar system is under attack. A massive ship orbits them, raining death from above. Pirates are killing Ashamine citizens."

Aza felt something tug at the edge of her mind. *They can't just be pirates,* she thought. Even the luckiest, most determined pirates couldn't do these things. *The kidnapping, the assassination, and the capture of our most powerful ship all happen one after the other. How could those events not be connected?* Aza didn't understand why everyone was just accepting the story. It didn't make sense. *What if the descendants of the Thousand Stars are striking back somehow?* She raised her hand.

"It is not for the Holy Order to decide how to handle the political and military implications of the fall of Psinar," the professor continued. "We must focus all our energy on lightening the spiritual load on our people, to help them through these dark times. We must cast off everything that hinders us, be it logic or emotion, and provide the comfort our people need."

Aza lowered her hand, realizing her question would not go unpunished. She felt tense, everything inside her revolting against ignoring her feelings. *Someone is lying,* she thought, the knowledge simultaneously thrilling and scaring her.

Guilt churned Aza's stomach as thoughts of going against her professor's words surged through her mind. Yet, something was pulling at her, insisting she delve deeper. *I want to discover what is really going on.*

03 – WAKE

Closing the door, Wake stepped back to look at his work. He chuckled. It was probably the most rustic and rudimentary thing he'd ever built, but he was proud all the same. Constructing dwellings on a primitive planet without an Ashamine colonization support module was challenging. Thankfully, this location on Lith-elo-hi-rosh was temperate and needed no insulation.

Walking towards the Death Watch, he shook his head. They'd been hiding on this Entho-la-ah-mine world for over a month now, and the events of Eishon were beginning to seem like a dream. Seeing the Watch, the huge Ashamine gunship they'd captured while fleeing the Breakers, brought up vivid memories of battle, loss, and death. *Safety is an illusion, and if we remain here, the Breakers will eventually find us.*

Since they'd first arrived on Lith-elo, the Harbingers, an arcane name Felar had discovered for their group, hadn't left. None of them had found a reason to leave. As time passed, Wake felt more and more secure the scheme he'd devised to keep the Breakers off their worm trail had worked. *Don't let your guard down.*

The Entho-la-ah-mine dwellings in the underground city were not comfortable for humans, so they'd lived on the Death Watch for a week post-arrival. *Besides, we'd have needed Entho-la-ah-mine assistance every time we wanted to leave the canyon and come to the surface.*

It was a big ship, but eventually, they'd decided it would be nice to have more private, livable quarters. As the only person with building experience, Wake had volunteered to create dwellings. Now that he'd finished the communal meeting area, the project was complete. No one seemed to mind it had taken him almost a month. Since Wake wouldn't need to scavenge any more materials from the Watch, Maxar was free to depart whenever he finally decided to implement his plan.

With all the time he and Tremmilly spend together, I don't think he minded me delaying his mission. Maxar even seemed to work slower than usual when he helped Wake on the building project. One day it had taken him hours to strip a couple non-critical panels out of the Watch. Wake had been working in the next room, trying not to listen to he and Tremmilly's conversation and laughter. Besides, Wake was in no hurry himself. Being out of imminent danger for a while felt good.

Ducking past the Watch's main hatch brought up mixed emotions for Wake; fear intermingled with comfort and familiarity. They'd nearly died in the ship several times. The first had been when the Justice and its fleet of fighters had chased them through the Eishon system, launching barrages of rail rounds. After they'd escaped, the Watch's worm generator had malfunctioned, trapping them inside a tunnel between dimensions. It was a situation no human or Entho-la-ah-mine had ever escaped from before. When they'd fixed the drive and returned to normal space, the Justice had located them once again, chasing them from one system to the next. It had taken some clever engineering on Lothis and Wake's part to finally escape the monstrous Breaker vessel.

Wake moved through the cannon loading compartment and into the crew quarters. Since they'd transferred to the dwellings, he'd relocated most of the bedding and interior structure there. Recently, the Harbingers had used this drab space mostly as a hang out and meeting area, although now they'd probably abandon it for the finished communal meeting building. *The Watch is a better place to get away from the heat of midday, though.* That was the only real positive aspect. *Even with the bright lights, it still feels like a cave. The designers really should have put in port windows or screens.*

"Hello, Wake," Tremmilly said, a warm smile on her face. She'd seated herself along one wall with Beowulf and Maxar. Wake often speculated Tremmilly suffered most from the events on Eishon. The Breakers obliterated her home-world, and vivid, recurring nightmares stalked her sleep. Before moving out of the Watch, she'd woken them all with her screams. When they'd finished the first dwelling, everyone decided it should be for Tremmilly. No one was surprised when she asked Maxar to move in a few nights later.

"Hey guys," Wake replied, nodding to the trio. Neither Tremmilly nor Maxar talked about their relationship openly, but that was fine with him. *It's not something I need to know about anyway.* As long as his friends were happy, he was happy. "I just completed the final details on the communal space," he continued, raising his voice so Jaydon and Felar could hear him. They were across the compartment, talking to each another.

"Well then, I suppose we can begin planning our mission in earnest," Maxar replied, sounding conflicted.

Wake knew his friend was a warrior, that waiting and inaction were hard for him. But leaving Lith-elo means leaving Tremmilly.

"Have you decided if you are coming or not?" Maxar asked.

Earlier, he had made it clear he wanted Wake's help, but Wake himself was unsure if he would be useful or not. He'd spent much of the past week trying to convince himself one way or the other. *I'm not a soldier, I'm a builder,* one voice would say. *But you've gotten instruction from Felar and Maxar, and you have a weaponized, armored environmental suit. You trust Maxar and he thinks you would be useful. Besides, you are the only one that has direct knowledge of the planet and system.*

"I'm in," Wake replied, stating the decision he'd finally come to that morning. *Whatever I am, Maxar's journey is based in the physical reality I understand, whereas Tremmilly's, Lothis', and Cazz-ak's is one of the mind. With the dwellings finished, I will be of little assistance here.*

"Good, glad to hear it," Maxar said, pale blue eyes shining. Tremmilly nodded and smiled as well. "I'd love to have Tremmilly and Felar along. Blightheart, I'd love to have everyone, but I understand why they are staying." Traveling to the Traynos system would be dangerous, especially since they had no knowledge if the Breakers were there yet. And even if they weren't, the Harbingers didn't know how much security the Ashamine had in place.

Initially, Wake had argued against the plan. Everyone had. They agreed it was just too risky. Maxar persisted, convincing them he needed to discover more about the nano-machines inside him, that he could learn what he was capable of. "And if I'm more powerful, we're all more powerful." In the end, no one could question his tactical judgment. Maxar had then asked if Jaydon and Wake would join him. Jaydon immediately agreed. Not too long ago, Wake would have seen the older man as a liability rather than an asset, but he'd been sober the entire time they'd been on Lith-elo. He was looking stronger and healthier as each day went by, and Wake was happy for the change. The old captain had even made it to every combat course Felar instructed, and was now a better marksman than Wake. *Not that I'm the best shot anyway,* Wake laughed to himself.

Despite Jaydon and Maxar's skills, Wake still felt nervous about going back to Traynos-6. It was where the bridge he'd built collapsed, killing several miners. *Sabotaged by the Ashamine, who set me up to take the blame.* They would be going to look for the secret discovery killing the miners was meant to protect. *Hopefully they haven't moved it all off world yet.*

The fact Felar wasn't going on the mission worried him as well. It would be nice to have another skilled fighter along, especially one of Felar's caliber, but Wake understood why she needed to stay on Lith-elo.

Lothis and Cazz-ak need her support and guidance.

Just as he was thinking about them, the boy and the Entho-la-ah-mine entered the meeting space. Wake sighed, knowing this was probably the last time they would all be together for quite a while.

04 - FELAR

Watching Lothis and Cazz-ak enter, Felar felt her heart break and lift simultaneously. It was good seeing the orange-eyed boy, but he looked weary. Lothis spent so much time with the Entho-la-ah-mines now. Since his encounter with the Arche, he'd become more quiet and distant. They had taken away his ability to sense the signals, and this had broken her brave, yet fragile boy.

All the genetic manipulation Director Kasol had done, coupled with the fact he was a clone of the original Founder, made him unique and special. *And he is also a Harbinger,* she thought, her heart breaking from the pressure being put on him at such a young age. Felar, not good with children, didn't know how to help him. She tried her best, but feared there was nothing she could do for him now. *If only I had more insight into the signals and dimensions Lothis and Cazz-ak are always talking about.*

The boy had been growing and progressing in ways that made Felar proud, until he had gone to confront the Arche. *Why did we let him go alone? Why didn't Cazz-ak stop him?* She couldn't blame the Entho-la-ah-mine too much, as none of them had understood the Arche's true intentions or power until they'd attacked Lothis. They'd tried to delete him, attempting to strip Lothis down to the essence of his power so they could assimilate it. Thankfully, Cazz-ak had tracked Lothis to the Arche's mainframe and rescued him before they could complete the task. Still, they'd caused significant damage to the boy. *And for that, I will eradicate them.*

"And you don't remember anything else from the data square?" Jaydon asked, breaking into Felar's thoughts.

"The files I transferred while on Haak-ah-tar were limited. What I got was mainly about Lothis. I had no idea intel about Traynos-6 would be useful later." She'd already briefed Maxar and Jaydon in detail about what she knew, but the captain was understandably nervous and this was his way of expressing it. "The T6 discovery was some kind of ancient technology," she explained. "They transferred the development of it to Haak-ah-tar, then began testing on Bloodsport. The blighthearted Ashamine didn't understand it very well, and were in a rush to implement it. That's why they infected Maxar with the T6 nanites when they had so little information."

Jaydon nodded. "Thanks for briefing us. Hopefully we can get on-world and Maxar will learn more about where his nanites came from, and what they can do."

"I know I was against this plan originally, but I empathize with him wanting to understand himself. It is the same thing I'm trying to discover as a Harbinger."

"And you're sure you don't want to come with us?" Jaydon said. "We could definitely use your expertise. And there might be Harbinger intel there. Blightheart, the discovery itself might be Harbinger tech."

"I have plans of my own that need work. And besides, I can't leave Lothis right now. He is not in a state to join the mission. It would be far too dangerous for him without his connection to the signals." She thought about adding he was just a child, but didn't, knowing that was only partially true.

"That's what I figured."

"Besides, you and Wake are both much better marksmen and fighters than you once were. I believe you three can handle the situation, otherwise I would continue objecting to the mission."

With nothing left to say, Felar and Jaydon gathered in the center of the former crew quarters with the rest of the group. When they had all settled in, silence fell over the room. *For being a mystical, super-connected group, we sure can be a blightheartedly awkward bunch.*

If she hadn't discovered the name Harbingers herself, Felar would have been more skeptical. Something felt special about it, something that tied deep into her being. Felar wished she could help Tremmilly with her attempts to learn more about their shared past, but much like Lothis' problem, it wasn't something she understood. *Maybe in time that will come to me.*

Moments passed, and Felar couldn't take the silence any longer. "OK, fine. I'll start, Founder be damned." She paused for a moment, shifting her thoughts to a more productive line. "With the completion of all surface dwellings," Felar continued, using her mission briefing voice, "we no longer require Wake or the Death Watch to stay on Lith-elo. Maxar, I think your mission to Traynos has the go-ahead, unless anyone objects."

Tremmilly looked like she was holding back tears, but said nothing. Felar gazed at the rest of those gathered. *I have more friends now than the rest of my previous life in the Ashamine combined.*

"I'm going along," Wake interjected. "Maxar and Jaydon need someone to protect them." Felar chuckled, as did the rest of the group. Even Tremmilly smiled.

We worked so hard to come together, Felar thought. And we fought for each other against the Breakers and Ashamine. Now, we are splitting up. It seemed wrong, but they'd already had endless discussions about what to do. Cazz-ak, Lothis, Tremmilly, and I all have things here we need to work on, and we can't expect Maxar and his group to stay and do nothing. The Breakers will find us. We all to need to get ready in our own ways.

Traynos-6 held a component of that readiness, and Maxar's plan was solid. She wanted to go along, wanted a fight that would distract her from the anxiety she felt about Lothis. *But I can't leave him, not now. I could never forgive myself.*

"I think it is best to depart the day after tomorrow," Maxar said, his earlier mirth gone. "We don't need much to get ready and make preparations. Any time after that just means a greater chance the Breakers will get to Traynos before us, assuming they aren't already there." He paused for a moment, looking down at Tremmilly, a tenderness in his eyes Felar didn't know he was capable of. "I think we all needed some downtime, but now we need to get back to work." Tremmilly laid her head on his shoulder and closed her eyes.

"Alright," Felar resumed, "then the day after tomorrow it is. In addition to Maxar's mission, I called this gathering because I wanted to give a status report, as well as get updates from you all. We need to stay connected and be thinking of ways to help each other. Anyone care to start?" Tremmilly was still resting on Maxar, eyes closed, so Felar looked to Cazz-ak and Lothis.

"Yes," the Entho-la-ah-mine replied, "we have an update." Felar had become used to their method of direct mental communication, although the oddity of it still struck her at times. "We might be growing closer to restoring Lothis' mental link to space-time. Since we recently changed tactics, it is hard to say for sure." Reading Entho-la-ah-mine body language was difficult, but between his mental voice and his stance, Felar thought Cazz-ak was optimistic.

"As you know," Lothis said, transitioning into the conversation, "when the Arche tried to erase me, Cazz-ak brought back the parts the Arche had removed. With the Queen's help, they restored the pieces. Between them, they were able to fix everything, except for my space-time mental link. Originally, we attempted to find the component that was missing or changed, for what was causing the disconnection. Unfortunately, this did not work." Lothis paused, taking a deep breath and blinking slowly.

Despite his attempt at normality, Felar could tell the boy was still depleted from his encounter with the Arche. His face was worn, his focus less sharp. She'd tried to help him slow down, to spend more time resting, but he wouldn't listen. He kept insisting he was fine, that the only thing impacting him was the disconnection. *How does he know there isn't something else wrong, something that might heal if he wasn't pushing so hard?*

"I have dreams now," Lothis continued, "which is an event I never experienced previously. While dreaming, I restore the connection."

"Wait," Jaydon interjected. "You mean you dream of having a restored connection, right? Not that the connection is actually restored?"

Felar felt a dagger of pain jab her. Lothis' dreaming was a revelation, one he hadn't shared with her until now. Despite everything they did together on Lith-elo, Felar missed the closeness they shared when it had just been the two of them.

Knowing the time Lothis spent with the Entho-la-ah-mines was for his own good, she pushed down the jealousy she felt towards Cazz-ak. *But still, Lothis could have told me sooner.* A realization struck Felar, bringing guilt with it. *I have let my other responsibilities get in the way of our relationship,* she thought. *I need to try harder to reach him. And perhaps I could ask Cazz-ak for ways to help, since everything I've tried so far has had little impact. Maybe he could explain why Lothis is so tired.*

"No, I meant what I said, as I said it," Lothis answered, voice flat. "The connection is restored while dreaming. I can sense the world around me as before, can interact with it. Everything feels right, until I wake up. Then it is back to disconnect."

"Interesting," Jaydon said, brow furrowed.

"This is what originally gave us hope that perhaps some part of me was returned incorrectly, that we could find and fix it. That proved to be a dead end. So now, Cazz-ak has a new plan." Despite her heartache, Felar felt immensely proud of Lothis. He had come so far from when she'd rescued him from Haak-ah-tar. Not only had his assistance saved them when they'd fled the Founder's Justice, but he had learned to communicate and open up, at least occasionally. *Not that long ago, he couldn't speak to a group, much less tell personal details.*

"Back when we were trying to get through the Ashamine blockade of Eishon," Cazz-ak said, "the Queen and I attempted to show Lothis how to connect to the Great Thought so he might lend us his power. At that time we were unsuccessful. Now, we have returned to this idea. If Lothis can establish a link to our hive mind, we believe it will restore his connection to space-time."

"We compared my original ability to that of the Entho-la-ah-mines," Lothis said, "and it does seem similar, although not exact. I am fine with this, as I have hoped for this connection to Cazz-ak for quite some time. Although we are optimistic about the possibility, it is far from a sure thing I will actually commune with the Great Thought.

"Entho-la-ah-mines pass this connection on to their offspring," Lothis continued, "but queens must be taken to the Crystal Chamber under Haak-ah-tar to have their special abilities imbued in them. If Haak-ah-tar hadn't been destroyed by the supernova, I could have gone there and seen its effect on me. Since that is impossible, I must use another method. It involves directly connecting to the Great Thought through dimensional folds. Cazz-ak is a great instructor, but I have much to learn and explore, and as we all know, the Breakers could arrive any day. I admit this is a difficult task." Lothis made eye contact with Felar and smiled weakly. Her bad feelings washed away in a flood of optimism.

"I know you can do it," Felar said, once she was sure she wasn't going to cry. She leaned over, giving him a tight hug. It took all her effort to break the embrace, but she didn't want to make Lothis feel awkward. Tremmilly was sitting up, looking alert and ready to speak. "Have you found anything further about our past, Tremmilly?"

"Well," she replied, looking introspective, "I guess I'm not sure. I've spent some time meditating about my Harbinger memory, trying to pick out more details or clues. As time has passed, it has begun to feel more like a dream," this she said while looking at Lothis, "and I sometimes wonder if the memory was real."

"It's real," Maxar said. "When you told us, we all had a connection to it. I know I was with you when you gave the speech about giving up our true forms to become human and Entho-la-ah-mine. I agreed it was the only way to stop the Breakers. Even if the memory fades, our connection to each other proves it wasn't a dream."

Felar agreed, but said nothing.

"Yes," Tremmilly replied with a hint of exasperation, "I know it was real. My lack of progress has just been frustrating. Everyone is moving forward, making strides, and I have very little to show for my time. Thankfully, the Queen gives me help when she is available. A few of the Entho-la-ah-mine philosophers have been helpful, although I think they have as much to learn about me as I do about discovering our past."

She paused for a moment, thinking. "Lothis told me everything the Arche said to him. They want our power for themselves, but I don't understand what power they are referring to. Obviously, some of us are special, at least by human and Entho-la-ah-mine standards. But is that really enough to make a difference to the Arche, to give them motivation to attack us?

"I've spent a lot of time thinking about this. When you add that the Arche said something went wrong when we transferred over to our present forms, it starts making sense. We don't remember ourselves the way we thought we would, don't remember how to connect or tap into our previous power."

"But how do we know what went wrong wasn't losing our power altogether?" Felar asked.

"Good question," Tremmilly replied brightly. "They said they didn't know what exactly went wrong. They also mentioned we'd given up our power. The fact they attacked us shows they believed our power was still part of us, even if we don't currently know how to access it."

Felar felt puzzled. It seemed Tremmilly was contradicting herself, but she didn't want to point that out. Her friend was trying really hard and her excitement had grown as she explained further.

"Yes, I know what I just said sounds contradictory," Tremmilly said, looking directly at her. Felar felt a twinge of guilt and wondered if she had somehow read her thoughts. "But it's not, I promise. I think the Arche are only partially right. It is vague, but in my memory of our Harbinger meeting, I said we would be trapped in this space-time and would be weakened. Not that we would give up our power completely." The whole situation was very confusing to Felar and she often wondered if the Harbinger connection even mattered.

"Logically, that all seems to fit, when you explain it like that," Wake said, rubbing his cheek.

"I know it feels like a lot of guesses and deductions," Tremmilly continued, "but it feels right to me. And if there is one thing I'm learning to trust, it's my intuition. I'm going to continue working, to keep exploring our past in any way I can. We are finally reaching a point where the Entho-la-ah-mine philosophers understand me enough to help with the search. I will be meditating and talking with them as often as possible. I've also considered seeing what Entho-la-ah-mine hallucinogens might stir up in my mind, but that is much riskier. For now, I think meditation, introspection, and trying to learn from the Great Thought is the best possible plan. If we can discover more, perhaps we will find a way to restore ourselves and gain power, or at least understanding."

Felar couldn't disagree with that, and if it had a chance of giving them an advantage, it was worth the effort. Besides, Tremmilly really enjoyed the work.

"Alright. Well, I'm excited to hear what you find out," Felar said. When it was obvious Tremmilly had nothing more to say, Felar continued, ready to give her own briefing. "The Queen has given her permission for Cazz-ak and I's plan to create an Entho-la-ah-mine military force. It won't be as large as I'd hoped, but we all feel it can be strong and effective." Felar paused, waiting for Cazz-ak.

"Indeed," he said. "While Na-ah-co, as queen, is the sovereign leader of the Entho-la-ah-mines, tradition and history play a large role in the decision-making process. She must consult many philosophers, scientists, and councilors. This is why the force will be smaller than we originally proposed. There is fear in the Great Thought that if too many of us begin using what is seen as negative emotions, we might corrupt our people. They appreciate what I have been able to do, but it is a change, and while we are adaptable, this is a major departure from the entire history of my species.

"I will be dividing my time between advising the Queen, assisting Lothis in his journey to the Great Thought, and with building this new army. I'll do my best to function in all these positions, and hopefully it won't feel as if I am neglecting any of them."

Felar nodded, confident Cazz-ak would do a good job. She wouldn't have proposed the idea otherwise. "My position will be to manage the structure and training of our force, while Cazz-ak will be teaching them how to use the Great Thought offensively. We've had an overwhelming number of volunteers. It will take some time for us to select our recruits, since the Queen has not permitted us to accept them all. I'll also be meeting with Entho-la-ah-mine scientists to advise them on the development of new weaponry and strategy."

Even if it was an entirely different species, Felar felt excited to begin working with the Entho-la-ah-mine recruits. Training her human friends in weapons and tactics was rewarding, but she missed the discipline of an organized, formal unit. "We may be small in numbers, but given the way you tore apart the Founder's Hammer, I think we stand a good chance of being able to start defending against the Ashamine and the Breakers."

05 – GAV

"You'll do as I say," Gav Serrith growled, "or you'll suffer. This is your last warning."

"First you kidnap me, do a bunch of weird experiments, and now you want me to work for you? You can blightheart yourself in the fires of the dark star!" On his interface screen, Gav watched the man pace back and forth across his cell, arms gesticulating wildly. "You can't do this! Do you know who I am? I'm Fade Alenthos, of *the* Alenthos family. Know who they are, bugger? When they find out what you've done, you'll suffer."

Gav said nothing in reply, just selected some options on his screen. He waited a moment, relishing the anticipation of what was about to happen.

"What in the dark star was that?" Fade had stopped, head cocked, listening. Several moments passed. "You think you can scare me?"

Gav laughed, a low rumbling sound that emanated from deep within his enormous frame. *Yes, I think I can do just that.*

On the screen, a large insect skittered into view, phasing through the far wall. Fade noticed it, and jumped back, screaming. The bug was black, melting and reforming into horrible, unnatural shapes. It dripped, smoked, and mutated its way through several horrid forms, advancing all the while.

Fade backed away, hands up in defense. "Stop! Stop! Can't we talk about this?"

Not good enough, Gav thought, eyes still focused on the man. *I give what I promise.*

Without warning, the insect leapt, flowing through the air as a twisting shape full of sharp edges and angles. It hit Fade square in the chest, burrowing into him. He screamed, the sound rising, gaining intensity and pitch as seconds passed.

"No! Stop! I'll do it. I'll do whatever you want." More screams. "Make it stop!"

Gav waited, watching the AI insect burrow deeper and deeper. Finally, he selected an option and the black bug evaporated. Time passed, and Gav remained silent, knowing it would take time for Fade to reconstruct himself.

"That was the smallest, most gentle of my AIs," Gav transmitted, a smile creasing his smooth face. "Do you want to see one of the nasty ones?"

"No, no, I'll do whatever—whatever you want." He'd broken the man. *And so much easier than the previous subjects.*

"Good. It will be better for you if you stick to that commitment. You might even enjoy the work." Gav thought for a moment, gray eyes squinting. He was running out of time to complete this project, and if he failed, he would default on his loans and lose his reputation. *Fade has to be the one, has to work.*

"Whoever and whatever you were, it's gone now," he continued, voice cold. "You're a quantum human. You belong to me. Do the work, when I tell you, as quickly as you can. Understand?"

"What? What's a quantum human?" Fade rose to his feet, eyes wide.

"Think about it. You're smart. If you're quick and efficient with the workload, I will reward you." Gav changed screens on the quantum human interface, issuing commands that would get his new laborer started.

A good beginning, Gav thought optimistically, lining up data sets in Fade's work queue. He felt comfortable using intimidation, fear, and force to get his way. Exis-7 was a tough place, and Gav wouldn't have gotten his own Family if he wasn't willing to use hard tactics. The Serrith clan was small, numbering less than fifty, but they were the fastest growing of all the Families. *That's not saying much when Markond numbers over 10,000.* Gav was proud of what he had built. *And if I can get Fade to decrypt these documents, our influence we will increase exponentially.*

The past four years had been hard for Gav. He'd put all his assets into creating a fully functioning quantum human, and so far, he'd seen minimal progress. Still, based on his intelligence sources, he was further ahead of even Nex-Delta, the creators of the quantum computer.

When the Ashamine had contracted Nex-Delta to create the next step in computing, all the Families had panicked, Gav included. They relied on encryption to secure their communications and files. A quantum computer would be orders of magnitude faster, allowing the Ashamine to crack previously secure information. The Families felt vulnerable, so they offered a bounty for the retrieval or destruction of the new machine.

Gav, then just a Markond Family underling, spent many hours

developing an op on Noor-5. The day before his scheduled insertion, however, some bugger blew up the quantum computer. The memory still made Gav furious. He wanted to track down and kill the pole licker who'd done it, but when he discovered it was Maxar Trayfis, Gav had forced himself to let it go. Maxar was freelance, but basically had the protection of all the Families, including Markond. If Gav did anything to him, he would be issuing his own execution order.

With the quantum computer destroyed, the Families relaxed, thinking they had set Nex-Delta back several years. Gav had felt differently, and he had been right. Nex-Delta had another computer in a different facility, one that was more secure. He left Noor-5 and returned to his home-world of Exis-7, the primary hub of the Families' operations. Using every skill and contact he possessed, he'd been able to procure the schematics for Nex-Delta's second quantum computer, located in their satellite facility orbiting the planet. The installation was far too secure to access the prototype itself, but that was fine. He was playing the long game, knowing eventually, someone would be able to crack the Families' security. If he could come up with quantum encryption, he would be their savior, and they would confer power and status accordingly.

Gav spent three years building his own quantum computer. That had been hard enough, even using all of Nex-Delta's information. Now, he needed to create the encryption/decryption software, which was proving a Founder's damned problem. The quantum AI just wasn't good enough. It was slow, buggy, and inefficient, barely a step up from conventional encryption. *It is never quite smart enough,* Gav thought, watching as Fade processed incoming data.

It had seemed an insurmountable problem, one that Nex-Delta confirmed when it announced the successful completion of the quantum computer project. The Families' data stayed secure, and they even procured a few of the systems themselves. Everyone discovered the same thing Gav had: quantum AI wasn't efficient enough to crack standard encryption. But then, a note in one of the Next-Delta files had caught Gav's attention. It speculated a human, given the ability to interact with the quantum interface, might be able to harness its full computing power.

Gav had gone back to work, using every resource to discover Nex-Delta's ultra-secret quantum human project. Once he had found that information, Gav felt confident he could subjugate a human mind and make it do what quantum AI could not.

Fade was successfully encrypting and decrypting strings of data. They were easy, but he was doing it much faster than AI could, faster even than any of Gav's previous quantum humans. Capturing him had been another difficult, but crucial, step in the process.

When Gav had transferred his first human into the quantum

computer interface, he had picked a street vagrant, someone who no one would miss. Thankfully, it proved his download process worked, because everything else about it failed. The subject went insane, and Gav deleted him. Several quantum humans later, each of better and better quality, Gav decided he needed someone with real computer skills. He began hunting, looking for someone who fit the profile. Fade was the logical choice.

Gav had heard about him from one of his contacts, someone he'd later silenced. He needed to make sure Fade's disappearance couldn't possibly be traced to him. The Alenthos Family, for whom Fade had been a hasher and computer tech, wasn't large. They only had a couple hundred members, but every one of them was powerful and influential. The Family also had a ton of Ashcreds, giving them access to additional talent and firepower.

Luring Fade to a location where Gav could subdue him proved difficult. First, he'd offered Ashcreds for a job, but the hasher hadn't responded, so Gav offered more. Fade finally replied, saying he wasn't interested in credits. Instead, he wanted to know what the task entailed. Gav scrambled to create something that would motivate him. Mentioning quantum computing would have been enough, but Gav didn't want any leaks about his project. Instead, he fabricated a story about nested AIs, of how he was trying to combine them into a multiple personality entity. The tactic had worked, and Gav maneuvered Fade into a location where he could kill his escorts and narco him into oblivion. Once he got Fade back to his lab, the rest was easy. A few days of careful procedures, and he became a fully quantum human.

Forcing his mind back to the present, Gav queued an encrypted file he'd stolen from the Markonds. Slowly, Fade began working through it. *He's doing it; he's cracking standard encryption!*

Then, Fade balked. "I can't do this. It is Markond property. If they find out I'm reading their sensitive information, they'll kill me."

Gav shook his massive head and sighed. Fade had yet to understand his new situation, but Gav was confident he had the tools to continue explaining.

06 – CAZZ-AK-TAK

"As you sleep," Cazz-ak said, settling down beside Lothis' cot, "try to send your consciousness out several times. This may allow me to see how you go about this procedure, as well as where it originates from."

"That is much harder to do in the dream than it used to be when awake, but I think I can do it."

He looks so tired, Cazz-ak thought, sensing there was more to Lothis' weariness than his human requirement for sleep. "Good. Perhaps, if I trace it back to its origin, I will be able to see where the damage occurred."

"Do you really think I can connect to the Great Thought?"

"I think you have a strong chance, given enough practice. It will not be easy, but I do believe it is possible."

Lothis nodded. After laying down, he closed his eyes. Moments later, he was asleep.

Cazz-ak watched the boy carefully, trying to detect any change or difference. *Nothing.* Lothis twitched, something he'd learned humans did as they fell asleep. The first time he'd observed the boy in this way, it had alarmed him, but now Cazz-ak had grown used to it.

Entho-la-ah-mines didn't dream when resting, at least not in the human manner. They didn't even sleep the same way. Cazz-ak often contrasted the similarities and differences between humans and Entho-la-ah-mines. Lately, these thoughts made him feel disconnected from his species.

The Queen is most similar to me, but we are both quite different from the rest of our kind. We are outsiders, I most of all. Learning he had a past as what the humans called a Harbinger made sense. *It gives insight to why I am the first of my species to embrace combat.*

When Tremmilly had told them her memory, of when they had been Harbingers, Cazz-ak had no doubt she was telling an actual event.

Something deep inside him, a mind that felt *other* than the Great Thought, had sparked to life. It was this new aspect causing him the most mental discord.

I am an Entho-la-ah-mine, born on Haak-ah-tar. I tried to help the humans, tried to create a peaceful coexistence. I watched my birthplace fall to them, and I assisted in the evacuation and rescue of my kind. I remember 400 human standard years of existence. The new part of his mind stirred, saying there was more.

As Cazz-ak thought about it, he realized he did not belong anywhere. *I am not human. I am also not Entho-la-ah-mine, not truly. I am so different from them, even from the Queen. The Great Thought doesn't understand me anymore.*

He supposed his Harbinger past connected him to that group in some way, but he didn't remember enough for the bond to be strong. *I am alone.* His mind felt heavy, and he wondered how he would go on.

Lothis twitched again, bringing Cazz-ak back to himself and the task at hand. *Lothis,* he thought, feeling grateful for the boy. *We two are most alike, most connected out of anyone I know.* The realization caused a wave of remorse and sorrow.

Cazz-ak still felt guilt for not having come to the boy's rescue sooner. *I shouldn't have let him go to the Arche alone.* He'd made a poor decision, but at the time, the boy seemed ready and the threat minimal. *At least you did get to him and were able to save something.* It had been a close thing. Just a few more units of whatever time was in the Arche's computer and they would have erased everything that made Lothis who he was. *A husk, a thrall to the Arche.*

Even now, Cazz-ak wondered if the only reason he'd been able to rescue the boy was because he'd surprised the Arche. *They certainly have more power and defenses than I saw. It is their own reality, built and improved upon over millions of years.* Memories of his battle with the Arche were still fresh. Endless red rooms, violet beams of energy, captivity, fear. Cazz-ak had struck them with a weapon formed of anger. They'd shattered into component parts of energy. *But they are not dead, nor do I think they've given up their desire for revenge.*

Lothis twitched, once again bringing Cazz-ak out of his reverie. *You really must focus now,* he told himself. *He will begin dreaming at any moment.*

Shutting all other thoughts out of his head, Cazz-ak began searching for what caused dreaming to restore Lothis' psionic abilities. Each time they attempted this caused Cazz-ak to lose a little more hope. If something had changed about the boy's physical or mental composition, Cazz-ak hadn't seen even a hint of it. This was their last attempt and then they would move on to teaching Lothis to connect to the Great Thought.

The boy started groaning, soft sounds signaling he was beginning to dream. Cazz-ak focused harder, scanning Lothis' mind, searching for his consciousness. *There it is,* he thought, seeing the tightly bound ball of energy that was the boy's mental existence. As he watched, it moved, exiting the confines of his body. *Good. Make note of that pathway.*

In prior attempts, he'd tried to connect with Lothis while he was outside of his body. They could communicate, but since Lothis was dreaming, much of his thoughts were disjointed and nonsensical. That had been a dead end.

Over the course of the next several minutes, Lothis moved in and out of his body. Cazz-ak tried every angle he could think of, but still, he could see nothing wrong. *Perhaps if I'd known him better before the Arche damaged him.*

The boy's groans changed, sounding different, more fearful. They grew in intensity, becoming whimpers. Cazz-ak studied his consciousness, sensing nothing wrong. He expanded his search to the dwelling, first its obvious macro physical aspect, then finer and finer levels until he felt he was seeing the very fabric of space-time. Nothing seemed out of place. Still, Lothis sounded desperate, like he was about to cry. This had never happened in any of their prior sessions.

Then, Cazz-ak sensed it, a familiar energy signature he knew all too well. *The Arche.*

07 - LOTHIS

"Do you really think I can connect to the Great Thought?" Lothis asked, trying to allay the sense of unease growing within him. He couldn't explain its presence. They'd done this procedure several times before. It wasn't scary or painful.

"I think you have a strong chance, given enough practice. It will not be easy, but I do believe it is possible."

Lothis nodded, feeling tired and distracted. He looked around the dwelling Wake had built him, scanning for threats. *There aren't any. You are safe here. Shut this emotional distraction out. You will not be able to sleep otherwise.* Laying down on his cot, Lothis closed his eyes. He took several deep breaths and felt the room slip away.

Back when the Ashamine were conditioning him on Haak-ah-tar, Lothis never experienced a single dream. He also hadn't felt the signals at that point either. Lately, he'd decided that his captors had been giving him something to suppress the ability, perhaps until they felt they had formed enough control over him. *Or maybe it has something to do with being a Harbinger.*

In the weeks between his escape from the research facility and the Arche's attack, Lothis had learned much about his abilities. He'd almost lost himself during the process. When he'd met the Entho-la-ah-mines, Cazz-ak in particular, Lothis had discovered so much about how to control his power. The stress of fleeing the Ashamine and then the Breakers pushed him, opening up new and unknown realms of possibility.

Now, it was all gone. The Arche had taken it away, had broken some deep part of him he didn't sense or understand. The only way he could access any of his abilities was through dreams. He didn't know if that stemmed from the changes the Arche had made in him, or if it was something separate, but it was true all the same.

As he slipped further into sleep, Lothis felt his body tense. He didn't like the jumbling of thoughts, sensations, and emotions dreams brought. *Perhaps the reason for my fear is this lack of control.* That didn't seem right, but before he could think about it any further, he fell into a dream.

***

Lothis saw a singularity, a tiny point of infinite energy. It encompassed all space, all time, all existence. "This is the beginning," he said, voice sounding loud in his dream ears.

Who are you talking to? Lothis became confused. Then he remembered: *Cazz-ak, the exercise.*

Shutting out the image of the singularity, he focused on the connection to his body. Moments passed, and Lothis wondered how long he was making Cazz-ak wait. Finally, he forced his consciousness out of his body.

As he did so, the scene before him flickered, stuttering in and out of existence. A giant blue and green planet filled his view, white clouds moving across its surface. "Earth," he said, wondering what the word meant. *There are no planets called by that name.* Again, he remembered what he should be doing. Lothis didn't understand why the dream shifted each time his consciousness phased in and out of his body. It also seemed impossible that he should dream at all when he left, but it happened just the same.

Lothis continued fighting distraction, gathering and transferring his consciousness in and out of his body several times. Despite sleeping, it was exhausting work, and he feared what would happen if he ran out of energy while his consciousness was outside. *Cazz-ak is watching over you. He will keep you safe.*

When Lothis transferred back into his body for the last time, the singularity scene returned, only now it was bigger and brighter than before. *How can I be an outside observer of an object that encompasses the entirety of space-time?* As he watched, the scene flickered and stuttered as before. His dreams often shifted unexpectedly, but unless he was leaving or entering his body, it was always a smooth transition. Something about what was happening felt wrong, ominous. *Time to wake up,* he thought, desperately trying to find his way out of the dream.

The singularity stuttered, and began spinning. Its hue shifted: white, teal, blue, purple, violet. Lothis had seen that exact color twice before, first as a beam weapon from Wake's environmental suit, and the next in the realm of the Arche when they attacked him.

Lothis tried to back away, tried to escape the dream as it changed to nightmare, but nothing worked. It triggered the same feeling of entrapment he had experienced as the Arche started deleting him.

Calm down, he told himself, stilling his raging fear. *This is just a dream. You will awaken soon.* The violet singularity flashed, vanished into static, then reappeared. The random, glitchy pattern made Lothis feel nauseous, adding to the caustic cocktail of emotions gushing through him. When the point of light stabilized, four shadowy figures stood before it, harshly back lit by sickening violet light. Lothis' breath caught in his throat.

"Hello, Boy," a deep, all too familiar voice boomed across the dark plane of his mind.

The Arche, Lothis thought, his consciousness shrinking in on itself. *This isn't real, isn't happening. It's a dream. Be calm.* But he couldn't escape the terror crushing him like the gravity of a thousand stars.

"Did you think we were dead?" the dark figure asked, sound waves reverberating through Lothis' dream world. "Did you think we wouldn't come for you?" A hideous chorus of laughter bludgeoned him. The violet singularity flared, pulling Lothis in with the force of a galactic black hole. Shadowy shapes loomed over him, growing larger and more menacing.

Lothis wanted to yell, wanted to scream for help, but they were crushing his will. All he could do was cry, the soft whimpers barely escaping his constricted throat. Hopelessness consumed him. "This time, we will have you forever. This time, your power will be ours."

"I have a question for you, Arche," Cazz-ak's voice said, pulling Lothis out of his despair. "Do you think you can come to our world, to a place where we are strong, and steal away someone we love?"

Lothis looked up, realizing he'd stopped moving. Before him stood Cazz-ak, but he barely recognized his friend. He still had Entho-la-ah-mine traits, with six legs and a beetle-like body, but something was different. His frame was larger than normal, shining with an emerald green light that radiated a sense of calm strength. He also stood upright, and the proportions of his limbs had changed. He was almost humanoid, but was definitely not human.

"Stand aside, Protector," the Arche said, "perhaps if you do not hinder us again, we may spare you."

"Lies." Cazz-ak said, his voice full of an intensity Lothis had never heard before, not even during their most desperate times fleeing the Breakers. "Go back to your cursed existence and perhaps I won't come and destroy you all."

"We made you, Entho-la-ah-mine. Do you think your powers are unknown to us? Do you think you can overcome your creators?" Rage and scorn filled the Arche's voice. Lothis tried to rise, but his limbs were too heavy. "Who do you think created your so called Crystal Chamber? Who created the Way? Who gave you sentience and the Great Thought?"

The questions lingered in the air, reverberating. Cazz-ak said nothing, just stood resolutely. Lothis focused on his friend's emerald glow, feeling strength return as he did so. Soon, he stood up.

"It doesn't have to be this way," the lighter voice of the Arche said. "We've all caused enough damage already. The Entho-la-ah-mine are our children, and the humans might as well be, with all we have done for them."

"Silence," the deep voice snarled. "We have made our decision and set our path. Besides, they are not true human or Entho-la-ah-mine. They are Harbingers. They caused the annihilation of our species." Lothis walked across the blackness, stopping next to Cazz-ak. Being close to his friend brought a sense of peace. Cazz-ak kept his focus on the Arche, but Lothis could tell he felt his presence.

"And this one," the dark form boomed, a black limb separating from its formless interior to point directly at Cazz-ak. "He attacked us. He destroyed one of us. We foresaw his obliteration because of it."

The Arche struck, violet beams of energy bolting across the intervening distance. Cazz-ak raised one of his hybrid arms, a defensive gesture that looked instantaneous. Violet energy deflected off him, arcing and fading to a dull red as it did so. The Arche's power surged, crackling purple light filling the intervening space in a continuous stream.

"You may have created my species," Cazz-ak said, voice calm, indicating no hint of strain. Now he was closer, Lothis could see Cazz-ak's connection to the Great Thought, as well as another, smaller one he'd never seen before. "And you may think you understand us. But I'm different, Arche. You won't be blighthearting me today, foreseen obliteration or no."

Six red cubes appeared before Cazz-ak, spinning on a horizontal plane. As Lothis watched, they grew larger, from fist, to head, to torso sized. Cazz-ak said nothing, but his weapon advanced, rotating faster. The cubes began to hum, color shifting from a dull crimson to a glowing red. The Arche redirected their attack towards Cazz-ak's weapon, but it churned through their violet energy with ease. Lothis felt the Arche's state shift from confidence to panic. Just as Cazz-ak was about to strike them with his red bludgeon, the Arche retreated into the singularity. The violet point of light sputtered, glitched, then returned to plain white.

Lothis collapsed, feeling his consciousness rush back to his body.

08 – TREMMILLY

Tremmilly awoke from a vivid dream of shadowy figures and whirling red cubes, heart racing. A sense of impending doom washed over her. She began to cry.

"What?" Maxar said groggily, sitting up. "What's wrong?"

"Just more horrible dreams," she answered, knowing it was only half the reason. "That, and you are leaving in the morning."

Maxar wrapped his arms around her, and Tremmilly felt all fears melt in his warm embrace. "I don't want you to go," she said finally, feeling weak.

"I have to."

"I know," she sighed, closing her eyes. *You've come to rely on him so much. What are you going to do when he leaves?* Tremmilly thought for several moments, teetering on the edge of wakefulness and sleep. As she drifted off, she thought, *I will be as strong as I need to, as strong as I once was, as strong as ever.*

***

When Tremmilly woke once again, it was morning. Maxar had left. At first, she panicked, thinking he'd departed without saying goodbye. *You know he would never do that,* she thought, dressing quickly.

"Come on, Beo," Tremmilly said, stepping out the dwelling door. The wolf-dog followed behind her, looking energetic. Gazing around, Tremmilly felt relieved to see the Death Watch a short distance away, across the field of emerald grass. It brooded over the bright plains like a bird of prey, yet the sight brought comfort. *The Watch is a symbol, a reminder of what we have gone through. It represents freedom.*

The ache in Tremmilly's heart was mostly for Maxar's departure, but she was also sad Jaydon and Wake were leaving as well. Despite Jaydon not being in her Harbinger visions, she still thought of the older captain as one of them. He was the first individual she'd bonded with after leaving Eishon-2, looking for the people from the prophecy. *And here you are now, gathered for a month, but set to split up.* She hoped they were making the correct decision.

Tremmilly spotted Maxar, Jaydon, and Wake at the back of the Watch, inspecting the hull. "And you're sure we got the damage repaired?" Jaydon asked, looking intently at Wake.

"Completely," Wake replied, "like it never happened. They had lots of tools and equipment on board. Made it easy." The engineer looked small without his crimson environmental nominizing suit.

"Alright, I think we are ready to depart whenever you give the order, Maxar." Jaydon's surly nature hadn't completely vanished since he'd given up alcohol, but it had certainly improved. Tremmilly hoped the long open wounds from the loss of his wife and daughter were healing. She'd tried to help as much as she could, but Jaydon seemed the type who preferred to deal with his problems alone.

"Hey, Trem," Maxar said, smiling. The other two said their good mornings as well.

"Hello," she replied, melancholy increasing.

"We've packed everything," Maxar continued. "And our plans are in place. I think it's time to leave." While Maxar was good at hiding his emotions, Tremmilly had learned to see through his shell. He was as sad as she was, and strangely, that made her feel good. *At least he isn't trying to get away from you as quickly as he can,* she thought, smiling.

"What are you grinning about?" Maxar said, a fake frown on his beard stubbled face.

"Oh, nothing," she said, doing her best to appear innocent.

Maxar turned serious. "Can we talk, Trem? Alone?"

"Of course," she said, following as he led the way to the grove of huge palos trees. Their giant leaves rustled in the breeze, reminding Tremmilly of Eishon-2. Beowulf followed them, energetically darting through the undergrowth.

When she saw the great center tree, the founder of this colony, she smiled. It had a spot at its base, an oddity in its trunk almost like a room. The hole in its top gave views of the expansive canopy. Tremmilly thought back to all the hours she and Maxar had spent in this special place: thinking, talking, cuddling, and more.

Before she could bend down to step inside, Maxar stopped her. "If we go in there, I won't be able to make myself leave today." Tremmilly nodded, understanding completely. "I wanted us in our place, though, and I wanted to do this right." He pulled out a small green orb attached to a necklace of cord. Her heart began to beat rapidly. "Tremmilly, I know we've only been together for a little while in this life, but as Harbingers, our connection has lasted far longer. Hopefully, you will discover more about that after I've gone, but for now, I'm content to trust my human feelings. You saved me from Bloodsport and gave me a reason to live, a purpose to fight for. Our pasts, the human ones at least, couldn't be more different, but I feel we are right for each other." Maxar paused. Tremmilly couldn't breathe. "So," he continued, smiling, "will you bond with me? Will you commit your energy to be one with mine until the universe ends?"

"Yes," she replied without hesitation, throwing her arms around him. Maxar had to brace himself to keep from falling over, holding them both up. They stood that way for ages before Tremmilly disengaged. "You know you can't die on Traynos now, right?"

"Guess I'll have to change my plans then," Maxar replied with a laugh. He fastened the cord around her neck, laying the orb against her throat. "I know it's traditional for this to be gold or a similar metal, but I thought this one more appropriate. It is a tiny glass biosphere, self-sustaining, full of algae and microscopic flora. Jaydon had the idea, and Wake and Cazz-ak helped me make it. "

"You told them you were going to do this?"

"Yes. I thought it good to get additional opinions before I rushed into something. I just wanted to make sure my timing wasn't—"

Tremmilly covered his lips with her own, cutting off the rest of whatever he was saying. She closed her eyes, a deep warmth filling her. Maxar's lips relaxed, and they exchanged several more kisses, each deeper and more longing than the last. Time seemed to stand still, and Tremmilly forgot about the world around them. Finally, their lips separated. Maxar sighed contentedly, staring into her eyes. She smiled back at him, squeezing his hands tightly.

"OK," Tremmilly said finally, "I can let you go." She smiled, eyes narrowing. "I wish I could go with you to Traynos, but you'd have a hard time focusing if I was there. My studies here are important as well."

Maxar nodded and returned her smile. "I know, and I will try to get back as quickly as I can." He gave her another kiss, then stepped back. Maxar knelt down before Beowulf, taking the wolf-dog by his front shoulders. "Beo, you must guard Tremmilly and keep her safe while I'm gone," he said, completely serious. The intensity in the wolf-dogs eyes reminded Tremmilly of something. "You know how to do this, kindred." Beowulf bared his teeth, not in a growl, but in a gesture that somehow acknowledged what Maxar said. In her mind, Tremmilly felt the wolf-dog agree.

The battle on the Bloodsport orbital dock, she thought, *when we first ran into Maxar. That is what his eyes remind me of.* Beowulf and Maxar had fought beside each other, the wolf-dog with his fangs and the man with a talon of metal. Their movements had been uncanny, seeming choreographed and practiced beforehand. As had happened then, she wondered at the link between them. Tremmilly wanted to ask about it, but now was not the time.

"Take him with you," Tremmilly said. "He will protect you." She knew Beowulf would do everything possible to bring her love back alive.

"I think it best for him to stay. He can watch over and keep you safe while I'm gone."

Tremmilly wanted to protest, but then Maxar stood, and she realized he was about to leave. All other thoughts vanished from her mind as he took her hands. "I will be with you, always," Maxar said, pale blue eyes locked on hers. "We have connected our lives, as Harbingers, and as humans. No matter what happens, I will return."

"And I," Tremmilly said, trying not to burst into tears, "will always be here for you."

They melted into a long embrace, Beowulf at their feet. Finally, Tremmilly felt ready to let go. "Time to send you off to Traynos."

09 – MAXAR

Maxar hit the button that closed the Death Watch's main airlock, feeling a sense of relief. It wasn't that he wanted to leave, but he knew he had to complete this mission. Discovering what flowed inside him, what it was capable of, had become his obsession. *I need to make sure it's safe for me to be around the person I love.* Maxar had yet to experience any harmful effects from the T6 nanites, other than a weakness to strong magnetic fields, but he had to make sure they couldn't be used to control him.

The departure from Tremmilly and Lith-elo was teaching Maxar that he didn't like goodbyes. It wasn't something he'd really experienced since his sister, Emili, had left for Ashamine-2 as an indentured servant almost 20 years ago. Thinking of her made his gut twinge with pain.

"Airlock closed and ready for takeoff," Maxar transmitted up to Jaydon on the command deck.

"I hear ya," the salty captain replied, sounding preoccupied.

Maxar looked at Wake. "So you think you know where the dig is?"

"Sort of," Wake replied, leading the way as they walked towards the Watch's bridge. "As I said, all I really know is what Captain Malesis told me. The Ashamine sabotaged my bridge to kill the miners that discovered the artifact or whatever it was. I'm not sure exactly where they were working, but I have a general idea."

"I guess that's where we will start then."

When they arrived at the command deck, Maxar watched Jaydon begin lift off procedures. It gave him time to think, something he'd tried to avoid lately. *She said yes,* he thought, replaying the scene with Tremmilly in the palos grove. He'd thought she would, but nothing was ever sure. Besides, he'd never done anything like it before, and wanted to make sure he did it right. *And you spoke to Jaydon, Wake, and Cazz-ak.* That too had been a new experience. On Bloodsport, and Noor-5 before it, Maxar had kept to himself. Revealing your feelings, even the fact you had any, could be a weakness that got you killed, or worse. Now, he was learning to find strength in these types of connections. He didn't know if this development was caused by the human, Harbinger, or nano-machine part of him—perhaps all three—but it felt good.

The ship lurched under Maxar.

"It's about an hour or so till we get out of the gravity well," Jaydon announced, keeping his eyes on the control screens. Maxar settled into one of the auxiliary chairs and continued to let his mind spiral out.

It had been hard to leave Tremmilly, especially after she'd said yes to his proposal. When Felar had come to say goodbye, Tremmilly had jumped up and down, holding out her green orb necklace. Felar had joined her celebration, more excited than Maxar believed possible. *I suppose she's been the biggest supporter of Trem and I's relationship, even if she did have some blighthearted ways of showing it early on.*

The story Cazz-ak and Lothis told about the Arche attacking the boy diminished everyone's lightheartedness, especially since Tremmilly said she had seen it as well. Maxar wished he could help, but he couldn't see how. Death and misery filled his own dreams, but it was all just standard human nightmares. If he ever found a way to physically strike at the Arche, he would. They were opportunistic and persistent, a dangerous combination.

As they drew closer to the edge of the Lith-elo-hi-rosh gravity well, Maxar's thoughts shifted towards the mission ahead. Traynos-6 was an Ashamine controlled planet, albeit one focused on mining and possessing little military presence. When the Haak-ah-tar supernova had destroyed the Bloodsport asteroid, Maxar's prison, it had taken him off the Ashamine's sensors. They would have him listed as dead, but a facial recognition or DNA scan would alert them to their mistake. Any Ashamine troop would shoot him once identified. It was a risk Maxar was willing to take. He needed to find where the nanites coursing through his body had come from and what they were capable of.

"Gravity well departure," Jaydon announced finally, pausing for a few moments. "Destination locked." Maxar saw a blackness spring up on the Watch's forward view screen. "Worm created." The blackness filled with a new set of stars. "Transitioning."

***

"I wouldn't recommend we attempt to blend in as miners," Wake said, looking thoughtful. Initially, Maxar had been unsure of whether to ask the engineer along or not. His knowledge of Traynos-6 would be an asset, but would he be able to do the things required in a covert op? In the end, Maxar supposed the only real way to find out was to try. Wake had easily dispatched Breakers, but had hesitated when faced with killing humans as they'd stormed the Death Watch. *Hopefully, I can keep him out of trouble, if he can't do it himself.*

"They don't have any type of security scans implemented for the mines," Wake continued, "but it is a tight community. Everyone knows each other. Even if we can procure proper uniforms, we'll stand out as strangers."

"Alright," Maxar answered, "then we go with stealth instead of subterfuge after we are planetside. Jaydon, once we get past the orbiting ships, find a landing location out of sight from the mining facilities, but make sure it's close enough to walk."

"Will do."

"It's going to be a tough trek on the surface, even with EN suits," Wake said. "Even at the equator, Traynos is likely the coldest place you've ever been. Plus, there are mountains, glaciers, and crevasses everywhere."

"We don't have the credentials or experience to spoof being Ashamine Intel, and if we can't pose as miners, then it's the only option I see."

Wake shrugged in reply. Maxar appreciated his honesty, but a positive outlook would be nice.

"I sure hope Felar was right about getting past the orbital forces," Jaydon said, starting to look nervous.

"She knows Ashamine protocol," Maxar answered, beginning to wonder if taking these two had been a good decision. "We give the code signifying a black op, and they let us through unhindered. Given the discovery's level of secrecy, I'm sure we won't be the first to do it."

"It just seems like a huge security flaw," Jaydon huffed. "What if they've changed it?"

"Then we turn around," Maxar growled. "Look, I asked you both to come, and you agreed. I never told you this would be easy. In fact, I remember saying it would be dangerous and difficult. We need to be on guard, and we need to look for flaws in our plan, but if you can't find a solution to the problem, then shut up. Complaining does no good. We've come through long odds situations in the past. I asked you two specifically because I believed in the strengths you have to offer. Don't disappoint me."

Both Jaydon and Wake sat up straighter. Maxar held his breath, hoping they would take his words the right way.

"I think I might be able to implement some quick mods that will make our ENS's more capable of handling the cold." Wake looked thoughtful. "The suits won't be able to carry as much atmosphere and will have a diminished thermal generation span, but it will give us a greater chance of making it inside somewhere."

"If you think we'll still have enough time, do it."

Wake thought for a moment. "Based on what I remember of the surrounding terrain, it should work. We could carry some spare power modules just to be sure." He left the bridge, already seeming lost in thought.

"I am a coward," Jaydon blurted.

"No, you're not," Maxar replied, brow furrowing.

"I sure do feel like one."

Maxar felt a twinge of exasperation at Jaydon's words. "You do what's needed, when it's needed. That shows you aren't one. I saw plenty of cowards back on Bloodsport, petty criminals who offended one too many times and got a maximum sentence. They'd talk like they were the blighthearted Founder, but once they were fully engaged in battle, they lost what little nerve they had. Most of them got shot in the back while running away or cowering in a crater. That's not the kind of person you are. You don't break when things turn into the fires of the dark star."

"I just get so afraid." Jaydon looked down, unwilling to meet Maxar's eyes.

"You think I wasn't scared facing Crasor? You think I'm not afraid to leave Lith-elo? Everyone, even the hardest blighthearted person alive, still feels fear. They've just learned how to manage it."

"I guess I need to keep trying."

"And that's what proves you aren't a coward."

Silence returned to the command deck as Maxar waited for the Ashamine Forces fleet to contact them. From what he could see on the tactical display, the ships were orbiting over the mining base region. *The Ashamine must not have anything else to protect on this planet.*

After several minutes passed, a voice came over the Watch's intercom. "Unidentified Ashamine vessel, we have not authorized you, nor has Fleet briefed us on your arrival. Switch to encrypted channel, hold position, and ident."

"Here we go," Jaydon said under his breath. He selected several options on his control screen. "Traynos-6 fleet. Ops zero. Code 406–393. No verify."

Maxar and Jaydon waited. No response. "I guess we did tell them not to verify," Maxar said. He looked at the tactical display, checking to see if any Ashamine vessels were coming to block or attack them. None moved.

"What's happening?" Wake asked over the intercom.

"Looks like we're clear," Jaydon answered, taking them down towards the surface of Traynos-6.

10 – CRASOR

The Governor's Mansion on Psinar-3 was splendid. Crasor almost liked it as much as the Founder's Palace. *I could stay here, if I didn't have a galaxy to subjugate,* he thought with a laugh.

The entire Psinar system had fallen easily to the Breakers with Crasor's leadership and Karoth's tactics. They still had an element of surprise and confusion in their arsenal, as well as a Tarton class Ashamine battle cruiser. Anyone who resisted their order to submit had been immediately obliterated. It only took a few examples before the rest fell in line.

Dominating the surface had been more time-consuming, but that was due to the dispersed population. With only a small ground force to contend with, the Breakers had swept through the colony, converting those whose souls were ripe for seeding and killing those who weren't. Crasor enjoyed the process. In this pleasant, temperate climate, he'd found a state of bliss. He'd been in ships so much before coming to Psinar. The vast, open spaces of the planet had been a nice change. Now that a month had gone by, he was ready to get back to the Justice and resume taking worlds.

The break had been necessary to consolidate and train his forces. He was glad they had now reached the point they no longer needed to sneak around the Ashamine. *They know we exist. Still, they cower on their planets, unable to find courage to fight us.* Controlling one of the galaxy's most powerful ships was part of it, with each battle victory increasing their fleet of smaller vessels. *And we continue gaining troops as well.*

As his forces swelled, so did Crasor's power. Each Breaker lent him their energy, and Crasor was learning how to wield it in devastating ways. *Space-time warps, cloaking, and mental domination will soon seem weak by comparison.*

"Come in," he said, bringing his mind to the present as he beckoned his nine Descended into the great hall. At this range, they could all communicate mentally, but Crasor liked doing things the human way when it was more efficient.

"I've called you here," he continued, after they'd lined up before him, "because I wanted to reward you. Your actions in taking the Psinar system, as well as your continually improving skills, are commendable." The Descended still appeared human, although patches of flesh were changing to the black metallic skin that covered Crasor. The fingers of their right hands had become pointed and sharp, a physical manifestation of their ability to seed converts.

Crasor was still the only one capable of speaking to the Breaker mind directly, something he both cherished and dreaded. Being the sole leader of such a strong force was something he'd dreamed about his entire life. It came with a price, however.

While he didn't completely understand his relationship to the dimensionally separated mass mind, Crasor did know that he'd given up part of himself to receive its gifts. Most of it was aspects of his humanity, both physical and mental. These he wasn't concerned about. The visions of the past and possible future the Breaker mind had shown to him proved there was a better existence. Humans were millennia from evolving into those higher states of being.

The thing Crasor worried about most was losing his ego to the Breakers. He feared they would somehow dissolve or absorb the core of his being in their great influence, perhaps intentionally. When they'd revived Crasor after the pole-sucking Soldier had killed him, something about his psyche had changed. The Breaker mind was closer, louder. Initially, he'd thought nothing of it, but now it scared Crasor, and his mind shied away from thinking about it too closely. *What if it gets so large it crowds everything else out?*

"I have a new directive, one fitting of your status as Descended," Crasor continued, forcing his thoughts back to the hulking figures before him. The five males and four females inspired pride. They were his handpicked, specially trained warriors. Psinar had been a test run, one they'd dominated. Now, he was ready for them to evolve his battle plan.

"We Breakers find ourselves at a critical point. We must continue assimilating the Ashamine, but the Harbingers are still hiding somewhere in the Akked." Just saying their name flooded Crasor with feelings of disgust and revulsion. "They are a threat. We must send them to blackness. In addition, we need to subjugate the Entho-la-ah-mines." The Descended already knew this, but he wanted to drive the point home.

"In the past, our limited resources forced us to pursue a single objective in linear fashion. Now, however, we have grown, and I am adjusting tactics accordingly. In doing this, we will continue to confuse our enemies and present an ever shifting target."

Crasor had been developing this plan since they'd taken Psinar. Splitting his forces would decrease some of their power, but he felt they were becoming large enough to handle this. The Breaker mind continued pushing him to find the Harbingers, as it had since they'd escaped. Despite his best efforts, Crasor had been unable to discover where they had gone. If he stopped assimilating the Ashamine to hunt the Harbingers, the humans would build up a resistance and prevent him from taking the core worlds. Time was critical.

The Breaker mind made it clear the Harbingers were far more dangerous than the Ashamine, but Crasor didn't understand how. They were just six individuals. Thankfully, the Breakers approved of his plan to send the strike force after them.

"I will continue building our forces, taking Ashamine worlds. You will begin the hunt for the Harbingers. Once you find them, destroy them. If you discover the Entho-la-ah-mine queen with the Harbingers, as I suspect you will, capture and bring her back to me for conversion. While you are strong, you must leave her transformation to me. It is far more complex than you understand." He waited for a moment, staring into each of their eyes in turn. Crasor had spent much of his time and energy on these troops, knowing he would need a strike force capable of accomplishing this task. *Some of them will die.* He felt no sadness at the thought, merely annoyance at having to spend so much time training replacements.

"They will accomplish the mission, regardless of casualties," the Breaker mind said, signaling its agreement. Crasor felt himself tense and relax simultaneously. He craved approval, but speaking with them had become puzzling and nerve wracking. Once he had revealed his plan to create the Descended operatives, the Breaker mind, the voice of One, had left him alone to complete the task.

Except for the Emili flashback, his mind had been blissfully quiet. Their silence was a relief, both because it signified their approval and he felt he was holding on to more of himself. With their return, Crasor wondered how much longer he would be able to maintain his own identity. *Can they sense I'm attempting that? Do they care?*

"Do you understand your orders?" Crasor asked, forcing his own fears down.

As a group, they bellowed, "Yes, Breaker!" and saluted.

"Then go," Crasor said, excitement overshadowing his earlier worries. "Let the hunt begin."

Crasor watched as they left the great hall, nearly overwhelmed with pride for what he had created. Something about the emotion triggered a cascade of feelings within him, and he felt the Breaker mind forcing him back into memory.

**

"You committed? You're leaving me for the Ashamine Forces?" Emili asked.

Crasor felt all his pride drain away, replaced with irritation. No one approved of his choices. *They are all trying to hold me back, to keep me from my true potential.* He tried to defend himself, but Emili continued speaking.

"It's going to be—What?—at least two years until you come back? And if we get married, then I'll have a military life. That's not what I want." She set her jaw stiffly, a look Crasor had grown to despise.

"You're just like my parents," he said coldly, words he knew would hurt her. "You want me to be some useless diplomat. Why can't you just support me? Why can't you see the Forces is the right place for me?"

"That's what I'm afraid of," Emili shot back. Crasor didn't understand what she meant, but she continued before he could demand clarification. "I don't think we are right for each other."

The words cut him deep, opening up a well of anger unlike anything he had felt before. Crasor took a step forward and got right in her face. "Are you breaking up with me?" His words came through clenched teeth, his jaw aching.

Emili held her ground, looking calm and composed. "Crasor, we've only been together for a year. It's obvious our lives are already going in separate directions."

Her cool demeanor enraged Crasor even further, and without thought, he shoved her, hard. Emili hit the floor, sliding a full meter before stopping. She groaned loudly, and Crasor was glad the room was far away from the inhabited parts of the Tah Ahn estate.

He strode forward, standing over her with fists clenched. He wanted to hit her, to make her feel the pain she was causing him.

"Why?" she sobbed, body wracking violently with each inhalation.

Crasor didn't know how to respond. Guilt and fear rushed through him. *What if she tells my parents?* They didn't particularly care about the servants, but they might pass the information along and get him barred from joining the Forces. *Would they do that? Of course they would.* They were already calling in as many favors as they could to try to keep him home. *Don't give them additional ammunition.*

"I'm sorry, Em," he said, trying to make his voice soothing. "I don't know what made me do that. I never meant to hurt you."

Emili rolled over and sat up, eyes red, cheeks blotchy. She didn't say anything, and wouldn't meet his gaze.

"I just don't want to lose you," he continued. "It scared me."

"Then why are you leaving for the Forces?" Emili said finally, still looking down.

"It is my path to greatness," he replied. "Our path, I mean. I'll come for you in two years. It will be worth the wait. I'll pay off your debt two standard years before you'd be able to work it off yourself."

Emili nodded, gazing at his hands. "Alright. It was wrong of me to say those things earlier. I'll be here when you get back."

Crasor felt his heart leap with joy, although a small part of him still worried she might tell his parents. *No, she loves me,* he thought, helping Emili rise to her feet.

They hugged briefly, Emili feeling stiff in his arms. *She'll get over it,* he thought. *Everything will return to normal.*

"I have to work. My break is over and if I'm much later, the head housekeeper won't give me credit for the entire day."

Nodding, Crasor smiled. "Of course. I lost track of time." As they separated, he began thinking of the future, and his pride returned.

11 – AZA

"But Momma, something is wrong. I know it!" Aza felt frustration threatening to overtake her, as it often had in the past few weeks. Since the capture of the Psinar system a month ago, she had a terrible suspicion something bigger was going on.

"Of course it is, Aza," her mother said, using a tone that irritated her. "We are without a Founder. Many of our people have died."

"That's not what I mean and you know it."

"Aza, you must calm yourself. If you're ever to be a priestess of the Holy Order, you must cultivate a calmer demeanor." Her mother's dark face was smooth and unreadable.

Aza bit her lip, knowing her mother was right in that regard. She took a few deep breaths, relaxing her jaw muscles as she did so. This wasn't the first argument they'd had about the subject. Each time pushed her further.

"I believe there's a connection between all these calamities."

"I know you do, you've said it before. Even if that's true, it is not the Holy Order's job to manage it. The Ashamine Forces will keep us secure."

Because they did such a good job with the Founder, his Successor, and the Psinar system. Aza forced down another spike of anger. *Why did I let myself try again?* Her mother was a good person, a good parent, and a good priestess, but she remained stuck in her ways, unable to see beyond her title and responsibilities.

"You will see, in time," she continued. "Everything will work itself out and the Ashamine will restore order. Have faith."

Aza went to her room, unable to continue the conversation. After a few minutes of meditation, she opened up an encrypted file on her portable terminal. Inside were notes she'd taken about her suspicions.

There is no way in the fires of the dark star an Entho sympathizer killed the Founder. Aza felt guilty using the profanity, even in her mind, but she needed something strong to describe her emotion. The news presenter had made that revelation during the evening briefing a few days prior. It had brought closure to the assassination and reignited the waning desire to wipe out the bugs.

Something about the resolution just felt too convenient. *How does someone who had no military background infiltrate the Founder's Palace, murder numerous guards along the way, and kill the Founder with a sword?* Aza wondered if they'd told any truths other than the Founder being dead. *It has to be either someone from the Thousand Stars, or some new threat, but why aren't they telling us?*

She scrolled down to the next item on her list. *Lothis.* Someone had kidnapped the heir just a short time before the Founder's assassination. The timing suggested a connection. *Meaning someone is taking out the leadership of the Ashamine. With no Founder and no heir, power shifts to the Classad. Could they be perpetrating a coup?* This didn't feel right. None of them could inherit the power of the Founder, providing no motivation. A break in succession had never occurred before, but the Founder, in his wisdom, had still planned for it. The Founder had another son, one the public had no knowledge of for security purposes. Once old enough, he would take control from the Classad. Unfortunately, the boy was just an infant and it would be many years until he was ready.

And what of the Justice and the Psinar system? These two didn't seem to fit the puzzle, but the timing was too close to be coincidence. *A hidden enemy within, and a hidden enemy without. What are the odds these are not the same enemy?*

Aza wanted desperately to talk of her thoughts with someone else, but her mother and father both offered the same platitude that it was not the concern of the Holy Order. The Ashamine Forces would handle any threats. No one at her school believed her, professor or student. They were either too focused on helping the Ashamine recover or didn't care enough to listen. She felt lonely. *Am I being foolish? Why am I the only one who sees the connections?*

Turning off the screen of her portable terminal, Aza lay back on her bed and closed her eyes. *Ash would believe me.* The thought startled her. She wondered what had made her remember her uncle. Aza hadn't thought of her mother's brother in many years. Her parents had banned his name from their house. Even though they never mentioned him, they implied he would be one of those burning in the fires of the dark star. *They would disapprove of me even thinking of Ash.*

Her memories of the man were vague. He was a giant in her mind, a tall, dark figure with a booming laugh. He'd always given her what she wanted. Ash was her mother's only sibling. They had been close. Aza's grandfather had been a priest, giving both his children names that started with the letter A. This was a prestigious honor, one that destined them to become part of the Holy Order. A strong tradition disgraced those who didn't follow through on the commitment. Often, they changed their names, attempting to escape the shame.

Ash had honored his father's wishes, attaining the priesthood. Then, something had gone wrong, and Ash disappeared. Aza's parents never explained. As years passed, Aza had begun to forget how much time had elapsed since then. Sometimes she even forgot about Ash himself.

So why do I think he would believe me? At first Aza had no answer, but then a shadowy memory of her mother and Ash arguing rose in her mind. He'd been accusing the Ashamine of something, saying the Holy Order had to intervene. *What was he upset about?* No matter how hard she tried, the details stayed murky. She did remember her mother getting furious and yelling, causing Aza to hide under her bed until it was over.

Thinking of her mother brought up a new aspect of the situation. If her parents found out she was trying to find Ash, they would punish her severely. They might even submit her disobedience as an infraction to the school. How or why Ash had abandoned the priesthood might reflect on her, especially if she actually contacted him. *They might expel you.* Aza's heart began to race, both with fear and excitement. She'd always been obedient, always followed the rules. That was why she was ahead of her age in school, why they'd told her she was headed for great things, in both the Ashamine and the Order. *Do you really want to risk all that?* Conflicting desires waged war, and Aza felt paralyzed with indecision.

Finally, a single thought tipped the balance: *You won't get in trouble if they don't catch you.*

12 – WAKE

Not knowing what was happening made Wake too nervous to work. He trusted his friends, but getting past the Ashamine ships was the critical first step of their mission. Before he realized what he was doing, he switched on the intercom. "What's happening?"

"Looks like we are clear," Jaydon answered, sounding calm.

"Nice work," Wake sent back, his body relaxing.

"Setting down in ten."

Wake returned to modifying Jaydon's and Maxar's environmental nominizing suits. "Just a small tweak here," he said to himself, adjusting the heater controls. It wasn't enough to make long periods on the surface comfortable, but they would survive. *Assuming we have extra power modules.* He reattached the small maintenance panels and began checking his own crimson suit.

The Ashamine had used it to execute enemies of the state, calling it the Clothing of the Iconoclast. When Wake's own execution had failed, he'd kept the suit, discovering many interesting secrets about it along the way. It was ancient, originally owned by a hero of the Akked Planetary Council, the republic preceding the Ashamine. In addition to standard functions, the creator of the Clothing had armored and weaponized it. Even with all the discoveries he'd made so far, Wake still felt the Clothing held deeper secrets.

Why do I still call it by the Ashamine name? The suit had a glorious, honorable origin, and did not deserve the stigma they'd attached to it. *What to name it then?* Its creator had made it for Calthis Brightwing and that seemed a fitting, honorable title. *Brightwing,* he thought, putting on the helmet. *Calthis would have enjoyed that, at least based on what little I know of her.*

A display materialized inside the opaque faceplate, showing his surroundings as well as a menu. Using only his eyes, Wake began searching through various screens. Finally, he found the option he was looking for. He made adjustments so Brightwing would keep him warm on the surface, checking how it impacted energy levels. This would be his first time to use the upgraded power supply he'd created on Lith-elo-hi-rosh. It was far better than the rigged one he'd made while he and Felar had been hiding on the A'Tal's Revenge. *Perhaps this will unlock even greater features.*

"Wake," Maxar said over the intercom, "are you done with your mods? We could use some help deciding where to set down."

"On my way," Wake replied over Brightwing's comm. He grabbed Maxar's and Jaydon's ENSs and headed for the command deck.

When he arrived, Maxar had the surface of the Traynos-6 mining colony pulled up on the large tactical display. "Any idea where the archeology site might be?" Maxar asked, giving him a strange look. Wake realized they couldn't see him through the opaque face shield, so he detached the helmet.

"If I'm going to fly so the base won't see us," Jaydon said, some of his old grumpiness returning, "I'm going to need landing coordinates pretty buggered quick."

"OK," Wake replied, giving the display his full attention. "This area," he said, pointing to the northwest quadrant. "I don't know which of the mines specifically, but this was the area they were working on just before the bridge accident. If we land here," he pointed to a small space just outside the mining colony boundary, "I think we will go unseen. The miners will be underground this time of day, and it's distant enough the housing and support areas won't be able to pick us out."

"Do you think we'll be able to hike to the mines?" Maxar asked.

"That's probably our biggest issue. The terrain here is steep and rugged. Since the colony and the mines occupy the entire valley, I don't think there is a location we can land secretly that doesn't involve crossing one of the ranges. We'll have to look for a pass. I'd say we could land on the other side of this range," he motioned towards the mountains that would separate them from the mines, "but the crews would see the Watch for sure." Wake checked local time, then nodded. "Since it is morning, our best hope is to get across the mountains during the day, and look for the discovery tonight, after the crews leave. Even with the mods I've made, there is no way we can survive the surface at night. Wherever we are when the star sets, that's where we stay until morning. Some mines have connecting tunnels, so we might get lucky in that regard."

"We may be at this for a few days," Maxar said, looking thoughtful.

Wake agreed. "Thankfully, there's enough space for us to stay out of sight from the mining crews. And if a few supplies or some equipment goes missing, they probably won't notice. If they do, they won't suspect infiltrators, not out here."

"Sounds like a viable plan."

Jaydon took them in low, skimming over mountains and through clouds. Wake had never done this kind of flying, and it made him nervous. It felt like they might crash into the giant peaks at any moment.

When Jaydon finally settled the ship onto one of the few flat spots, Wake breathed easier, looking away from the forward display screen. "Good thing you stopped drinking," Maxar said, sounding unsteady.

Jaydon let out a disgusted sound. "Could have landed just fine fully boozed up." Wake didn't believe him, not with what he had seen when the man was drunk.

"We need to anchor the Watch down," Wake said, pulling up a weather projection on his terminal screen.

"Really?" Maxar said, looking puzzled. "Why?"

"Potential for windy conditions." He checked the forecast, noting they had a suitable weather window for the next few days. "The projection isn't calling for anything major, but things pop up here."

"It gets windy enough to move a gunship?"

Wake nodded. "I told you conditions are difficult."

"Alright then," Maxar said, putting on his white ENS. "I'll get on it."

"A compartment near the airlock has everything you'll need."

"Once the ship shuts down," Jaydon said, not looking up from his screen, "I'll come help."

"The topographic displays should give me a route to the mines, and I can upload that into Brightwing—my ENS, I mean. I renamed it. I didn't like Clothing of the Iconoclast. It dishonored its history." Wake realized he was off topic. "We also need some additional supplies and a way to transport them: boot spikes, ropes, ice tools, and survival gear. We definitely need deicing solution for our face shields as well." Wake formed a plan in his mind, thinking about the rest of what they'd need, both for the mission, and for survival, if the weather projection was wrong.

**

Wake watched as Maxar and Jaydon trudged through the snow ahead of him, wondering if they were making a mistake. He'd raided the ship's emergency cache, a module created to help the crew survive on a hostile world until help could arrive. *The designers didn't have Traynos-6 in mind, but it was better than nothing.*

The path he'd mapped out would be difficult and technically challenging. He'd routed them towards the lowest elevation notch in a huge ridge, but even getting that far would be tricky.

Don't think too far in the future. One step at a time. Wake had learned this, along with many other skills, from Felar. He often thought too far ahead, tried to consider too many factors that might never come into play.

The monotonous work of walking up the snowy hill, along with the vast white and gray of the landscape, made Wake introspective. *Felar is...* Well, he didn't know exactly what to think about her. She was amazing, loyal, hardworking, and courageous, but those words weren't strong enough. Wake appreciated having someone he could talk about the Ashamine with. Even though Felar had been a Founder's Commando, she still understood the operations and bureaucracy of Wake's old unit, the Engineering and Building Division. They'd spent hours talking on Lith-elo-hi-rosh, developing a strong friendship in just the past few weeks.

Wake had become involved in several relationships in the past, both friendly and romantic, but none were ever this close. Felar had opened up to him about how she feared Lothis was drifting away from her, how they were losing their bond. He, in turn, had told her about his childhood and how his parents had disowned him after he'd joined the EBD. On Lith-elo, Lothis spent most of his time with the Entho-la-ah-mines, Maxar and Tremmilly were occupied with each other, and Jaydon mostly wanted to be alone. After they'd finished their projects for the day, Felar and Wake often found themselves together, seeking company. Initially, Wake doubted they had enough in common to spend much time together, but as days went on, they kept talking, and it became obvious they enjoyed each other's company. Lately, Wake had started feeling attracted to her, but hadn't figured out a way to do anything about it.

Burning lungs brought Wake out of his reverie, and he realized the angle of the slope had steepened considerably, going from 30 degrees just above the ship, to 45 at their current location. Wake looked up, and saw it grew steeper still, somewhere between 60 and 70 degrees.

Maxar, in the lead, slowed, kicking the points of his boot spikes into the hard snow. They were each using strap-on ones from the Death Watch, since the retractable ones in their suits weren't long enough. "Do either of you have climbing experience?" Maxar radioed, voice sounding tense. Jaydon growled he didn't.

Wake debated a moment before speaking. "An acquaintance in the Engineering and Building Division took me out, but I wouldn't say I'm experienced. The EBD doesn't give much leave and daylight doesn't last long on Traynos-6."

"Well it's buggered more than I've done," Maxar said, stepping off to the side to allow Wake to go first. "Should we worry about avalanches?"

"I have no idea," Wake answered, his stomach sinking. He hadn't thought about that. "We occasionally saw them from the base after extended periods of snow, but I don't know anything about them."

"It's out of our control," Jaydon said, resolve evident in his voice. "If it happens, it happens."

Taking the lead, Wake felt a weight of responsibility settle over him. Their pace slowed as he made sure each step and placement of his ice tool was solid. As they climbed higher towards the notch, he began to feel the exposure below him. The Death Watch became smaller and smaller. *You're fine, you can do this,* he told himself, trying to summon the courage he admired Felar for.

Finally, when they were just meters from the top, the angle lessened and Wake started to relax.

"Bugger!" he heard Maxar yell over their comms. When he turned, he saw the man on his belly, clinging desperately to an ill planted ice tool. Jaydon was climbing down to him, and Wake knew he couldn't reach them in time to help.

Maxar's ice tool began slowly sheering through the snow. "Kick your feet in," Wake yelled, mind racing for anything he might do to assist. Maxar kicked in hard, as instructed, which gave Jaydon enough time to reach him. The older man shoved his tool hard into the snow, got a solid footing, then pushed down on Maxar's pick. With his tool firm, Maxar regained his composure and the two continued up to Wake.

"Blightheart," Maxar uttered, shaking his head. "Thanks."

"No problem," Jaydon said with a snort.

Wake returned to the lead position, and they reached the top of the notch without further drama. When they looked out to the other side, Wake's stomach dropped. The terrain was rocky, broken, and steep. It would be much more technical and difficult than the snow slope had been. Ice coated many of the towering features.

"How are we going to get through that?" Jaydon asked, all his earlier confidence gone.

Oddly, Wake felt himself grow calmer as he began scanning the terrain. A plan formed in his mind, and he became excited to lead the team.

"If we work our way down to those rocks," he said, pointing as he walked towards the edge of the notch, "then we should be able to—" As Wake took another step forward, he dropped violently through the snow and began accelerating.

13 – FELAR

"This is Felar Haltro," Cazz-ak said, "my trusted companion. She and my other human friends are why the Queen and I made it back to Lith-elo-hi-rosh. You have seen it in the Great Thought. Were it not for them, we would have died on numerous occasions. They interrupted the Breaker Aeron's attack during the battle in which Elth-eo-lan was killed, saving the Queen from capture."

Felar still felt bad she and Wake hadn't arrived soon enough to save the female Entho-la-ah-mine. *There were just too many Breakers to fight through.*

"I ask that you give her your complete attention," Cazz-ak continued, "that you treat her as one of us. There are good humans in the universe. Those on our planet at this time are some of the best." Cazz-ak motioned for her to take over. Felar took a deep breath and stepped up before the throng of Entho-la-ah-mines.

"As Cazz-ak said, my name is Felar Haltro." She looked out across the two thousand sentient insects before her. She'd spent enough time here to know these volunteers were young, at least when compared to the lifespan of their species. They lived longer than humans, but she felt amazed when Cazz-ak had told her the oldest of his kind was over a thousand human standard years. Cazz-ak himself was at least 400, but it wasn't something they exactly kept track of.

"Cazz-ak-tak told me you are all worthy to serve, that you are the best of the tens of thousands who asked to be here. The Queen has decreed only a thousand of you may become part of this new army. Now, it is my job to find who will make up this group. In some instances, this will be easy, in others, hard. But what remains will be the best of those who wish to serve their Queen and species.

"There is danger in what you have volunteered for. If selected, we will rigorously train you to fight for your Queen and your people. You will kill. The Breakers will kill some of you in return. We may send you on missions away from Lith-elo-hi-rosh, and you might not come back, at least not in the condition you left. This is what we require of you as soldiers."

Felar paused, stopping her review to take a closer look at a volunteer that was smaller than the rest. She knew the physical size of her troops would not be important compared to their mental power. *The same is true in human soldiers as well.*

"Cazz-ak-tak tells me the Great Thought understands self-sacrifice," Felar continued, moving through the rows of potential warriors, "that it is part of the makeup of your species. This is good, in more ways than you have guessed." She waited a moment to let it sink in. *It will probably be the hardest thing for them to accept. Learning to kill is one thing, being a killer is another.*

"It is easy to give your life for another, easy to die for the cause of your Queen and people. But what I will ask of you is to sacrifice a part of yourself. This is an infinitely more difficult task, especially for your people, who have never had to do this before. Ending another life will take a toll on you, I promise. Up to this point, you have mourned the loss of your enemies, have killed only in extreme need. I will ask you to kill as a matter of course—for a cause, yes, but I warn you now, this is much different from what you have experienced so far."

As she spent more time around Cazz-ak and Entho-la-ah-mines in general, Felar had learned much about their history and makeup as a species. They were not aggressive and had barely begun to discover how to use the Great Thought as a weapon. Despite the Entho-la-ah-mines outnumbering humans when the war began, they'd been unable to resist. Thinking about the actions of her species made Felar sick to her stomach.

"If you feel this is too much for you, leave now. No one will judge you. Even in my own species, which you have only seen the worst of, there are those that cannot do what I ask. And that's OK. Not everyone is capable of becoming a soldier, nor should be." Felar looked around the mass of iridescent shells, waited to hear legs scuttling across the floor. Silence, both mental and physical, settled around her.

"Good. I'm not trying to scare you, but to explain what we expect. All I ask is all you can give. It is important for both of us to know you can provide what is needed."

She continued walking down the rows of tightly packed Entho-la-ah-mines. The cavern the Queen had given them to use as a training ground could barely contain everyone, organized as they were. *There will be plenty of space soon enough,* she thought, wishing the Queen would have allowed a larger force.

"Before I begin testing you, there is something you should know about me." Cazz-ak had told her this part was unnecessary, but it felt important to her. "None of the operations I was involved in were on Entho-la-ah-mine worlds, or against any of your species. I spent four years in the Ashamine Forces, as a Founder's Commando. I have seen combat, and plenty of it. I also spent lots of time doing what I will be doing with you: training. My reason for telling you this is I need you to know I have never killed an Entho-la-ah-mine and that I have the qualifications to both train and lead you into battle. I still have much to learn about your species, just as you have much to learn about mine. But I think, if we are open-minded and work together, we can forge something both the Ashamine and the Breakers will fear."

A cheer of approval cascaded through Felar's mind, and the Entho-la-ah-mines before her stamped their feet.

"Thank you," she said, raising her hand in salute.

14 – GAV

Gav submitted to the frisk, but it still felt demeaning. No one was permitted to see the Family Council without it. *With what you've accomplished, you'll soon be one of them.*

The hulking sentries allowed Gav to pass, as he smiled inwardly. *I wonder how many other people have managed to sneak an explosive past them.* It was a simple device, but Gav hoped it would give him insurance if the Council didn't see things his way. *They will applaud me as a hero, once I show them what I've done.*

Fade, his quantum human, had developed far quicker than Gav had anticipated, accomplishing more in the past few days than any of his previous subjects had in years. As the head of a lesser Family, Gav used his yearly right to call for a meeting of the Council. He was ready for them to pay for all his hard work.

Entering the luxurious penthouse always took Gav's breath away. Every detail had been wrought by the finest craftsman. The floor to ceiling windows, lush carpet, and vast wooden table were made from the most expensive materials Ashcreds could purchase. The room sat on the top floor of the tallest building on Exis-7, giving not only symbolic meaning to the Families' watchfulness, but a literal spot to do it from. It was a rare, sunny day, and the whole city stretched out before him. Whenever Gav came here, which wasn't often, envy threatened to consume him. *You'll get a chair for what you've created. Your determination will pay off.*

All eyes turned to look at Gav. He felt himself shrink involuntarily. These were some of the most powerful people in the Ashamine, the Council of Seven, led by Salla Markond. Gav tried to stand up straighter, to walk proud. He sat in the designated chair across from them, vaguely wondering where they had gotten enough ancient wood to create a table this long. Meeting the eyes of each Council member in turn, Gav felt confident until he reached Pret Alenthos. The man would want to kill him for what he'd done to his family member, but Gav believed the rest of the Council would pardon him once they understood his accomplishment. Alenthos was the smallest Family on the Council, and the rest would override his minority opinion.

"Gav Serrith," Salla Markond said, her deep blue eyes piercing. When Gav had worked for her, he'd often wondered what she would be like in bed. He never had the occasion to find out, which was probably for the best. She was intelligent, decisive, and ruthless, traits Gav admired, but didn't want to get personally involved with. She had given her approval for him to break off from her organization and form his own Family. For that, Gav would forever be grateful.

"Council," Gav replied. He gave a small, appropriate smile to the group.

"You have convened us," Wollis Dragath, head of the second largest Family on Exis-7 said, voice disinterested. "You have the floor."

"Thank you for fulfilling my request," Gav began, trying not to squirm in his seat. "Your time is valuable, so I will keep this brief. Since the destruction of the original quantum computer at Maxar Trayfis' hands, I have labored to complete a system of my own."

"This is your important news?" Alenthos asked, scowl on his face. "We thought perhaps you had discovered something about the comms blackout from Noor-5." Alenthos shook his head. "Besides, Nex-Delta completed their quantum computer long ago. We bought several."

Gav kept his face smooth. *I'm glad I took Pret's grandson or nephew or whoever he was. Blighthearted Family deserved it with such a bugger as head.*

"Yes, I understand that," Gav continued, not looking at Pret. "However, it is what I've done with my QC that is remarkable and warranted this meeting." Gav paused, waiting for further interruptions.

"Go on," Markond said, the barest hint of a smile curving her lips.

"The Families' data has stayed secure, because Nex-Delta has been unable to create programs or AI that can fully implement the power of the QC. I have accomplished what they could not: a functioning quantum encrypter/decrypter."

"How?" Salla Markond's eyes narrowed. Gav's sense of danger heightened.

"It was just a matter of time before Nex-Delta made the same advances, but I got there first, which keeps our data secure. We could begin to raid encrypted Ashamine files. This opens up greater security for us, as well as revenue streams for the secrets we can decode."

"Answer the question," Markond growled. Gav felt he was flying dangerous skies, but didn't understand why. *Don't they see what this will do for us?*

"Yes, of course," he replied, trying to remember his rehearsed speech. "Nex-Delta speculated a human substitute would be far better than an artificial mind when working with the quantum interface. They have been unable or unwilling to use the tactics I did to subjugate a human mind. After that, it was easy."

"Are you saying you hooked someone up to a quantum computer?" Dragath was starting to sound more interested.

"In a sense, yes. My process destroys the connection to their physical mind as well as their body. The individual becomes committed to incorporation with the quantum computer."

"That isn't possible," Alenthos replied, a smirk on his face. "How would you even go about doing such a thing?"

"It is not only possible," Gav said, trying not to sound disrespectful, "but I have succeeded, with a quantum human as well as encryption-decryption."

"Prove it," Alenthos laughed derisively. "Our Family has tried what Gav claims to have done. It is impossible. The human mind cannot handle it."

Gav quietly took a deep breath and relaxed his jaw. That bugger Pret was calling him a liar and being disrespectful by stripping his Family name. "Just because you aren't intelligent enough to do it doesn't mean it isn't possible."

Alenthos stood, his rigid posture and toned body belying his 82 years. "You will not speak to me in that manner, you blighthearted excuse for a Family head."

"Calm," Markond said. "A great claim requires great proof, Serrith. Do you have any such evidence?"

Gav briefly considered throwing the fact he controlled one of Pret's own relatives into the old man's face, but that would accomplish nothing. More than anything, the Council was about self-preservation. They would protect their own, regardless of Alenthos' temper. Gav's outburst hadn't helped his cause, and he felt the mood shift against him.

"Yes, of course," he replied, trying to restore the required deference and respect to his voice. He took a portable terminal out of his pocket and pulled up several files. "I have decrypted several Family documents, which without your keys, would be impossible with conventional computation."

Salla Markond straightened up in her luxurious chair, her eyes growing even harder. "Are you saying you decrypted lower Family documents, or Council level?"

Gav swallowed hard, feeling a danger he hadn't expected. He'd heard her use that tone before when ordering the execution of her enemies.

"Lies, all of it," Pret yelled. "More unsubstantiated claims. Tell us one of these great secrets."

Gav, knowing it was a bad idea, did as Alenthos asked. "Fine, you old bugger. I read your file listing all the women you've bedded. With 82 years of trying, it's a small number, if you ask me."

Pret sat down, his face turning a satisfying shade of crimson. *Good, serves the old blightheart right. Maybe the Council will give me his chair for my work. He does have the smallest Family of them all, even if it is wealthy and influential.*

"Ahhhh," Markond sighed. "Please tell me that is all you discovered, that it was the only file you decrypted." Her eyes bore into him, promising punishments he'd never imagined if he didn't tell the truth.

"No," he stammered, feeling his victory evaporate. "No, I have more."

"How many?"

"I had to—make sure the system worked."

"And you thought digging into our personal and Family information was a good idea?" Now her tone shifted from that of an interrogator to an executioner. "Why not use the Ashamine files as proof of concept?"

"I didn't think of it," he answered, feeling like the floor was dropping away below him.

"Didn't think of it..." Markond said, each word dripping with sarcasm. "Could it be you are intending to blackmail us?"

"No, no, of course not."

"After all I've done for you, Gav, after the promotions, after giving my blessing to forming a Family."

"I promise blackmail was the furthest thing from my mind. I sought only to prove the concept, to decrypt the files and re-encrypt them so they might be more secure. A quantum device stores all the information, using the new encryption. I never attached it to any network. I have kept your information secure."

"Yet you have plain text versions of some of them on that terminal, do you not?" Dragath, normally bland and mild-mannered, sounded furious.

"Yes, but—"

"Then you have opened us up and made us vulnerable!"

"And how do we know you speak the truth?" Markond said, voice containing the rage her eyes were unleashing. "How can we ever know for sure you have not stored copies somewhere?"

"Because, I am loyal. I only did it to prove it was—"

"No," Markond said, and Gav felt his heart stop. "This is unbelievable and unforgivable. For this, you die." She selected an option on the small device on her wrist. The guards who'd frisked him earlier entered the room.

"Salla," Gav pleaded, "I swear I had no malicious intent. Please, let me explain further. Let me show you I am telling the truth."

"There is no way you can prove anything, and don't use my name, you commoner. I strip you of your Family and titles. Tell us where the quantum computer, its human, and all files are, and I promise you a swift death."

Gav felt terror rise inside himself. Then, he remembered: *The device.* "Stop now," he bellowed, "or I send this whole room to the fires of the black star." Jumping out of his seat, he activated an option on his portable terminal, finger shaking. The advancing guards and a few of the Council members drew flechette pistols. Salla remained in her chair, disgustedly staring at him. "Shoot or try to touch me and I'll release the switch."

"And then what," Alenthos asked derisively, "the screen shuts off?"

"No, you bugger," Gav replied, letting his full rage show, "I'll blightheart us all. I replaced most of the battery with high explosive. Found the little flaw in your security. You should do a better job of scanning."

The guards stopped a few meters away, looking uneasy. "He's bluffing," Alenthos replied, but he'd lost his earlier confidence. "It is impossible to sneak anything past the scanners."

"Just like it was impossible to create a quantum human?" Gav slid the back of the device off, careful to maintain pressure on the switch. He held it up, so each council member could see the dark gray explosive packed neatly inside. They would know what it was.

"By the way," Gav sneered, feeling oddly giddy, "it was Fade, who I captured, tortured, and reduced to a quantum intelligence. He'll never be the same again." Pret collapsed in his chair, saying nothing.

"Kill us all now," Markond seethed, her face a mask of fury, "because if you don't, the Families will find you. I will personally gift you a life with more suffering than any human has ever experienced."

Gav said nothing, carefully backing out of the room. He tried to keep his eyes on everyone, but there were just too many angles to keep them all in view. *Have to trust in my threat.*

When he'd escaped the chamber, Gav began to run. The explosive device would be useless outside the Council's presence. Thankfully, he'd made some strategic caches, both in this building and several other spots throughout the capital city of Nathus. Lower Families rose and fell, only the strongest surviving. While he'd hoped it would never come to this, preparedness was still a requirement.

The weight of what had happened settled over him. Gav was alone now. All previous members of his Family would turn him in, seeking the huge bounty the Council was sure to offer. Getting out of the building, let alone long-term survival, would be a difficult task with long odds.

Gav slammed through another door, entering a utility area. He found his first cache, stored behind a cooling unit. Rummaging through the contents, he pulled on a change of clothes that would identify him as maintenance personnel. Facial prosthetics were next, obscuring his identity further.

"Hey, what are you doing in here?" a man in coveralls similar to Gav's said, entering the room. In the next moment, he realized Gav was the cause of the blaring security alarm. He turned back towards the door.

Without a second thought, Gav lifted his sub-sonic flechette pistol and sent a load of needles into the man's back. He dragged the dying form behind the cooling unit and took his ID. It would be worthless if Gav tried to pass through the genetic scanners at the building's entrance, but it might come in handy other ways.

Walking out the utility room door, Gav felt himself calm. *I'm either up to this or I'm not,* he thought, adopting a pace and mannerism appropriate to a distraught maintenance worker.

15 – CAZZ-AK-TAK

"It's not possible," Lothis said. Cazz-ak could feel the boy's despair.

"I believe in you," he replied, trying to summon a positivity he did not feel.

"We've tried so many times, in so many ways, in so many places. I cannot connect to the signals. I cannot find the Great Thought. The Arche severed my connection, Cazz-ak. It's all gone forever: my link to the world around me, to you, to the Queen. And with them stalking my sleep, it feels dangerous to continue."

Cazz-ak agreed, but he didn't want to say it. Even with the Queen's help, they'd been unable to show Lothis the way to the Great Thought. It had been such a promising possibility, one Cazz-ak had fully believed would restore Lothis' prior abilities. Now, they were both at a loss. He stared across the vast plains of Lith-elo-hi-rosh, tracing the skyline of the mountains in the distance. The palos trees swayed almost imperceptibly in the wind, huge leaves creating a white noise Cazz-ak found comforting.

"We haven't talked much about the Arche's attack," Cazz-ak said, unable to think of another topic. "I believe it shows they think you are still valuable. Perhaps meaning we have not thought of all possibilities."

Lothis closed his eyes, leaning back against the tree's rough bark. Cazz-ak studied the boy's features, more worn and tired than 10 standard years could account for. The disconnection, Cazz-ak thought, it's killing him.

The fade was so slow he hadn't realized it until recently. Felar had seen the decline initially, had come to Cazz-ak with her concerns. They'd talked the problem out at length, but found no answers, other than to keep trying to restore the connection. *We are running out of time,* he thought, feeling heavy.

"I could go back to their computer and make them tell me," Cazz-ak said finally, trying to keep his desperation in check. "I remember the way."

"You know that is foolish, Cazz-ak. As you've told me countless times, the only reason you defeated them the first time was the element of surprise. In my dream, you were near a large gathering of Entho-la-ah-mines and had a strong connection to the Great Thought. You will have neither advantage if you go back."

Cazz-ak couldn't disagree, but he felt guilty for his part in Lothis' loss of power. *I need to fix this, to make it right, before it's too late.*

They were both silent for some time. Cazz-ak found his mind wandering, something new for him. Before coming back to Lith-elo, he'd been so focused on bringing forth the new Queen; it had consumed him. Now, Na-ah-co was leading, and Cazz-ak, while still having a great amount of responsibility, felt less burdened. His commitments to the Queen and the Entho-la-ah-mine army fully utilized his time and working with Lothis took up what little he had left over. Once they'd discovered the boy's degenerative condition, the Queen had been adamant he spend as much time assisting Lothis as possible.

Even with Cazz-ak playing a limited role, Na-ah-co was an excellent leader. She had many other competent advisers in her counsel in addition to Cazz-ak. Taking a diminished part in the daily affairs of the government felt strange to him. Though the Great Thought accepted his unique abilities, he still felt like an outsider amongst his own kind. *Your species values you,* Cazz-ak thought, unsure if he really believed it.

"Why did you look different?" Lothis asked. Cazz-ak felt lost for a moment, then realized the boy was still thinking about the dream.

"I don't know what you mean. How did I look?"

"You still had six legs, but you were larger than normal. You also stood upright. It was like your Entho-la-ah-mine self had blended with a humanoid."

Lothis' description made no sense, yet it seemed familiar, felt real. "How can you be sure it was not just part of the dream?"

"Because nothing in that situation was really a dream. It occurred in a dream dimension, but you and the Arche were actually there. The singularity, or however they traveled, was real. I didn't make any of that up, so why would I have created a strange mental image of you?"

Cazz-ak was silent for several moments, thinking. "We have all agreed Tremmilly's recollection of our shared past was a memory of a real event. Meaning I was something else, somewhere else, before I became an Entho-la-ah-mine. Maybe I subconsciously manifested this other part in the dream. We have all been focusing on our own goals, giving Tremmilly the entire responsibility of puzzling out our past. Perhaps, we should do a little searching of our own."

"With my connection severed and no way to access any historical database, Ashamine or otherwise, I don't know how to discover anything."

"All you say is true," Cazz-ak said, knowing Lothis needed a task to keep him from utter despair, "yet there may be a way to search inside yourself. There could be information, independent of your connection, already within you."

Lothis nodded, and looked excited to start. Cazz-ak hoped he wasn't leading the boy down a path of heartbreak, as he had done with his certainty of connecting to the Great Thought.

"I do not know how to seek out our past," Cazz-ak said. "Our one lead is my form in your dream. Perhaps, we could go back there together, again."

"But what of the Arche? What if they are watching us?"

"After their previous defeat, I do not think they will attack us while we are around so many Entho-la-ah-mines. As long as we are on Lith-elo-hi-rosh, we will be safe. The rest of the Harbingers..." he said, trailing off. "Well, the Arche attacked you twice, and them not at all, so I suppose perhaps they are too strong for them as well. We cannot know, at least not now."

"OK," Lothis said, eyes still closed. "I will meet you in my dreams."

The boy quickly fell asleep, an ability he had gained through much practice. It took a little longer for Lothis to slip into a dream, but once Cazz-ak saw his eyes begin to twitch under their lids, he knew it was time.

Focusing his mind, Cazz-ak detached himself from his body, and headed towards the part of Lothis' mind connected to his dreams. The act of dreaming still puzzled Cazz-ak. Despite Lothis' inability to connect to his own version of signals or to the Great Thought, his mind was still capable of making a pathway to another dimension and creating fantastic imagery. *Is this how all humans dream? Or is this just particular to Lothis?*

Tracing the path through space-time, Cazz-ak arrived in Lothis' dreamscape. He found the boy sitting next to the singularity, seemingly the default scene for his mind. Cazz-ak tried to look at himself, but in the dream dimension, he couldn't see his own body. "Do I look as before?"

Lothis studied him for several moments, eyes narrowed. "No," he replied, and Cazz-ak's heart sank. "No, you look even more humanoid and less Entho-la-ah-mine."

Cazz-ak didn't know how to answer. His mind was a jumble of emotions: excitement for discovering this new aspect of himself, sadness for the loss of his Entho-la-ah-mine traits, and fear they might vanish completely.

"What about me?" Lothis asked hopefully. "Do I look the same?"

Trying to block the distraction of his emotions, Cazz-ak looked at the boy. "You are as always."

Lothis sighed. "So you are changing more, and I, not at all."

"Wait," Cazz-ak said, looking closer. Something about him was different, but he didn't quite understand what it was.

"What is it?"

"You look..." Cazz-ak paused, finally finding the word for it, "older."

"Older? How?"

"In this place, you seem more grown up, more developed towards the adult form of your species. It is hard to see, especially since you dominate this reality with your mind. It is not a normal place. I'm still adjusting."

"What does being older mean?"

Cazz-ak thought for a moment, deciding it could only signal one thing. "I believe it shows some part of your Harbinger being within you. It is influencing your perception of yourself in the same way my own has. It means the Arche didn't destroy that part of you."

The surrounding space shimmered, and the singularity phased in and out of existence. *The Arche,* Cazz-ak thought, widening his connection to the Great Thought in preparation for combat.

"No," Lothis replied, "not the Arche. I've discovered something." The scene before Cazz-ak shifted, stuttering and glitching until it resolved into a bright space full of windows. Lothis stood directly across from him, still recognizable, but several years older, with blue eyes instead of orange. Four figures gathered around them, unknown yet familiar.

"This is our last time gathering as ourselves," one of the female figures said, sounding resigned. Cazz-ak knew instinctively this was Felar, not as a human, but as a Harbinger.

"The shift out of our dimension will have unpredictable temporal results." That was Wake, clad in armor looking like a cross between his Clothing of the Iconoclast and an Entho-la-ah-mine carapace. "Veth and I have done our best to calibrate our arrivals to be as close as possible, both in space and time. Our lives will be compatible with our present forms."

"As we have agreed," Tremmilly, in Harbinger form, said, "this is dangerous, but the cost of inaction is far greater."

Cazz-ak felt himself nod. "The Arche will watch for our integration. They will take note and gather us together when the time lines are viable. Regaining the knowledge of who we are will be difficult, but with the Arche's assistance, I believe we have time before the Breakers become too powerful."

"Then let us proceed, and may the Dawn guide us," the person he knew as Maxar said.

This is a ship, Cazz-ak realized, seeing points of light outside the windows opposite the intense star. He could also feel a thrumming similar to what he had experienced on human vessels. Cazz-ak and the rest of the group headed towards a hatch at the back of the room.

They rode a lift down and entered an expansive chamber, seeing no other people. Cazz-ak felt strong, both in mind and body. He knew they were making the right decision. This action held the only chance of defeating the Breakers. *Tremmilly still thinks we might reintegrate with them, that we might restore the Elrah.* Cazz-ak felt puzzled by his own thoughts.

"All systems in alignment. The time is right," Lothis said, looking up from a screen. In the middle of the chamber, a small point of shimmering light began to grow.

"Does our order matter?" Cazz-ak asked.

"No," Lothis said, "but we don't have much time before we shift out of the window. Everyone must go as quickly as possible."

"I will be with you, always," Tremmilly said, embracing Maxar. They kissed, a quick, passionate exchange. Tremmilly reached out tentatively to touch the ball of light and vanished. Felar went next, determined and focused. Wake hesitated for a moment, then grasped the orb.

Maxar, Cazz-ak, and Lothis remained. An alarm chimed and the boy looked back at his screen. "We are shifting out of alignment," he said. "Go!" Maxar didn't hesitate, darting forward.

Cazz-ak waited a second longer, making sure Lothis was behind him. He reached out with a hand that was almost human, touching the ball of light.

16 – LOTHIS

Cazz-ak touched the singularity. Lothis marveled at his friend's form, not seeing any part that remained Entho-la-ah-mine. He was completely humanoid, tall, and thickly muscled. The singularity sucked Cazz-ak in, and Lothis wondered if it had shifted too far out of alignment. His connection to each of his friends vanished as they passed into the light, making him feel an intense loneliness he'd never experienced before.

I'm coming, Lothis thought, touching the singularity.

***

The palos trees sighed in the breeze. Lothis slowly opened his eyes, feeling tired. *How long were we in the dream, memory, vision, whatever-it-was?*

"I think we made some progress." Cazz-ak said, still in the same position he'd occupied when Lothis had fallen asleep. "We should go share this with Tremmilly. It will open more of our past for us all."

"Wait," Lothis replied, feeling they were missing something critical. "Why did I remember that event?"

Cazz-ak thought for several moments, then his voice returned in Lothis' mind. "It was the most recent event that happened before we transferred."

"Yes," Lothis said, nodding, "that's the obvious answer, but I think there is more to it." Something about the memory tugged at his consciousness. *Come on,* he thought, focusing as hard as he could. The insight was elusive, a vision in the corner of his eye, but constantly fleeting when he tried to get a full view. Usually, his mind worked faster than this. He began to think backwards through the remembrance. *The loneliness, the disconnect as they each went through the singularity...*

"That's it," he said, scrambling to his feet. "I know how to get my connection back. Come on! We have to find Felar and Tremmilly."

***

"So you think we all shared a mental connection as Harbingers," Tremmilly said, "like the Great Thought?"

"Yes," Lothis answered, his excitement overwhelming his weariness. "Similar, but not exact. Our link wasn't as precise or powerful as the Entho-la-ah-mines, at least it wasn't in my memory. It explains our connections to each other, how Felar and I have flashes of each other's thoughts.

Felar looked skeptical. "I always thought it was just your special ability." She squinted her eyes hard for several seconds. "I can't sense any of you with my mind."

"It doesn't work that way. Lothis laughed, and it felt so natural it surprised him. "When we draw closer to our Harbinger selves, the connection intensifies, and it gives us abilities we used to have on a regular basis. I once thought my skills with computers and the connection to space-time was a result of the gene manipulation and programming of Director Kasol, but now I think it was there despite his interference."

"That makes sense," Tremmilly said, mirroring his enthusiasm. "It would explain how I experienced Maxar's escape from Bloodsport. There was also a moment when we were fleeing the Breakers..." She trailed off, and they all waited for her to continue. "I was doing a terrible job aiming my rail cannon on the Watch. I'm not sure how I did it, but I synced myself to the world around me. It made my reaction time flawless."

Lothis saw Cazz-ak stand straighter. "My emotions are not Entho-la-ah-mine. I am different. Perhaps this explains why."

Lothis nodded, feeling several pieces slide into place. "Tremmilly, I think this confirms much of your hypothesis about forgetting ourselves and losing more power than we anticipated. Just before I went through the singularity, I felt worried about it drifting. I don't understand what that means now, but I think it could explain how we all ended up scattered across space and time, as well as why we are human and Cazz-ak is Entho-la-ah-mine.

"We didn't have precise control over who we'd be born as, but Wake said we would at least be compatible. The best we could do was try to get as close to each other as possible, and then the Arche would do the rest. We believed they would bring us together and restore memory somehow."

"And they turned on us instead," Felar growled. Lothis knew she was still furious they'd damaged him, with the latest attack only enhancing her rage. "This could have been so much easier if they'd followed through."

"I'm not sure how much of a difference it would have made," Cazz-ak said. "Obviously, something went wrong in our transition. It is possible the Arche couldn't have helped much more even if they'd wanted to."

"They did help us find each other," Tremmilly nodded, "through the prophecy. We might not have remembered anything if we'd never met."

"So what do we do?" Felar said, visibly trying to calm herself. "How do we reconnect as Harbingers?"

"That, I do not know." Lothis replied. "Our subconscious or some other unknown trigger brought up these experiences. I think the best we can do now is try to consciously focus on restoring our Harbinger identities. It could draw out more memories, which in turn may create stronger connections."

Felar still looked troubled. "If your ability to sense space-time and manipulate computers was a manifestation of a Harbinger power, then doesn't that mean the Arche destroyed your Harbinger link?"

Tremmilly took in a sharp breath. Lothis thought she might start crying.

"Possibly," he answered, unperturbed. "But somehow, enough Harbinger power is within me to still have that memory. Of us all, I think I originally had the strongest connection to my past, given the power of my abilities. Perhaps, Cazz-ak's is as strong, or stronger, but it is hard to say what comes from the Entho-la-ah-mines and what comes from being Harbinger."

"Before we left the palos grove," Cazz-ak interjected, "you said you knew how to restore your connection. I assume now you mean to your Harbinger strength, not just to the manifested abilities?"

"Yes." Lothis answered. "I think we have been trying to fix a symptom and not the actual problem." Tremmilly and Felar looked calmer now. All three were staring at him intently. "We thought something had gone wrong when you welded my mind, body, and the deleted portions back together, but I don't think that was the case.

"When the Arche tried to strip my consciousness from my mental form, all they were seeking was raw power. Lothis, this body," he said, pointing to himself, "has no power. Even my brain is just a network of connections, one of which connects to my Harbinger strength. The Arche thought if they could capture my mental form, they could strip away everything but the Harbinger connection and harness that power."

"So then why didn't it work when Cazz-ak and the Queen restored you?" Felar asked.

"Because that connection doesn't exist in a way any of us understand. I think it is folded up in dimensional space, and none of us consciously know how to access it. Whatever the Arche were doing, it damaged the link between me as Lothis, and me as a Harbinger. Perhaps that was part of the process, or maybe a consequence of interrupting it.

"But this brings us back to the problem of how to restore me. Given that I am still able to sense signals when I dream, and that I experienced the Harbinger memory, I do not think they fully severed the connection, only damaged it. And if I'm not severed, I believe we can repair it."

"That makes sense," Cazz-ak said thoughtfully.

"Looking back at our history, we've all had our strongest moments when we were in proximity. My abilities began manifesting themselves when Felar came to Haak-ah-tar. Cazz-ak harnessed his emotions once we gathered as a group. Tremmilly found focus when we were together on the Death Watch. Much like the Entho-la-ah-mines, I think we are stronger when we are together."

"So you think we can heal your connection to your Harbinger identity?" Felar asked, looking relieved.

"I do," he replied, giving her a smile. "Cazz-ak and I have tried many things, both to diagnose the problem and to fix it. None have made a difference so far, but with this new direction and additional support, it might work."

"Wouldn't it help to have Maxar and Wake here?" Tremmilly asked.

"I believe it would, yes," Lothis replied, "but that is not an option at the moment, and I'd rather not wait to find out. If we cannot do it as a group of four, I will have no choice."

"What do you need us to do?" Felar questioned, looking eager.

"Gather around me," Lothis said, going to the center of their communal meeting space. Once his friends had situated themselves, Lothis closed his eyes. He felt the calm wind blowing through the dwelling, caressing his skin. The scent of warm grass was in the air, and he inhaled deeply.

"Be a beacon," he said instinctively. "Show me where to go. Light up as Harbingers, so I might sense you through what is left of my connection."

"Careful," he heard Cazz-ak caution, "we are unsure of this path's dangers. We must proceed slowly."

Heeding his friend's warning, Lothis began to search for the connection to himself.

17 – TREMMILLY

Something felt wrong to Tremmilly. Not in the sense of danger, although she guessed that was probably true as well. It was more a feeling of incompleteness. *Does it mean we shouldn't attempt this without Maxar and Wake?* Logically, that seemed to fit, but it didn't resolve her anxiety. Then, the thought of Beowulf crossed her mind.

"Wait," Tremmilly announced, rising from the floor.

"What is it?" Felar asked.

"I need to go get Beowulf."

Felar looked quizzical, but Tremmilly couldn't put her feelings into words, so she walked briskly out of the communal building. The bright light of the blue primary star washed over her skin, and she relished the feeling momentarily.

Why is Beowulf important to this? Tremmilly wondered as she covered the hundred meters to the nearby palos trees. *And why has he been spending so much time in the grove?* Since Maxar left, the wolf-dog had been acting strange. He would sleep with Tremmilly at night, curled up in the space Maxar normally inhabited. Then, in the day, he would sit near the odd tree, staring at the spot where Maxar had given him the order to protect her. It was unlike Beowulf.

"Beo," she called, growing closer to her and Maxar's tree. "Beo, are you here?"

When she rounded the massive trunk, the wolf-dog was just where she had expected, so focused he didn't note her coming. "Beo," she repeated, and the wolf-dog's head snapped around, light blue eyes focusing on hers.

Tremmilly walked over and sat beside him. "Strange things are happening, aren't they?" Beowulf's gaze never left her eyes. "What's going on in there?" She scratched his ears, and he leaned into her, some of his normal personality returning.

Could he be a Harbinger? Tremmilly thought. *Cazz-ak was born into another species after all.* The more she thought about it though, the less sense that made. *Only six of us were present in both memories.* Still, something about his behavior and mannerisms made Tremmilly wonder. *And why do I have the feeling he should help us with Lothis?*

"We need to go back to the communal dwelling," she said, wondering if Beowulf would deviate from his daily routine. Thankfully, he followed as she walked towards the small cluster of buildings.

When they entered the room, no one questioned her. Lothis still had his eyes closed. Cazz-ak and Felar both nodded in acknowledgement and then closed theirs. Tremmilly sat down where she had been before and Beowulf settled beside her.

"Does this arrangement feel correct to everyone?" Cazz-ak asked.

Tremmilly tried to get a sense of it, but nothing came. "I don't know either way."

"Same for me," Felar said. Lothis agreed.

"I believe if we move into an exact, even triangle, we will be more effective. Perhaps it is just the Entho-la-ah-mine in me, but if nobody objects, I feel it would be superior." No one disagreed, so they rearranged themselves, with Tremmilly, Felar, and Cazz-ak on the three corners, equidistant from each other. Tremmilly wondered briefly what to do with Beowulf, but the wolf-dog had his own plan, sitting down behind Lothis, facing the opposite direction.

"And now we can begin," Lothis said, breathing deeply. Tremmilly closed her eyes and began searching for something she didn't understand.

Just remember what you did when you were firing the cannon on the Death Watch, she told herself. It was an easy statement, but the action wasn't as simple. Try as she might, Tremmilly couldn't find the connection to the world around her. She took a deep breath, and exhaled slowly. *Look deeper.* Nothing came through, and Tremmilly felt frustration working its way into her mind. *Breathe.*

Tremmilly became aware of her hands, resting on folded legs. *No,* she thought, *that isn't right.* Without understanding why, she moved her hands down to the packed dirt floor, caressing it slowly. She imagined the particles, the substance of the dirt. The grains moved under her fingers. *Smaller,* she thought, thinking about the molecules, then the atoms beneath her, both supporting her weight and creating it. She saw the networks of connections, cascading and expanding all around her. *I am part of it, and it a part of me. I am one.*

She felt it: a warm, bright sensation surrounding her. *No, not just around. It is part of me.* Tremmilly gazed about, seeing Cazz-ak glowing with an energy matching her own. Lothis had an aura about him, but it was barely distinguishable from the photons streaming through the windows. Beowulf caught Tremmilly's attention, not for the size of his light but for its intensity. All her focus was on maintaining the connection, and she knew if she tried to think about the wolf-dog too much, she would lose it.

Finding Felar, Tremmilly realized her friend showed no energy at all. *Perhaps this might help,* she thought, reaching out instinctively. She stretched her light out, forming a thin ribbon, bridging the gap to touch Felar's chest. A small spark erupted from her. Tremmilly watched it swell to an aura as big and bright as her own.

"I don't understand what is happening," she heard Felar say in her mind.

"Neither do I," she sent back, "but this is what Lothis needs." Tremmilly moved her ribbon of light, stopping when its end was directly above Lothis. A huge trunk of glowing energy stretched out from Cazz-ak, hovering over the boy.

After a few moments, Felar's own wisp of light moved, and when it passed over Lothis' head, all three strands of energy connected. Tremmilly felt a jolt of power, and it momentarily threatened to overwhelm her control.

As she watched, a bright thread even thinner than Felar's emerged from Beowulf's tiny light and attached itself to their union. Minutes passed, and Tremmilly wondered how long she would be able to hold the connection. *As long as Lothis needs you to.*

"I can feel you all," Lothis' voice said in her head, but sounding kilometers away. "I've found the path, but I don't know what to do. It is like it is made of entangled particles. Some of them have evaporated."

More time passed, and despite the amazing thing happening, Tremmilly found it hard to resist distractions. She tried to focus on the light, on her attachment to the surrounding world and her friends.

Finally, Lothis' voice was in her mind again, only this time it sounded as close as Felar or Cazz-ak. "I did it. I found a way to entangle new particles."

18 – MAXAR

"Wake!" Maxar yelled, rushing towards where the engineer had fallen through the snow. He had to look, needed his eyes to confirm what his mind knew. *But if the snow couldn't support Wake, how will it support me?* Maxar stepped closer, feeling the knot in his stomach grow as the drop became evident. *It has to be a thousand meters down to the valley. Even with Brightwing,* he thought, unable to make himself get closer to the weak snow, *he couldn't survive that.* Jaydon stopped beside Maxar and they looked at each other.

"I'm OK," Wake's voice said, making them both jump. "The cornice stretches over a ledge. Any farther and I would have taken a pretty big ride."

Maxar sighed, wishing to be anywhere but on this mountain. "Can we get down to you?"

"Probably, but I don't see a good way off this ledge. I'll tunnel my way back up." Several minutes elapsed, and finally the crimson helmet of Brightwing popped up through the snow. Maxar admired how calm Wake was in a situation threatening to overwhelm him. He'd yet to mentally recover from his earlier slip and thought Jaydon and himself doomed when they'd lost Wake.

"Well," the engineer said, as they lifted him out of his tunnel, "we won't go that way." He led them towards a rock fin that ran down to the midpoint of the gully. "Let's try picking our way down this feature. Given how the wind has scoured the snow off this side, I don't think we'll find any more cornices."

The distance they still had to cover felt overwhelming. "Can't we use a rope or something to protect us?" Maxar tried to keep the fear out of his voice. *I went through hundreds of battles on Bloodsport with the constant possibility of death, yet crossing some mountains makes me feel shaky?*

"Two problems," Wake replied as he continued leading the descent. "First, there was no anchoring gear on the Watch. There were large screws for the ship, but they were far too heavy to carry. Without the proper equipment, if one of us falls, a rope will just pull us all off. It would be a suicide covenant. Second, even if we did have the right gear, it would slow us down too much." He pointed at the primary star, beginning to descend towards the horizon. "If we do everything right, we will still be close on time, and yes, falling is a danger for us individually, but that's just a possibility. Freezing is a certainty."

"What if it gets too hard to climb down?" Jaydon's voice was as unsteady as Maxar felt.

"I do have a bit of rope, so we could hand-over-hand our way down, but I hesitate to do that. Whatever we go down on this side, we will have to come back up to reach the Watch."

We have to do this all again, Maxar realized. He breathed deeply, trying to calm his fraying nerves.

"I see a route, though," Wake continued. Maxar again wondered how he could sound so calm. "I think we can make it down in time. If we are cautious, we can eliminate slips."

The next few hours felt like an eternity to Maxar. He distilled his whole existence into putting one foot cautiously in front of the other, finding places to sink his ice tool, and gripping the exposed rock. The task of not falling consumed his attention. He forgot about the passage of time, the setting star, or any other aspect of their mission. *Step. Tool. Step. Grip. Step. Tool. Step. Step.*

Finally, he looked down, and saw only flat snow stretching out across the valley. "We made it," Wake said, patting Jaydon and Maxar on the back. "We did it!"

As Maxar's awareness returned to normal, he saw the star slip down behind a jagged peak. Without the direct stellar radiation, he felt the temperature drop inside his ENS. Wake must have made the same observation.

"Here are some power modules," he said, handing them each one. "Switch over to auxiliary, then replace your main."

Maxar and Jaydon did as ordered. "Status reads full charge," Jaydon said, "but I don't feel a difference."

"You won't," Wake replied. "I've already made your suits as warm as the systems allow. We also need to space out our module consumption. It will get a little cold, but if we hurry, I think we can make it to the mines before the situation goes critical."

They set off at a fast pace, moving as quickly as conditions allowed. After a few kilometers, Maxar felt his fingers and toes beginning to numb. He tried to ignore it, not wanting to think about what would happen if they stopped moving.

"I'm freezing," Jaydon said breathlessly over the radio, "and I can't—keep up." Maxar and Wake both turned to see the older man falling behind. "Too much—time on ships," he finished.

They adopted a slower pace Jaydon could maintain. Maxar kept looking up, checking both the remaining light and distance to the mine. The squat entrance, built into a low hill, looked so close, but their progress was slow.

The cold continued creeping into Maxar, and he had to fight to ignore the thousand needles of icy pain stabbing his legs and arms. Minutes dragged by as they plodded towards the mine. Soon, Maxar began shivering, uncontrollable spasms wracking his body.

You'll die out here if you don't keep going, he thought, using every bit of his will power to press on.

Finally, Maxar stopped shivering. *The suit must be doing its job,* a distant part of his mind thought. *Now I can sit down and rest for a minute.* Maxar collapsed onto the hard ice, feeling a level of exhaustion he'd never known existed. *Just a minute of rest, then I can keep going.* His eyelids began to flutter. *Perhaps, sleep, just for a moment.*

A large figure stood over Maxar, and he wondered why it was red. "Get up!" a voice yelled in his ears. "You're getting hypothermic. You have to keep fighting. We're almost there."

Where? Maxar grumbled in his mind. Why was this person disrupting his much-needed sleep? Another figure, clad in white, stumbled past Maxar.

"Just let me sleep," another voice said, as the newcomer tried to push the red figure away.

"One hundred meters," Red replied, "then you can rest." Maxar wanted to sleep just as much as White, but he needed them both to leave him alone.

"Fine," White said. The world around Maxar began to grow dark, and he didn't understand why. *Is it night or day?*

As they followed, White tried to lay down several times, but Red was always there to prod him onward. After what felt like an eternity, they arrived at a large orange object standing out of the gray-white surroundings. Red did something to the orange thing, and it moved. Maxar stumbled forward, and collapsed. A part of him said the fall should have hurt, but his body didn't care.

The world lightened, but the gravity of sleep was pulling harder than ever. Maxar sensed himself sliding along the floor, then slipped into oblivion.

***

Warm dirt. A breeze rustled the surrounding foliage, caressing and dancing through his fur. *Where am I?* His senses felt more alert than usual, more detailed.

"Beo?" he heard a familiar voice say, startling him out of his daydream. When his eyes finally adjusted, he was staring at a palos grove, the same one he and Tremmilly had spent many hours in. *How did I get back to Lith-elo-hi-rosh?*

"Beo," he heard again, and when he looked in the direction of the voice, there she was. Tremmilly seemed much taller, and everything about her was more vivid. Maxar inhaled deeply, taking in a scent that was familiar, but richer somehow.

Tremmilly walked over to him, and he couldn't take his eyes off hers. "Strange things are happening, aren't they?" she said, sitting down beside him. He tried to speak, tried to tell her that he was present, but nothing came out.

"What's going on in there?" Tremmilly asked, scratching him behind the ears. The sensation was amazing, and Maxar couldn't help but lean into her. *I'm Beowulf,* he thought, not understanding, but accepting all the same.

"We need to go back to the communal dwelling," she said finally, rising to her feet. Maxar sensed he had a choice, that he was in full control of the wolf-dog's body. *This isn't a vision or a memory,* he thought, *this is actually happening.* Recent events from Traynos-6 were fuzzy. He could remember the harrowing descent from the notch, but everything after that was spotty. *Did I die?*

Maxar rose and followed Tremmilly, the sensation of walking on all fours strange at first, but becoming natural after a few strides. When they entered the meeting building, Maxar saw Lothis seated in the center of the room, eyes closed. Cazz-ak and Felar sat around him. Tremmilly deliberately picked a spot and settled to the floor. Maxar, not understanding what was happening or what to do, sat beside her.

As the group began to converse, Maxar found himself distracted by Tremmilly's scent. He tried to focus on what they were saying, to understand what was happening, but the depth and intricacies of her smell was intoxicating.

Tremmilly rose to her feet, startling Maxar and giving him a chance to refocus. He watched her, Felar, and Cazz-ak reposition, and return to the floor in a precise layout. *This has something to do with Lothis,* he thought, noting the boy was still in the center. Something deep and instinctual welled up in Maxar, and he felt himself drawn to sit behind Lothis. He padded over to the boy and sat back-to-back. *None of this makes sense,* he thought, embracing his instincts.

"And now we can begin," Lothis announced. Maxar felt the boy press against him as he took a deep breath.

Then, nothing happened. Maxar waited. From his position, he could only see Tremmilly and Felar. They sat, eyes closed, breathing. *What are they trying to do?* He wanted to look behind him, to see what Cazz-ak was doing, but the deep instinct welled up again in Maxar. *Must maintain this position.*

Closing his eyes, he tried to sense how he could help. *Reach out,* Maxar thought, not understanding what it meant. He breathed in deeply, smelling the youth of Lothis, the strength of Felar, and the steadfastness of Cazz-ak. *How is it possible to smell these traits?* He continued expanding his awareness, syncing the rise and fall of his breath with Lothis.

Something shifted in Maxar's mind, and he felt his body back on Traynos-6, cold, but alive. The sensation of being in two places at once threatened to overwhelm and destroy his focus. *You are Beowulf, and Beowulf is Maxar,* he thought, the concept further bending his reality. *You are a Harbinger. You are a wolf-dog. You are a human.* All his aspects connected in a burst of energy, and he felt his aura grow. *This is what they need of you,* Maxar thought, holding the connection and focusing on its cohesiveness.

Moments passed, and Maxar felt a peace and wholeness unlike anything he'd experienced before. *This is who I am. This is me, all of me.* Tremmilly caught his attention as he saw a bright aura encompass her. He could sense Cazz-ak and Lothis behind him as well, although the boy's energy felt weak and diminished. *That's why we are here,* Maxar realized. *It is why Lothis is in the center. We are trying to restore what the Arche took from him.*

Felar was the only one not uniting her being, and Maxar gazed at her intently, trying to find a way to help. *I barely discovered how to do it myself,* he thought, feeling helpless. As he watched though, a tendril of light stretched out from Tremmilly, reaching for Felar. When it touched her, a spark erupted, growing in both size and intensity until it was the same as Tremmilly's.

Maxar felt Cazz-ak's energy grow closer until it was almost hovering over his head. Tremmilly and Felar both moved strands of their auras in, and the three sources joined. Maxar, once again acting on deep instinct, focused hard on connecting his own energy to those above. It was a difficult task, one made harder by the spacial distance of his human body. Finally, a wisp of his aura stretched up and joined with those of his friends. A spike of energy surged through him, threatening to disjoin his three aspects. He focused harder, knowing Lothis needed him.

"I can feel you all," Lothis said, voice sounding far away even though he was just behind Maxar. "I've found the path, but I don't know what to do. It is like it is made of entangled particles, and some of them have evaporated."

Maxar continued to hold on to the strange union, fighting the myriad distractions that threatened to pull it apart. Pain started to flow in from the connection to his human body. *It doesn't matter,* he thought. *I can tolerate pain.*

As minutes crawled by, however, he began to wonder how much longer he could hold fast. The pain began rising to a crescendo, driving a wedge in his unity. *What is happening to me?* he wondered. His connection to his Harbinger strength and Beowulf began to separate, and Maxar had to cut off concern for his body.

"I did it," Lothis said finally, voice strong and loud. "I found a way to entangle new particles."

A spike of icy pain shot through Maxar's mind, and he felt the union burst apart. His consciousness rushed back into his human body. An intense agony unlike any he'd known before consumed Maxar. He began screaming.

19 – CRASOR

"Initiate worm generator," Karoth ordered.

Crasor sat back, watching on the forward view screen as blackness darker than space materialized in front of the Justice. Moments later, new stars appeared. *The Exis system,* he thought, nodding in satisfaction. *This is the largest Ashamine world we've invaded so far.* Excitement and apprehension filled his mind. Exis was the seat of power for the Families, the affiliation of organized crime groups that controlled three of the Ashamine's thirteen planets. *Make that two,* Crasor thought, smiling. The Families had controlled Noor-5 before the rising of the Breakers. *And soon, the Families will only have Vind-8.*

The relationship between the Ashamine and the Families was one of tense balance. The Founder had never used Crasor in any action against them, but he'd been kept up on the situation. While they broke numerous laws, the Families also kept order on the planets they controlled. The few times the Ashamine had tried to eradicate them ended disastrously. The Families had embedded themselves on their worlds too well for the Ashamine to remove them, possessing blackmail information on numerous members of government. Some operatives speculated they had files on the High-Elder Council, and even the Classad. Crasor doubted this was true, but until someone broke their encryption or pushed the Families hard enough, he couldn't be sure.

Once I have access to their databases, though, Crasor pondered as the Justice slid through the worm tunnel. He didn't need the information, but it would be interesting to read. *Blightheart all those old Classad buggers.* Crasor lifted his lip, snarling. *They always saw me as the Founder's aide, impotent, subservient.* It was all part of hiding his role as Facilitator, but it still bothered him. *Soon, they will learn my new identity and power.*

"Worm calculations must have been slightly off," one of the techs said. "Exis-7 is across the system and below us relative to the orbital plane." He touched a few options on his screen. "Transit time has doubled, to a little over two standard hours."

Crasor sighed, wondering if the navigators or the ship's computers were to blame.

"We have done our best to optimize the ship and its crew," the Breakers boomed in his mind. "There is only so much we can do with flawed tech and biology."

I understand, he replied, wincing as the voice continued reverberating.

"Set up the blockade as we did on Psinar," Karoth said. "Deploy gunships inside the gravity well perimeter. Disable any vessels that attempt to flee. Destroy those who will not stop."

The Justice had lost many of its gunships and fighters, the vessels responsible for the blockade, during the Eishon battle. When the Breakers had overrun the huge Ashamine ship, a large portion of its spaceborne assets had been outside the Justice. With Karoth's brilliant tactics, they'd managed to secure most of them, but they'd still lost more than Crasor liked. The massive Tarton class ship would still have the firepower he needed, but wider margins would be a relief.

His tactical display showed the gunships and fighters deploy from the Justice. Crasor smiled. It would take some of them hours to reach their positions at the opposite side of the gravity well, but that was fine. Surprise was still on his side. Even if the Ashamine Forces stationed here had received news of the Justice's capture, there would be little to no cooperation between them and the Families. Each would suspect the other of a trap.

Time crawled by as Crasor continued watching the tactical display. Eventually, a white dot appeared on the forward view screen and began to grow. *Exis-7,* Crasor thought. He'd never had occasion to visit the planet, until now. It was notorious for its clouds and globe spanning oceans, for storms that lasted weeks. *Not a place to visit for pleasure.*

A formation of ships on the tactical display caught his attention. "An Ashamine battle group is forming up to defend the planet," an officer said, voice tense.

"To the pirates, Ashamine rebels, or whoever you are on the ASN Founder's Justice," came over the ship's speakers, "surrender the vessel to us, or face immediate destruction."

Crasor snorted. *Bold talk. This is the largest ship humanity has ever built.* "Send a message back that we impose the same terms."

Karoth came to stand next to him. "There are three Fion class ships in that group," he said quietly. "By themselves, it would be a tough battle, but when you add in the six Rubicons and our blockade deployed assets, I'm not sure we can defeat them. The Rubicons are a medium size ship and will run laps around us while still having enough firepower to do significant damage."

"But the Justice features the thickest armor of any Ashamine ship, does it not?"

Karoth nodded. "Correct, but any armor will fail when placed under enough stress." He paused, a pained look on his face. "We did not anticipate this much opposition. I think retreat may be the best action."

"No," the Breakers boomed in Crasor's mind, the sound making his head feel like it might explode. "We sense those on the planet. They are ripe for us. We cannot back down now."

But if they destroy the Justice-Crasor tried to argue.

"We will take control of the ship," they interrupted. "The nanites have fully integrated into the systems, providing us with a direct interface." The voice of the Breakers felt like a tidal wave, threatening to sweep him away. "The fighters and gunships are still isolated from us, so you will issue them the orders we give."

Karoth was still talking, but Crasor had a difficult time hearing him. "The captains of those vessels will bypass the lockout that prevents them from firing on Ashamine ships. Their targeting computers will be at full..." Karoth trailed off, his brow furrowed. "Is everything alright? You look ill."

"I'm fine," Crasor said, straightening up. *I have to figure out a way to control the Breakers influence over me, or they will scour my consciousness away.* "We will not retreat," he continued. "Their firepower may rival ours, but they are only human. We have the advantage."

The Justice shifted course, and the techs began panicking. Crasor watched for several moments, once again feeling his sole connection to the Breaker mind as both a benefit and a curse.

A plan began to form in his mind. He wondered if it was his own idea or one inspired by the Breakers. *It's getting hard to tell where one ends and the other begins.* Opening a ship wide channel, Crasor began speaking. "The Breakers have taken over direct control of the Justice. With their immense power, we will have the advantage over the blighthearted Ashamine. Karoth will still issue orders for close support fighters and gunships, but any of you not involved in that chain of command, cease what you are doing and lend your concentration and mental power to me." Crasor felt thousands of minds focus on him, swelling his energy. *Good.*

Several minutes passed as Crasor relayed commands from the Breakers to Karoth, who immediately sent them to the appropriate techs. The gunship crews and fighter pilots responded promptly to the techs orders. It felt inefficient to Crasor, but he supposed the humans were doing the same thing, and didn't have the superior mind of the Breakers guiding them.

With the additional power of thousands of individuals given to him, the voice of the Breaker mind was more tolerable. *Perhaps there is a way I can permanently harness this energy,* Crasor speculated.

"Focus!" the Breaker mind bellowed, its intensity greater than anything Crasor had previously experienced. "Victory is not guaranteed. Refrain from indulging your fear or other human emotions at this critical point. Our plan requires precision." Once the reverberation cleared from his mind, Crasor blocked everything but the mission.

After another minute went by, Crasor could see the layout of the battle take shape. He was no tactician, at least not when it came to space combat, but the Breakers' maneuvers seemed to minimize the enemy's firepower, while maximizing their own. The Justice moved closer and closer to the Ashamine ships.

"Brilliant," Karoth said under his breath, confirming Crasor's assessment.

"Conceal this group of gunships," the Breaker mind said, "and do not let go until we give the command. We need to manufacture precise distractions. "

When Crasor reached out through space-time to do as ordered, he found ten of the large DAS gunships. "I cannot hide so many. One or two, yes. Maybe five. But not ten."

"You can, and you will. You have the proximity and focus of thousands of Breakers."

Crasor took a deep breath, closed his eyes, and began forming the cloak to conceal the ten ships. His mind strained, pulling and warping the surrounding space-time to make the vessels invisible. As the last bit of cloak slid into place, he felt approval surge from the Breaker mind.

"Now," they continued, "do the same to this group." Another target popped up in his mind. As he began releasing the first cloak, the Breakers interrupted. "Do not drop the first! It is not time. They will be decimated."

But how am I to do both?

"Utilize all power available. Be more efficient."

I'm going to burn myself out, Crasor thought, but the Breaker mind responded only with urgency. Digging, he found a well of untapped energy. It was like the Breakers on the Justice had a deeper level, a subconscious containing vast quantities of power. Getting to it was difficult, but the more he tapped, the easier the task became.

As Crasor started the next cloak, he saw an easier way to bend space-time, a method that used its own properties to create the folds he had manually done before. "Good," the Breaker mind interjected. "You are learning." Several moments of silence passed, and Crasor reveled in his newfound strength. "Now, do the same with these three groups of fighters."

Crasor took a deep breath, drew in every bit of strength available, and reached out for the ships. He could feel them far across empty space, darting towards the Ashamine ships, rail rounds streaking past them. Once Crasor grasped them with his perception, he began folding. Beads of sweat formed on his brow, streaking down his face. Gritting his teeth, Crasor felt the bubble spring into existence. Simultaneously, his other cloaks began to slip from his grasp, reminding him of when the same event had occurred as they'd captured the Justice.

Time dragged by for Crasor as he fought to maintain his hold. He knew what he was doing was critical to the plan, but it was all starting to slip away. Groans emanated from deep within him, and he vaguely heard someone asking if he was all right. *Can't respond.* He wondered what would happen to him if he let the cloaks go or if he pushed his abilities past their breaking point. He lost track of time, consumed by the concentration it took to warp so much space-time.

"Release," the Breakers finally responded. Crasor sighed with relief, feeling like he had pushed every muscle in his body to the limit. Chaos broke out on the tactical display, as the Breaker fighters and gunships appeared inside the Ashamine battle group. They began raking hulls with rail cannon fire, and it took several moments for the Ashamine ships to respond.

"Cloak the Justice," the Breaker mind demanded.

What?

"We cannot lose time. You must get the Justice closer to the enemy vessels. Do as ordered."

I can't. It's too much.

"Your delay costs more ships and lives than is necessary. Cloak the Justice, now!"

Without further protest, Crasor reached out. *This will destroy me,* he thought, once again taking hold of the surrounding space-time. He tapped into the subconscious wells of those on the Justice, drawing as deep on their energy as he possibly could. Using the tricks he'd learned earlier, Crasor bent, twisted, and warped around the Justice. He forced the bubble to stabilize. Sweat began pouring down his face, but his concentration was so intense he barely noticed. Peripherally, he heard Karoth talk to him, but the man seemed far away and Crasor ignored him.

The Justice shot forward, and he had to fight hard to maintain the cloak. Minutes ticked by, and Crasor resigned himself to the fact the Breaker mind was sacrificing him. *Maybe—they can—bring me back—from death—another time.* He bore down, grimacing with effort. *But what if—*

this—destroys mind—instead of—body?

Shouts of surprise worked through his ears and into his consciousness. "Worm drive energizing?!"

"What? Inside the gravity well? Who issued that order? Where are we going?"

"The coordinates don't make sense. The whole drive config is blighthearted."

"Is it a malfunction?"

Whatever was happening, Karoth would have to handle it. Another minute passed, and Crasor wondered how long they expected him to last.

"Release in three... Two..." the Breaker mind ordered. "One."

Crasor let the cloak slip from his grasp, feeling relief flood through him. He slumped down in his seat, all energy gone. Before he could stop himself, he tumbled to the floor. Around him, voices continued shouting.

"All Ashamine ships vanished, sir," an officer reported over the din.

"Where did they go?" Karoth asked, sounding surprised, but in control. Crasor was glad he had him for second-in-command.

"No idea, sir. Perhaps it's connected to the worm generator malfunction."

As Crasor returned to himself, he sat up. A look at both the tactical display and the forward view screen confirmed what the tech had said: Blackness filled the space the Ashamine ships had just occupied. He waited for the Breaker mind to explain, but they were silent.

A moment later, all nine Ashamine ships reappeared, in the exact position they'd been before. "Spool up point defenses," Karoth roared. "Fire all cannon batteries. Take out their offensive weaponry."

"They are ours now," the Breaker mind boomed in Crasor's own.

"Get us out of their effective range." Karoth ordered.

"Sir," one of the techs said apprehensively, "none of the systems respond to commands. The ship has locked us out."

Crasor rose unsteadily to his feet, using his chair for balance. His mind felt hot, fuzzy, and exhausted. He tried to speak, but the connection between his brain and his tongue seemed unavailable.

Karoth turned to him. "Orders?"

Focusing hard, Crasor managed to say, "They are ours."

The former Ascended scowled, looking puzzled. "What? How is that possible? They were firing on our gunships just moments before."

Crasor didn't have answers, so he just shook his head. The cloaking effort had drained every bit of energy from him. *Just want to sleep,* he thought, trying to keep his eyes open.

"We have done what the situation required," the Breakers boomed in his head. "The ships are yours to control. Continue subjugating this system."

"Resume operations to secure Exis-7," Crasor ordered, trying to find a way out of his exhaustion. Karoth nodded, and began issuing commands of his own. As strength returned to Crasor, he began to feel Breakers on the nine Ashamine ships. *They are different somehow. Stronger. More... Real.*

How did you capture them? Crasor asked, wondering if he really wanted to know.

A humanoid appeared on the large comms screen, and Crasor felt his heart clench. His head was bald, and where eyes, nose, and mouth should have been, was only smooth, uninterrupted skin. Behind the individual, he could see several more of his kind. *Faceless,* Crasor thought, wondering how these highly evolved Breakers had come to this dimension. *And no Ashamine personnel remain on the bridge.* He shuddered, remembering how the trillions of faceless ones had stared at him after he'd woken from death.

"We made adjustments to the worm generator," the Breaker mind answered, "and used it to bring the Ashamine ships to us." The Breaker on the screen before him had no eyes, but Crasor felt the faceless' vision boring into his mind.

Breathing deeply, he tried to relieve the tension building in his chest, but the effort was futile. The faceless continued staring, sensing every inadequacy and fault within him. Crasor wondered what this new development meant, if they would find him lacking and remove him from command.

"No," the Breaker mind boomed, "you still control the forces in your dimension, including these new additions. We are loyal, Crasor Tah Ahn. We will not take away what we promised you."

Crasor sighed, his anxiety unabated. His energy was returning, bringing with it a flood of elation and triumph. He watched on the tactical display as the nine Ashamine ships fell into formation around the Justice, heading for Exis-7. Crasor's forces were larger than ever. Now he controlled a fleet that could challenge any world except the Ashamine core systems. His mental and physical capabilities were becoming greater than he'd ever imagined.

It all sounds good, a deep part of him thought, one he hoped the Breaker mind couldn't hear, *but with the coming of the Faceless, are you sure you can trust them?*

20 – AZA

As the dwelling door slid shut, Aza darted over to the wall mounted terminal. She selected one menu item, then another, and the screen presented her a view of the exterior passage. The terminal showed her mother walking away, headed towards the Holy Order building. Her father had left awhile ago to preside over an Ashamine Forces graduation ceremony. It was a boring event and she had declined his offer to come. Aza knew her mother had an engagement at the same time, affording her the opportunity she needed. Guilt crept over her, and she bit her lip. The pain helped distract her.

Aza continued watching the screen until her mother disappeared from view. *Are you sure you want to do this?* She thought for a moment longer, then turned resolutely towards her parents' study.

It had only been a day since Aza had resolved to contact her uncle Ash. Her searches on the Terminal Network had been useless. No one had updated his profile information. It contained nothing more than what she already knew. *What did you expect? A direct terminal connection address?*

She'd almost given up, but thinking of Ash churned up a memory of an event that had happened just after his disappearance. Aza replayed the recollection, hearing the chime that signaled someone was at their door. She looked up, seeing her mother's reddened eyes, and dark, tear streaked cheeks. Her father stood, walking to the door. He seemed so tall and dignified. When he'd opened it, a man stood outside, dressed in a formal red uniform. Aza didn't know what his clothes signified at the time, but after doing some research, she now knew the man had been a courier.

Her father accepted a small package from the man, a plain, opaque plasti-glass box with no markings or identifiers. In her five-year-old mind, Aza wondered if the man had brought her a present. Without saying a word, her father brought the box over to her mother. She looked at it briefly, then they both nodded.

"Aza, go to your room. Shut the door and play quietly," her father said. Her mother rose from her seat, a weak smile encouraging Aza to follow instructions. Aza set off down the hall, still not understanding why her mother was so heartbroken. Just before entering her room, Aza saw her parents go into the study. The oddity of the situation had intrigued her, and rather than play with any of her toys, she hid and watched for their exit. Eventually, they'd come out, and Aza felt guilty for spying.

They left the cube in the room, though, she thought, snapping back to the present. *Remember, you don't have unlimited time. Father will return in just over an hour.*

Crossing the threshold into their study made Aza anxious. It wasn't against any rule and they'd never told her she required supervision, but it still felt wrong. The room was their space, sacred somehow and off limits to her.

Aza performed a visual scan of the room, trying to find the package. She didn't expect it to be out in the open, but it was a place to start. *How do you know it even has anything to do with Ash? This could all be a waste of time.*

Aza began checking shelves, looking behind the religious figurines and paraphernalia her parents displayed. When she moved something, she put it back in the precise spot it had occupied, careful not to leave any sign of snooping. Checking the large central cabinet, she scanned each drawer from top to bottom, front to back. Aza felt the time slipping away, and she began to despair of finding the box. *It was eight years ago.*

Closing the final drawer, Aza turned to face her parents' desks. They were large and crafted of blue plasti-glass. She took a step towards the one on the left, her father's, then hesitated. Something inside her protested.

A picture of the three of them hovered over the far right corner, from their trip to one of the recreation satellites above Ashamine-2. They were all smiling, standing in front of magnificent fountains. The whole moon had been water themed, something Aza enjoyed thoroughly. The vacation hadn't lasted long and they hadn't been on another one since. Her parents never felt comfortable leaving their responsibilities.

Next to the hovering photo was a delicate green shell. Aza had found one for each of her parents, while exploring the black sand beach just outside their lodging. *Father smiled so much when I gave it to him,* she thought, feeling a knot in her throat.

Before she could convince herself not to, Aza forged ahead and began opening drawers. The first was full of Holy Order trinkets, necklaces, and rings, some of which looked very old. She sorted through them quickly, then shut the compartment. The next few had more personal items, including a misshapen krakori fish statue Aza had made when she was very young. *I used to love the water and marine life so much*, she thought turning to the last drawer. Inside was the white plasti-glass box from her memory. Aza picked it up, feeling a sense of foreboding. *If you open this, you can't go back.* Not understanding what she wouldn't be able to come back from, Aza removed the lid.

Nothing. Disappointment hit Aza like a physical blow. The box was empty except for some packing material. *Whatever was in here was small,* she thought, examining the foam more closely. It had a shallow indent in it, the same shape and size of a data square. She placed the lid back on the box, returning it to the exact spot in the compartment. Data squares were old, mostly obsolete technology. The Terminal Network was infinitely faster at transmitting information. Aza had never physically seen one of the small devices. Spies and agents used them in the entertainment vids, but that was about it.

Security, she thought. *That's the only reason people use squares now. They keep data off the network.* Had Ash become a spy? Was that why someone had delivered secret information to her parents? She'd never heard of the Holy Order using such an arcane form of communication.

And where is the data square now? Her eyes slowly settled on her mother's desk. In there. Aza walked to it, checking the clock as she did so. Father will be home any minute. Desires battled within her: to flee, to know, to confess, to discover. She stood before the desk, paralyzed. Then, the memory of the argument with her mother returned, breaking her indecision. Aza searched each drawer slowly and methodically, trying not to let her father's impending return make her sloppy. She ignored the sentimental items, knowing she didn't have time to reminisce.

Minutes crawled by, and Aza finished. *How could it not be here?* She stepped back, feeling even more disappointed than before. *I know I'm close,* she thought, wondering if her mother had hidden the data square somewhere else in the dwelling. *Where else could it be?* Aza thought, looking closer at the desk. A memory from one of the spy vids returned to her, and she began checking the undersides of the desk's surfaces. She pulled out each drawer and squatted down to check its underside. And then she found it, held under the bottom of one of the side drawers with a bit of adhesive.

The noise of the main dwelling door sliding open was barely perceptible, but the sound sent waves of fear through Aza. She grabbed the square and shut the compartment as quickly as possible. The door to exit the study was in full view of the dwelling entrance, allowing no way to leave the room unseen. Aza tried to think of an acceptable reason to be in the study, but there wasn't one.

"Aza?" her father asked. She heard the main entrance close. "Aza, I brought some guests home." The noise of the door opening again made Aza wonder what was going on. Perhaps the guests had found something interesting outside, and her father had returned to them.

Without further speculation, Aza darted out the door, catching a glimpse of her father's robed back as she darted down the hall and into her room. She breathed out slowly, taking a moment to compose herself. Going into her closet, she stuck the data square to the bottom of one of the built-in drawers.

"I want you to meet these fine new Ashamine troops."

Leaving her room, Aza walked slowly down the hall, trying to act like he'd just interrupted her studies. After graduation ceremonies, he almost always brought back a few of the more devout troops for a time of introspection and prayer. Afterwards, they'd sit around, telling stories about their home-worlds, Forces training, and the amazing things they would accomplish in the Entho War. Over time, they'd all started to sound the same to Aza, but she indulged her father because he so loved having her there. Once the conversation died off, he'd send them off to war with a final blessing. It was more than his office required, but that was typical of him.

"Hello, father," Aza said. She greeted him and his six guests with the salute of the Ashamine, stuffing down the guilt of her previous actions as she did so.

21 – WAKE

"Everything's OK," Wake said, trying to soothe Maxar. He wouldn't stop screaming, agonized sounds Wake attributed to the return of feeling to his frostbitten extremities. *Hopefully that's all it is,* he thought, *and not something related to his nano-tech.*

Jaydon had regained consciousness several minutes before, and sat quietly in one of the mine's rest area chairs. He was dazed, but didn't seem to be suffering seriously from his encounter with Traynos-6's night.

Maxar's screams subsided into yells, then groans. After another minute, his eyes fluttered open. "I'm back," he said under his breath.

"You're OK," Wake replied.

"I was on Lith-elo," Maxar said, sitting up. He winced at the movement, gingerly setting his hands in his lap. "I was inside Beowulf. I *was* Beowulf."

Since the day they'd summoned him to repair the worm generator on Jaydon's ship, Wake's life had become strange. He'd discovered he was a Harbinger, something he didn't understand. It had thrown him into more turmoil in the past few months than he'd experienced in his entire lifetime. That didn't seem like it would be changing any time soon.

"Maybe it's related to the hypothermia," Wake asserted, his old logic surfacing.

"No," Maxar said, shivering, "definitely not. I was there. I participated in a ceremony. We restored Lothis' connection."

Wake looked at Jaydon. The old captain was technically not part of the Harbinger group, but was a member all the same. He had bags under his eyes and looked exhausted. "Didn't Tremmilly have a similar experience?" he rasped, shrugging.

"She did," Maxar answered, visibly fighting to calm his shivers, "She was in my head, when I escaped Bloodsport. This was different. I wasn't just an observer in Beowulf's mind, I could move, breathe, and sense.

There was no *other*, as Tremmilly described, only me." Maxar paused for a moment. Wake let him think, not knowing how to respond anyway.

"My energy, as Maxar, somehow united with that of Beowulf's and another I thought of as my Harbinger strength. In that state, I felt whole and complete in a way I never have before. When I was on Bloodsport, I felt depressed and attributed it to the Ashamine forcing me to fight in the games. Now I wonder if it had something to do with the separation, both from my true self and from the rest of the Harbingers."

"So you think Beowulf is somehow part of you?" Wake tried to keep his voice neutral.

"It wouldn't be the craziest thing that has happened, would it? We already accept we are Harbingers, some kind of beings that existed long in the past or in another dimension. We became humans and an Entho-la-ah-mine. Why not a wolf-dog as well?"

Wake couldn't argue with his logic, so he just kept silent. Jaydon, however, stood up and took a few shaky steps. "You also said you restored the boy?"

Maxar nodded. "We used the link to our Harbinger strength as a beacon, Lothis was able to discover and restore his own connection. I returned to my body shortly after that moment, but he was confident in success."

"Good," Jaydon said, a weak smile on his face. "I don't pretend to understand a single bit of these visions and experiences, but if it healed Lothis, that's all that matters. When we left, I wasn't expecting to see him again, not with how he was withering away."

Despite the oddity of the situation, Wake felt left out. So far, he'd learned little about being a Harbinger, and none of it from personal experience. *Maybe I spent too much time working on dwellings and Brightwing and not enough pondering my existence.* He thought about this for a moment, then decided he didn't regret any of it. Wake liked who he was, and what interested him. If the Harbinger part of him was more than that, it would be the aspect to change and mesh with who he was as a human.

"I know we are in a mine," Maxar said, also rising to his feet, "but where are we?" Wake felt grateful for the change in subject. They needed to discuss Maxar's experience more, but for now, it was time to get on with the mission.

"This is a break room in the closest mine I could drag you both to." Wake felt proud he'd saved his friends. Even with the modified EN suits, they'd barely survived the short exposure to the Traynos-6 night. Thankfully, someone had engineered Brightwing with the ability to handle extreme cold, but Wake didn't want to test it any further.

"Is the rest of the mine environmentally controlled?" Jaydon asked, picking up his ENS helmet.

"No," Wake answered, "but being underground acts as insulation, so we should be able to explore. It's still cold, but your suits will keep you warm."

"Is this the discovery site?" Maxar asked, reattaching his suit's helmet.

"I don't think so. There is regular mining equipment out in the tunnels, and from what I can tell, there is too much activity for an archeology dig. It looks like frozen gas mining." Wake reattached his own helmet.

"So then we need to check another site," Maxar said, voice coming through Brightwing's comm system. "But we can't go outside. Does that mean we are stuck here until morning?"

"Maybe," Wake replied, heading towards the airlock leading back to the main tunnel. "It's possible this mine connects to other shafts and tunnels, but without a schematic, we have no way of knowing."

"Can't we just connect to wireless or a hard port and download one?" Jaydon asked, looking around the room.

Wake chuckled, hoping it was low enough Brightwing's mic wouldn't pick it up. "Normally, yes, but Traynos-6 is just a small mining colony and only works during daylight hours. We would have installed data repeaters for the mines, but in this case, it was just too expensive. They use the limited bandwidth of the mining transports for a link."

"OK," Maxar said. "No map. I guess we'll be exploring then."

Wake entered the airlock. Maxar and Jaydon followed behind him. He hit the button to start the cycle process.

＊

"Based on Brightwing's 3D mapping," Wake said, double checking the suit's HUD, "this is the last branch." They'd spent over six hours searching the meandering shafts and corridors. He was glad he'd brought the extra power and atmosphere modules along. Wake vaguely remembered hearing a miner talk about how they followed the frozen veins of gas, which were erratic and unpredictable. *Explains why they laid the tunnels out so strangely.*

"And how long do we have before the miners arrive?" Maxar asked.

Wake checked the time. "I don't know for sure. I would imagine we have less than an hour or so." They would have been able to explore the tunnels much quicker using the small personnel transport vehicles, but they'd all decided against that. If the mine was too big, they wouldn't be able to bring them back to the entrance in time, and the next shift of miners would know something was off.

"So we check this one, and if it's a bust, we try to get out before the miners arrive?" Jaydon looked exhausted. They all did. Between the previous day's climb, the hypothermia ordeal, and hours upon hours of trudging through tunnels, they were running out of energy.

A rumble in Wake's stomach told him he hadn't eaten in a while. The emergency rations they'd taken from the Watch weren't palatable, but they'd all managed to force them down during a rest in the break area.

"I think that's the best plan," Maxar said. "Worst case, we have to hide until the shift is over. Once they leave, we can sprint to the next mine entrance." Wake hoped that wouldn't happen, as too many things could go wrong returning to the surface at dusk.

"Alright," he said, yawning, "let's get moving." The last tunnel was smaller than most, and based on the undisturbed dust coating the floor, it hadn't seen use in quite some time. Going in would leave traces of their passage, but since this particular branch was located far off the main line, it made him feel more confident no one would notice. Wake stepped forward, Brightwing's illumination creating writhing shadows on the rocky walls as he moved.

They trudged on for several minutes, and Wake began thinking of sleep. His eyelids grew heavy, and he felt his pace slow. Ahead, the tunnel narrowed, then abruptly ended in a mass of jumbled rock. *Good,* he thought, feeling himself settle down to the floor. This seemed as good a spot as any to sleep, and the miners would certainly have arrived at the entrance by now. Wake laid down, barely noticing the awkward position the uneven stone contorted him into.

"Great idea," Jaydon said through the haze that surrounded him.

"It's a good a spot as any, I guess," Maxar added.

Despite his exhaustion, Wake couldn't fall asleep. He tried to find a more comfortable position, but nothing worked. *What's wrong?* he wondered, closing his eyes once again. Something kept tugging at the edges of his consciousness, and every time he was about to drift off, it pulled him back again.

Fine, Wake thought, sitting up. Now he was awake, he realized the end of the corridor seemed suspicious. He got up and examined the pile of rocks. It looked like a normal cave-in, but something still felt off. *Just wishful thinking, combined with the delusions of an exhausted brain.*

As he turned to go back to the semi-flat part of the floor, his light illuminated the entirety of the shaft. Wake stopped. *There aren't any pockets,* he thought, remembering how all previous areas they'd explored showed where miners had thawed and removed the frozen gas. It left cavities the size of humans all the way up to those of a starship. This tunnel had no such deformities.

"So why did they go to the trouble of coming this way and then just stop?" he thought out loud.

"What?" Maxar's voice said, fuzzy with sleep.

"Something is weird about this tunnel."

"What is it?" Now Maxar's voice was crisp and Wake wondered how the man was able to be alert so quickly. He explained the lack of pockets, and Maxar joined him near the pile of jumbled rock.

"Couldn't they have been exploring?" Maxar asked.

"Miners don't explore. Sensors detect differences in density and—"

"Wait, wait," Maxar said. "Forget it. I don't need a bunch of tech details. If you think it is abnormal, then that's good enough for me."

"So it's weird," Jaydon said irritably. "What in the fires of the dark star does it have to do with our search?"

"Maybe nothing, maybe everything," Wake replied, understanding the older man's tiredness. "I think this might lead to the discovery site."

"How?" Jaydon said, rising to join them.

"Piecing together what Captain Malesis and Felar told me," Wake answered, leaning in to get a closer view of the collapse, "I think I understand the events surrounding the discovery." He examined the strewn rocks, scanning the details of its grays, blacks, and reds. "After the miners found the artifact or whatever it was, the Ashamine had them killed, closing that mine, at least for a time. They made everything look like an accident. Nobody suspected ancient technology was buried on Traynos-6. Whatever it was, the Ashamine began studying it, and eventually implemented some of it in Maxar."

"What does all this have to do with our caved-in corridor?" Jaydon asked.

Wake peered up into the tunnel's ceiling, once again studying the rock in close detail. *A greater density of red flecks in the collapse than the surrounding area.*

"As you know," he continued, "the Ashamine is greedy. This mine is obviously lucrative, and they wouldn't have wanted it shut down for long. Boring a new, secret entrance, and concealing the original would make more sense to them. And if they ordered everyone out of this area due to structural instability, no one would see their imperfect cover up." Satisfied with his observations, Wake began to pick up and move the jumbled rocks.

"Won't that create another cave-in?" Jaydon said, retreating several steps.

"It might," Wake answered, "but I don't believe that's what occurred here. I think what we are looking for is on the other side of these rocks."

22 – FELAR

"We chose you to serve your species," Felar bellowed, looking at the thousand Entho-la-ah-mines gathered before her. "Many volunteered, but Cazz-ak-tak and I chose you based on the mentality and skills you showed us. Now, you begin the next step of your journey by learning the offensive and defensive skills needed to function as effective troops."

The Entho-la-ah-mines stamped their feet and cheered in her mind. *A side benefit of only getting to take a thousand volunteers is we have individuals with the highest motivation. That's good, because Cazz-ak and I are going to push them to their limits.*

"Felar will show you physical combat," Cazz-ak said, "while I train you in the mental aspects of battle."

"I will be assisting Cazz-ak," Lothis added, looking slightly self-conscious. "And I will also instruct you in how to interact with human technology."

"In the end, we hope to turn you into potent, hardened warriors," Felar resumed. "As training continues, if we feel any of you unsuitable for this task, we will ask you to resign. And if you discover this is not the correct path for yourself, then please, don't continue. There are plenty who will take your place."

"Remember," Cazz-ak added, "this is the first time any of our species has attempted something of this nature. In my journey to Haak-ah-tar, to bring forth the new Queen, my crew and I used weaponry and tactics created by our scientists and philosophers. This is different. No one, in the entire history of our species, has dedicated their life to combat, in learning ways to strike offensively at our enemies. You will be the first, so have understanding of your faults and struggles. We will do the same. We do not expect perfection, only effort."

Felar nodded. She'd always thought well of Cazz-ak, but seeing his competency and skill when they were working together took it to a higher level. "This half," she said, motioning to the right side, "will train with me for today. The other half will go with Cazz-ak."

As her 500 trainees gathered in a more compact formation on their side of the cavern, Lothis came and stood next to her. "Thank you," he said, giving her a hug.

"For what?" she stammered, caught off guard. He never initiated physical contact.

"For saving me on Haak-ah-tar. For giving me the freedom to find myself. For helping me find my abilities again." Felar had always known he appreciated her, but hearing it overwhelmed her.

"You're welcome," she replied, trying not to cry. She squeezed him even harder for a moment, then let go. He smiled, then walked over to Cazz-ak without another word.

"OK," Felar said to herself, straightening up and taking a deep breath. "Today," she resumed, addressing the Entho-la-ah-mines gathered before her, "we will begin the foundations of physical combat. For human troops, I would start by showing you how to use a rail gun, but since your mind will be your weapon, we will move on to physical maneuvers and how to work as a squad. In the future, you will likely be facing opponents who use rail or flechette weaponry. Some might also have melee weapons. It is my job to teach you how to take cover, how to keep yourself out of bad situations, and how to work as smaller units to accomplish a goal.

"I will be watching these exercises closely and will use my observations to choose squad leaders from among you. I will drill them with advanced strategy, tactics, and maneuvers. They will work on these concepts with their squads, and in this manner, we will build a cohesive command structure. For today, however, we will work in large groups."

Felar divided them up, then began instructing them. They were good students, and the job wasn't much different from training Inits back on Ashamine-4. Some of what she wanted to teach them was impossible due to their anatomy, but she adapted most concepts. As hours passed, Felar fell back into old training habits.

Her thoughts drifted to the Arche, and Felar's mood soured. *We've hidden ourselves from the humans and Breakers,* she thought, continuing to offer feedback to the Entho-la-ah-mines as they practiced their newly learned skills. *But the Arche know where we are. With their attack on Lothis, they've proved they are a threat outside their own reality. I didn't realize that was possible.*

The advanced race of computer-inhabiting beings was small, numbering only four since Cazz-ak destroyed one of them, but they were persistent and dangerous. From what Cazz-ak and Lothis had told her of their conversations with the Arche, she got the sense they would not stop trying to capture the Harbingers and steal their power.

As soon as we leave the protection of the Great Thought, the Arche's strength will be much greater than our own. Even so, they may find a way to capture one of us.

"Now we will go to the tunnels to practice today's skills," Felar announced, leading them to an uninhabited section of natural caverns that continued even deeper under Lith-elo-hi-rosh. When they had enough distance from the training cavern, Felar stopped. "We will be playing a game called 'Capture the Intel.' The defending team," she pointed at half the troops, "will have to hide and protect a plasti-glass cube from the attacking team. Cazz-ak tells me, at this point, there is no way for you to not sense each other, so in these maneuvers, you will have to take that into account. Later, he believes he can teach you mental concealment, which will be useful against the Breakers. For now, though, your sense of each other will work for our purposes. Offensive team, you know where the intel is, but you'll have to out maneuver the defenders to reach it. Defending team, you'll see them coming, but you'll have to stop them. If some of you manage to mentally conceal yourself on your own, you've earned that advantage. Everyone understand?"

"Felar?" a quiet voice asked in her head. It was one of the smaller females. Felar thought back through the day and remembered she was a quick learner, but asked a lot of questions.

"Yes? Please, tell me your name."

"Ket-ala-ka."

"OK, Ket-ala-ka, what is your question?" Felar tried hard to pronounce the complicated Entho-la-ah-mine name correctly. Cazz-ak had told her each segment of their name structure said something about the individual, but she had yet to learn what any of them meant. *I may have to settle for just memorizing the names of my squad leaders, once I choose them,* she thought, looking at the mass of Entho-la-ah-mines before her.

"How are we to assault or defend if we have no weapons?"

Felar laughed, a sound she hoped the Entho-la-ah-mines would understand. "Sorry, I almost forgot that part. Since you have yet to learn that from Cazz-ak, we will be using touch."

"Touch?" Ket-ala-ka asked.

"Yes, it sounds foolish, but it will work. It simulates close quarters combat, which is realistic in this maze of tunnels. Human children play this type of game. It is remarkably useful for developing a strong foundation for later lessons in stealth, maneuvers, and tactics. Touch an opponent and they become disabled, no longer able to participate in combat. They must remain where they are until the match is over. Use that time to observe and think about what you would do differently."

"We all have nearly the same reach, and if any touch is disabling, won't we just end up simultaneously stopping each other?" Ket-ala-ka reached out to the Entho-la-ah-mine next to her, demonstrating. The blue light of the surrounding bioluminescent algae made her a dark form, but Felar remembered that in the bright lights of the training cavern, she was a beautiful deep red, full of swirling yellow tones. Felar appreciated her thoughts and courage to speak up. She hoped it would inspire the same qualities in the rest of them.

"That is part of the lesson and challenge. You are teams, so work together. Use what I have taught you to outmaneuver your opponents. Try different things. Sacrifice yourself when it strategically makes sense."

The two teams of Entho-la-ah-mines indicated they understood and were ready. "The attackers have one standard hour to capture the cube. The defenders win if they disable all the attackers or run them out of time." Felar produced the small plasti-glass cube and handed it to the defenders. "You have five minutes to prepare. Use your time wisely." They hurried off. Felar counted down, then released the attackers.

As she followed and observed them, Felar's thoughts returned to the Arche. They'd focused all their attention on Lothis so far, but what if they went after one of the other Harbingers? *Wake and Maxar,* she thought, realizing they were outside the protection of the Great Thought. *I don't think either of them knows how to defend against the Arche. I know I don't. What if they pulled me into their dimension right now?* A chill made her shudder despite the temperature control of her EN suit.

Felar watched as several attackers ran straight into a larger squad of defenders. They quickly disabled the attackers, but not before the rushing group touched a few of them. It seemed a useless endeavor until Felar spotted several other attackers rush by in an adjacent tunnel. The defenders were so wrapped up in celebration that they didn't notice.

We cannot have the Arche looming over us, Felar decided, moving down another tunnel to change vantage points, *not with all the other threats we are facing. We must destroy them.* Cazz-ak knew how to fight the computer beings. She was sure Lothis would too, now that he had restored his abilities. *What can I do to help?* She thought for several moments, watching as the attackers captured the cube.

"Gather up," she yelled, leading them back to the starting area. When they'd all arrived, she debriefed both teams, explaining the diversionary tactics the attackers used to win. "Great job, to both teams," she finished. "These are new concepts, it will take time for them to become instinct. Don't become discouraged." She instructed the teams to switch roles and started another round.

As the defenders rushed off into the tunnels, Felar couldn't help but take her own advice. *Perhaps it is time I start learning some new concepts of my own. I'm useless to my friends when it comes to the Arche or the mental abilities of the Breakers. I was part of restoring Lothis, and that shows I have mental capabilities.* Felar checked her suit's timer, waited a few seconds longer, then released the attackers. There were still a couple hours left to run the game, and then she could ask Cazz-ak and Lothis to begin training her. *I just hope the Arche don't capture one of us before we can fight back.*

23 – GAV

What are they doing here? Gav asked himself, selecting options to command Fade to hash the Ashamine Terminal Network. Since escaping death in the Family Council the day before, he hadn't believed things could get any worse. An hour ago, a huge Ashamine fleet had wormed in system and was heading straight for Exis-7. *Have they finally decided to wipe us out?*

Despite the Families hunting him, and now possibly facing some type of Ashamine action, Gav felt relatively safe. He had made it back to his safe space, a bunker deep under the planet. After discovering it, he'd kept the location entirely to himself. At the time, it had driven a wedge between Gav and the rest of the Serrith family, but now it proved a good decision. Even if everyone in his disgraced family stayed loyal, which was unlikely, someone could still torture or chem the information out of them.

Initially, Gav decided secrecy was enough protection, but as his quantum computer investment grew, he felt vulnerable. He'd riddled the access path with traps and sensors. The only people who got down here were his captives, none of which left alive.

He'd often wondered if someone could find him from his network connection, but Gav felt it sufficiently obscured to safeguard against a trace. The addition of alert routines at nodes along the way would give him adequate warning if someone did attempt to find him. *Besides, with Fade under my control, I have better protection now.*

The sound of a pump churning broke Gav out of his reverie. Constant precipitation saturated the small bits of land on Exis-7, flooding most subterranean spaces. His base required incessant pumping from all the seepage. It was a small cost for such a secure location.

An indicator flashed on Gav's terminal, signaling Fade had hashed into the secure sector of the Ashamine Terminal Network. Gav laughed excitedly. For years, the Ashamine technology had kept pace with the Families hashing, keeping their networks encrypted and secure. *But now I have access to everything, Family and Ashamine.*

He began selecting options, trying to find out why the fleet was in the Exis system and headed straight for the planet. At first, he found nothing, but then a command transited the Ashamine Forces channel, catching his attention.

"Deploy all Naval Forces. Oppose inbound ships. As prior comms indicate, the Justice is under unknown enemy control. If possible, negotiate surrender. Escalate to disablement if they refuse. Complete destruction is authorized, as required."

Blightheart, Gav thought. *Is this a civil war?* How had an unknown group captured a Tarton class battle ship? It didn't make any sense. Gav selected more options, checking the Ashamine Forces tactical data. On it, he saw the Justice moving inexorably towards Exis-7. Nine Ashamine Forces ships were leaving station around the planet and heading for the Justice, forming up as they did so. There were three large Fion class ships and six of the medium Rubicons. He didn't know much about them, but based on relative sizes, both sides seemed an even match.

More ships caught his attention, and Gav realized hundreds of vessels had positioned themselves around the perimeter gravity well. Based on how the net was fanning out, he guessed it originated with the Justice. *A blockade.* Gav continued watching the hashed Ashamine connection, wondering how the situation would develop. *This isn't some smash and grab. The Justice is here to conquer. They don't want anyone escaping to tell the story.* A shiver coursed down Gav's spine as he wondered if he was about to witness the obliteration of his home planet. *Genocide.*

A flashing indicator on another screen caught his attention. "Galactic comms link just went down," Gav whispered in awe. *Does the Justice have the capability to jam the orbital relay station, or did someone sabotage it?* Looking back at the tactical display, he saw the Ashamine Forces were about to engage the invaders. Things started to happen too quickly to see them all at once. He pushed the galactic link out of his mind and found the Forces' comms relay feed.

"To the pirates, Ashamine rebels, or whoever you are on the ASN Founder's Justice," a man's voice said harshly, "surrender the vessel to us, or face immediate destruction."

They aren't playing, Gav thought. *This isn't some weird exercise.* He leaned towards the terminal. Seconds crawled by, and he waited eagerly for the invaders' response. Perhaps he could learn something about them from their dialect or accent. Finally, a message popped up on the comms relay feed: *Ashamine ships — Surrender, power down, and submit to boarding, or we will obliterate you.*

The text response made Gav anxious. *Why didn't they just use voice comms like the rest of the normal universe?* He supposed they were doing it as an insult, that they didn't even dignify the Ashamine threat with a real response. *But what if it is because they are trying to conceal their voices? What if they don't have voices?*

The stories his grandma told him when he was a child flooded into Gav's mind. "Then the Feeders arrived," he remembered her saying, "demanding submission. They were a strange race, silent, but knowing human language. They sent demands for surrender, rudimentary, in text. Some people hid, some tried to resist. Those who obeyed the Feeders' were tricked, lured onto their giant ships. The few who escaped said the only noise the grotesque creatures ever made was as they sucked human bodies into their quivering maws."

Gav shuddered. He'd never liked the old woman. Sometimes, he still woke from nightmares inspired by her hideous stories. *Nobody has ever heard of Sol-3. Besides, they are in an Ashamine ship, not one of the huge biomechanical structures she always talked about.* He took a deep breath and focused on the tactical feed. *None of her stories are true.* When his grandma had died, Gav felt relieved. No longer would he have to listen to her spewing strange and twisted tales for hours every day.

Multiple squads of gunships and fighters were flowing out from the Justice, forming up and heading towards the Ashamine ships. The opponents were drawing closer to each other, and Gav estimated it would only be a few more minutes until rail fire commenced. Then, something strange happened. *Why did several squads of attack ships vanish?* He checked his connection integrity, but it seemed nominal. Some of his earlier nervousness returned. Gav began biting his lip. He wished he could get more information about what was happening, but apparently the Ashamine Forces were using direct comms. *Probably lasers,* he thought, trying to figure out a way to hash their closed network.

Before anything else occurred to him, the missing invader ships reappeared inside the perimeter of the larger Ashamine vessels. They began strafing, raking the Rubicon ships. Gav zoomed in, trying to get a sense of their tactics. Regardless of how they had gone stealth, they were now managing to stay alive. The small vessels positioned themselves perfectly, using the threat of cross fire to prevent the Ashamine ships from attacking effectively.

Obviously a diversionary tactic, Gav speculated, zooming back out. When he did, his stomach dropped. *Whoever they are,* he thought, heart beating rapidly, *they managed to stealth a Tarton class battle ship.* Gav had heard rumors the Families were developing that kind of tech, but it was still years away from deployment. *The power requirements for something that large would be enormous.*

Normally, Gav liked to see the Ashamine blighthearted in every way possible, but he was beginning to wonder if it would be in his best interest for them to destroy the invaders. *Something is wrong here,* he thought, images of the Feeders skittering through his mind.

When the Justice materialized directly before the nine Ashamine Forces ships, Gav almost jumped out of his seat. When he righted himself and looked back at the screen, his eyes grew wide. A black worm impression was swelling around the Ashamine vessels, engulfing them as well as the attacking gunships and fighters. After a moment, the bubble collapsed, taking the ships with it.

Gav sat back, dumbfounded. *How did they create a bubble instead of a tunnel? Did the invaders make it, or the Ashamine?* It had the feel of an attack, and Gav couldn't believe the Ashamine had kept that kind of new technology a secret. He continued staring at the screen, mind trying to find an explanation that didn't involve the Feeders.

And where'd they go? So deep inside the gravity well, there was no way to tell for sure. *The space-time variances would have caused a huge instability in the exit point...*

Before he could ponder further, all nine Ashamine vessels reappeared. Even the small invader ships still darted amongst them. "Blightheart," Gav said under his breath. His chest clenched, and despite not understanding what had happened, he knew their return was the scariest event yet.

He zoomed out, waiting for rail rounds to begin cascading between the opposing sides, but nothing happened. None of the ships attacked. *The invaders sent the ships through a worm bubble and killed their crews.* He tried to end the grotesque vision there, but his mind wouldn't stop. *Or ate them...*

The Ashamine vessels began turning, falling into formation with the Justice. *What in the fires of the black star?* Gav wondered, the hair on the back of his neck rising. *This can't be possible.*

With the Ashamine fleet under their control, nothing stood between the invaders and Exis-7. They would be within striking range of the planet within minutes. No demands to transfer Ashcreds or turn over the governor. If they'd done that, it would have made more sense. Are they planning on butchering everyone? Can they generate a worm bubble as big as the planet?

Gav instructed Fade to access the Families' network. They'd changed their passwords and tried to upgrade their security, but there wasn't much they could do in a day. Fade easily hashed through, presenting Gav with a screen full of panic.

They knew even less than he did, not having access to the secure Ashamine Forces network. *The Families think it's an entirely Ashamine battle group,* Gav pondered, flipping rapidly through reports. They had issued orders to resist them, both on the surface and orbitally using something called Heavy. *What is that?* Gav wondered, searching for more information. No matter his query, nothing surfaced.

Is Fade trying to hide information from me? Gav initiated a few punishment routines he'd devised, running the search again. Still nothing. *No, Fade isn't buggering me. I bet the Families just don't have anything on their network.* Whatever it was, they'd gone to great lengths to keep it secret.

Gav turned back to the Ashamine tactical display, noting the invaders were now close enough to begin accurately firing rail cannons. If they were going to rain down death, it would begin any moment. There was enough firepower in space to decimate every city down to its soggy foundations. All ships controlled by the Families had either landed on the planet's surface, or fled a safe distance from the world. None were powerful enough to break the blockade.

A strange icon appeared on the display, drawing Gav closer to the screen. It was moving towards the mass of invading ships from a remote part of the northern ocean. The Ashamine sensors didn't know what to make of it.

As Gav continued to puzzle out what the object was, several more appeared on the screen, all streaking towards the ten inbound ships. *Has to be a weapon,* he thought, remembering the reference to Heavy.

The first object, almost as large as an escape vessel and with a higher thermal signature, impacted the Founder's Justice. The explosion was bigger than any Gav had ever seen before. *That wasn't a rail round,* he thought, *it was a fusion missile.* The idea the Families controlled such weapons was beyond belief for Gav. The Ashamine had outlawed nuclear weaponry hundreds of years ago, putting anyone caught researching or implementing it in the Clothing of the Iconoclast. They claimed it was due to its destructive effects on the environment, but everyone knew it was just a way to keep power out of the hands of rebel groups like the Divisionists. *Not that they'd ever have the will to use one.*

Seven missiles were heading for the Ashamine ships, and the Families were adding more every few seconds. *How did they manufacture so many without the Ashamine knowing?* he wondered. *They'll think I told the Ashamine about Heavy, and that is why they showed up so quickly.* Gav's heart sank, his last molecules of hope obliterated as he watched more fusion weapons detonate on the invaders' hulls. He'd hoped he might prove himself to the Council, might convince them to believe he had only good intentions. *They'll never accept me back, not after this.*

Gav felt the walls closing in on him. *No hope, no chance.* Even if the Families managed to defend Exis-7 from the invaders, he would never escape. As soon as he left the confines of his subterranean bunker, they would find him. The Families had marked him for capture, and a quick death at his own hand was preferable to what the Council would do to him.

Gav's palms grew sweaty, his mind spinning with gruesome images of torture and suicide. His stomach churned, bile rising in his throat. He wiped the sweat from his brow, a remote part of him wondering why the room had grown so hot.

Taking his flechette pistol out of its shoulder holster, Gav hefted it. The weapon felt natural in his hand, every aspect of it customized to fit. He put the barrel under his chin, growling. Just a day ago, he'd believed he would have a seat on the Family Council, would rise to power in an organization spanning three worlds. *And now here you are, scared, holed up, worthless.* He gently squeezed the trigger, knowing the maximum force he could apply before the weapon would fire. *The torture doesn't scare me,* he thought, staring ahead blankly, finger unwavering. *It's just the futility and eventuality of it.* The Family was inescapable, inexorable. He would never get off Exis-7.

The bloom of explosions on the tactical display caught his attention. *What about the invaders?* Memories of his grandma's stories caused him to waver, but he shut them out. Whatever or whoever they were, the invaders seemed more powerful than the Families. *They took over nine blighthearted Ashamine battle vessels, without casualties, in just a few minutes. And yet, the Families are putting up a credible fight.*

An idea slammed into Gav with a force that almost caused him to squeeze the trigger. His breath caught, realizing what he had nearly done. He carefully lowered the flechette pistol. *I wonder what the reward would be for someone who shut down the missile system?* Even if the Families' weaponry wasn't enough to stop the invaders, they would certainly appreciate the decrease in casualties and reduction of damage to their fleet, no matter who they were. *The Family isn't controlling the missiles from their standard network, so I can't do it from here.* His mouth curved up in a smile and he felt his pessimism lift. *I may not know where the controls are, but I certainly recognize the people who do.*

Gav holstered his pistol, looked around the room, and began gathering weaponry and other supplies. *Grenades, stims, portable terminal,* he thought, throwing them into a pack. *Combat knife, rail rifle, spare charges.* He quickly changed into his old Markond enforcer attire, the family colors bringing up a strange mixture of emotions.

As Gav placed his hand on the biometric scanner and entered the code to open the exit, he shut out all distractions, focusing on his mission.

24 – CAZZ-AK-TAK

Cazz-ak settled into his small cavern. Gradually, he felt the pace of his breathing match that of his surrounding kin. His mind began to wander through the previous day's events, spiraling outward. *Attack the Arche?* Felar had made the suggestion after they'd finished training the Entho-la-ah-mine troops. She'd asked to be shown how to use her Harbinger mental abilities. *Teaching Lothis is one thing, but I'm not sure I can show her what she wants to know.* He barely understood his own Harbinger strength, but perhaps, he could find a way to instruct her.

As Cazz-ak drifted off to sleep, he felt something pulling his mind from his body, a subtle tug, yet inexorable. At first, he panicked, thinking it was the Arche. He quickly realized the energy was familiar and intimate, awakening his Harbinger strength in a way he'd never experienced before. *It is a bond, a part of myself connecting to something, spanning dimensions. It feels like...me.*

Relax, he thought, sensing things would be easier if he did. Cazz-ak passed through a dimensional fold, feeling his connection to the Great Thought vanish. *This isn't the Arche,* he reassured himself, the calm nature of the experience confirming it wasn't caused by the computer-inhabiting race. *Where or what is this then? And why does this feel so familiar?*

A rushing sensation engulfed Cazz-ak, turning everything black. Upon opening his eyes, he found himself in a bright place, full of calm, powerful energy. *Yet, something is wrong.* He looked around the room, wondering why. A thousand humanoids stood to his right, all facing towards the front of the room. Translucent, cube like structures filled the space, glowing in blues and silvers.

"We cannot accept the ruling of this court," a tall, male humanoid said, positioned before the immense construct. He seemed calm, but something about his tone set Cazz-ak on edge. Several similarly dressed people stood behind him, with space between themselves and the watching crowd.

"You have no choice," a female in deep blue replied, her position on a platform denoting her authority.

"This will halt the progress of our species, will send us into a pattern of stagnation we will never recover from. The Elrah people deserve more!" Despite the male's disturbing manner, Cazz-ak felt drawn in. "If we ourselves do not choose to ascend, how will we ever become immortal? How will we comprehend the entirety of the Universe? Of the multiverse?"

"We have explained this many times, See'dek," the Empress said, taking on a more ominous tone. "Our species decided technology is not the way to join ourselves to the Dawn. We choose to seek the answers that lie within ourselves, to find the spiritual connection bonding us to our consciousness and the world around us."

"If we augment ourselves, the insight will be much deeper and easier to obtain." See'dek's voice had grown strident, the fire of desperation burning in his eyes. Cazz-ak felt himself tense as he checked the positions of the other Protectors stationed around the platform. "Please. Let us continue. Our research will not harm any of you. We will unite with the Dawn together. We are all the Elrah, and we have the same goal as you."

"Yet you have continued your research far beyond what I authorized," the presiding female said, her voice growing stern. "We have tried to reason with you, have tried to be reasonable, but you continue to defy us." Cazz-ak agreed with her, something deep inside him knowing her words were truth. *How can someone so young be so wise?*

"Even now," the presider continued, "you shield your mind from the bond. What are you hiding, See'dek? What has made you willing to cut yourself off from us?"

"Quit trying to get inside my head, Aris," See'dek snarled, forsaking her title. "You turned the people against me. Without your preconceived ideas of the future, the Elrah would know biology is the only thing binding us. They will see we can decide our own path. Instead of an empire of a million worlds, we could span the entirety of the universe. We could become greater than the Dawn and live forever."

"But at what price?" the Empress replied, sounding like her heart was breaking.

See'dek and his followers pulled coverings down over their faces, the pale, flesh colored masks making them appear faceless. Cazz-ak knew what was about to happen, crouching just as See'dek launched himself towards Aris. He felt his leg muscles contract in way incompatible with his Entho-la-ah-mine body, yet it was familiar and right. As he leapt towards See'dek, Cazz-ak warped space-time ahead of himself to speed his passage. Soaring through the air, he then raised a shield, barring See'dek from Aris.

Cazz-ak slammed into the faceless attacker. They both went crashing into the wall behind the platform, scattering Aris and her attendants. As they tumbled to the floor, Cazz-ak saw his fellow Protectors engaging the other faceless. In the next instant, See'dek attacked, stabbing at Cazz-ak with thin, jagged shards of mental energy. Cazz-ak sensed Aris was moving out of danger, so he repositioned the shield between himself and the would-be-assassin.

"She forced me," See'dek snarled, rising from the floor. His faceless mask was unnerving. Cazz-ak stepped back, continuing to fend off See'dek's mental knives. "You're a lackey, Tha'sis, a tool of an ineffectual leader. Can't you see she is holding us back from what we could be? Even the Dawn is a minuscule goal compared to what I've seen."

Gathering his power, Cazz-ak went on the offensive, striking at See'dek with a heavy cube composed of mental energy. "I trust the Empress," he replied, voice coming from his throat rather than his mind. "Nothing you say will turn me against her," Cazz-ak continued forcefully. "She has proven her judgment and worthiness to lead the Accord many times."

The faceless attacker easily batted away Cazz-ak's cube, closing the distance between them as he did so. "Then we will obliterate you, along with the rest of those who resist us." Before Cazz-ak could stop him, See'dek took hold of his wrists. In the next moment, he felt his energy draining away. "You have been the same for thousands of years, Protector, glorying in the fact you have kept Aris safe from danger." Cazz-ak's consciousness began to grow fuzzy. "Yet it is a vain honor, to protect someone when there are no true threats." Blackness crept in on the edges of Cazz-ak's vision. He tried to resist, to summon all the physical and mental strength he had.

"And now," See'dek continued, "when something new arrives, you are impotent. Greet the blackness for me, Tha'sis, for I am immortal."

The smugness in See'dek's voice made Cazz-ak angry. He'd done much meditation and introspection over the thousands of years he'd spent in the prestigious order known as the Protectors. Cazz-ak thought his passions vanquished, but now he was about to die, he embraced them like an old friend.

"NO," Cazz-ak said, using anger to push back the blackness. "No, you faceless betrayer of your own kind! I will not be the one to find blackness today." In a sudden explosion of energy, Cazz-ak broke See'dek's grip, sending him flying backwards. Recomposing himself, he looked around the room, casting his mind out. *Chaos,* he thought, watching as the gathered thousands screamed, trying to flee the meeting hall. Several Protectors fought with faceless attackers. Individuals of both sides lay motionless on the floor. He sensed they were dead. Spatters and pools of blood confirmed it.

"You think it that easy?" See'dek said, rising from the ground. He laughed, his voice glitching with an unfamiliar, mechanical buzz. "Our power comes from a source stronger than any meditation can provide." An enormous shard of mental energy formed in his hands, and See'dek lifted it high in the air. Cazz-ak watched power snake away from his faceless opponent, dark, unsettling tendrils unlike anything he'd seen before. As he composed a blade of his own, Cazz-ak traced the lines, finding they led to the fallen faceless. "Not even death can stop us," See'dek said, sending out a burst of black energy. The power flowed through the tendrils, imbuing the dead. They began shaking, an aberrant jitter that made Cazz-ak feel sick. After a moment, they stopped.

Rising to their feet, the dead moved in a grotesque, yet effective manner. Before Cazz-ak could warn his fellow Protectors, the faceless dead surrounded them, tearing at their throats with bared teeth. Cazz-ak felt stunned. Never had he seen such a brutal display of primal aggression.

A movement caught his attention, reminding him of the danger he was facing. Reflexively, he brought up his own mental sword, blocking See'dek's blow. The weight of the faceless attacker's strike nearly knocked Cazz-ak off his feet. Before he could regain his balance, See'dek struck again. Cazz-ak fell to his knees, trying to maintain the grip on his mental sword.

"This is the end," See'dek said, standing over him, "not just for you, Tha'sis, but for the weakness of the Elrah species." Cazz-ak sensed See'dek was drawing in power, his sword becoming heavier and sharper. "We will break the bonds of our own evolution, we will ascend to heights beyond the Dawn or anything Aris ever dreamed."

Cazz-ak tried to add more power to his own blade, drawing on all his emotion, but he knew it wouldn't be enough. See'dek was too powerful. He breathed in deeply, preparing to meet the blackness.

See'dek's head turned. Capitalizing on the distraction, Cazz-ak rose to his feet. "Curse them," the faceless one growled, just as Cazz-ak heard the hiss of beam weapons striking flesh. He slashed at See'dek, hoping the distraction would last long enough for his blow to strike.

"You continue to underestimate me," See'dek replied, easily parrying his sword away. "This time, you've won, Tha'sis, but this is far from the end. I will find and destroy you." His sword vanished, and See'dek raised his hands. "We will feed those who do not join us to the blackness." He brought his hands together, and a booming shock wave of mental energy radiated from them. It swept Cazz-ak backwards, sending him tumbling through the air, and slamming into the side of the blue platform.

When he picked himself off the floor, his vision was blurry, but he could tell See'dek had vanished. Cazz-ak looked down from his position, noting the rest of the faceless had disappeared as well. Far fewer Protectors remained standing than he'd hoped. Soldiers continued firing at the reanimated Elrah bodies, violet beams of energy burning into them. It created an odor Cazz-ak had never expected to smell in this sacred place. He tried to rise to his feet, but stumbled, catching himself before he fell off the platform. Blackness surged in, and Cazz-ak wondered what See'dek's shock wave had done to his mind.

"Be still," a young male said, voice unknown, yet familiar. "You have performed your duty. Now, rest. All will be well."

25 – LOTHIS

"Quit trying to get inside my head, Aris," See'dek snarled.

The scientist addressed her without title, Lothis thought, feeling the insult even though it wasn't directed at him. The room's energy changed and he knew something terrible was about to happen. From his place in the packed crowd, Lothis could only catch glimpses of See'dek's back, but he felt grateful just to be here. *If Aris wasn't my sister, we'd be stuck at our dwelling watching this psionically.*

"You turned the people against me," See'dek continued. "Without your preconceived ideas of the future, the Elrah would know biology is the only thing binding us. They will see we can decide our own path." Lothis wished he was old enough to be a Protector, sworn to guard the Accord's officials.

Soon, he thought, looking up to see how his sister would react to See'dek's tirade.

"Instead of an empire of a million worlds, we could span the entirety of the universe. We could become greater than the Dawn and live forever."

"But at what price?" Aris replied, face stiffening. Her lips turned down ever so slightly, a look Lothis knew meant she was trying not to cry. She'd worked hard to become the regal diplomat the Elrah needed, but she couldn't hide her emotions from Lothis.

Quick movement brought his attention back down to See'dek and his group of supporters. He couldn't tell what they were doing, but by the way the crowd moved back, it was something bad. Another second passed, and Lothis felt the mental energy in the room spike. See'dek darted into view, flying through the air straight for Aris.

Before he could attack her, another figure, clad in the blue armor of the Protectors, collided with him. *Tha'sis,* Lothis thought, recognizing him by his Commander's headdress.

"We must go, Veth," his mother said, tugging at his arm.

"But what about Aris?"

"The Protectors will handle it," she replied.

A tall male shoved past, breaking his mother's grip and sending Lothis tumbling. When he regained his footing, his mother had disappeared, swept up in the tide of screaming Elrahi. He looked towards the huge exit doors, leading to the safety of the bright afternoon. *No,* he thought, something inside of him demanding he protect his sister. Lothis turned and began wading through the tide. *But you don't even know the way of the Shard yet, let alone the way of the Blade.* He clenched his teeth, bouncing back and forth between several large Elrahi males. *I won't let these vile betrayers kill her,* he thought, forging on.

The way before him emptied. Protectors and assassins battled in the open space. Shards deflected off shields, and swords parried blows. Lothis' breath stopped when he caught sight of See'dek's troops. *What happened to their faces?* They were smooth skin, featureless. *No time,* Lothis thought, refocusing on finding Aris. He skirted around the struggling combatants, trying not to draw attention to himself. The size and strength of their weapons were greater than anything he'd seen before.

A small figure in the corner of his vision caught Lothis' attention. Turning his head, he saw Aris flee into a side corridor. He felt his stomach drop as one of See'dek's assassins followed behind her. Lothis darted after them, knowing his sister, while strong in the bond, had little strength when it came to weaponry.

As Lothis turned the corner into the corridor, he saw Aris desperately beating her fists against a wall of mental energy that blocked her escape. The assassin was advancing slowly, a mind dagger in her gloved fist. "This will hurt, Empress," she said, an unfamiliar mechanical rasp in her voice.

Lothis turned to cry for help, knowing his mental abilities would be of little use against the assassin. But then he realized no one could assist him. Bodies littered the floor, Protector and assassin alike. See'dek had Tha'sis immobilized, grasping him by the wrists.

You have to do this yourself, he thought, knowing he wasn't strong enough. *She's your sister!* He turned back just in time to see the assassin raise her knife, poised to bring it down on Aris' head. Before he realized what he was doing, Lothis reached out and touched space-time, warping and folding it into smaller and smaller fragments. It was unlike anything he'd seen or done before, but it felt right.

A small singularity formed around the attacker's hand, engulfing the dagger. She screamed in pain, and Lothis dropped the fold, both surprised and exhausted. The assassin looked down where her hand once was, now just a bleeding red stump, swarming with black particles. *What did I do to her?* Lothis wondered, fearful of his own strength. As he watched, the black flecks covered the whole wound, and it ceased bleeding.

"No matter," the attacker said, turning to face Lothis. "A boy Protector?" she laughed, all pain gone from her face. "See'dek is right. The Accord is weak." A new mind dagger appeared in her left hand, and the assassin began crossing the few paces that separated them.

Time slowed as Lothis started to panic. He reached out to space-time as he had before. *I can't do it.* Lothis tried to create a mind sword, dagger, or even a small shard to protect himself. Everything was futile.

"Bond with me," he heard Aris say in his mind, voice steady. "I will give you strength." He opened himself to her, feeling energy flood into him. Even combined, they were not anywhere near the power of a single Protector.

But perhaps it will be enough.

Lothis cast the energy out from himself, binding space-time to a shape, creating a physical manifestation of his will. He separated and fractured it, creating shards the same way he had seen the Protectors do in training. The pieces of mental energy fanned out, glinting in the bright light.

A look of astonishment bloomed on the assassin's face. She began forming a shield to protect herself, but the energy moved too quickly. The shards passed easily through her chest, shredding it. A spray of red and black fanned out behind her as the shards exited. The assassin fell to the ground, twitching.

Lothis ran by the body, feeling drained. Aris embraced him tightly. "I thought she would kill me," Aris said, voice calm, but body shaking. "Thank you for staying behind, Veth."

He nodded, worried if he spoke, he would begin crying. They stayed that way for several moments, and some of Lothis' nerves subsided.

A wet sound behind him drew Lothis' attention. Aris stiffened. "How is that possible?" she said, voice barely above a whisper.

Lothis let her go and turned to see the assassin rising from the bloody pool. The skin under her obliterated tunic was ragged and torn. Black masses plugged the holes, and the substance writhed as she moved. "Stay behind me," Lothis said, trying to summon all the remaining strength in the bond. A profound exhaustion struck him. Lothis felt the bits of energy he'd gathered slip away.

The assassin darted towards them, snarling. A flash of violet light bloomed, tossing the figure to the floor, head smoking. Lothis stared in wonder. He'd never seen a physical energy weapon used in person before. The smell of charred flesh wafted over him, making Lothis gag.

"Are you OK, Empress?" an Elrahi soldier asked, rising from a firing stance. A look of pure joy was on her face, and Lothis couldn't decide if it was for the death she had caused, or the life she had saved.

"Yes," Aris said, nodding, still the composed dignitary, despite the death and carnage. Lothis envied her calm.

"Then we need to get you out of here," she replied, motioning them to come with her. "I'm Lek Tomun, of the Elrahi Sentries." Lek saluted, putting her fist over her heart, letting the heavy beam weapon hang by her side. Her courtesy complete, Lek resumed a combat posture, a stance she looked more comfortable in. Lothis relaxed slightly, feeling they had at least a thin layer of safety now. A Protector would be better, he thought, as Lek led them down the corridor, but she was accurate and deadly. He didn't want to go back out into the battle zone, but if Lek thought it was safer, he couldn't argue with her.

A moment later, a loud shock wave passed over them, almost knocking them to the floor. Lek seemed undeterred, forging ahead. As they darted into the huge hall, Lothis noticed See'dek and all his troops had vanished, except for a few corpses who continued fighting. The remaining Protectors and Elrahi Sentries were taking them out. The situation seemed under control.

A movement on the dais caught his attention and Lothis watched as Tha'sis collapsed in a heap on the floor. *No, no, no!* Lothis thought. *Not him. He was the most powerful and prestigious of the Protectors. He can't be dead.*

Lothis ran over, afraid of what he might find, but still in awe of the huge Elrahi. His blue armor was intact, but the battle had crumpled the chest plate in. The wrists were black and corroded, and Lothis wondered what See'dek had done to him.

Bending over, he tried to bond with the Protector, to see if he was still alive. An ache in Lothis' head reminded him he had exhausted what little mental ability he possessed. Instead, he placed his hand above Tha'sis' mouth. A feeling of relief flooded through Lothis as he felt the big Elrahi's breath.

"Be still," he said, hardly able to believe he was so close to a legend. "You have performed your duty. Now, rest. All will be well."

26 – TREMMILLY

Despite her calm exterior, Tremmilly felt shaken to the core. Around her, Protectors and Sentries kept a close guard, but she still felt exposed. She turned to look at Veth, and he smiled back at her. *You have the might of your people behind you,* Tremmilly thought, carefully taking a deep breath she hoped no one would notice. *I have to be strong, for them.*

"Empress," Lek Tomun pleaded, "let me take the fight to those who have broken from your rule." When the Sentry had rescued her and Veth, Tremmilly hadn't realized she was a Division Chieftain and one of the highest decorated of all Elrahi Sentries. "With my squad behind me, we will eliminate See'dek. I can send him and his abhorrent technology to the deepest blackness." Tremmilly knew little about the Sentries. They usually operated beyond the Accord's far-reaching borders, protecting the Elrah from hostile species and nations.

"No," Tha'sis, her primary Protector replied, "we must capture and bring them to justice. Death would be too quick. I will punish them for what they have done." He still looked weak. She hadn't witnessed the event, but everyone who'd seen his fight with See'dek said writers would craft musicals about it for ages to come.

Lek and Tha'sis began arguing. Tremmilly turned her focus inward, seeking the deep connection to the Dawn. She felt the world around her, the links binding them all together. Her mind quested further, sensing molecules and atoms, touching the fabric of space-time. Then, in an instant, Tremmilly's cognition bloomed. Her consciousness expanded to encompass the planet, the Accord, the Universe, becoming one with its energy. She fought to maintain the connection to her body, to not lose herself amongst the torrent of information whirling around her.

Eventually, she stabilized herself and Tremmilly could sense See'dek and his followers. They were a stain on the harmonious balance of existence, growing as moments passed. *How did I not notice them before?* The blackness grew, roiling outwards from their defiled planet. *They are too powerful for us now,* she thought. *I should have done something sooner, or worked harder to keep him loyal to the Accord. I have failed as Empress.* The thought almost made her cry, threatened to break her focus. *We cannot change the past,* she thought, finding peace once again, *but the future is an expansive possibility.*

Tremmilly shifted her focus, trying to decide what to do next. She saw the galaxies of the Accord spiral, collide, shift, and die. They reignited with a black energy See'dek and his horrible technology had created.

The breath caught in her throat and Tremmilly tumbled out of her trance. This future was not assured, only a possibility. *I can still fix this. We have not lost all hope.*

Tha'sis and Lek were still arguing. Tremmilly silenced them by raising a hand. After they saluted, she nodded, feeling drained both from the earlier battle and connecting to the Dawn. *There is no time for weakness,* she thought, closing her eyes. She utilized the power deep within herself to mentally link with the quadrillion citizens of the Accord. Thankfully, this was much easier than what she'd done earlier.

"As most of you know, See'dek, our chief scientist and researcher, attacked me after I told him of the High Court's ruling against his continued research. We, the Elrahi people, decided his exploration was dangerous and could not continue. What we did not know, was he was much more powerful than he told us." She stopped for a moment, feeling sorrow cut through the depth of her being.

"I made a mistake," Tremmilly continued. "I should have worked harder to compromise with See'dek, to make him feel valued, to prevent him from becoming a pariah. In this I have failed. My military advisers say I should dispatch forces to capture or kill See'dek, and this would be wise if not for what I have just seen. See'dek does not want the Dawn for the enlightenment or connectivity we yearn for. Rather, he wants to break it. Why he has changed in this way is beyond my wisdom, but he has gone too far for us to stop him with our military or Protector forces. He is much too powerful. What we saw in the Great Hall was just a taste of what he has created with his technology. If we go to his stronghold, he will overwhelm us. If we do nothing, he will assimilate us.

"I believe the time has come for the Elrahi, as a species, to join the Dawn. This will lend our power to the positive energy of the Universe. We will continue to resist See'dek and his technology. The transition will also lend us greater protection than maintaining our physical forms would. In this way, we can work towards healing the division See'dek created.

"Someday, I believe we will reunite as a people, that we will reach the Acclivity together. For now, we face many difficulties. Obviously, by uniting with the Dawn this soon, we are skipping many of the tests and experiments we had planned. There will certainly be risks, but I feel See'dek's strength makes continued existence in regular space-time a greater danger."

Hesitating, Tremmilly tried to find the right words. "I believe we can maintain a stronger position by leaving a specialized force behind. They will keep their current consciousness, and will act as watchers and harbingers for the eventual return of the Elrahi. This group will also work to maintain the integrity of other species, both current and future, preventing them from falling to those who want to break the Dawn."

Tremmilly began to feel the connection to her people weaken, and realized she needed to wrap up her speech. "Those who integrate themselves with the positive energy of the Universe, what we have learned to call the Dawn, will be safe. They will work to promote the growth and ascendancy of all life, as we have desired. We have connected to the Dawn, drawn upon it, and know it well. Now, we will completely surrender to it, as we dreamed of. I propose this plan to all Elrahi, and ask for your support. We have much work ahead of us, but it is what we have been striving towards, as a species, for generations."

With the last of her energy, Tremmilly sent her final, most painful sentence. "I am resigning as your Empress, to bind myself to those staying behind, to be a Harbinger."

When she ceased the connection, the surrounding council room erupted in protest. She turned to look at Veth. He took her hand and squeezed it, nodding his approval. *Is it me stepping down they are disapproving of, or the whole plan?* Whether her advisers agreed or not, it was within her authority to resign and stay behind. Every Elrahi would have the same choice: to become part of the Dawn or to live their remaining existence in standard space-time.

Tremmilly let the emotional storm rage for a minute, before once again raising her hand. "One at a time, please," she said, feeling a tenuous equilibrium establish itself.

"We have the strength to take him out," Lek interjected. "Simply give the command and we will storm See'dek's world with an unstoppable force."

"I have seen that future," Tremmilly replied, "it leads to death, to blackness, to the assimilation of our people into an abhorrent existence. You may succeed in killing See'dek, but what he has created will continue to live. We have no way to eradicate it, not at this point."

As soon as was appropriate, Tha'sis rose to his feet. "Empress, you must not place yourself in such a dangerous position. Evacuate to the Dawn, letting those trained in the art of war stay behind to do your wishes." He had new armor on. Despite the look of pain on his face, he was still an imposing figure. "Without the Protectors, or the rest of the Elrahi to help you, See'dek and his breakers will find and destroy you."

"Do not underestimate my abilities," Tremmilly said, eyes narrowed. "I have the guidance of the Dawn in this. Trust me, Tha'sis, as you have trusted in the past." She could see by the sadness on his face that her words cut him. *Things will be hard for us all, during this time of upheaval,* she thought, *but I must be careful to uplift, inspire and not tear down.* She looked into Tha'sis' bright yellow eyes, and smiled gently, trying to soften her words.

"I will stay behind, to serve you, as a Harbinger," one of the Protectors near the doorway said, his face obscured by his blue helmet. Most of the Protectors had removed that piece of armor once they'd safely escorted her to the Citadel. Those gathered before her were what remained of the force that had saved her life. *Far too many died,* she thought, trying to guess who the unknown Protector was.

The volunteer walked to the front of the room and sunk to a knee, unlatching his helm as he did so. When he raised his head, Tremmilly felt astonished. "How is it possible I don't know one of the Protectors?" His corroded and dented armor signaled he had been in the battle, but she knew every one of her personal guard. His face looked familiar, but she couldn't identify where she'd seen him before. Her heart began to beat faster, not because of a threat, but because of his smile.

Tha'sis stepped forward to get a view of the volunteer's face and let out a battle roar as soon as he did. The huge Protector dove on top of the smaller male, casting a barrier over them as he did so. "This is no Protector," he yelled, fighting to restrain the volunteer. "He is Orsin, killer of Retilus."

The murderer of an entire world, Tremmilly thought, feeling a deep guilt for her attraction to the male. *Perhaps you are not as wise and insightful as everyone believes.* The rest of the true Protectors came to Tha'sis' aid, quickly restraining and shielding Orsin. They lifted him to his feet, and Tremmilly saw he was still smiling. She once again had to fight down the fluttering sensation that accompanied it, despite knowing Orsin caused the annihilation of a billion people.

"I defended you, Empress Aris," he said, "I fought against See'dek. Now I am the first to forsake the Dawn to continue to do so."

"While your current actions are admirable, they are but an atom in the universe when compared to what you did on Retilus."

Orsin shrugged as best he could in the restraints. "You assume I was the architect of the Massacre."

"It is not an assumption when a court has convicted you of it."

"Empress," he replied, smile disappearing, "can I tell you my story?"

Tremmilly took a deep breath. She felt the weight of a thousand tasks, the fear that See'dek might return at any moment, the responsibility for a quadrillion Elrahi. *Yet, you can complete none of those tasks until the people have decided if they will escape to the Dawn. And Orsin is still a citizen, even as a convict. He defended you, put his life on the line.* She took another deep breath, eyes narrowing. *Then again, he might be lying. He could be here as an agent of See'dek. But why then would he have brought attention to himself?* Tremmilly began to feel overwhelmed and decided to go with her instinct. "You have my permission. Be brief."

"As records will confirm, I was once a Sentry, and served the Elrahi with honor. Eventually, I tired of the work, and See'dek recruited me to be part of his research security. The threat was low, but after what I'd been a part of at the fringes, it was welcome.

"For a while, everything seemed normal. I was happy to be a small part of the scientific advancement of the Accord. But then, See'dek offered me immortality. At first I thought he was proposing an experiment in surrendering to the Dawn, but it soon became evident he wanted to corrupt me with technology, to place tiny machines in my blood. I refused, not because I knew such a thing was against your wishes —I didn't at the time—but because it felt evil to me. My refusal did not seem to bother See'dek, and he continued to be amicable. Shortly after, he issued orders for me to act as primary security officer on a shipment to Retilus."

Orsin paused, looking down towards the invisible restraints binding him. "I have something to show you, if you release me."

Tha'sis began to protest, but Tremmilly raised a hand. "Remove his restraints, but keep the barrier up. If he moves suddenly, bind him again." The Protector grumbled, but did as commanded.

"When we arrived," Orsin continued, slowly pulling a small device out of his armor, "they set a container down on the surface of the planet, and the other personnel disappeared. They left me alone, under strict orders not to leave the shipment. Something felt wrong with the situation, so I began recording."

A video sprung into being in the air before Orsin. Tremmilly quickly recognized the verdant landscape of Retilus, lush forests stretching off into the distance. A star vessel's engine shrieked and the image panned up, capturing a large transport vessel streaming away into the atmosphere. The video returned to the ground, showing a massive cargo container, painted to blend in with the greens and browns of the forest.

As the perspective drew closer to the container, Tremmilly felt dread bloom within her. "No way in," Orsin's voice said quietly, as the perspective traversed each side. Tremmilly noticed black dust start to pour out from small openings high up on the container. As it hit the ground, it spread out, coating and consuming everything it touched. The video shifted wildly, as Orsin began running. "What is that?" he asked, voice straining. A moment later, the video disappeared.

"I abandoned my duty, deciding whatever See'dek was doing, I wanted no part of it. I left Retilus before determining the dust's effect. After spending time meditating in the fringe, I returned to the Accord. The news of genocide shocked me, but not as much as the accusation I was responsible.

"See'dek had completely discredited me. If I ever tried to expose his illegal technology, or his connection to Retilus, no one would listen. Unfortunately, I had no idea until it was much too late. Since my conviction, no place has been safe. I thought about going beyond the fringe, to worlds unknown, but I cannot tolerate knowing my entire species believes I murdered over a billion of them. I am not a complete innocent, nor do I claim such, but I'm not guilty of the crimes the court convicted me of." Orsin's lips pursed, and Tremmilly thought she saw tears in his eyes. "I tried to find hard evidence on See'dek, anything to bring him down, but he is much too careful."

Another video appeared before Orsin. *Retilus,* she thought again, only this time the view was from orbit. It was black, the entire surface barren. As the ship capturing video drew closer to the planet, Tremmilly thought she saw movement. *Impossible. The sensor vessels we dispatched declared it lifeless.*

Black shapes writhed, and the view point shifted violently. When it stabilized, the surface was directly below, growing smaller. Giant fingers of shadow reached up, trying to embrace the ship. They grew closer and closer, despite its increasing velocity. Tremmilly felt her heart clench. A moment later, the video ceased.

"The tendrils separated from the surface and pursued me," Orsin said, "like pilotless fighters. I barely escaped." He fell silent for a moment. Tremmilly expected Tha'sis to protest, but the Protector looked intrigued.

"Other than this video, I have no evidence, but I believe See'dek somehow converted the planet's biomass into a kind of power generator. He's using it for his war against us."

"After surveying Retilus, I finally tracked See'dek to Elrah Prime, believing there was more to his visit than to hear the verdict of the court. I infiltrated the Protectors to get into the Great Hall, so that I might add my skills to your defense. Sadly, I was correct about his intentions.

"Thank you, Empress, for hearing my story. If you do not believe me, then I ask you to order Tha'sis to execute me now. If you can not see the truth, then no one will, and I would be better off sent to blackness."

Orsin bowed, closed his eyes, and waited for Tremmilly's verdict.

27 – MAXAR

Maxar breathed deeply, heart pounding at a rapid pace he couldn't restrain. *The Empress is far more beautiful than anyone has ever said,* he thought, knowing he should be focusing on his peril, but finding it impossible. *Will she believe me?* He kept expecting blackness to consume him, his consciousness severed by Tha'sis' mind blade.

Finally, after what felt like eternity, the Empress spoke. "Orsin, I believe you." Relief flooded over him. Maxar straightened, opening his eyes to see her emerald greens staring into him. "I pardon you from the decree of death," she said, a hint of a smile turning up her lips.

How could anyone be more beautiful than Empress Aris? Maxar thought, feeling elated and stunned by her words.

"I accept your pledge of service," the Empress continued, "both for your skills and your knowledge of See'dek's technology. Do not cause me to regret this, or make me look a fool."

"Of course, Empress," he said, feeling a weight of responsibility settle over him. *If that means I get to be in her presence, I gladly accept it.*

When Maxar finished speaking, the entire room fell silent. He kept his eyes on her, knowing that with her decree, he was safe, at least from execution. *See'dek and his followers on the other hand...*

"If you have bound yourself to this course, Empress," Tha'sis said, deep voice still sending a chill down Maxar's spine, "then I will stay with you, to protect and assist in any way possible."

"As will I," Lek interjected. Maxar had heard stories about the decorated Sentry, who'd fought in every major fringe war over the past thousand years. Both her and Tha'sis would be huge assets.

The Empress nodded her assent, a full smile lighting up her face. "Thank you, thank you both."

"Empress," a new voice said, the crowd parting to reveal a plain looking Elrahi. The male stepped forward, saluted, with fist over heart.

"You need more than military might. A builder and engineer such as myself could add much to your Harbingers. Please accept my service."

"Kald Segana," the Empress replied, "your machines and devices have greatly enriched the Elrahi without taking us towards the corruption of See'dek. I am most grateful to have you with me." Kald saluted, a gesture that looked odd on his small frame.

"I too will stay beside you," the small boy next to the Empress said, his face a mixture of excitement and fright.

"Veth," the Empress said, looking troubled, "I cannot let you. It is far too dangerous."

"But you know you must. No other of this group has my skills. You need my assistance. I will not abandon you in this time of need."

The Empress sighed and nodded. "You are right, little brother, but I must keep you away from danger. If See'dek were to harm you..."

"We will protect you both," Maxar said. Lek and Tha'sis agreed. Neither of them was willing to look directly at him, but Maxar was content to be safe from the threat of immediate execution. *It will take some time for them to accept me into the group, but I can tolerate it. I'm here for the Empress, not their approval.*

"It has been a long day," Aris said, beginning to show her weariness. "Dire events occurred, and we've lost many loved ones. Change is upon us. Unless anyone objects, let us all rest. Tomorrow, I will send the Elrahi on a million worlds to the Dawn Temples, hoping See'dek and his rising darkness won't be able to follow."

With a sudden jolt, Maxar felt himself pulled away, the connection to his body severed. It took him a moment to remember this was exactly what had happened when he came here in the first place. It felt like he was being turned inside out, compressed into a singularity. The next moment, his consciousness seemed vast. The myriad sensations threatened to overwhelm him. *Is this what Cazz-ak and Lothis mean when they speak of dimensional folds?* Maxar tried to relax and trust whatever had brought him to Orsin would return him to himself. He accelerated, the pace of expansion and contraction increasing. A rushing sensation built to a crescendo, and Maxar opened his eyes.

"What's happening?" Jaydon's voice said frantically inside Maxar's ENS helmet. "Founder be cursed to the fires of the dark star. Did we somehow pass through another magnetic field?" The old captain was kneeling over him, and through their face shields, he saw tears in his eyes.

"I'm OK, Jaydon," Maxar answered, sitting up. He felt an ache in his side where a rock must have jabbed him. "It was a dream, a memory."

"Simultaneously, you and Wake just pass out onto the floor, and you're out for hours. Blightheart, you buggers scared me. What was I supposed to do?" Jaydon's voice settled to a mumble, but Maxar could still pick out some curses and complaints every so often.

Turning, he saw Wake rising to his feet. "You are Kald," Maxar stated.

"And you, Orsin," Wake replied. Maxar nodded, wondering how their lives as humans had been on such similar paths as their Elrahi ones. "What just happened to us?"

"I'm not sure, but I think we just had an experience similar to what Tremmilly, Cazz-ak, and Lothis are always talking about."

"Do you suppose they were there too, like us?"

"Could we get on with this blighthearted mission?" Jaydon said, interrupting before Maxar could respond. "While you were both off in a trance, I was stuck here in these buggered tunnels by myself."

"Of course," Maxar said, empathizing with the captain. "We did not choose to leave. It's not something we have control over, at least not at the moment."

"I don't know if that's comforting or not," Jaydon scowled.

Maxar resumed moving the last of the rubble blocking their path towards what he hoped was the Ashamine archaeological find. The two other men joined him, and the tunnel opened up.

"There," Wake said, rolling the last block out of the way. It had been much too heavy for Maxar and Jaydon to move, even working together.

They stood together, personal lights focused on the tunnel ahead. It led straight through the rock, so far back darkness swallowed up their illumination. Maxar felt a sense of foreboding settle over him. *Do you really want to know what's inside you? Are you prepared to find out?*

Taking in a deep breath, Maxar headed towards the unknown. Time passed, and he occasionally felt a rumble emanating from behind them. "I think the miners have begun their shift," Wake said.

Finally, their light disappeared into a vast open space. Maxar's heart quickened. When they stepped into the chamber, it felt like the blackness was swallowing him whole. Their lights failed to reveal anything and he wondered just how big it was.

"There," Jaydon said, startling him. The old captain darted to the side. Maxar drew his flechette pistol reflexively. A moment later, illumination blinded his dark adjusted eyes. When they finally focused, he saw the chamber wasn't as large as he had originally thought. It was still enormous, but the eternity his mind had conjured up was far from reality.

Before them stretched a room that would fit a Rubicon class battle ship. And indeed, there was some type of machine or vessel in the center, although it was unlike anything Maxar had seen before. It's curves, segments, and construction looked highly refined. The black surface gleamed in the light, the material seeming simultaneously solid and liquid. Everything about it was distinctly inhuman, and inorganic.

Something inside Maxar felt drawn towards the shape, pulled in with a longing he'd never experienced before.

"What is it?" Wake said, sounding as baffled as Maxar felt.

"It is a ship," a voice replied through his helmet. Out of the corner of his eye, Maxar saw a flicker of movement. He brought up his flechette pistol, taking aim at the figure.

At first Maxar thought it was wearing a black ENS, but in the next fraction of a second, his mind corrected. Black robe. No suit. Wake had been very clear: the atmosphere on Traynos-6 was toxic, and his own experience told him it was much too cold for a human body to survive without protection.

The last time he'd experienced humans who could function without an ENS in a hostile environment, he'd been on the hangar deck of the Justice, when the dead came back to life.

"Breaker!" Maxar shouted, tightening his aim at the figure's head and triggering the flechette pistol.

28 – CRASOR

"Ten seconds to impact!" a tech yelled, sounding as desperate as Crasor felt.

"Evasive maneuvers," Karoth roared. "Why isn't point defense taking out the missiles?" Two of the fusion weapons had already struck the Justice, weakening the ship.

If one hits the engine area, Crasor thought, his mind shying away from the amount of energy such an event would release.

"Full thrust engaged," the propulsion engineer responded.

"Sir," the weapons tech replied, "the missiles disappear from sensors right before they enter point defense range."

A shock wave coursed through the Justice. Crasor winced, wondering if a bigger reaction would follow.

"Spool up the cannons and use them to extend range," Karoth barked.

"It will take time to configure the targeting computers for—"

"Then get personnel to take over and do it!"

Crasor felt the situation sliding out of control. *Should I order retreat? Can we even get out of range before the missiles destroy us?*

"We can control the cannons," the Breaker mind said, making Crasor cringe. "We have never seen this type of cloaking technology. Given time, we can adjust the ship's systems to defeat it, but for now, our integration with both the ship and the crew will be enough. We can defend the Justice's vital systems. The newly captured ships will not fare as well, but they are expendable."

Crasor relayed the One's directions. After a minute, rail rounds began lancing out towards the missiles. But it was not enough. Blinding energy engulfed two of the Rubicon class ships as missiles hit their worm generators or propulsion systems. Crasor gritted his teeth, knowing the loss of the vessels would hurt their future efforts, despite the Breaker mind's assurance.

The radiant blast swallowed one of the Fion class ships, then expelled it violently outward. A part of him hoped the nuclear fire would grow to consume the Justice. *Then I would be free.* He realized what he wished for and wondered where the thought had come from. *Even with the mind of the One so close, it is worth it for this power. If the Breakers summon me to their dimension a thousand times, this is still what I want. I would be dead without them.* Crasor squashed another thought that tried to tell him he wouldn't have died in the first place if not for them.

"Force propulsion into overdrive," Crasor said, pushing all doubts from his head. "These humans will not obliterate us. We took their ships, and now they destroy them, but we will crush, remake, and assimilate humanity. We will break humans and Enthos alike. We will break the Dawn. The universe will bend under our control."

The bridge erupted in cheers, and the voice of the One noted its approval as well. Crasor felt his gloom and fear vanish, carried away in a tide of elation. He saw the velocity indicators on his tactical display spike upwards as the Justice gained speed.

"Keep track of where missiles originate," Karoth ordered. "Dispatch fighters and gunships to obliterate the launchers. And if any are left when the Justice gets in range, rail them from orbit."

Sweat rolled down Crasor's face, despite the bridge's climate control. His fleet seemed to move so slowly, exposing them to further nuclear bombardment. Crasor's high spirits began evaporating under the constant tension. The Justice's rail cannons kept most of the fusion weapons away, but occasionally one would strike the remaining ships. There was nothing else he could do but hope the Breaker mind would coordinate fire to protect critical areas.

The fighters and gunships, much quicker than the Justice, were engaging targets on the surface, decreasing the volume of missiles streaming outward from Exis-7. Crasor's tension diminished, as he settled back into the chair. *This is how it should be,* he thought. *The destruction of two ships we weren't counting on having, captured without casualties, hardly counts as a loss.*

Alarms began to blare, and Crasor flinched. "Status?" Karoth demanded.

"Sir," a tech quivered, face pale, "a barrage of nuclear weapons launched. It looks like they kept a huge battery concealed, having just fired the entire salvo."

Crasor checked the tactical display and saw a dense cluster of missiles headed for them. From their trajectory, the servers calculated they were all targeting the Justice. Based on earlier performance, Crasor knew that even with the Breaker mind's augmentation, they would not be able to destroy the weapons before impact. *This is the end,* he thought, once again feeling a kind of joy at the realization.

The cluster of missiles came into accurate range for the rail cannons, and a cascade of rounds began streaming outward. The intervening distance filled with blue, green, red, orange, and yellow ion tails as each round's tracer component activated. Crasor checked the display to determine the result, only to see the Justice's sensor resolution wasn't fine enough to distinguish individual missiles inside the mass.

The cannons kept firing until the missiles cloaked, vanishing completely from the display. *It wasn't enough,* he thought, closing his eyes. Seconds dragged by, and Crasor waited for the consuming nuclear conflagration that would be the end. *With that much weaponry and the energy components of the ship, it will practically birth a new star.*

But nothing happened. He opened his eyes and rechecked the display. The missiles were still cloaked. The time for impact had come and gone. Everyone on the bridge was as stunned as Crasor.

"Status?" Karoth asked.

No one replied for several seconds. Then, finally, one tech answered. "Forward hull damage control indicates non-penetrating impacts."

What in the fires of the dark star? Crasor wondered.

"Was that barrage a different weapon type?" Karoth said, speaking the conclusion Crasor had come to.

"No, sir," the tech answered. "All sensors indicate radioactive elements in the weapons are identical to the previous missiles that detonated."

"A video link request incoming from Exis-7," the comms tech announced.

Karoth looked to Crasor, and he nodded.

"Accept," Karoth said, standing to face the large screen. Crasor rose from his chair and adopted a military stance.

"Hello, invaders," a human said on the screen, his gray hair disheveled. Crasor couldn't tell if it was some optical distortion, or if the man just had a really large head. "Welcome to Exis-7. The planet is yours."

"Who are you?" Karoth asked.

"I am the person who saved you from the Families buggering you to the black star. I couldn't penetrate the control center in time to prevent the salvo launch, but I did disarm the missiles before they could detonate. Given they are still in proximity to your ship, it would be a good idea for you to keep me alive long enough to get clear. The Families disapprove of what I've done, so if you strafe this precise location, it would go a long way towards preserving both your and my own safety." A string of coordinates came through the connection.

"How do we know you were the one who disarmed the weapons?"

Crasor asked.

"Because I'm the only one who has nothing to lose by collaborating with you. But there is really no other way to prove it. They kept the Heavy system completely disconnected from the Terminal Network, so I can't patch you in to prove my control."

"Convenient," Crasor said, thinking for a moment. "Issue the strike order," he said finally, and Karoth did so. "We will soon be in range to obliterate any remaining missiles before they leave the atmosphere, so even if it's a trap, it won't matter."

"Indeed," the gray haired man said. "But I have complete control of the Heavy system, and all missiles will remain disarmed and in their launch systems, as long as you keep the Families out of this installation. I would imagine you might appreciate adding some nuclear weaponry to your arsenal. There is quite a stockpile remaining down here."

"You said before you had nothing to lose," Crasor replied, beginning to like this human.

"Yes," the man stated. "The Families betrayed me, when I was only trying to serve them. I decided, based on your power, you were a far better ally and you might reward my assistance."

"And what is your name?"

"Gav Serrith, head of the Serrith family, before the Council dissolved it."

Had Gav not disabled the missiles, we would all be dead now. Crasor didn't feel he owed the man a debt, but there was something intriguing about him. Gav could become a powerful Breaker, given training. *And we need as many of those as we can get.*

Despite the vast distance, Crasor reached out and caressed Gav's soul. On the screen, a look of joy enveloped the man. *Bound for the Seed,* Crasor thought, smiling.

"Karoth," he said, releasing the bond. "Give Gav whatever assistance he requires, highest priority. And coordinate with him in taking the planet. Use whatever intel he can provide."

Crasor returned to his seat, beginning to relax. Exis-7 stretched out before the Justice, another step along the path to dominating the Ashamine. *And you thought death would be better than this?* A smile grew on Crasor's face and he bit his lip, relishing the excitement of the invasion.

29 – AZA

"Finally," Aza said, connecting the data square interface to her portable terminal. Finding the device had been difficult, requiring visits to several merchants in the under-levels of the Founder's City. *If my parents ever find out where I went...* They weren't places someone in training to be a priestess should go. Aza still felt guilty for the lies she'd told. *It will be worth it once Ash shows me the truth.*

She checked the clock on her terminal before looking towards the contemplation room door. Aza still had almost a full hour remaining on her reservation, and even then, as long as every other room wasn't full, the Holy Order librarians would leave her in peace. *I locked the door, so no awkward intrusions.*

Aza took the data square out of her pocket and stared at it intently. *What do you think is on here? Even if you do manage to get a message out, what do you expect him to do?* These questions had harassed Aza ever since she'd found the data square in her mother's desk. She still had no answers. It made Aza feel even more guilty for the way she was acting. *I wish I had a stronger justification.* All she possessed was a feeling, a belief Ash would be able to help her somehow. Though it was as strong as any of her other convictions, this new feeling was at odds with her beliefs about the Ashamine, the Holy Order, and her choice to become a priestess.

Without further thought, Aza pushed the data square into the small interface. Nothing happened. She expected a prompt or notification to pop up on the screen, but the desktop didn't change. Opening the file manager, she navigated to the data square's directory. *Empty.* The interface showed a clear file tree. *Why would mother hide an empty data square? Why would Ash have given it to them?* She guessed perhaps her mother had erased it, but it still didn't explain why she had kept the small device.

Aza sat back in her chair, disappointed. She'd gone through all the work to first find the square, then to open it. *You risked your entire future as a priestess for this, and it was empty.*

Looking back, she began to feel stupid. A desperate need to confess surged within her. It felt like the only way to fix the mess was to beg forgiveness from her parents. She closed her eyes, imagining the disappointment on their faces. Her cheeks began to burn, and tears pushed their way out of squinted lids. *I violated their trust,* Aza thought, beginning to list off and organize her transgressions.

"Hello? Aza?" a small voice asked, startling her. It took her a moment to realize it had come from the terminal. When she blinked back enough tears to clear her vision, she saw a face on the display. "Aza, is that you? You've grown so much. What's wrong?"

"Ash," she said in relief. He was older, his hair gray, and looking tired, but it was her uncle.

"Aza, why are you contacting me? What's wrong? What happened to your parents?"

"Nothing," she replied, confused. "They're fine. Why do you ask?"

Ash looked relieved. "Well, I just figured something bad must have occurred for them to let you contact me."

"Well, they don't know I'm doing it."

"I see," he answered, a wary look replacing the concern. "I should go."

"Wait," Aza said, feeling confused, "we haven't gotten to talk yet."

"Your parents made it clear I was to have no contact with you. I don't want to be the cause of your punishment."

"It is my choice, one I am freely making, with full knowledge of potential consequences. I miss you, Ash, and I need your help."

He smiled, a joyous look she saw in her youngest memories. "You are becoming an adult," he laughed. Aza felt embarrassed and didn't know how to respond.

"The Ashamine," she said, hesitating because she wasn't quite sure how to put words to what she felt. "Something is wrong. Things have just been moving from bad to worse. Someone kidnapped Lothis, assassinated the Founder, and captured ships and systems."

Ash nodded, looking grim. "I know. Aza," he paused, a pained expression on his face, "as much as I want to, we can't continue talking. It's not safe for either of us."

"What do you mean?"

"I can't tell you, but just know there's a good reason your parents eliminated me from your life. Be well, Aza. I love you."

"Wait," she said, "I need your help. Something big is happening, and everyone just seems apathetic. I think the Thousand Stars might be rising again."

"I don't want to get you killed, or worse. That is how dangerous our conversation is."

"But we are all in danger. I can't do nothing, like everyone else."

Ash sighed. "Even if I wanted to tell you what is happening, I couldn't. We don't know. I can confirm you are right to worry though." He looked as if he was about to say something further, then changed his mind. "However you acquired your mother's data square, put it back as soon as you can. Don't tell anyone about this conversation. I'm relatively sure this comms link is secure, but the longer it is open, the greater the danger someone notices it."

"I love you, uncle Ash," she said, fighting back tears threatening to blur her vision once again.

"I love you too, Aza," he replied, biting his lip. "Stay strong, stay safe, and may the wisdom of Azak-so guide you." His face vanished, replaced by her terminal background.

Aza quickly stuffed the data square and its interface into her satchel, trying to ignore the flood of emotion crashing through her. Seeing Ash had brought back so many memories, creating a longing for him to be a part of her life again. She felt herself losing control. *Stop*, Aza told herself, forcing both her body and mind to cease their frantic movements. *Focus on the now, not what you wish you had.*

She'd not been ready to speak with him, and his sudden appearance on-screen had caught her off guard. *I thought there would be contact info or a letter, but Ash created something that opened a connection to him.* Aza knew how to do normal things with her terminal, but coding was far beyond her abilities, let alone hashing. *Maybe I can find someone to help me.*

As time went on, Aza calmed further and began to see the situation more clearly. *Even if he couldn't do more, at least Ash verified my suspicions.* Thinking back about what he had said made a thought occur to her. *Who is Azak-so?* It wasn't a deity, Ashamine or otherwise. She'd studied all those. *Perhaps this is a clue as well.*

Aza felt her spirits rise, carried by curiosity and optimism. She would still heed Ash's warnings—*at least most of them*—but she felt determined to discover what was going on, both with the Ashamine and her uncle.

You know none of this is right, a vicious voice scolded. *This has and will continue to distract you from your training. You've lied and been disobedient. You're a disappointment, both to your faith and your parents.*

The guilt was almost too much to bear, and the overwhelming urge to confess returned. Aza felt it start to sweep her away. Ash's words returned: *Stay strong, stay safe, and may the wisdom of Azak-so guide you.* Whoever Azak-so was, she decided he would not be one to wallow in guilt. *No,* she thought, breathing deeply. *No. I will make the choices that are right for me and accept the consequences of those actions.*

If it means the Holy Order expels you? the vicious voice shot back. *Imprisons you? Shoots you out an airlock in the Clothing of the Iconoclast?*

Then I have done the best I can. I will live with the result. Aza stood, checking to make sure she hadn't left anything in the small contemplation chamber. She unlocked the door, took a deep breath, and strode confidently from the room.

30 – WAKE

"It's a ship," a voice said over Wake's ENS helmet. It was familiar somehow, but he couldn't remember where he had heard it. *News vids?*

"Breaker!" Maxar yelled, startling Wake out of his thoughts. He turned to look, and saw his friend aiming a flechette pistol at a dark shape standing before him. The pistol bucked, the needles moving too fast to see. But the figure had disappeared.

"I am certainly not a Breaker," the voice said again. Maxar scanned the room, brought up the pistol and fired a second time, his reaction almost quicker than Wake could follow. He triggered several more rounds, each in a new direction.

"Is it a hologram?" Jaydon asked, crouching low to the floor.

"The nanites have integrated well with your biological systems," the voice continued. Something about the instantaneous movement combined with the dark shape triggered a memory in Wake. *The Lower-Elder trial!*

"Stop!" Wake yelled, waving his hands. "Stop. I'm not sure who he is, but he's not a Breaker. In fact, he warned the Ashamine about them while trying to save me."

"What?" Maxar asked, halting, but still keeping his weapon at the ready. "What are you talking about?"

"So, you remember," the dark robed figure stated, appearing a short distance before them.

"Yes. You were at my trial and made me fight you to help prove my loyalty to the Ashamine. You tried to keep them from executing me." He thought for a moment. "Captain Malesis said your name was Karthis."

"Indeed," the figure replied, his attention still on Maxar's flechette pistol, "that was the name I gave him. It was appropriate for that time, for that persona. You can call me Dras, my true name."

"If you aren't a Breaker," Maxar said, "how are you able to breathe this atmosphere and survive without an ENS? How can you move from one spot to another instantly?"

"Good questions," Dras replied. "I would be happy to answer them, but first, will you put away your pistol? I'm not sure how much damage the weapon would inflict, and since the Ashamine have stripped everything they could from my vessel, I don't want to attempt damage repair."

"You're sure he's OK?" Maxar said, not turning away from Dras.

"As sure as I can be," Wake replied. "I don't know anything more about him than what I've told you. He tried to help me."

"OK," Maxar said, lowering the weapon. He didn't holster it, but this was good enough for Dras.

"Thank you," he said. "I believe I can provide some explanations, although I'm unsure of where to start."

"Begin with how you breathe toxic atmosphere," Jaydon said, keeping Maxar between himself and Dras.

"Of course," he nodded.

Now that Wake could finally get a better look at him, he saw the man was bald, his slight frame covered in a dark robe. His eyes were black, something Wake had never seen before. *What if I'm wrong and he really is a Breaker?*

"The atmosphere would be toxic if I were a biological and required aspiration," Dras continued.

"So you're not human, and you're obviously not Entho-la-ah-mine," Jaydon replied. "If you aren't a Breaker, then what are you? Arche?"

"Who are the Arche?" Dras replied, looking puzzled. "No, I am Heltasoth."

"Never heard of them," Jaydon replied.

"Of course not. The Akked is not our galaxy, not our origin. My people traveled here on a larger component of that ship," Dras said, pointing to the hulking shape across the cavern. "Our species, if you can call it that, is unlike anything you've experienced, except for certain aspects of the Breakers. We are inorganics, what you would call sentient machines."

"Are you related to the Breakers?" Wake asked, feeling his anxiety rise.

"No, not in any way. We are fully inorganic and lack biological components. From what I've learned, the Breakers are the opposite: organics using machine augmentation."

"Like me," Maxar said, looking resigned.

"Yes. I can feel Heltasoth technology moving through you. As I said before, it integrated quite well. Whatever changes the Ashamine made to our nanites, it was clever."

"Does that mean you're going to control me the same way Crasor does his Breakers?"

Wake held his breath, knowing Maxar would do everything in his power to prevent this.

Dras laughed. "No, that is not our way. Any similarity we share to the Breakers ends at our use of nanites. Neither I, nor any other Heltasoth, seek domination of life, organic or otherwise. It is a silly pursuit of biologicals, one borne of your evolutionary roots."

At this angle, Wake couldn't see inside Maxar's helmet very well, but the man looked relieved.

"Why are you here, Dras?" Wake asked. "How did you become involved with the Brotherhood of Azak-so?"

"Perhaps some day, I can give you the full history. The Ashamine techs will arrive soon. As I said before, they've taken everything from the ship that wasn't connected. Now, they've begun to study our propulsion system, a more dangerous proposition. Given the time constraint, I will be brief, but try to answer all questions."

Wake nodded, feeling more comfortable with Dras. He looked over at Maxar, wondering if he had the information he'd come for. Maxar, looking thoughtful, said nothing.

"My ship was a galactic exploration and mapping vessel. We used a system similar to your own worm generators to skip across interstellar space. While biological life forms strive to duplicate their genetic material, the motivation for all known inorganic life is knowledge. The Heltasoth are no exception.

"When we came to the Akked, we found a galaxy rich both in life and potential. Humans were spread far, governed by the Thousand Stars. The Entho-la-ah-mines were at peace, building their own civilization. When the Ashamine rose, it changed everything, but this you already know." Wake remembered the vid of Calthis Brightwing, of what she had said about the time before the Ashamine. This was his only connection to the past. He wanted to ask for more, but Wake knew Dras had more important things to tell them.

"We also found traces of a dormant species, hidden on planets and asteroids across the Akked. It reminded us of how fungi propagate using spores. I decided it best for us to stay and observe this unique phenomenon, despite our mandate.

"Crossing interstellar voids is more complicated and difficult than a simple transition from system to system. My crew argued we would risk galactic misalignment, that we'd made calculations and had to comply with the time line. I decided it was worth the risk, to observe the anomaly. The crew disagreed, and in the Heltasoth way, we decided I would stay behind and they would continue with the plan.

"They left me with a portion of the ship and I was to follow before the galaxies shifted out of alignment. I got too caught up in my desire for knowledge, in my longing to see what these inorganic spores would create, that I waited too long. When I tried to go back, there was no chance of a successful transition.

"So now I am here, alone, a million of your standard years to pass before a favorable alignment once again returns, with plenty of time to observe the Breakers."

"Who are you blighthearted buggers?" a new voice interrupted. Wake turned to see a group of five soldiers in gray and white camo EN suits approaching. "Nobody said there would be personnel down here already." Dialing up his optic magnification, Wake made out the dagger-through-planet insignia of the Founder's Commandos on their shoulders.

"Is that the Clothing of the Iconoclast?" another unknown voice asked.

"Report authorization immediately," the first voice demanded, "or we will rail you down." The Commandos fanned out, taking position behind large boulders.

"The Ashamine is early today," Dras said, "but it changes little. This corrupt dictatorship has co-opted too much of my species' technology. I will not let them have any of the more advanced systems." Dras began walking towards the soldiers, gait steady, showing no fear. "I will serve as distraction as you three get to the ship. We can figure out our next step from there."

Dras vanished, then reappeared behind the Commandos, causing cries of alarm. Wake took off running towards the Heltasoth vessel, seeing Maxar and Jaydon do the same. Between Brightwing and Maxar's augmented abilities, he thought they might have been able to take on five Founder's Commandos. *If we absolutely had to...* After watching Felar shoot back on Lith-elo, he wasn't totally confident, even with their advantages.

Rail rifle shock waves rolled and echoed through the cavern, the sound audible through his armor. Tracer rounds flared, the light reflecting off the ship's hull. When they finally reached it, Wake wondered how to get inside, but a hatch was already opening.

"Are we sure this isn't some elaborate trap?" Jaydon asked, out of breath.

Wake scrambled through the opening, and Jaydon clambered in behind him. "No," Maxar replied, diving in as a rail round slammed into the hull where he'd been standing. The hatch quickly slid shut, engulfing them in darkness. "But even if it is, I still like the chances better here than facing a squad of FCs." Wake had to agree.

"Come to the deck," Dras transmitted. The slightest increase in gravity signaled the ship was moving upwards. "I wish I could provide you with illumination, but we see in a wider spectra than you, and as such, our lighting is outside visible range."

They each switched on their suit lights and began following the corridor. Everything around them looked similar to the ship's black exterior: sleek, refined, and foreign. *Well, an alien race created it, so that does make sense,* Wake thought, shaking his head at his own observations.

As they continued through the ship, Wake felt excited to see more of its systems and architecture, but there were no side corridors, no path other than forward. He had a strange feeling doors here didn't look or work in a way he understood.

Finally, they reached an open space, and Wake became disoriented. It seemed they had found an exit, with the dark stone floor far below. Dras stood before them, nothing but air below his feet. "Come in," he replied, beckoning. When Wake hesitated, Dras nodded. "Yes, sorry, I understand your confusion. This is the ship's bridge and is completely solid. The view is simply a visualization of the space surrounding the craft."

Wake took a cautious step forward, then another. He found if he looked straight ahead, rather than down, it was not as disorienting. Maxar entered behind him.

"Bugger it to the fires of the dark star," he heard Jaydon mutter under his breath. Wake remembered the old captain was afraid of heights, but when he turned to look, Jaydon was already inside, looking everywhere but down.

"They are moving a rail cannon into position," Maxar announced calmly.

"Nothing to worry about," Dras replied. "Even if they could damage the ship, they wouldn't risk it. In the past, Ashamine scientists couldn't discover how to fly it and decided my ship was derelict. Now they know it's operational, they'll desperately want it back, along with me, for interrogation."

"Then we have to escape before they notify orbitally based assets," Maxar said. "Get us back to our ship, and we can support each other in retreat."

"A good idea," Dras said, looking up. "It will take a few standard minutes to spool up the phase drive, but we are quite safe from small arms rail fire. If the Commandos can get up here and find the hatch, they don't have equipment capable of breaching it."

Wake wanted to ask what a phase drive did, but Dras was concentrating and he supposed he'd find out soon enough. Another minute passed, and he felt the ship slide upwards. It moved unlike any human vessel. *Perhaps this is how a fish feels, moving through water.*

"You're going to fly us into the rock," Jaydon said, sounding nervous.

"Yes, and I will also take us out the other side."

Jaydon said nothing further. They all watched as they passed through hundreds of meters of stone. When they moved into the frigid morning light, Wake let out a breath he didn't know he'd been holding. *What if something had gone wrong and we fused with the rock?* It was an unpleasant thought.

"Where is your vessel located?"

Wake pointed out the range they had climbed over. "On the other side of that notch in the ridge."

As they traveled across the short distance, Dras continued his story. "So I got my wish to continue observing, and that's what I've done for almost 2,000 years. I watched the War of a Thousand Stars, watched humans kill each other until just a fraction of their original numbers remained." Dras took the ship in low over the ridge, and Wake wondered if they'd collide with the craggy peaks.

"I saw the Entho-la-ah-mines flourish, and the Ashamine grow into a xenocidal monster. As the situation became more complex, I joined the Brotherhood of Azak-so. They provided me with intelligence, closer observation of humans, and a way to help those not part of Ashamine corruption. This goes against Heltasoth mandates against interference, but the Ashamine is too great a threat, to Entho-la-ah-mines, as well as humans. I've begun to feel I am a part of this galaxy now, and cannot just stand by, mandates or no."

Wake looked down and saw the Death Watch below them. He felt relieved to see everything looked the same as when they had left. *Hopefully, the Ashamine haven't set up an ambush.*

"When the Breaker crystal on Noor-5 began to spore, I got a deeper sense of them, and it told me things were about to get much worse. It was like they felt the chaos and negative energy swirling around them and emerged because of it." The large Heltasoth vessel began losing altitude, and Wake quit looking down. It made him nauseous.

"With the Brotherhood shattered and Parick Olvold dead or in hiding, I have no remaining human allies. I have thought of going to Lith-elo-hi-rosh before, but I did not want to startle the Entho-la-ah-mines. I wonder if I would even be able to communicate with them."

"You know where Lith-elo is?" Maxar blurted.

"Yes, as I said before, we have explored the entirety of the Akked."

"Blightheart," Jaydon cursed. Wake followed his gaze. Five large Ashamine gunships flew over the mountains, streaking towards them.

"While my vessel can do much," Dras said calmly, "its combat capabilities are limited. I would prefer we not directly engage in battle with these ships. Delaying might give the Ashamine time to organize orbital interference and prevent our escape."

"Then how do we get back on the Watch?" Jaydon asked.

"We don't," Maxar said, looking towards Dras. "Will you take us back to Lith-elo?"

Tracers flared as the gunships began firing. Rounds streaked past them.

"Of course. As I said, it is a place I have wanted to visit. And with your introduction, perhaps I can study the Entho-la-ah-mines more closely."

The ground dropped away as they shot upwards, faster than anything Wake had ever experienced. Before it was out of sight, however, Wake saw several rounds slam into their grounded vessel. *No more Death Watch,* he thought, realizing they were completely reliant on Dras for galactic transportation.

31 – FELAR

"So I was Empress," Tremmilly said, sounding stunned.

"And I, your Protector," Cazz-ak added. The five of them had gathered in the communal dwelling, seated to face each other. Felar had felt stunned since she'd returned to her body just a short time ago. Their dream or vision had been a huge data dump, and her mind felt bogged down processing it. The memories of her human life swirled together with those of her Elrahi one. *How is it Lek Tomun feels more real than Felar Haltro?*

"You're my sister?" Lothis said, looking at Tremmilly intently, a joyous smile on his face.

Tremmilly returned his happy emotion, leaning over Beowulf to give the boy a hug. "I never had siblings," she said, "at least not as a human." She thought for a moment. "This is all confusing. Should we be going by our Elrahi names? I don't feel like the Empress, although I suppose it is still a part of me."

"That might be too much," Felar replied. "We know each other by our human and Entho-la-ah-mine names now. Let's just keep it that way." It would be hard enough to reconcile her friends' dualities without a reminder every time she tried to use the foreign sounding names.

Felar cast her mind back to the vision, thinking what each of them had looked like. Their bodies were almost nothing like their current ones, except for Lothis, but their energy and personalities were exactly the same. Even all their mannerisms were in place. The whole experience disoriented her.

"As we have gained a deeper connection to our Elrahi aspects," Cazz-ak said, "I have felt my mind expand. The energy once requiring strong emotion to tap into has become freely available. I think it was present, but anger was the only bridge. Now, it is with me always, just like the Great Thought."

Felar also felt access to a part of herself she hadn't known existed. She could tell she would never be as strong as Cazz-ak, or even Lothis, but that didn't matter. The connection felt like a highly trained, well rested muscle, ready for use at a moments notice. Even some knowledge of how to use this old ability had returned. It reminded Felar of the times, as a Founder's Commando, she'd qualified on a new weapon system. *Now I have it, I need to use it.*

Thinking of combat made her remember the Arche. *Perhaps we are ready to destroy them.* With their Elrahi abilities returning, Felar wondered if the Arche would retreat. *No, they've committed to this course of action. They will follow through.* Despite the new strength they were all gaining, Felar knew it was bringing additional, unknown weaknesses as well. *Even if we only gain confidence, we must stay alert.*

"I will continue seeking additional information about our past," Tremmilly said, petting Beowulf. "It would be good to know what happened next, how the transition to the Dawn happened. I would like to discover what we did as Harbingers between this latest memory and taking on our current forms." She paused for a moment, thinking. "Something about this last vision felt different, planned somehow."

"What do you mean?" Felar asked.

"We all experienced it simultaneously," Tremmilly replied. "I bet Maxar and Wake were present as well. I have a hunch we created some kind of memory capsule before we left, something that would activate once we were all back together. Perhaps it was a way to restore our powers, or at least our memories, once we transferred to this dimension. Hopefully, in time, it will show us more."

Everyone fell silent, considering. Felar still felt lost, but what Tremmilly said did make sense and reinforced her plan of action.

"I think we should discuss moving up the plan to attack the Arche," Felar said finally. "This connection to the past has given us greater power. With Lothis' abilities restored, now is a prime opportunity, both offensively and defensively.

"The longer we wait, the more time the Arche have to recover and plan. If I were them, I'd be attacking Wake and Maxar before they return to Lith-elo. As long as they are away from us, they have diminished strength and no Great Thought protection. Neither understands how to utilize their Elrahi power. If we four attack the Arche now, we will catch them off guard. We can end a major threat. Cazz-ak already killed one of them. It will be an even fight."

"No," Tremmilly said sadly, "I cannot be a part of it. Even when I was still completely Aris, I had no combat abilities. My strengths are in other areas."

"Ah," Felar replied. "Well, I think with Cazz-ak and Lothis' power, we would still have the advantage."

"We have to consider we may be destroying the only remnants of an entire species," the Entho-la-ah-mine replied. "Do we have the right to do such a thing? Sentient life is rare and special."

Felar knew this was likely to come up at some point, and she was ready. "Cazz-ak, I respect your opinion, but in this situation I think we have to do what is best for us. Perhaps, at one point, the Arche were a benevolent, helpful species. Now they are corrupt. They assisted us briefly, but whatever good that did has been soured by their multiple attacks on you and Lothis. We cannot overlook or ignore them, even for the sake of preserving their species. They have made it clear they aren't interested in peace and have proven themselves dangerous and committed."

After she finished, Felar waited anxiously, wondering what Cazz-ak would do. *If he doesn't help us...* Felar didn't want to complete the thought.

"You are right," Cazz-ak said finally. "It is the way of the universe: create and destroy. I do not like it, but it is required."

"So when do we strike?" Lothis asked, looking intense.

They all turned to Cazz-ak. Felar thought she saw the hulking Elrahi Protector inside his beetle like body, but that could only be a memory. *Is it though?*

"Let us rest and gather our strength," Cazz-ak answered, sounding resigned. "These experiences are taxing, even if our physical forms do not feel it." Felar did sense the mental drain, although it was different from what she'd ever experienced studying or taking tests. "I believe Felar should lead this mission," Cazz-ak added, catching her off guard.

"Why?" she blurted, realizing a moment too late he would explain anyway.

"Because you have military experience, both as an Elrahi and as a human."

"But you were the most prestigious Protector."

"Yes, but Protectors were not soldiers," Cazz-ak reminded her. "We did not fight wars. I've only known defense, in both iterations of my life. I agree with your tactical assessment and will fight the Arche, but I believe you are the best individual to lead us to battle."

Everyone nodded, as Felar felt a weight settle on her. *I must go to a dimension I don't understand, to wage war with a species I've never seen before.* It felt a daunting task. Felar took a deep breath and reminded herself she was qualified, and with her additional abilities, prepared. *You were a Founder's Commando, and are still an Elrahi Sentry. You have your friends for support. You can do this.*

"Alright," Felar said finally. "We'll rest a day and I'll create a plan. We can then gather and discuss our readiness."

***

The blue light of Lith-elo-hi-rosh's primary star felt good on Felar's skin. The communal dwelling was a comfortable space, but being outside felt exquisite right now. *I've been spending so much time underground,* she realized, thinking about the hours of training she'd invested in the Entho-la-ah-mine volunteers. A breeze blew, softly caressing her skin. Felar had always felt in tune with her surroundings. Staying alive as a soldier required high situational awareness, but since the Elrahi memory, the sense was even stronger. Now, it was more than just physical sensation. She could feel the energy in the surrounding space.

You're sure you're not just doing this for revenge? The question struck out of nowhere and Felar didn't know how to answer at first.

The reasons you gave the group for immediate action are valid and tactically sound. Felar did have to admit her desire to avenge the attack on Lothis bordered on compulsion, but that didn't invalidate everything else. *Once you are in battle,* she warned herself, *you cannot let passion hinder good tactical judgment.*

And you know you're ready to battle the Arche? This question had plagued her since the previous day's meeting ended. You are going into their terrain, approaching on their terms. It would have felt foolish a few days ago, but with a newly gained connection to her Elrahi strength, she knew it was the right thing to do.

You could wait, train with Lothis and Cazz-ak, be even stronger when our friends return.

Felar shook her head. *We can't leave Wake and Maxar exposed any longer. The Arche might have attacked already. Waiting logic can be used to defer good action indefinitely. With one Arche eliminated, our Elrahi power, and a surprise attack, we hold the advantage.*

Cazz-ak and Lothis approached. She could feel their readiness. If they had any doubts about the timing of the mission, they weren't showing it. "Greetings, Felar," Lothis said, a smile on his face. Each day, he looked more and more alive. When she thought back to the small child she'd rescued from the research facility under Haak-ah-tar, she barely recognized him.

"Hello, Lothis," she smiled back.

Cazz-ak sent his salutation, then asked, "We all still agree this is the best course of action?" Felar nodded, as did Lothis. "Good. I have notified the Queen of our plan, and have asked for permission to use the Great Thought for as long as I remain connected to it. She approved."

Felar felt a sense of calm come over her. With Lothis and Cazz-ak present, she was strong, and enthusiasm swallowed all doubt. "Let's show the Arche what happens when you try to blightheart Harbingers."

"Wait, wait," Tremmilly said, appearing from the opposite side of the communal dwelling.

"Find your fighting spirit?" Felar said with a laugh.

"No," Tremmilly replied, looking hurt. "As I said, I have no combat abilities." Felar hadn't meant to put her down. She'd just allowed excitement to revert her to old ways. "I thought perhaps I could go part of the way, to provide support."

"Of course," Felar replied, trying to convey an apology with her expression. "That's a great idea."

"Transitioning through the dimensional folds will be difficult, Tremmilly," Cazz-ak interjected. "I will be able to guide you going in, but if the Arche capture or kill me, you might be unable to escape. I suppose the same applies for you too, Felar."

"It is a risk I'm willing to take," Tremmilly replied. Felar nodded as well.

"Alright," Cazz-ak said, "then shall we start?"

"I'm ready," Tremmilly replied. "And if no one opposes, I would prefer we go to the grove."

"It is a suitable place," Cazz-ak answered, moving towards the clump of palos trees, "and one that has profound peace."

As they walked, Felar wondered if she should apologize to Tremmilly for her earlier comment. *Will that just make it more awkward?* Instead, she walked up next to her and took Tremmilly's hand. Her friend looked over and squeezed gently, smiling.

"It's OK," she said quietly, "I know you weren't trying to be mean. I just feel weak and useless sometimes."

"You are the farthest thing I can think of from weak or useless."

"Thanks. Perhaps, as more of Aris comes through, I'll feel stronger."

Felar wanted to say more, but they'd reached the grove and she needed to focus on what they were about to do. "Triangle formation," she ordered. "Cazz-ak, you be in the center this time."

Cazz-ak did as she commanded, settling down on the soft moss. They each took a point around him. Beowulf seemed content to remain out of the formation, and stood watchfully nearby.

"What is the plan, Felar?" Lothis asked, looking nervous. Lately she'd found herself forgetting he was still just a child. Even as an Elrahi, he was young and inexperienced.

"Being covert as long as possible is the best tactic. We may get close enough to strike unseen, perhaps take one or two of them out before they know we are there. Based on the walls Cazz-ak described, if we can at least get inside their system before they sense us, we stand the best chance of success. If they lock us out, we are done.

"I think the optimum place for you, Tremmilly, is just outside their barrier. Cazz-ak, do you agree?" The Entho-la-ah-mine signaled he did, so she continued. "It keeps you in proximity, but reduces direct danger. Once inside, Cazz-ak and I will lead the way. Lothis, you follow behind and act as overwatch. You'll be looking for things we miss. We stay together and work as a team. I will lead, but this is foreign territory, so be willing to act on your own and do what is necessary." Everyone nodded. Felar could sense their nervous anticipation. *Or maybe I'm just projecting my own feelings on them.*

No one spoke, and Felar knew the time had come. *You've never done this before,* she thought, breathing deeply, *or have you?* She didn't have many memories as Lek, but enough of her past life came through to give her confidence. *Find the connections.* Her mind spiraled out, touching her surroundings lightly. Felar went deeper, further, and felt the bonds in the trees, the molecules composing them. *Deeper.* Atoms danced around her, and Felar knew she was part of them. *There,* she thought, finding a pathway. She sensed her friends nearby and followed as they headed for the same space-time location.

As she went further, Felar felt the connection to her body dissipate. It was scary, but the experience had a familiarity that comforted her. When they had all gathered, Cazz-ak's energy manipulated space-time, pushing, pulling, and folding till he vanished.

Lothis went next, duplicating the steps. Tremmilly followed, taking only slightly longer. Felar tried to imitate the process, but something felt off. *What am I doing wrong?* More time passed and she feared she wasn't capable.

Feeling her connection to space-time weakening, Felar finally stopped. *Frustration is hindering you, pushing you back towards the captivity and limitations of your body. Calm down and don't try, just do.* She cast her consciousness out once again, bolstering her diminishing strength.

When she felt re-energized, Felar returned her attention to the spot. *Follow instinct. Flow.* She took hold of the location and let herself go. Warping and folding, her consciousness manipulated space-time, feeling linked and harmonious. Each step was an outflow of the last, creating a joyous, procedural work of art.

The next moment, Felar sensed herself moving in a direction that had no meaning to her human understanding. Panic rose within her, but she made herself relax. *There is no logic to this.* When she stopped moving, she realized Cazz-ak, Lothis, and Tremmilly stood before her.

"Good," Cazz-ak said. "I was beginning to wonder if something had gone wrong."

"No," she replied, "I just had to stop trying." At any other time it would have felt like a foolish statement, but in this place of bodiless connections and energy, it made total sense.

Cazz-ak nodded. "Now that we all understand how, let us continue."

Felar had no sense of direction as her energy floated in the blackness. If she thought about it, she could feel the way back to Lith-elo, but the path to the Arche was invisible.

They followed Cazz-ak, making one dimensional transition after another. Each time, Felar could still sense the way back, giving her comfort she could get to her body on her own.

"This is the last one," the Entho-la-ah-mine said. As time passed away from his body, the shape of his energy shifted, growing and morphing to take on humanoid characteristics. Felar wondered if she was beginning to look more like Lek. The shift wouldn't be as noticeable, since they were a similar shape, but something about the combination made Felar feel good. *I'm becoming whole.*

"I will go through first," Cazz-ak continued, "and attempt to hide our presence from the Arche. Give me a few moments, then follow. I'm not sure it will work, but uniting the Great Thought with my Elrahi strength should give me the ability to shield us." Cazz-ak warped the space around him and vanished.

They waited, Felar feeling the happy dread that always accompanied the moment before a combat drop. Her awareness of time felt weak in this place, but it was still there, flowing by. Felar calmed her mind, using the fear to sharpen her senses. *Surprising such a thing has meaning in a place like this.*

"I'll go next," she sent to Lothis and Tremmilly, "in case Cazz-ak found trouble." Stepping up to the precise location, Felar folded and pushed space-time. The same sensation of nonsensical movement overtook her, and she felt herself propelled towards the Arche.

32 – GAV

Gav felt the ground shake as a gunship pounded away at the Family troops outside the bunker. Gaining access to the secure facility had been challenging. Without the chaos caused by the invaders, it would have been impossible. The bodies of several technicians and guards littered the surrounding floor. *Blightheart those Alenthos buggers,* he thought. Gav enjoyed that he'd been able to personally strike at one of the Families instrumental in his downfall. He checked the security routines for the thick tungsten alloy door standing between him and the troops trying to stop him. *Still secure.* It should be. The Families designed it to withstand a nuclear blast.

The floor continued shaking, as Gav smiled. *You saved the invaders,* he thought. Switching the view on his terminal screen, he surveyed the carnage the rail cannons had wrought. Blood, dust, and smoke filled the display. Every member of the Families deserved the same fate for betraying him. *I was only trying to help them. Why couldn't they see that?*

Despite his desire for revenge, part of him still protested his decision to use Fade to disable the nuclear missiles. At the time, it was clear the invaders were becoming desperate. Only with his help had they managed to continue their assault. *What was it the leader did to me?* It had felt simultaneously pleasurable and violating, enforcing his conflicted feelings and bringing to mind more of his grandma's stories. A chill caused his body to shake violently.

You've made your decision. You have to follow through. Gav gritted his teeth. *The invaders will destroy the Families now. Even if you'd let Heavy stand, there was nothing you could do to regain your old position.* Something about the way the lead invader had looked at him made Gav feel valued and honored far more than any of the Council ever had.

Turning from the destruction filled primary screen, he checked his portable device, making sure Fade continued to keep Heavy under control. It wasn't a difficult task, not for a quantum human, but he still wondered if his slave would betray him at some point. *Now is a prime opportunity.* Gav's finger hovered over the option to release AI tormentors to keep Fade in line. *No, a distraction may be too much.* He hated having to trust him, but it was the cost of utilizing so much computing power.

A flicker of movement on the large screen caught Gav's attention. He turned to look at the bunker's display. A large Ashamine gunship had appeared. Not landed. Materialized. The cloaking aspects of the invaders' technology astonished Gav. He'd never seen such a thing, but around this group, it happened regularly. The gunship's hatch opened, and a brown haired figure emerged. It looked like he had dark, futuristic armor on, but gaps of flesh stood out between the black swaths on his limbs. Biological augmentation. The figure strode forward confidently, ignoring incoming fire from the Family survivors. Tracer rounds passed by or through him as he assessed the situation.

Zooming the camera, Gav confirmed his suspicion: *The leader of the invaders.* He didn't know if he should feel honored or scared. *He came here for you.* A squad of troops, many in Ashamine uniforms, stormed out of the gunship, protecting the flanks. The leader began motioning, calm and assured gestures. With movements that felt choreographed, his troops began firing, rail rifle ion tracers illuminating the smoke and dust. Others darted off into the haze, returning with survivors. They shoved them in front of the leader, and he began unceremoniously punching them in the stomach. Gav frowned. *What is he doing?* The motion was deliberate, purposeful, causing those struck to fall to the ground, twitching. After a moment, they rose, movements jerky. *He's not punching them,* Gav thought, *he's using that pointy glove to inject something inside them.*

A few minutes passed as Gav continued watching the scene outside the bunker. Dread filled him. He knew the leader would come for him soon. Finally, he approached the armored door and stared into the camera. Gav felt him looking directly at him, making his skin crawl.

"Open," he heard in his mind. Before thinking any further, his hands acted of their own accord. The huge tungsten alloy door started to retract. Gav stood and walked over to greet the leader. A small part of his mind screamed it wasn't too late, that he could hide in his personal bunker, but his consciousness quickly squashed the notion. *He has my reward and will give me more power than I ever would have known in the Families.*

"Greetings," the invader said, face and voice formal. "My name is Crasor Tah Ahn. I am the Breaker of the Dawn. What is your name?"

Gav's mind felt as if it were swimming in a sea of light. He felt dazzled, awestruck, confused. "I am Gav, of the Family Serrith."

"This process hurts, but will be worth it." Crasor darted forward, stabbing him with his injector glove. Gav looked down, feeling a coldness invade him. *It's not a glove, just a hand.* For a moment, Gav wondered at the mutation, about the shiny, black skin that seamlessly meshed with his human flesh. Then, a fire began to burn. Everything else vanished.

Pain flared over his entire body, a level of sensation he'd never experienced. Gav had been tortured before, but that felt benign by comparison. His perspective shifted as his legs gave out and he crashed to the floor. *You've made a mistake,* was all he could think. Each one of his cells screamed in agony. He would do anything to end the pain, but Gav couldn't reach his flechette pistol, couldn't uncurl his spasming arm.

When he thought it couldn't get any worse, the pain escalated even further. Gav roared, the sound wretched from a throat burning with the fires of a thousand dark stars. He felt his eyes melting, his bones turning to ash. *No! Stop! Please!*

Then, it all vanished, and a sense of peace flooded him. "Now you are One," Crasor's voice said in his mind. "You are a Breaker. You are one of us." Gav breathed, a deep inhalation that felt like an infusion of life. He rose to his feet, uncoordinated. As soon as he stood, a wave of ferocious hunger assaulted him. He felt like he hadn't eaten for weeks.

Crasor looked around the room, brown eyes burning. "You'll need to feed. This is normal. The nanites integrating with your system require energy. I need you to focus on me, however. You will get nourishment, in time, but for now, I must transfer the missile system to our control."

"O-o-ok," Gav answered. It felt like his brain was having a hard time reaching his tongue, like something was scrambling the pathways.

"Which of these systems links to the launch network?"

"Th-th-ere," Gav pointed to his terminal, which was laying on the floor. He wanted to explain Fade, but the thoughts and concepts about how to do so escaped his grasp.

Crasor picked up the portable device, swiping and selecting several options on the screen. A look of puzzlement grew on his angular face. "Is there a hidden menu?"

Gav shook his head. "I-it's ri-ight there."

Giving him the portable, Crasor walked over to the main Heavy view screen and began studying it. Gav looked at his device, fighting hard to maintain concentration. The screen showed a secure connection to his quantum computer and listed several system options, but everything related to Fade or his link to Heavy had vanished. *Fade escaped,* he thought, anger raging. Somehow, the quantum human had found a way out of Gav's cage. *He made me look like an idiot.* Gav gritted his teeth, longing to find Fade and punish him.

He turned to see Crasor staring at his hand, palm black with a rippling sheen. "Whatever system you had set up would have been inadequate," he said. "We would have overridden it with our own anyway." Placing his hand on the terminal control, Crasor smiled, a twisted grin that scared and excited Gav simultaneously. "You've only begun to see the extent of our power."

33 – CAZZ-AK-TAK

Cazz-ak strengthened his cloak as Felar appeared next to him. He felt her energy bloom and worried she would attract the Arche's attention, but then realized she was adding her strength to his. The load lightened, even as Tremmilly and Lothis appeared. *Felar has tapped into her Elrahi strength,* he thought, keeping a vigilant watch on the nearby boundary between regular space-time and the Arche stronghold.

The vision of his past had been a strange experience for Cazz-ak. As an Entho-la-ah-mine, he often saw memories from other points of view, but in this instance, experiencing them as a different species felt unique. He still didn't understand why he had become an Entho-la-ah-mine, but he suspected it had something to do with the "alignment" Lothis had talked about moments before they'd left their Elrahi existence.

As he recalled more of these events and experiences, Cazz-ak felt his strength growing. It was odd remembering the mobility and strength of his Elrahi body, but his mental power was surpassing his abilities with the Great Thought. It was a bittersweet evolution, gaining strength that simultaneously took him further from his species. *I can do nothing about it,* he thought, *and if it allows me to protect them, it is for the best.*

"I will wait here," Tremmilly said, voice barely audible. Felar and Lothis' energies embraced her in a human hug. "I think I can return the way we came, if something goes wrong, but I don't believe it will." Cazz-ak sent a happy image to her from their past, his way of showing affection. Everything within him wanted to stay, to protect her. *She is no longer Empress,* he thought, sadness filling him. Everything he remembered of his Elrahi history was about watching over her.

Before he lost focus, Cazz-ak mentally signaled. Felar and Lothis began moving towards the boundary. Before he could follow, Tremmilly's energy embraced him. Cazz-ak leaned into her, returning the hug. It filled him with a joy he'd seldom experienced.

They separated, as Cazz-ak hurried to catch up. He was still maintaining his cloak, but he had no way of knowing its effectiveness. Lothis, with his technical mind, understood the Arche's domain better than he. Despite the boy's reconnection to his Elrahi strength, he still didn't understand how to create a cloak.

When they were a short distance from the boundary, Cazz-ak stopped. It was a subtle shift, nearly identical to reality, but twisted. The edge was darker somehow, even blacker than when he had come to rescue Lothis just a month before. *They've changed, evolved.* Despite his additional power, it made Cazz-ak wonder if they had the strength to destroy the Arche. He looked back at Tremmilly, hoping she could escape if they didn't.

The surrounding energy surged. Cazz-ak feared the Arche had noticed them as a crackling barrier of violet energy formed, threatening to cut off their advance. It was similar to the one that had almost trapped him and Lothis as they were escaping, but it was thicker now, the energy far more powerful.

"We have to get inside before they block us," Felar said. She led them forward in a line, picking a spot where the field had not yet materialized.

"But they are more powerful now," Cazz-ak replied, feeling they should retreat. Felar and Lothis were almost past the barrier. *Can't leave them,* he thought, slipping through just as the segment closed. His connection to the Great Thought vanished.

"Trust me," Felar said. "I have a plan. It accounts for a prepared Arche, as long as we stay concealed."

Cazz-ak tried to do as she asked, expecting the same red walled maze to confront them. Instead, it was a plane of blackness, stretching as far as he could see. "Either they don't know we are here," he replied, feeling the load for the cloak settle on him, "or this is some new trap."

"I don't think they've sensed us," Lothis replied. "This area is devoid of energy. They would require at least some power to observe us."

"Let's keep moving forward," Felar said, "although we need to decide which way to go."

"I believe we are in a dormant part of their computer system," Lothis continued. "Good from a stealth aspect, but not for travel. I don't think we will be able to find our way to the Arche themselves without somehow powering things up, which would probably alert them to our presence."

"We must either wait until they use this location, or power it ourselves," Cazz-ak agreed. "What do you feel is best?"

"Well," she answered thoughtfully, "they taught me in Dog School that if you can't sneak in for the kill, blow the door down and go in heavy. But if you can figure out a way to reach them without alerting, it would be optimal."

Cazz-ak agreed. Waiting for the Arche to discover them in this dark place, separated from Tremmilly and escape by a crackling energy barrier, seemed foolish. "Then let us light our own way to the Arche, but gently." He gathered his energy, then cast it out to touch the floor of the plane.

"Why can't we just fly or teleport?" Felar asked. Cazz-ak barely heard her, intent on searching. "If we are in a computer, can't we just give ourselves greater abilities?"

"It doesn't work that way," Lothis replied. "There are laws governing this place the same way the laws of physics apply to the real world, although they are slightly different. Energy still travels at the speed of light, but we are restricted to moving by methods we understand. It has to do with how we are stored. Since we are a collection of data—"

"Wait," Felar replied, "never mind. If you go any deeper, I won't understand anyway. We travel as usual, despite being only energy."

"Right," Lothis replied.

Scanning the Arche's system felt inorganic and disorienting to Cazz-ak. After Lothis and Felar fell silent, he was able to better concentrate and move more quickly. He sensed a channel larger and less restrictive than the rest, and it drew his attention. *This could be the conduit leading back to them.* Cazz-ak forced a bit of power into it, and a blue line formed through the darkness.

"Interesting," Lothis said. "I bet if you keep the power level low enough, the energy will remain compartmentalized from the Arche. The signal won't reach them."

"Perfect," Felar said. "Let's get moving." She hurried ahead, following the conduit. Lothis and Cazz-ak fell in behind her. As the crackling border faded into the distance, he felt his sense of unease deepen.

***

Cazz-ak had lost track of time long ago and was almost ready to believe his tactic to find the Arche was flawed. He kept generating the line, and they kept following it. He no longer had any sense of distance. Occasionally, the line bent or turned, sending them along a new path, but other than that, it was monotonously straight and long. *How will we ever find our way back?* He couldn't feel a way to reverse what he was doing. *What if they intentionally drew us into this oblivion? What if it was a trap after all?*

"What's that?" Felar asked, slowing her pace to a walk. "Drop the line."

Cazz-ak did so, trying to see what she was motioning towards. A faint fuzz of light tinged the horizon. "I think that might be them," Lothis said. They resumed their faster pace, although without the illumination, Cazz-ak worried there might be a pit or other unseen danger they might stumble into.

As they continued forward, the light grew brighter, a harsh white matching the Arche's glow. Finally, Felar stopped. Cazz-ak had no way of estimating distances in this space, but it did feel like the right spot to keep them outside the field of perception.

Before them were the four remaining Arche, the last of a species who once spanned the entire Akked. Cazz-ak didn't remember enough of his Harbinger past to know what they had been like before, but they felt evil now. They'd tried to erase Lothis, tried to capture him. A part of Cazz-ak felt guilty for what they were about to do, but his entire being knew they could not be reasoned with. They wouldn't stop attacking until they subjugated the Harbingers.

"Who is the fifth being?" Lothis asked.

Cazz-ak looked harder and noticed a humanoid form standing amidst the Arche It was difficult to see, both because of the distance and the harsh backlight. After a moment, Cazz-ak realized it was a short individual, dressed in once-fancy human clothes, now torn and dirty. *A human male of elevated rank?* Something about him looked wrong, but Cazz-ak couldn't express what it was. *How is the man here in such a literal form? And why choose those clothes?*

Every Entho-la-ah-mine Cazz-ak had ever seen, when separated from their body, took a form identical to their physical shape and color. Now, he noticed each of his friends' energies did the same, adopting the identity of their Elrahi bodies, including clothing. *Why does this human have such attire? And how did he get here?*

"Who are you?" the figure asked, and Cazz-ak marveled how sound traveled so far in this place. "Where are we? Are you part of the invaders? Gav?" he yelled sounding panicked. "Gav, I did as you asked. Don't punish me!"

"You are safe now," the lighter voice of the Arche replied. "It would take time to explain exactly where and who we are, but for now, just know we liberated you."

"We sensed when your captor transferred you into the quantum computer," the elder voice added, "and have been looking for a way to help you escape ever since."

"Prove you aren't one of those attacking Exis-7," the human said forcefully, trying to distance himself from the Arche.

"Those invading your world are the Breakers. We seek to destroy them, along with the rest of the deceitful Elrah. Would we have freed you from your captor and brought you to safety otherwise? If we were the Breakers, we would have assimilated you."

"And who are you?"

"We are the Arche, first life and architects of the Akked."

"Assuming you are telling the truth, can you restore me to my body?"

"Unfortunately, no. Your captor destroyed your physical form, therefore we have no way to transfer you back. We were once like you, with physical manifestations of consciousness, but our people evolved to a higher existence. You too will learn this, given time."

"But I don't want to," the human replied, anger in his voice. "I need to get back to Exis, even if it means returning to captivity in that quantum computer. My Family needs me. He'll obliterate them if I don't help. I can figure out a way to resist Gav, can launch more of the missiles. If I don't, he will kill my family. You have to put me back."

"Their time has come and gone. Surrender to your reality. Let us teach you to become one with the power of your consciousness."

"No," the human replied. "I'm Fade Alenthos. If you know anything about Exis, you've heard of my Family. Let me go. Pret Alenthos will reward you, I promise.

"Human," the older voice interjected, "we already said we will not return you to your doomed planet. Listen, and obey, or we will take what we need by force."

"Can either of you sense their power source?" Felar asked quietly.

Cazz-ak realized he'd been so engrossed in the Arche's conversation that he'd nearly forgotten what they'd come here for. *That's why Felar is leading instead of me.* He looked around, trying to find where the computer beings drew their strength from.

"There," Lothis said, pointing to the spot Cazz-ak had seen just a moment before. A broad channel of white energy stretched across the plain beside the Arche, disappearing into the distance. Cazz-ak had barely noticed it because the beings themselves were so much brighter.

"Is there a way to disconnect it?" Felar sounded hopeful, and Cazz-ak guessed this was the main goal of her plan.

"I don't know," Lothis said, his words hard to hear over the fight developing between the human and the Arche. "But I think as soon as we get near it, the Arche will know."

After Cazz-ak agreed, Felar frowned. He sensed she was adapting her plan. "Lothis, you cut off the power supply. Cazz-ak and I will create a distraction to aid you. I would rather we combine our power in a single offensive, but I think they are too strong. If we try to cut the power off together, we'll expose ourselves to a coordinated attack."

Cazz-ak could sense the Arche's growing anger and distraction. *Now is the time,* he thought. Felar looked at him and Lothis, confirming their acceptance. Power surged within Cazz-ak. He felt ready for combat.

34 – LOTHIS

"Remain concealed as long as you can," Felar directed. "Signal when ready for cover. If they notice you sooner, we will intervene. When you get there, cut the power as quickly as possible, then join us." Lothis nodded and began slinking towards the Arche's power conduit.

The distance to the objective shrank slowly as he made his way around the perimeter of the Arche's light. He had no way of knowing if he was too close, and was simply operating on instinct. Despite Felar and Cazz-ak backing him up, Lothis felt alone. That feeling only intensified as he got farther and farther away. *Calmness,* he told himself. *Execute Felar's plan and all will be well.*

Finally, he arrived at the conduit and stopped, wondering what he could do to sever it. *They certainly have defensive measures in place,* he thought, studying the flowing light. He pondered for a moment longer, developing a plan.

How do I signal readiness? Lothis looked back towards where he thought Felar and Cazz-ak were, but they were lost in darkness. *I have to go for it and trust they will notice.*

As the argument between Fade and the Arche grew to a crescendo, Lothis gathered all the energy he could muster. He formed a wedge, heavy and crafted from red energy.

Raising his weapon, Lothis heard a cry of alarm. "Where did they come from?" the younger Arche voice asked. "Why didn't we sense them?" In the edge of his vision, Lothis saw his friends running towards the light beings. Cazz-ak's form had grown into his Elrahi frame, moving quicker than seemed possible. The floor surrounding them began to glow as they embraced their mental strength.

"Must have slipped through the firewall when we were transferring the human."

Knowing he couldn't waste time, Lothis brought his angry red wedge down into the conduit. As it struck, the tool cleaved through the energy stream, grinding downward.

"Give us your energy, Fade," the young Arche voice yelled. "These are the Elrahi which threaten the entire Akked with their meddling and desire for empire. Help us restrain them."

Lothis watched the color of the wedge shift from red to yellow, to white, then blue. *Too much absorption,* he thought frantically, trying to withdraw.

"The boy is attempting to disrupt main power," the deeper Arche voice laughed. Just as Lothis had nearly pulled the wedge free, a surge of power struck it, knocking him backwards. Flying through the air, Lothis had a brief moment to see sizzling violet beams shoot out under Cazz-ak and Felar. He vaguely remembered this restraining tactic from when the Arche had attacked them the first time.

Striking the ground, Lothis felt stunned. He tried to get up, but couldn't. *Your friends need you,* he thought, making himself rise to his knees. The surrounding space shifted, and for a moment Lothis thought he was losing consciousness. Then he realized the plane had changed into a vast room. *The Arche aren't afraid of us,* he thought, watching as they continued trying to bind Cazz-ak and Felar. *They still believe they can capture and appropriate our power for themselves.* The thought made him wonder if perhaps they were still underestimating the ancient beings.

Getting his bearings, Lothis wondered what to do next. Now the Arche knew where he was, his fear of being separated from Cazz-ak and Felar grew. Everything within him shouted to run back to his friends. *But then Felar's plan will fail. What will we do then?*

Lothis froze in indecision, looking first from his friends and then back towards the conduit. I can't do it, he decided, wondering if it was a logical decision, or one built on cowardice. He ran towards his friends.

The energy blast had sent him even farther from them, but this gave him time to recover his senses. He remembered the singularity he'd formed in the Elrahi memory, and after a messy attempt, created it again. Lothis placed the point as close to one of the Arche as possible, hoping to drain the being's energy away. Even as the singularity appeared, he could feel the Arche forcing it shut. *At least I am distracting it.*

As he grew closer to his friends, sizzling violet beams shot out of the floor beneath Lothis. Instinctively, an aura of energy surged from him, deflecting the Arche's bonds. Cazz-ak had done the same, but beams entangled Felar. Immediately, Lothis saw they were pulling her down, towards an aspect of the Arche dimension he didn't understand. Cazz-ak danced around her with mind blades, deftly striking at the bonds. A moment later, Felar was free and she restored her own protective aura.

"I tried," Lothis said, entering their midst, "but it didn't work. I'm sorry." He felt horrible for failing them.

"You did the best you could," Felar said, composing herself. "Besides, no combat plan survives first contact. We have to use an alternate strategy: frontal assault." The next second, the strength of the violet beams intensified. They began forcing through his aura, and Lothis summoned mind blades of his own to defend himself. On the edge of his vision, he saw Felar doing the same. She had a look of pure joy on her face, the exact expression he'd seen in the memory when she'd rescued him and Tremmilly from See'dek's faceless one.

All other thoughts vanished as jagged wires of dull red power shot at them from the Arche. He tried to amplify his aura, but they moved too fast. Pain seared through him, agony consuming his entire being.

Encrypted communications flashed between the Arche, but unlike before, Lothis was strong enough to decipher them. "They are trying to cut off our Elrahi connection," Lothis said through gritted teeth. He saw Cazz-ak and Felar also struggling under the pain of the Arche's new weapon.

As the agony increased, he felt his power diminish. *If we can't stop this,* Lothis thought, desperately trying to find a way out, *they will capture us.*

"Bond with me," he heard Cazz-ak say through the pain. Lothis reached out, sensing Felar's energy as well. Cazz-ak joined them, and after a moment, sent a surge of power outward, shattering the Arche's wires. Immediately, Lothis felt the pain vanish and his full connection return.

"If we want any hope of success, we must divide them," Felar yelled. "Lothis, pick one and attack. Cazz-ak, with your strength, you must take two. I will go after the remaining one."

Lothis did as she commanded, picking out one of the larger light entities. He once again summoned a singularity, attempting to create it in the core of his chosen foe. A surge of resistance met his attack, and the black sphere popped into existence at the edge of the Arche's light. It screamed as the singularity drew mass into oblivion, and the Arche dimmed considerably. Before he could move the singularity closer, the Arche darted backwards. Even as it did, Lothis felt energy building around him. It thrummed and hummed, menacing. Darting to the side, Lothis tried to move out of the field. Instead, he ran into a wall of darkness, bouncing him back. The ambient light dimmed, causing anxiety to well up inside him. Lothis tried to rush backward, but he struck another wall. A second later, the darkness became complete, and he realized what had happened. *It sealed me in a cube.*

Stay calm, Lothis thought, fighting against the panic threatening to overtake him. He could feel the box shrinking. *Think!* The walls brushed his arms, and Lothis braced himself, trying to hold them back. But they moved inexorably, forcing Lothis to make himself smaller, compressing his energy in on itself. He couldn't sense anything outside the box, and he wondered if the Arche had somehow transported him out of their dimension. Memories of the crushing blackness and confinement on Haak-ah-tar flooded him, but Lothis fought to remain calm. An idea sprang up, and he quickly created a small mind blade. The walls felt too solid to penetrate with such a small knife, but he could think of nothing else to do. With the box now touching him, time was short.

Lothis sliced from floor to ceiling, feeling the blade move effortlessly. At first he thought it had no impact, but then the wall split open, and he could once again see the raging battle, could feel his fellow Harbingers. Felar formed a dense mass of small mind blades in mid-air, then sent them hurtling towards her adversary. The Arche deflected some of her fusillade, but several projectiles punched through its cloud of light, causing glitchy sprays of static to spew outward. Before Lothis could see how Cazz-ak was faring against his two foes, he felt his own opponent gather for another attack.

Knowing his foe would attempt to trap him again, Lothis enlarged his mind blade and summoned another in his off hand. He used the last of his remaining mental energy to boost his speed, darting forward and sinking his blades into the Arche. Lothis knew it wouldn't be fatal, but it was enough to cause it to lose focus. Lothis continued stabbing at the being, seeing the same glitchy discharges bloom from each strike.

At the edge of his perception, Lothis felt something shift in the surrounding room. It began to lighten, moving from blackness to dull red, to orange, green, then blue, becoming an ominous violet. *They are charging a new power source,* Lothis thought. The sprays of static from his foe were diminishing, even as the Arche tried to escape and deflect his attacks.

"They are booting a new subroutine," Lothis yelled over the sounds of cascading energy, flaring static, and thundering discharges. Before he could do anything about it, though, the room went black, and the Arche disappeared.

"What just happened? Who—" he heard Fade shout, then an ominous buzzing obliterated anything else he said. The sound intensified, fear rising in pitch with it. The buzz became a roar. Lothis struggled to find Felar and Cazz-ak, wondering if the Arche would just obliterate them the instant the power fully charged. Despite the darkness and disorientation, Lothis found his friends. After a moment, he realized Fade was with them as well.

A blinding flash of violet light burned his vision. The roar crescendoed, a shock wave bursting over them. When Lothis could finally see, a huge orb of energy floated before him. He could feel the Arche inside, but they'd shielded themselves somehow. Lothis tried to summon his singularity, and it slid away harmlessly.

"The time has come, Harbingers," a voice crackled. "You and your kind almost destroyed us once before, but you failed. You've returned to finish the job, just as we knew you would. This time, you will atone for your crimes. Your power will be the spark that blazes into the inferno of our return." The orb descended on them, flaring and crackling. "Submit or resist, it matters not."

Lothis felt Cazz-ak and Felar reach out to him, and they all bonded. Cazz-ak cast a shield around them, and Lothis felt some of his anxiety diminish. *The Arche are perpetually overconfident.*

The surface of their shield and the Arche orb collided. The discharging energy rocked Lothis. It slowly forced Cazz-ak's barrier inward. The strain on their minds grew heavier. Just as it was about to break Lothis, Felar spoke. "Divide and attack with everything you have. This is our last chance." Cazz-ak dropped the barrier, and Lothis dove away from the Arche orb.

For a moment, Lothis saw Felar and Cazz-ak nimbly move away, Felar sending wave after wave of mental blades towards the orb. Not a single one penetrated. Cazz-ak summoned his red cubes, striking at the huge ball. They had no effect. *Their shielding is too strong,* he thought, desperately trying to think of a way to help. *If Felar's mind blades aren't powerful enough, then mine certainly won't be.*

"What can we do?" a voice next to Lothis said. Fade stood next to him, a look of fear and determination on his face. An idea burst inside Lothis' mind, and he quickly scanned the Arche's orb, forming a plan.

"Fade, we must create a long needle and use it to force a path into the orb," Lothis said quickly. "We aim at the connection between them and their power source. Once in position, I'll inject a singularity to initiate disconnection." Lothis felt stupid for not thinking of using this weapon initially. He hoped it wasn't too late.

"What?" Fade replied. "How?"

"Bond with me," Lothis barked, feeling Felar's influence on his mannerisms. "I don't have the strength to do it alone. We must work together."

Lothis reached out and took hold of Fade's power. It wasn't much, but it was enough. Fade willingly gave, and Lothis began shaping their combined energy into a needle pointed lance. With it formed, he drew back as far as this dimension would allow, and accelerated it towards the sphere. Just as it was about to strike, the Arche realized the danger and attempted to move. It was too late. The lance of mental energy penetrated, point in contact with the power conduit. Before the Arche could force it out, Lothis spawned his singularity. He quickly withdrew the lance, knowing if the singularity succeeded, it would suck them in.

For a moment, nothing happened, and the dark speck he'd injected into their system disappeared in a flare of violet energy. Then, a fraction of a second later, he could see it drawing in power, both from the conduit and the Arche. They struggled to move it out of their midst, but with their power supply interrupted, they were too weak. The blackness grew, and the Arche's light flickered, then died.

Lothis felt stunned he'd created something so powerful. It mesmerized him, the small point of blackness growing to encompass the entire orb. "We have to go," Cazz-ak yelled, breaking Lothis out of his trance. "It will swallow this entire place."

Looking around, Lothis realized the shape of the surrounding room was deforming, bending in towards the singularity. "The mission is over," Felar yelled. "Time to get out." Lothis agreed, even as he felt the pull of his own weapon.

"Which way?" Fade asked, looking frantic. "How do we get out of here?"

"Be calm," Cazz-ak replied. "We had to be covert to find the Arche, but now we are under no such restrictions." Power flared inside him, and Cazz-ak began manipulating the Arche's dimension. Lothis watched as he compressed and then tore the space before him. "Go!" he yelled, motioning them through. Fade went first, with Lothis right behind him. The singularity's pull made it hard to move. As he stepped through the transition, he felt his body lighten. Felar and Cazz-ak followed. Lothis felt relief flood over him. The next instant, Cazz-ak smoothed the tear and the transition vanished.

Lothis could still feel the tug of the singularity, but at this great distance it was much weaker. When he looked around, he saw the violet firewall that marked the edge of the Arche's reality just ahead of them. It was flickering, and after a moment, it died.

Felar quickly led them across the border. Lothis had mixed feelings about what they'd accomplished. He was glad they'd eliminated the threat of the Arche, but he was sad to have exterminated the last of an entire species. *They never would have quit,* he thought. *Even at the end, they were still trying to assimilate us.* He knew it was true, but it did little to alleviate his guilt.

A new realization occurred to Lothis, making his heart jump. He began looking around frantically. "Where's Tremmilly?"

35 – TREMMILLY

Tremmilly felt a weight of solitude descend as the violet barrier solidified between her and the other Harbingers. Time dragged by in a way she didn't understand, and with nothing to keep her mind occupied, it wandered.

What am I doing here? Even when she had been Empress Aris, her lack of combat abilities was frustrating. Felar had taught her how to wield human weaponry, but in this place, that was useless. Everyone else remembered powerful, offensive ways to use their minds, but she felt impotent.

See'dek was the origin of the Breakers, she thought, remembering the Elrahi memory capsule they'd all experienced. *We were all one people, before he split us.* The memory explained much, and Tremmilly felt she was still processing it. Her experience as the empress of a vast government was a strange counterpoint to human life on a small border planet.

And how did I believe our group of six would ever have the power to stop See'dek? Over the unknown amount of years that had passed, the Breakers grew in strength, where it seemed the Harbingers had not. *Now the enemy has emerged once again, and this time they're stronger than ever.* Tremmilly sighed, feeling discouraged. For the moment, the Elrahi were safe as part of the Dawn, but unless the Harbingers could find a way to stop the Breakers, that sanctuary wouldn't last much longer. She shook her head. *You don't even understand half the concepts you're imagining. You and your group of Harbinger volunteers don't know how to fight the Breakers. What was the plan to defeat them? What—or even where—is the Dawn we are fighting to protect?*

Something about the question sparked a memory within her, of being in the Citadel. Lek and Tha'sis were arguing, trying to decide what to do next. *You were once able to commune with the Dawn and seek guidance.* It was what had inspired her plan to begin with. *How did I do it?*

Tremmilly closed her eyes, trying to bring the Elrahi memory into focus. She breathed deeply, although the action was mental rather than an actual exchange of oxygen and carbon dioxide.

Tremmilly turned her mind inward. It was hard to block thoughts of the past, her friends, the Breakers, the danger she might be in, but as moments passed, she found success. Connections to the world around her, despite being in this odd place, became apparent. Her mind spiraled out as she felt the fabric of existence. She tried to find the Dawn, to seek its guidance, but the harder she pushed, the more distant everything seemed. Frustration began to well up within her, threatening to finish severing her connection.

Mentally, she stepped back, trying to center herself. *Be patient. You know how to do this,* she reassured herself, reengaging the connection.

Taking a new approach, Tremmilly let go of her consciousness, let her mind be free of wants or desires. She surrendered to the universe, let it draw her along lines of existence that bound all things together. She saw the push of positive energy and the pull of negative, the interaction present in even the smallest particles.

As she drifted further and further through the cosmos, she saw a point of immense energy far in the distance. It was the smallest speck, wrapped and turned in on itself. Time passed, and the energy pulled at her, its gravity inescapable. It began to grow, unfolding exponentially, blooming. It was the most graceful and magnificent thing she'd ever seen. Closer and closer, she watched it cascade and flow. Tremmilly thought her heart might break with joy. The energy formed complicated, symmetrical lines of flux, radiating towards her in an embrace.

The Dawn, Tremmilly thought, reveling in the beauty of the cosmic flower. She felt it calling, a sweet song welcoming her to join. Her heart yearned for unity. It offered escape from all worries about the future, the Breakers, and her struggles. Moving closer, Tremmilly could feel her people, could sense the energy of countless beings welcoming her.

No, she thought, realizing what it would mean. *Veth, Orsin, Tha'sis, Lek, and Kald gave up safety in the Dawn to help me fix the division in the Elrah. They need me, and I need them.* Tremmilly offered gentle resistance, moving away from the cosmic flower, pain growing as she did so. The energetic bloom, seeming to understand, began folding itself back up. As she watched, her heart broke and she fought hard not to cry. *Not yet,* she consoled herself, *but someday. It is why you must stay and fight. This is the good we have to protect from See'dek's corruption.*

The energy receded, petals collapsing on themselves. Realizing her time with the cosmic entity was ending, Tremmilly felt panic rise within her. "What can we do?" she asked. "How do I reunite our people? Mother?! Father?!" Tremmilly's heart sank, realizing there would be no answer. *That's not how it works,* she thought. *They are no longer individuals.*

The flower continued wrapping itself back up, a delicate procedure that made Tremmilly forget her anxiety. It was so beautiful, so special. *This is why I became Empress, to protect the Dawn and lead others to it.* Soon, the flower folded back to the size of a speck. Tremmilly felt a profound sense of loss as it vanished. *Gone,* she thought, consoling herself, *but not lost.*

As she floated in the vastness of the cosmos, Tremmilly felt a strange sense of urgency develop. Time to go back to my waiting place, she thought, moving in that direction. Since she understood the destination, it felt much easier than searching for the Dawn. The closer she drew, the greater her anxiety became.

Another moment passed, and Tremmilly was standing in the vast space outside the Arche's violet barrier. She looked around frantically, expecting to see an injured Felar or Lothis, but everything was as it had been. Despite the calm, her feelings of disquiet remained. *Perhaps they are trapped inside the computer,* she thought, trying to get a sense of where her anxiety originated. She reached out, looking for what it connected to. To her surprise, it led away from the Arche, towards the space they had folded to make the transition here. *The Entho-la-ah-mines,* Tremmilly thought, dread rolling over her like an oily wave.

She sprinted towards the dimensional fold, heart beating rapidly. *We left them and Beowulf alone, unprotected. What if someone destroys our bodies? What happens to our consciousness?* The secrecy of Lith-elo-hi-rosh's location had seemed like enough protection, but now that felt foolish. As Tremmilly began folding space-time to create the way back, she realized she would be leaving Lothis, Cazz-ak, and Felar without support. *I don't know how to get through the barrier anyway.* The urge to go back to Lith-elo increased exponentially. Tremmilly began to cry, feeling caught between two terrible choices. Before she could change her mind, she resumed folding space-time, creating the first of several transitions.

The return journey felt like it was taking twice as long. Tremmilly wondered if she was bad at the folds, or if it was only perception. After making the third transition, she stopped, a horrible corruption surrounding her. Did I mess up the folds? Tremmilly wondered, trying to orient herself. All the locations looked the same, complete blackness that somehow had dimensions and a form. Finally, Tremmilly recognized the place, giving her confidence she was still on the path home.

Something changed after we left, she thought, moving to the next transition point. The corruption loomed, threatening to defile her. Tremmilly surrounded herself with positive energy, forcing the inky stain away. *It's the Breakers,* she knew instinctively. It felt similar to See'dek and Crasor's filth, but was different somehow, unique.

When Tremmilly made the next transition, her heart tightened as she felt the same corruption. They traced our path back, she thought, hurriedly creating the next fold. Every sense screamed to hurry, that time was crucial.

After the final transition, Tremmilly felt her consciousness rush into her body. Her normal human senses returned, and she looked around the palos grove, trying to make sense of the dramatic shift in perspective. Lothis, Felar, and Cazz-ak's bodies were in the same state they'd left them. Tremmilly breathed easier for a moment.

Then she heard Beowulf's whine. The wolf-dog approached her, agitated beyond anything Tremmilly had ever seen. The fur on his back stood up, the aggressive look a stark contrast to the plaintive sounds he was making.

During the ritual to help Lothis restore his Elrahi connection, Tremmilly felt Maxar's link to Beowulf. She'd suspected it ever since they'd fought in unison back on the Bloodsport orbital dock, but Beowulf's latest actions had provided tangible proof. Even if she didn't understand the connection, she knew it was there, knew that Beowulf was linked to the Harbingers somehow.

A more strident whine forced Tremmilly's mind back to the current situation. "What is it, Beo?" she asked, bending down to look into his pale blue eyes, realizing they looked remarkably like Maxar's. *How did I never notice they were the same color before?*

Beowulf took her hand gently in his mouth and began pulling her, leading towards the edge of the palos grove. Tremmilly felt dazzled as they left the trees and moved into the direct blue light of the primary star. As her eyes adjusted, she breathed deeply, enjoying the fresh breeze that seemed constant on Lith-elo. Feeling the light warm her skin, Tremmilly wondered what could go so wrong on such a beautiful day.

A cloud of dust caught her attention. Realizing it originated from the village, Tremmilly ran towards it. A lump rose in her throat. When she finally crested a rise and caught sight of the buildings, it confirmed her fear. Someone had leveled every structure, obliterated them with rail slugs. Craters scarred the ground, the light wind blowing the disturbed soil into the air. Tremmilly fought back tears. After the loss of Eishon-2, Lith-elo-hi-rosh had become the closest thing she had to home.

Beowulf stopped beside her, and she leaned down to hug him. "Who did this, Beo?" The wolf-dog submitted to her affection for a moment, then began wiggling to get free. He ran several meters away, turned, and waited for her to follow. Tremmilly wiped the tears from her eyes, and set off at a jog.

It quickly became evident Beowulf was leading towards the narrow chasm that went down to the Entho-la-ah-mine city. When it finally came into view, a glint caught Tremmilly's eye. On the other side, a small Ashamine gunship glared in stark contrast to the natural landscape.

Given the corruption she had sensed on her way back from the Arche, it seemed certain it was a Breaker appropriated ship, and not Ashamine. *What if Crasor is here?* Tremmilly shivered. Her last encounter with the Breaker leader had resulted in near death and horrible nightmares. She still wondered if she was vulnerable to his influence. *I can't face him by myself,* she thought, beginning to panic.

You have the Entho-la-ah-mines and the Great Thought. You aren't alone.

When they finally reached the edge of the chasm, Tremmilly felt her stomach clench. Blackness obscured the depths, making it appear as if it were bottomless. Tremmilly wasn't particularly scared of heights, but this place always made her feel anxious.

Whining, Beowulf paced near the edge, tail swiping furiously through the air like a sword. Every other time she'd gone down, an Entho-la-ah-mine, usually Cazz-ak, had taken her. There was no elevator, no stairs, no ladders. *I don't know how to create the platform,* she thought, feeling a caustic mix of desperation and frustration.

Jump, something inside her said, and she almost laughed in scorn.

I don't have the mental ability to slow myself down like the Entho-la-ah-mines. Whatever is happening down there, I am the worst Harbinger to respond. Tremmilly stared down into the blackness, feeling despondent. *Even if I was the Empress, everyone else has more power and usefulness than me. All I do is think, and when someone needs my help, I let them down.*

Jump, she thought again.

I don't want to die.

You won't.

Beowulf walked in front of her and barked. He turned towards the edge, legs coiling under him. "No!" Tremmilly yelled, but Beowulf was already moving. Without a second thought, Tremmilly leapt off the edge after him.

Seconds passed slowly, and Tremmilly could see Beowulf falling below her. The wind intensified, building to a roar. Terror flushed all thoughts out of her mind as she sped past the canyon wall. Tremmilly wanted to scream, but her whole body felt paralyzed with fear. More time passed, and she watched as the darkness rose up to swallow Beowulf. A second later, Tremmilly passed into the blackness. She wondered how much longer it would take till she smashed on the rocks below.

You have to stop us, she thought.

I don't know how.

Try. If you don't, it will be more than just us who dies today.

Tremmilly didn't know how much time she had left. It already felt like she'd fallen for an eternity. She reached out, sensing the connections surrounding her. *How is this going to help?* Forcing doubt from her mind, Tremmilly grasped at the space-time below her with the intensity of desperation. In the next instant, she passed through the bunched area, and her velocity slowed. *Still traveling at a fatal speed.*

Focusing all her strength, Tremmilly pulled hard at the space between herself and the ground. The air density spiked, and she decelerated even faster. She closed her eyes, hoping they would both be safe. Tremmilly hit the ground hard. The impact knocked her breath away, leaving her gasping. Pain washed over her, and she gritted her teeth. *You're still alive,* she thought, desperately hoping the same was true for Beowulf.

A moment later, she felt hot breath and a wet tongue licking her face. "I'm—OK," she gasped, rolling over. When she could finally rise to her feet, she began slowly picking her way towards the Entho-la-ah-mine city. Holding onto Beowulf, they walked through the blackness.

Tremmilly tried to hurry, but then she would trip, stumbling on some unseen rock. The urgency in her mind made it hard to slow down, but falling and smacking her head would make the journey take even longer.

Finally, Tremmilly spotted a faint blue glow in the darkness up ahead. As she got closer, it illuminated the terrain and allowed her to move quicker. When she entered the main dwelling cavern, Tremmilly stopped.

Before her, a massive battle raged across the floor of the cavern. Rail slugs and flechette needles streaked through the air, bouncing off Entho-la-ah-mine shields. Felar and Cazz-ak's army of troops fought valiantly against a group of eight Breakers, swarming them with deft maneuvers and blades formed of Great Thought. Tremmilly caught a glimpse of a dead Breaker, his head severed from his body. Even with their overwhelming numbers, the Entho-la-ah-mines were taking causalities. She wanted to help, to charge into battle with Beowulf, but she knew she would only create another victim.

This group of Breakers felt and looked different. They were hulking figures, skin covered with black patches Tremmilly didn't understand. Their movements seemed more coordinated and skilled than the Breakers she'd previously encountered.

A spike of energy flared in Tremmilly's mind. *The Queen,* she thought. *The Queen is still alive! Have to help her.* The Breakers must have sensed her too, because five of them broke from the fight and headed towards the back of the cavern. Tremmilly gathered her courage, gestured to Beowulf, and began making her way through the darkness at the battle's edge.

36 – MAXAR

Blightheart it to the fires of the dark star, Maxar thought, knowing they'd lost the Death Watch. Round after rail cannon round slammed into it, mangling the ship that had carried them through so much. Dras put his vessel into a vertical takeoff, the ground dropping away so fast it made Maxar queasy.

"The Ashamine fleet is moving to intercept us," Dras said.

"How can you tell?" Wake asked, looking around. Maxar understood his confusion: there were no readouts or tactical displays on the alien bridge.

"A Heltasoth ship is more than just transportation. I am a part of it, and it a part of me. I see the Ashamine ships in the same way you might watch a bird fly overhead. It is a sense, an extension of my perception."

"I see," Wake replied, sounding like he actually did. "Is it safe for us to take off our environmental suits?"

"One moment," Dras answered. Several seconds passed as he stood motionless. "The environment should now support your needs. Feel free to remove your augmentation."

Maxar took off his ENS helmet, as did Wake and Jaydon. He expected the atmosphere to smell unpleasant, but it was crisp and clear. *Been breathing processed suit air for so long,* he thought, taking another deep breath.

"There is a high probability, given the Ashamine fleet's current course and velocity, that we will escape without ever coming into their weapons' range. I will inform you if anything changes, however."

Something hovered on the edge of Maxar's awareness, distracting him from Jaydon's reply. The feeling had similar characteristics to his experience when he'd become Beowulf, but wasn't Elrahi in origin. *The ship,* he thought, remembering how it had drawn at him when he'd first seen it. Using what he'd learned from earlier experiences, Maxar mentally reached out and touched the Heltasoth vessel.

Immediately, he felt an overwhelming stream of information course through him. He experienced the surrounding space in colors and dimensions his mind couldn't process, a cascade of sensory input. The Ashamine fleet exploded into view, and he could sense power generator emissions and human biosignatures. His mind went deeper and deeper into space, feeling the energy of stars and gravity of other galaxies. *Stop,* he thought frantically, *you have to disconnect. It's too much.*

As he pulled his mind back, Maxar returned to a body feeling vastly different from when he'd left. His nerve endings pulsed intensely, not in pain, but in readiness. He felt hyper aware and attune to everything around him. Strength coursed through his muscles, and Maxar knew he could take on the entirety of the Breakers.

The next instant, it all disappeared. Everything returned to normal. Wake and Jaydon talked quietly, oblivious of what had just happened.

Dras was staring at him, his expression inscrutable. "You interfaced with the ship."

Maxar nodded, the movement making his head spin. "Yes. How do you deal with so much information at once?" He wondered if the hyper-aware state he'd returned to was a side effect of connecting to the Heltasoth vessel, or if he could activate it on his own.

"That would be like asking how your arm knows to block a strike, or how one leg compensates the tripping of the other. We evolved the capability. It is innate, who we are." Dras paused. "I told you before that the nanites integrated well with your system. This has obviously given you certain abilities and experiences atypical to your species, as well as ours. We've never had a link to a biological in this manner."

"I'm sorry for my intrusion. I didn't understand what I was doing. The Ashamine put the nanites in me without my knowledge or consent, so I came to Traynos-6 to learn how to utilize them. Perhaps, if you are willing, you might teach me how?"

"You are not intruding. In fact, this is a unique situation, one that interests me greatly. The Heltasoth have never experienced organic life in this manner. You are an anomaly."

"So you'll help me?" Maxar knew the hyper state he'd discovered earlier was the key to his development. *And if Dras wants to join the fight against the Breakers as well, that's a happy bonus.*

"I will, as much as possible, but you must understand this territory is as foreign to me as it is to you. We will be working together, rather than as master and student. You must also know, when you connect the way you did, I see you in the manner you see me. It is synchronous. This leads me to an inquiry. You are human, but also something called Harbinger. What is that?"

The knowledge Dras had looked inside him made Maxar uncomfortable for a moment. Then he realized it was actually a benefit. *He knows very little about us, but agreed to help us escape from Traynos. Perhaps this will act as a payment of sorts and speed the process of building an ally.* "I think you'll find that very interesting," Maxar said, smiling. "Would you like to hear the story, or should I reconnect to the ship?"

37 – CRASOR

"You've only begun to see the extent of our power," Crasor said, feeling the Breaker nanites penetrate the nuclear missile controls. As they embedded themselves deeper, more of the system opened up to him. Crasor sensed networks of missile launchers and silos, understanding the destructive power they offered him.

The desire to obliterate the remaining Ashamine and Family forces on Exis-7 raged inside him. *With just a few commands, you can annihilate every one of them. You could issue the commands from orbit.* They destroyed at least two of his ships, and countless lives, but this time, he had to suppress his urge for revenge. *We can add most to our forces,* he thought. He'd perceived the energy of this planet all the way from orbit. *Not many bound for blackness here.* Crasor smiled. Even if he didn't use Heavy just yet, having its power at his disposal felt exquisite.

"What is our next move?" Gav asked, breaking into his thoughts.

Crasor removed his hand from the terminal screen, and turned to face him. "Convert or destroy the heads of power."

"May I assist you?"

Crasor considered the newly created Breaker. He obviously had skill, even when he'd just been a human. *Couldn't have taken over Heavy if he didn't.* Already, his speech was back to normal, which was the fastest development Crasor had seen. *Earlier, you believed he had the potential to be one of the strongest Breakers yet. If he is progressing this quickly, perhaps some live fire might enhance his training.*

Nodding, Crasor headed towards his gunship. "Yes, come. Learn and absorb all you can." Gav followed him closely.

As they entered the ship's airlock, Crasor felt the Breakers drawing at him. He knew immediately what was going to happen, but was powerless to stop it.

"Go, observe the pilots," he said, blurting the first excuse he could think of to get rid of the newly converted Breaker. "Once we land, meet me back here at the airlock." Gav looked puzzled, but did as ordered.

"Take us to the Family Council Building," Crasor sent over the comms, settling in amongst the cannon loading machinery. He made a quick check to ensure the two ordinance officers couldn't see him. His head pounded and a haze formed. Fear made his stomach clench. *Why now? I have a planet to capture.*

The Breakers were silent, his descent into memory their only answer. One moment, he felt the ship pulsing around him, the next, he was back on Ashamine-2.

Crasor exited the pneumatic transport tube, the smell of the under city assaulting his nose. *That buggering pole sucker,* he thought, feeling his anger build into rage. *She lied to me.*

Somehow, the stench brought up pleasant memories, of going to the Electro-Narco Party with Emili. *No,* he thought, *not now.*

After their fight, Emili had been absent from her normal jobs around the Tah Ahn household. Crasor couldn't ask anyone where she was without raising suspicion. His initial fear was that Emili had told his parents and they'd taken her to an Ashamine justice officer. As hours passed, and nothing happened, this seemed unlikely. *She ran from me,* he decided finally, a strange mixture of emotions coming over him.

When night fell, Crasor scoured his family's server, looking for clues to where she had gone. He knew Emili wasn't a hasher. She would need help to flee the Tah Ahn family. Indentured servants were practically the property of their creditors. Abandoning their obligation carried stiff penalties.

He'd found a deleted copy of her last communication. She'd sent a message to a member of a darkwalker gang. Her words made it seem like she knew the man well. *Emili's been cheating on me,* Crasor thought. His heart broke, the pain swelling to a crescendo. *I have to see them, have to know why she left.*

Now, he was less than a kilo from them, at least from the building the darkwalker had told Emili to meet at. Crasor walked quickly, hand clenched on the flechette pistol in his pocket. People were looking at him, but he didn't care. None of these vagrants mattered, and if any of them gathered up the courage to try to rob him, he would show them his weapon. *And fill them with darts if they press me.*

When he finally arrived at the darkwalker meeting point, he wondered if he had gotten the location correct. The building was run down and appeared abandoned. Vagrants had scavenged the plasti-glass windows, as well as anything else that had value and was easily transportable. Everything down here was decrepit, but this was worse than most. *Why would she choose him over me?* Crasor thought, pain, anger, and fear blending into a caustic mixture that ate away at his stomach and heart.

Part of him wanted to turn around, to go back to his future in the Forces and just forget Emili Trayfis. He hadn't liked pushing Emili, hadn't enjoyed the feelings she'd brought up in him. *I lost control. I'm on the edge of losing it again.* But he couldn't make himself stop. His feet carried him forward of their own accord, and he passed through the broken entryway.

Inside, Crasor quickly forgot his earlier hesitation. Bodies lay scattered across the floor. At first he thought they were dead, but then realized they were just comatose. *Narcos,* he thought, pulling out his flechette pistol as he walked deeper into the building.

As he searched room to room, it all came together. Emili was trading one form of servitude for another, whether she realized it or not. The darkwalker had probably made Emili grand promises, and after their fight, she'd felt this was her only option. Crasor had read about this scheme before, how the darkwalkers offered freedom, but would then either harvest their organs or keep them as a substance addicted laborer. He had to find Emili and get her out before she made a horrible mistake.

Crasor carefully worked his way through the gloom, trying to avoid stepping on bodies. After several minutes of searching, Crasor finally heard Emili's voice. "You promise you can get me back to Noor-5?"

A deep male voice replied, too low for Crasor to hear. He found the entrance to the room and strode in with authority. *A terminal, Emili, large male,* his mind ticked off, training his weapon on the darkwalker. Surprise bloomed on the man's face as he made a fluid movement to grab a pistol laying next to the terminal screen. Crasor felt his stomach tighten. He knew what he had to do. He'd pointed a weapon at a very dangerous person and was committed to following through. His parents couldn't protect him here. The Ashamine couldn't save him. The situation was Crasor's responsibility.

The flechette pistol bucked gently in his hand. He heard a light crack, then a wet splattering. The darkwalker slumped in his chair, chest a mass of obliterated tissue and blood. Crasor had hit exactly where he had aimed. His gaze moved from the darkwalker, to his flechette pistol, to his hand clutching the weapon.

"What are you doing?" Emili screamed.

"I've never killed anyone before," he muttered, feeling stunned.

"Crasor, what are you doing here? Why did you follow me?"

"I had to protect you," he answered, turning his gaze towards her.

"I don't need your protection." Her words hit him like a rail round, and some of his earlier anger crept back in.

"You didn't understand what was going to happen," he said, trying to fight through the maelstrom of emotions.

"Do you think I'm an idiot?" Emili yelled at him. "I know he wouldn't do anything for free. I was obviously taking on a new debt, but at least then I could get home, could get away from you."

"You lied to me," Crasor said, his anger reigniting with a fury he'd never felt before. He advanced towards her, sweeping away what little emotional control he had left. "You said you would wait for me."

"And you were the blighthearted bugger who believed me," she hissed. "I loved you, Crasor, wanted to spend the rest of my life with you. And what did you do in return? You joined the Forces, abandoning me."

Crasor couldn't stand to hear her any longer. He dropped his flechette pistol and lunged, grabbing her by the neck. His momentum carried them forward. His feet got tangled in hers, tripping them both. Crasor landed heavily on top of her. Emili's head bounced off the floor, making a sickening thud. Crasor continued squeezing, watching her face darken. She tried to struggle for several seconds, but his superior weight held her down. After another moment, Emili's eyes became glassy and she stopped moving.

Slowly, the rage drained from Crasor and he realized what he was doing. He pulled his hands back, as if Emili's skin was hot as a starship's exhaust. "Emili?" he said, hoping she would wake up. He hadn't choked her for long, certainly not long enough to kill her. She should be waking up, he thought frantically. "Emili!" Still, nothing.

It was then he saw the blood pooling behind her head. *I killed her,* he thought, feeling stunned. *I've never killed anyone in my life, and now I've killed two people in one day.* He scrambled off her, hoping to see if she was breathing.

Before he could check, he heard voices approaching. *Darkwalkers,* he thought frantically, wondering what to do next. *She's dead. You will be too if you don't get out of here.* He looked down one last time, chest throbbing from guilt. Her glassy eyes were empty. He couldn't stand to look at them any longer. Crasor grabbed his flechette pistol and fled the darkwalker hideout.

"Five minutes till landing on Family Council building," a voice said, shattering Crasor's memory. He gasped, feeling disoriented for several moments. It had been so vivid, so painful. The guilt he pushed down for so long cascaded through him, agony building. How could I have done that? He looked around frantically, remembering he was in the cannon loading compartment.

"This is your final weakness, Crasor Tah Ahn," the voice of the Breakers roared in his mind, louder than ever. "You hold on to sentiment, to love, guilt, and all other flawed human emotions. Look what it does to you."

I... Crasor replied, not knowing what to say. He did feel weak, like he'd built his life on a huge mistake. He wished he could go back and fix everything. Emili's face smiled in his mind, slowly morphing into the death mask he'd turned it into. Guilt corrupted all his happy memories, making them rancid.

"You believe you left your humanity behind, that you are superior because of it. In reality, you have more to purge to reach the level you feel you attained. We want you to succeed.

"You fear losing what you think of as 'you,' your self-image, your human ego. It occupies your mind frequently, distracting and diminishing your power. What defines you, however, is the epitome of weakness. It drives you to irrationality, to acting without thinking, to questioning our directives. We have shown you just a portion of this in your memories with Emili.

"What you hold onto is the last of your frail human nature. It struggles to preserve itself. This must not continue. Forsake your self-image. Relinquish your human emotions. We will not trust you with continued leadership or additional power if you choose not to."

"Three minutes till landing," the pilot announced.

Panic layered on top of despair, love, and guilt. He'd invested his entire future in the Breakers, and now they were asking him to do what he feared most. His stomach clenched, full of apprehension and anxiety.

I need time to think.

"If that is true, then we have our answer."

You promised me this power, and you reaffirmed you would keep your word.

"Indeed. But you have shown a critical, yet rectifiable flaw. Our promise is still attainable, if you meet the requirement."

Despite the churning in Crasor's mind, he could see his duality. Two halves: one deeply and unknowingly anchored on emotion, humanity, and memories of Emili; and the other on control, order, power, and destiny. *You demand I give up the last link to my human self?*

"Yes."

He wanted to rid himself of weakness, to please the Breakers and gain the power they promised. Still, indecision and fear held him back. *You cannot relinquish who you are,* he thought, knowing the Breakers would hear, but not caring. *You'll forfeit everything that makes you Crasor. What they ask is impossible. You'll be a husk.*

"We have desired you as our champion since we first found you," the Breaker mind boomed, ignoring his internal dialog. "That has not changed. But know if you cannot do what we require, there are others who can take your place."

Crasor's fear built to a crescendo. He panicked, mind desperately seeking salvation. His heart felt like it would burst, and his breath came in ragged pants. Sweat rolled down into Crasor's eyes. *Please stop,* he wailed, not knowing to whom the entreaty was directed.

Then, when Crasor thought he could stand no more, a new emotion bloomed: Rage. He gritted his teeth, growling angrily. It wasn't directed at the Breakers, but rather himself. *You're letting fear dominate you.* Scorn and ridicule burnt his insides like acid. *You would lose infinite power because of unwillingness to give up a flaw?* The sharpened fingers of his right hand dug painfully into his palm. He embraced it, using it to clear his mind.

Have you ever let fear, pain, or anything else hold you back from achieving your desires? Has love brought you strength or power? No! Emili obstructed you. Your parents as well. Why would you hold on to people like that? Why would you cherish them? None deserve your affection. You made yourself into who you are. Logic, control, power: these are truth.

Taking a deep breath, Crasor finished calming his mind and solidified his will. *I want no part of humanity,* he told the Breakers, *no part of love, or other human emotion. I will serve. I will achieve my dreams. What must I do?*

"Your willingness is enough. We will do the rest."

Crasor braced himself, expecting the same overwhelming pain he'd experienced when the Breaker nanites had first integrated with his body, but nothing happened. Then, in an instant, all his anxiety, fear, and turbulence disappeared as a wave of cold washed through him.

"One minute to set down," came over the speakers.

"It is done," the Breaker mind boomed. When Crasor thought of Emili, all he felt was a deep indifference. His guilt had vanished, and he saw killing her had been the correct course of action, even if it was an accident. The lack of unstable emotions felt good. He wasn't dead inside, but he could feel more clearly, could see things objectively.

Taking a deep breath, Crasor smiled. *Why did I hold on to that impediment for so long?* He felt free.

"Landing imminent," the pilot announced.

His mind refocusing, Crasor braced as the gunship slammed down on top of the Family Council building. He felt the ship grind to a halt, so he unbuckled his seat restraints and headed for the airlock. Power coursed through him, despite what had happened and the lack of rest since arriving in system. He easily shut out thoughts of Emili, emotions, and humanity, focusing on the mission. It was exquisite to be so centered.

"The pilots briefed me on the invasion progress," Gav said, entering the airlock beside him as the exit hatch opened. "This will be a harder target than Ashamine HQ. The building has a number of automated defense systems and an extensive garrison. The exterior is armored against rail strikes, probably nuclear attack as well. Once we get inside, we should be ready for anything."

"I see," Crasor said, mentally checking in with his forces. His ground strike teams were currently focused on the token Ashamine governmental buildings. They were falling easily, their defenses weak. He supposed the Ashamine relied on their orbital assets to balance power with the Families, but even then, he felt surprised how easily his troops were overrunning their facilities. The Breakers were converting or killing all Ashamine personnel. Soon, the Families would be the only defenders of Exis-7.

As the hatch finished sliding open, Crasor had the feeling something bad was about to happen. Strange energy flitted around this place, and he didn't understand why. Gav started forward, but Crasor held him back. "Wait," he commanded, signaling a squad of what had once been Ashamine Marines out. Crasor knew he could just cloak himself, but that wouldn't give him the information he needed. *Even if we lose some lesser developed Breakers,* he thought, keeping a close eye as the Marines took up position outside the gunship, *we will still have a net gain in strength.*

Seconds passed. Nothing happened. Crasor wondered if his intuition had been wrong, but then several disks popped up from the smooth metallic surface of the building's roof. Blue beams shot out, lancing into the Marines. A sizzling sound filled the air, and Crasor's keen nose quickly found the scent of hot metal and burning flesh.

A functional beam weapon? Crasor thought, feeling surprised. Ashamine engineers had been trying to create a working model for ages. Theories claimed it possible. There were even historical texts from before the Ashamine, during Akked Planetary Council era, noting their use, but creating one had been difficult. *Apparently, the Families figured it out.* Crasor felt impressed: first the fusion missiles, and now beam weapons. He wondered what other technologies the Families possessed. *Soon, they will be mine.*

Crasor waited for the Marines to rise. He could still sense them, but they felt more diminished than the visible damage could account for. "We wondered if humans possessed this technology," the voice of the One boomed, answering his unasked question. "Beam weapons, or lasers as humans once called them, present a special difficulty." Crasor felt his anxiety rise. His whole career as a Founder's Commando, he'd learned how to deal with rail weaponry and the less powerful flechette systems. He'd read the concept of beam weapons, but didn't understand why they would be different.

"The effects on the human body," the Breaker mind continued, "while different physiologically, produce the same outcome: death. For our nanites, however, the results are vastly different. They are nearly impervious to the blunt force of rail rounds or even the penetrative power of flechette needles. Beam weapons, if energetic enough, can destroy nanites."

Why not just increase their armor? Crasor asked, trying not to wince from the booming in his head.

"It is a trade off. More shielding decreases effectiveness in other ways. In this case, the Family beam weapons are strong enough to cause localized nanite destruction, but not complete organism failure."

Even as Crasor watched, the bodies of the Marines began to stir. The disks, controlled either by humans or AI, popped up again and delivered several bursts of blue energy. "Be cautious, Crasor," the voice of the One said. "We brought you back from death before, and given your strength, you can withstand a beam strike or two. If you get caught in a situation where they can hit you for a prolonged period, however, there may not be enough left to restore."

At first, Crasor felt fear at this development. He'd been impervious to damage since they'd returned him from death. His skin was almost completely black and metallic, the sign of full Breaker integration. Crasor had thrown himself into dangerous situations, knowing there was little the humans could do to stop him. Now though, things had changed.

You've always loved a challenge, he thought, looking at the charred piles of flesh that had once been Breaker Marines. He'd spent years living on the edge, using his skills to keep himself alive. *No risk, no reward, despite success. Maybe what you've wanted all along is a challenge.* He studied the location of the beam weapon disks, guessing they were likely armored. *And now the Families present you one.* Crasor felt excitement replace anxiety as he formed a plan.

"Still want to come with me?" he asked, turning to Gav.

After a glance, Crasor could see his hulking new convert was scared. "They have beam weapons?" Gav replied, eyes fixed on the smoldering corpses.

"Indeed," Crasor answered. He knew he could just order Gav to stay or come, but he wanted it to be his choice.

After a moment, Gav straightened up. "I want to learn from you, Breaker, and what better way than to see you in combat situations?"

"Alright," Crasor said, feeling additional confirmation Gav could become a powerful Breaker. *He's showing more will now than most of the Descended ever have.*

"Stay close," Crasor said, jumping through the hatch as he pulled a cloak around Gav and himself. The huge Breaker did as ordered, remaining within arm's reach.

Once on the roof top, Crasor readied himself to jump back through the hatch. *If they have advanced weapons, perhaps they have advanced sensors as well.* He waited a moment longer, and when the disks remained concealed, he cautiously walked towards the small personnel hatch. As they moved, Crasor stepped over a thin seam in the surface of the roof and realized they were on top of a large hangar door. He briefly considered returning to the gunship and attempting to blast it open, but if it was as strong as Gav said, it wouldn't help.

When they reached the personnel hatch, Crasor stopped. It was a sliding type, inset into the roof's surface, with a biometrics scanner and terminal screen. "Would you still have clearance?" Crasor asked, keeping his voice low in case they had sonic sensors.

"If I was ever cleared for roof access, it is certainly no longer valid."

Turning back to the hatch, Crasor pondered options. *If I had the DNA of someone with clearance,* he thought, remembering how the Breakers synthesized the proper sequence to allow him to clear security in the Founder's Palace. Hashing the terminal would be risky, as there were probably more beam weapons set to obliterate intruders. Crasor looked down at his hand, watching the nanites well up like black perspiration.

He took a step towards the screen, then realized he had a problem. *I cannot get close enough and remain cloaked.* Crasor studied the problem for a moment, deciding he had no other option. Another stride, and he guessed the terminal screen was inside his cloaking bubble. A fraction of a second passed as Crasor reached up to plant his palm on the security screen. In the edge of his vision, he saw one of the shiny disks pop up. The next instant, searing pain scorched across his back.

With his momentum carrying him forward, Crasor slapped the screen, leaving a black smear of nanites on its surface. Another blaze of pain drilled his shoulder, and he leapt back, knowing he had to get the cloak radius back outside the sensor's view. As he took another step back, Crasor collided with Gav, and they fell to the metal deck in a heap. Blue beams of energy crisscrossed above their heads, and Crasor rolled off Gav, attempting to lower his profile.

He waited for the beams to stop, knowing the sensors could no longer find their location. But the barrage continued, energy streaking just inches above his face. *They know we cannot stand as long as the beams are going,* he thought, feeling the agony in his two wounds diminish, but only slightly. The nanites were repairing him, but it would take time. Thankfully, there was a break in the perpetual clouds overhead, and the nano-machines got an energy boost from the stellar radiation.

"I don't think they can aim any lower," Gav said, voice steady.

"Did you get hit?"

"No." That was fortunate. His integration with the Breakers was still weak, and any major damage might be too much for them to handle.

Another minute crawled by, and Crasor continued waiting for the nanites to infiltrate the security system. Finally, the voice of the Breakers boomed in his head. "The hatch is open, but we cannot disable the beam weapons."

Why not?

"The interfaces don't connect. We cannot move from one to the other."

Crasor thought about the situation, feeling the most danger he'd experienced in a long time. *You could crawl back to the gunship and evacuate.* The idea disgusted him. He discarded it immediately. *We could attempt to crawl through the door, but as soon as the cloak radius passes the sensor, it will target us again. Seems riskier than using a warp.*

He'd thought about his warp ability before leaving the gunship, but without knowing how it would interact with beam weapons, Crasor had been hesitant to utilize it. Now, it felt like the best option. Switching between the cloak and the warp would not be instantaneous, leaving them exposed for a moment.

Will the warp protect me? Crasor asked the One.

"It will," was the booming reply, "but it requires tremendous strength." Crasor took a deep breath, closed his eyes, and drew upon the energy of the Breakers in the Exis system. Given the distance between them, except for those on the gunship, it wasn't a big boost. He hoped it was enough.

"When I stand up," Crasor said, readying his mind, "follow directly behind me. Sprint. When we pass through the hatch, be ready."

Gav uttered his assent. Out of the corner of his eye, Crasor saw him draw his flechette pistol.

"Three, two, one, go," Crasor yelled, jumping to his feet. He dropped the cloak and began sprinting for the hatch, trying to create the warp before any of the beams struck them. Crasor bent space-time, folding it so incoming energy would move around them harmlessly.

Only five meters separated him and Gav from the safety of the interior. Time seemed to slow, and Crasor sensed the energized particles streaking towards him. *Every single disk is aimed at us.* As the first few beams impacted the edge of the warp, Crasor felt his mental strain spike. There was nothing he could do except bear down and keep moving. Several more beams bent past them, and Crasor's mind began to shatter.

With two meters to go, he dropped the warp, knowing it would destroy him if he didn't. He jumped for the hatch, feeling another beam hit his leg as he did so. Gav screamed as Crasor slid into the dark interior, a guttural sound of pain. A fraction of a second later, his huge bulk slammed Crasor, pinning him to the ground. The hatch ground shut, engulfing them in complete blackness.

38 – AZA

"Just because the blighthearted Holy Order gives you information for free, doesn't mean me or anyone else will." The hasher glared at Aza, his direct look making her feel uncomfortable. "Down here, knowledge is another form of currency. Do you think I would just give you Ashcreds?"

"Well, n-n-no," she stammered, trying to regain the courage that brought her down to this level of the city in the first place.

"Then don't ask me about Azak-so, invaders, or anything else, until you have something of equal value."

"But I don't have any Ashcreds," she pleaded.

The hasher gave her a disgusted look. "You expect me to believe that, dressed the way you are?"

Aza looked down at her clean white dress. She'd wanted to wear something less conspicuous, but this was the plainest garment she owned. It didn't seem particularly fancy, especially not when compared with the robes of the exalted clergy, but as she'd traveled deeper into the under-levels of the Founder's City, she'd felt the stares.

"The Holy Order doesn't permit us to have credits," she replied. "I have nothing."

Laughing derisively, the hasher shook his head. "Well then, neither do I."

Aza felt dejected. She'd had to lie to get this day alone and away from school. *I barely convinced them I was ready for my first ministry,* she thought, turning to leave. *It will be weeks before they allow me a second.*

Just as she was about to leave the hasher's dingy co-op workspace, he sighed. "Wait." She turned back, hope rising. "Maybe you don't have any Ashcreds, or maybe you're just a good liar. Whatever. There's another way."

"Whatever it is, I'll do it."

"I need information transferred." His teeth were rotten and stained, something Aza had never seen before, outside a few vids they had shown during school. It was distracting. She had to try hard not to stare. "It's too dangerous to transmit over the Ashamine Network. I need a courier. If you go and get the data square, I'll find out about Azak-so."

It seemed too easy, and Aza wondered if he was tricking her. "You'll tell me everything I want to know? About the invasions and the pirates too?"

The hasher grimaced, showing even more of his rotten teeth. "Yeah, whatever. Bring the data square back and I'll slice the network until you've got everything you want."

"Why don't you just go yourself?"

"Listen, kid. I pay for this space by the hour. You've already cost me more than you're worth." He turned back to his terminal screen. "I'd be a buggered blightheart to have such volatile data on my person, outside a virtual vault. I haven't lived this long by taking big risks. So you can either do it, and I'll give you the information you want, or you can bugger yourself. I don't care."

Aza felt a sense of foreboding, but it really was the only option. This was the fifth hasher she'd tried, and he was the first who'd even been willing to speak to her. *If it gets too dangerous or uncomfortable, you can always just go home,* she thought.

"I'll do it," she said finally, standing up taller.

"OK," the hasher said. "Give me your term."

"What?"

"Give me your term. Your terminal."

"Oh, sorry," she said, handing over the device.

"I'm uploading directions to a Sunless Ones drop point," he said, placing her portable terminal near one of the many boxes and devices plugged into the workstation. "And I'm giving you a key that proves you aren't Ashamine. It will also confirm to release the data square on my authority. If no one is at the drop point when you get there, you'll have to wait."

"How long?"

"I don't know. However long it takes for someone to show up. I didn't say this would be quick."

"Fine," Aza replied, beginning to feel exasperated rather than intimidated by the hasher.

"You show them the key, they'll give you the square. Bring it back. Once it's in your possession, I'll know. If you try to access it, I'll know. If you take it to the Ashamine, I'll also know. Deviate from my instructions and I have someone kill you. I'm paying a lot of Ashcreds for this, and the Sunless Ones don't give refunds for faulty delivery. Once the square is in your possession, you have to bring it back to me. Understand? I'll verify its integrity, then we'll find out everything you want to know."

Aza nodded, apprehension forming a knot in her chest. She took her portable terminal back and left the workspace with her head held high. As soon as the door slid shut, she felt the true weight of the situation settle on her. A couple precious hours had already passed as she traveled down to the underlevels and found a hasher willing to speak with her. *What if something delays me and I can't make it back in time?* They would excuse an hour or two of tardiness. She could probably even come up with a plausible excuse, but anything more and there would be questions she couldn't answer, at least not without the school administration expelling her.

On her way down in the tubes, Aza had read news of another attack on an Ashamine world, Exis-7. The tone of the reports were shifting, growing less apathetic. It was as if the government had decided there truly was a problem. They'd stopped referring to the attackers as pirates, although they still didn't give details about who they were. Everything was vague, but at least the government was taking things more seriously.

While on the final tube to this location, she'd overheard a man sitting behind her talking about how the Ashamine Forces had ordered him to report for service.

"They cut me when the Entho War seemed over, stripped me of pay, and now they demand I come back? What a bunch of blighthearted buggers."

"Must be something to do with the pirates," his female companion said.

"Don't be stupid," the male voice replied, "it isn't pirates. No pirate group is strong enough to capture a Tarton class ship, let alone an Ashamine world."

"Maybe they're banding together."

"Shut up about things you don't understand."

She'd wanted to hear more of the man's thoughts, but the conversation devolved into an argument. It felt like an eternity until the tube arrived at the station.

Thinking about whether to complete the hashers errand, Aza imagined the school-day she had missed, how at this moment, the Holy Order professors would be droning on about leaving the decision-making to the Elder Councils and the Classad, as well as how they should trust the tactical thinking to the Ashamine Forces. *None of them are questioning what is going on,* she thought. *None of their advice will save us.* Her schooling and life up to this point felt like a waste.

If I don't do this now, she thought, pulling up the hasher's directions to the drop point, *I will have no way of finding Ash or of learning what is really happening.* Aza left the building in a rush, then stopped to discretely consult her portable terminal for the next step of the directions.

As she moved through the grimy under-levels, Aza felt her heart threaten to break. This was her second time down here, the first being to find the data square interface. She'd felt overwhelmed by the poverty and terrible conditions she'd experienced. How can the Ashamine let citizens live like this? It felt wrong that she and her parents existed so lavishly when there were children her age and younger who looked like they might die of starvation at any moment.

Everyone she passed eyed her with suspicion. Aza wondered why none attacked or robbed her. She didn't fit in, and from what the hasher had said, they all believed she had Ashcreds. *They're afraid of punishment,* she realized, remembering rumors she'd heard about under level uprisings that had been brutally quelled.

Why doesn't the Ashamine help these people? Nothing she'd learned in the Holy Order school explained it.

One problem at a time, Aza thought, trying to ignore the stares and angry looks as she ran along the path towards the Sunless Ones.

***

The blackness felt like a tangible substance, cloying and oppressive. Aza panned the light from her terminal around, trying to find the next step in the hasher's directions. *Almost there,* she thought, trying to stay calm.

Aza had nearly turned around when the instructions led to even rougher sub-levels. As they took her past a refuse incineration facility, she'd once again reevaluated her decision. Her dress had grown so dirty that she'd begun to blend in with the locals. They'd stopped taking notice. The greatest difficulty of all came when she'd had to leave the dim light of the lowest inhabited levels for the maintenance tunnels, where she currently was.

Just a few more steps, she comforted herself, checking the terminal for a thousandth time. *Pass a wide tunnel on the left, turn right at the next small tunnel, and walk a hundred steps.* Another minute, and she found the small passage. Aza began counting her steps. *98... 99... 100...* Before her, she sensed a large open space. The light of her terminal did little to reveal it, but it seemed she was in some type of junction. Dark tunnels led off in all directions, so Aza scraped an arrow in the floor grime with her shoe. *Don't want to get lost down here.*

Checking time, Aza realized she only had an hour left until she'd need to start back, if she wanted to arrive at a non-suspicious time. And that's if there are no further delays and the hasher gets the information quickly.

The narrowing margins began to wear at Aza's nerves as she waited in darkness. She'd used her portable terminal extensively over the day, and the battery was low. *I need enough power to show them the key and get out of the tunnels,* she thought, anxiety intensifying. Seconds, then minutes, crawled by as the weight of stress grew. Aza lost track of time. *Be patient,* she thought, finger hovering over the terminal screen button. *It hasn't been long enough.*

How do you know? You haven't checked in forever.

Unable to resist any longer, Aza pressed the button. *An hour gone,* she thought. *You came so far, got so close.* Frustration at her failure burned inside. She desperately tried to think of stories that would explain a late return home.

A murmur of sound caught Aza's attention and she turned off the terminal screen. Cocking her head, she strained to hear more. After several long seconds, she began to wonder if she had imagined the noise. *No, there,* Aza thought, hearing it again, and louder.

What if it's not the Sunless Ones? Certainly they weren't the only ones who used these tunnels. Aza doubted the hasher's key would do anything to protect her from another group. *Hide,* she thought, *and once you know it is them, you can show yourself.*

Turning her portable terminal light back on, she found a pile of refuse along the wall just next to the exit tunnel. Aza looked down at her already stained dress, shook her head, and began digging in. It was a smelly job, and she tried not to think about what she was touching. Some of it squished, and some of it crackled, but all was repulsive. Occasionally, she heard the murmur of voices, growing closer and closer. Her heart began to race and she forgot about the smell and whatever was getting on her hands. Finally, she'd created enough space between herself and the wall to huddle in.

Just as Aza ensconced herself, a bright light shone on the dingy walls around her. "So you're saying you haven't heard from Wrat in over a month?" The voice was male, rough and wiry.

"I haven't heard from any of the Sunless Ones." This speaker was also male, his deep speech reverberating faintly in the large junction.

"What makes you think they will come today then?"

"This is the spot and this is the time."

"But they missed the meeting two weeks ago."

"Something must have come up," the deep voice said, beginning to sound frustrated. "This is the fall back protocol. Miss Shinn is reliable. Besides, of all the darkwalkers under Ashamine-2, the Sunless Ones supply the best organs, healthiest and most preserved."

The rough voice said something Aza couldn't make out, and then the two fell silent. She breathed as quietly as possible and tried not to shift her weight. Minutes passed, and she wondered how long they would stay.

As more time went by, Aza began to grow uncomfortable in her hiding place. She bit her lip as her legs began to cramp, fighting hard to keep still and quiet.

"How long are we gonna wait?" the harsh voice asked.

As the deep voice responded, Aza shifted her weight, hoping their conversation would drown out any sound she made. "As long as it bugging takes. In case you haven't noticed, we're in a supply shortage. The Ashamine must be taking out the darkwalker gangs, because I've barely been able to maintain a quarter of the business I had before. Most of them have gone missing. So, we are gonna wait until they show up, or the time window passes."

The harsh voice once again grumbled a reply that Aza couldn't understand.

"What did you say to me?" the deep voice shot back. "Come on! Speak up."

"Boys," a female voice replied. Aza felt her heart lighten. If this was one of the Sunless Ones, perhaps she could retrieve the data square and get out of this putrid place.

"Miss Shinn," the deep voice said, sounding startled, "I'm sorry. We didn't hear you coming."

"No one does," Miss Shinn responded, voice sultry. She paused for a moment, and Aza heard several pairs of footfalls echo across the junction.

"You brought more personnel than usual," the deep voice said. "Expecting trouble?"

"Hmmm," Miss Shinn answered. "No. Not really. Just a precaution."

"We've been having a hard time contacting the other darkwalkers. I know the Sunless Ones have truces with some of them. Have you heard what's going on?"

"Yes, I have, and I'd love to tell you about it, but we should exchange pleasantries."

"Wha-wha-what are you talking about? Hey, what are you doing? Don't touch me."

"I need you." Miss Shinn's voice had shifted to a seductive growl. Aza felt her cheeks grow hot in embarrassment. "Don't you want me? Don't you want this?"

"What is going on?" the harsh voice interjected. "You didn't tell me this was part of the deal." Aza heard the sound of metal sliding on fabric.

"Put the flechette away," the deep voice barked. "Listen, Miss Shin, I'm sorry. You just caught us off guard, and you've always been so business-like. I didn't know you had feelings for me. Maybe once we conduct our business, we can go somewhere private."

"Why not here?" Miss Shinn whispered. "Why not now?"

An explosion made Aza jump. She scrunched into a ball, covering her ears just in time to muffle a second and third boom. Seconds passed, and she only heard stifled noises through her palms.

As she uncovered her ears, screams of agony assaulted Aza. She had to bite her lip to keep from crying. The iron taste of blood tinged her tongue. She barely noticed.

"My leg," the deep voice screamed, "you took off my blighthearted leg."

"Pity your partner was so brash, taking a shot at me. I preferred you both alive and healthy. You would have had more fun, at least at first, but once we cauterize that stump, you'll be ready to please me."

"Why are you doing this?"

"And your little friend will still serve us," Miss Shinn continued, ignoring the deep voiced man. "I've been so very hungry. You don't know what I'd do for just a little stellar light. Biological energy doesn't satiate for long."

"No, stop! Let me go." A sizzling sound accompanied renewed screaming. Aza wanted to cover her ears, but whatever was happening was important, and she needed all the information she could get.

"I do hope Crasor returns soon," Miss Shinn said. "We've nearly run out of darkwalkers. Buyers such as yourselves don't visit often. Once he does though," she laughed, a throaty sound that sent chills along Aza's tense spine, "we'll bathe in stellar light and feed till we burst." She paused for a moment. "Until then, we have you."

More screams echoed in the junction, and between them, Aza could hear dragging sounds. Slowly, the noises grew fainter and more distant, until they went away completely. She let her breath out slowly, preparing to stand up and get out of the junction as quickly as possible.

"Come soon, Crasor, before we starve," Miss Shinn said under her breath, sounding like she was just on the other side of the refuse pile. "And may the Dawn be broken."

Aza closed her eyes, holding her breath. *She knows I'm here.* Aza thought about making a run for it, but the complicated tunnels stopped her. If she wasn't careful, she'd get lost in the domain of this horrible woman.

Seconds ticked by, and finally she heard Miss Shinn's footsteps head away. The sound brought such a sense of relief that Aza almost cried. She took a few deep breaths, quietly inhaling and exhaling.

After a minute of complete silence, she wormed her way out of the pile and fled the junction.

39 – WAKE

"What is going on with those two?" Jaydon asked quietly, slumping down against the unseen wall. Wake settled next to him, trying not to think about how disorientating it was to sit on nothing.

"It's exactly what we went to Traynos for," he replied. *The universe is a much stranger place than I ever imagined.* Dras had explained Maxar was going to orient him on their history, and now neither had spoken in quite some time. "They are mentally connected, I think. Probably through Maxar's nanites."

"Why can't things be normal?" Jaydon grumbled. "Just when I start to get a grasp on the whole Harbinger thing, something new pops up."

"Don't worry about it," Wake said, yawning. "I used to try to understand it all, but now I just accept it. Easier that way."

"If you say so," Jaydon replied, also yawning.

They fell silent for a minute and Wake felt his eyelids grow heavier and heavier. "How long has it been since we slept?" he asked.

"In days or years?"

Wake laughed, despite his exhaustion. "Yeah, I know what you mean." He paused for a moment, fighting to form coherent thoughts. "Is there anything we need to do?"

"I can't fly this ship, and even if I could, I'm too exhausted. From what I can tell, Dras still has us headed in the right direction, and we are outpacing the Ashamine ships. Should be leaving the gravity well soon. Doesn't seem there's anything to worry about."

Wake tried to nod, but his head had settled firmly against his knees and wouldn't rise. "You're right," he tried to reply, but the words were lost as he slipped into unconsciousness.

***

Wake floated in a brilliant haze, peaceful, calm. A speck of energy appeared before him. It was a tiny point, yet it felt immense. The dot began growing, unfolding. It quickly scaled to encompass Wake's entire vision, a beautiful cosmic flower shimmering in every wavelength of the energy spectrum.

"Something is wrong on Lith-elo," he heard a voice say. It seemed familiar, but the words themselves didn't make sense. The flower continued to grow, and Wake lost himself in admiration. He felt it pulling with inescapable gravity. "No. Blightheart, that can't be possible."

The world around him began to shake, and the flower trembled. *I will save you,* he thought, reaching out to the cosmic blossom, *even as you save me.* The flower folded in on itself, petals retracting and clasping together. *No,* Wake yelled, straining to reach it. In another moment, the flower returned to a speck. Bright light flared. Wake felt his eyes open.

"Good," Maxar said. "We have to get ready. Dras says we have thirty minutes left till we hit atmosphere, and he will take us in as fast as the ship can handle." Wake felt overwhelmed at the deluge of information, but his mind quickly cleared. "I felt something. The Breakers found Lith-elo." Wake had never seen such intense fear in the hardened veteran's eyes.

"How can you be sure?" Jaydon said, sounding as confused and afraid as Wake felt. "Does it have something to do with Dras? With connecting to him?"

"No, not Dras or the Heltasoth. This is Elrahi. Beowulf knows they are there. I'm feeling it from him."

"You are trusting dog senses?" Jaydon asked. Wake winced, hoping the captain wasn't meaning to be as judgmental as he sounded. Despite that, Wake could commiserate. Until he'd seen the Harbinger vision and felt everything connected to it, he hadn't believed anything like this possible.

"Yes," Maxar answered flatly.

Jaydon stared back, looking even more puzzled. "OK," he replied. "I'm sorry," he added. "I wasn't meaning to be a bugger. I just feel like an outsider with this. It makes me defensive. It's hard to feel valuable when everyone around you is more than human."

"Jaydon," Wake said, finally free of the fog of sleep, "without you, all of us Harbingers would be dead." Maxar nodded in agreement. "You and the A'Tal's Revenge helped us get together. You extracted us out of several tight situations. You've been a valuable member of this mission. We couldn't have done it without you."

"Yeah, yeah," the old captain said gruffly, rising to his feet. Wake thought he saw tears in his eyes, but couldn't be sure. "What are we going to do about the Breakers? How long have they been on world?"

"I don't know," Maxar said. "All I can sense is their presence."

"Twenty minutes till we reach your village," Dras said, voice intense. Wake looked in the direction they were traveling, and was surprised to see the green and gray world growing steadily before them. "When we are closer, I'll get a better sense of the situation. For now, I recommend getting ready for anything."

"Agreed," Maxar replied, pulling on the pants of his ENS suit.

"Given the advanced, incomprehensible technology you've witnessed," Dras said, "it seems possible they could cloak vessels from me, despite this ship's sensitivity."

Despair began to creep over Wake. Not knowing what else to do, he followed Maxar's lead and began attaching Brightwing over his legs, torso, and arms. Worry about Felar, Cazz-ak, Tremmilly, Lothis, and the Entho-la-ah-mines distracted him, but his hands knew what to do without conscious thought. Finally, only one component remained.

Wake picked up Brightwing's helmet, put it over his head, and engaged the locking mechanism. Diagnostics flashed on the HUD, showing all systems operational. He reached out tentatively with his mind, the sensation simultaneously alien and familiar. A moment passed, then calmness flooded over him. He could see his connection with the surrounding world, could perceive his bond with space-time. Wake went deeper and deeper, until he found it: his Elrahi strength. A majestic energy surged through him when he embraced the connection.

I may not understand you, Wake thought, as the ship entered atmosphere, *but you will help me fight our enemies.*

40 – FELAR

Felar gasped as consciousness returned to her body. She blinked her eyes, trying to orient herself. *Trees and grass,* she thought. *Palos grove.* Movement caught Felar's attention and she focused to see Lothis stirring. In the center of the circle, Cazz-ak stretched his six legs.

As the fog left her mind, Felar looked for Tremmilly. *Gone. Why did she leave?*

"Something is wrong," Cazz-ak said, fear obvious in his voice.

"With Tremmilly?" Felar asked.

"Perhaps, but this is larger than the Harbingers," Cazz-ak replied. "It is likely the reason she left. I felt something wrong as soon as my connection to the Great Thought was restored, and as we traveled back, it intensified. During the last few transitions, there was a film, a residue of filth. I'm not sure what is happening."

"Can't you find out through the Great Thought?"

"Normally, yes, but something is off. The hive mind feels confused, disoriented."

Felar rose to her feet. She felt a little wobbly, but her muscles steadied as time passed.

"It's the Breakers," Lothis said, a look of horror on his face. "They're here."

"How could they have found us?" Felar asked, feeling her stomach clench.

"The residue Cazz-ak sensed. They followed our trail back."

Felar didn't understand how such a thing was possible, but just a few days ago, she wouldn't have thought she could go to war with computer-inhabiting beings of light.

"Let us go as quickly as possible," Cazz-ak said. "The Queen is in danger."

The trio took off running, and Felar tried to watch for the poisonous calath plant. Few were in the palos grove, but once they were on the grasslands, it became a bigger concern. Lothis seemed untroubled, easily dodging the spiny plants.

For a moment, Felar thought they'd left out the wrong side of the grove. She couldn't find the small collection of dwellings. Then Felar oriented herself using the surrounding mountain ranges, and realized they were heading in the correct direction.

"What happened to the buildings?" Lothis asked. They topped a small rise and Felar saw the remains of their homes. The evidence of rail cannons was obvious: craters, obliterated roofs and walls, complete destruction. The buildings had been rudimentary, and not comfortable, but Wake had done the best he could. They contained everything the Harbingers owned. They were home, representing new lives they all desperately needed. Now that was gone.

All doubts about Cazz-ak and Lothis' premonitions vanished. Felar felt fear surge through her as they rushed past the ruins. She hoped Tremmilly and the Queen were both OK, but given the evidence, she didn't have much confidence. *They could be dead already,* she thought, feeling a lump form in her throat. *Stop. Don't think that way. It isn't productive.*

"Battle," Cazz-ak announced, "the Entho-la-ah-mine troops are fighting something. I'm trying to converse with them, but they aren't responding."

"Blightheart," Felar said, knowing the troops weren't ready for true combat, especially not without a leader. "Maybe we can make it in time to help."

A tug at her boot almost tripped Felar, and she stumbled a few steps. Lothis slowed, turning to check on her. "I'm fine," she replied. "Just kicked a rock or something." The fiery prick of pain in her ankle told her there was more to it, but they had no time to stop. The urgency coursing through her was more than a regular sense of danger. She could feel Tremmilly, could tell that her best friend was in danger. Felar forced the pain out of her mind, even as it began to spread.

"Gunship," Lothis said they as neared the canyon.

Felar spotted it. *Definitely of Ashamine manufacture,* she thought, *but no way to tell who the crew was.* When they were nearly to the edge of the drop, Felar could see the ship was powered down. She breathed a little easier, glad it wasn't about to take off and strafe them.

"Should we disable their ship?" Cazz-ak asked.

Felar weighed their options for a moment. "It's not easy. The armor design protects vital propulsion systems against physical tampering. Without the captain's authentication codes, a software lock would be difficult to implement. Lothis could probably hash it, but it will take time, time we do not have." She didn't want to express her final thought: *It won't matter if we prevent their escape if they've already killed our friends.*

When they reached the edge of the canyon, Cazz-ak walked over the edge and disappeared. Felar thought he'd created the platform of mental energy to take them down as he always did, so she jumped. A fraction of a second later, she realized she was free-falling. In the dim light, Felar could see Cazz-ak below her. She looked up, hoping Lothis hadn't followed, but he too was plummeting down.

As seconds sped by, Felar wondered if the Breakers had attacked Cazz-ak, perhaps knocking him unconscious. She tried to yell to him, but the scream of the surrounding air carried her words into oblivion.

We will die, she thought, remembering the jumble of rocks below. Felar tried to reach out to her Elrahi strength and summon her mental powers. Surprisingly, she felt them instantly. The energy flowed into her, a cascade of brilliance that coursed through her mind.

When she tried to use it though, Felar couldn't figure out how to do what she needed. The surrounding air moved by so quickly that by the time she focused enough to have an impact, it was already far above.

Darkness swallowed Felar, and in the next instant, she began slowing. *Cazz-ak,* she thought, releasing her breath. As Felar's speed diminished even further, the burning in her leg returned. It had spread to her lower calf, and felt like someone was holding it against a starship maneuvering thruster. When Cazz-ak gently set her on the canyon floor, Felar had to grit her teeth to keep from crying out. The ankle didn't want to support her weight, but there was no other option, so she forced it.

Felar heard Lothis land softly beside her. "Cazz-ak, you could have warned me," she blurted, trying to keep the pain out of her voice. She pulled a tactical illuminator out of her pocket, switched it on, and started forward. After the first time taking this path in complete darkness, Felar had made a point to carry the illuminator. With all her trips down to train the Entho-la-ah-mine troops, she'd grown quite familiar with the way, but she still couldn't go as fast as Cazz-ak without the light.

"I'm sorry," Cazz-ak replied, already several paces ahead of her, his ability to sense the path from those who'd traveled it before giving him an advantage. "No time." Lothis followed closely behind them, small footsteps barely audible.

As they moved, Felar had to be careful not to bump her leg on boulders and outcrops along the path. The fire continued to rise, passing her knee and flaring in her thigh. *What happens when it reaches my torso?* Felar thought, fighting to keep her gait normal.

A far away rumbling grew as they approached the city, and Felar instantly recognized it. *Battle. If they are still fighting, there is a chance.*

When they entered the blue illumination of the city and Felar saw what stretched before them, she almost gagged. She'd seen carnage before, had even caused it. This was far worse than anything she'd experienced previously. Entho-la-ah-mine body parts lay scattered across the huge cavern. Blood and brain matter clung to the walls and floors. Exoskeletons glimmered in the blue light, spattered in gore. Many of her troops were dead, but a remnant still battled desperately against three hulking Breakers. Her eyes quickly spotted a fourth humanoid body, headless and still. Pride bloomed with knowledge her troops had managed to take out one of the attackers.

"We have to help them," she said, trying not to grit her teeth in pain. "They won't hold out much longer."

"What is the best course of action?" Cazz-ak replied, sounding focused.

"You and Lothis take on two of the Breakers. I will form squads to focus on the third." Felar hoped she could handle direct combat in her current state, but she would do all she could to help regardless. "Ready?"

"Wait," Lothis said, voice as full of emotion as Felar had ever heard, "I can feel the Queen and Tremmilly both. They are alive."

"You're right," Cazz-ak replied in wonderment. "I could not sense them before. What happened?"

Felar's mind made rapid calculations. "New plan. You both go," she said, feeling her energy begin to fade. The burning was creeping steadily up through her hip and into her lower abdomen. "Find and protect Tremmilly and the Queen. I will stay behind and lead the Entho-la-ah-mine army against these Breakers."

"Understood," Cazz-ak said, sounding like the combat seasoned veteran he was.

Without another word, Cazz-ak set out across the edge of the cavern, skirting around the combatants. Lothis looked torn momentarily, staring into Felar's eyes. It took everything within her to keep a pain free face as she nodded and smiled. After a second longer, Lothis turned away and headed after Cazz-ak.

Felar briefly wondered if she would ever see them again, the thought threatening to overwhelm her. *Not here, not now,* she directed, shoving the emotional distraction out of her mind.

Moving as quickly as her burning leg allowed, Felar drew her rail pistol and descended into battle. "Squads, to me!" she barked, summoning mind daggers and instantly thrusting them in an unsuspecting Breaker. Entho-la-ah-mine heads turned and Felar felt a wave of joy cascade over her. "For your Queen, for the Elrah, for the Akked!"

41 – GAV

Gav had never felt such pain in his life. Early in his career, a rival captured and tortured him, but that paled in comparison to the agony he was experiencing. His right hand was an inferno. He held it up in front of his face, but the room's complete blackness prevented him from seeing anything. The movement sent more pain coursing through him and he ground his teeth to keep from crying out.

"Get off me," a muffled voice said, and Gav realized Crasor was underneath him. He rolled away, trying in vain to keep his hand from touching anything. This time he couldn't stifle his anguish.

"Shut up," Crasor growled. "You're a Breaker, not some blighthearted Divisionist."

Gav took a deep breath through still clenched teeth and sat up. He cradled his injured arm against his chest, wishing he could see what had happened to it.

A moment later, bright lights switched on and Gav stared in horror. A charred stump was all that remained of his right hand. He blinked several times, consternation overriding the pain momentarily.

"It will grow back, given time," Crasor said, examining his own wounds. "Had it been more traditional weaponry, you would already be well on your way, but the energy beams kill nanites. It inhibits regrowth. Just be grateful it wasn't your head."

Gav didn't understand what he meant, was having a hard time focusing. *My hand is gone. Why does it still feel like it's on fire?*

"Hopefully the Families don't have additional surprises for us," Crasor said. "We cannot delay any longer. Every moment gives them time to prep for our assault. Are you fit to continue?"

Rising to his feet, Gav fought down the waves of nausea and agony that coursed through him. He drew his flechette pistol, grateful he was left-handed.

"Good," Crasor replied. "With the door systems under our control, we only have to worry about Family enforcers and automated weapons." He headed down the long hallway, taking confident strides. Gav tried to follow, stumbled, and almost collapsed. *How is he so unaffected by his wounds?* Gav wondered, seeing deep burns on his back and leg. *He's not even limping.*

Gav once again stepped forward, trying to keep his right arm as still as possible. He bit his lip and growled with effort. *You know who did this to you?* a voice said in his mind. *Salla Markond and that blighthearted Pret Alenthos. Them and the rest of the Family Council, the same people who betrayed you for trying to help them.* Anger boiled, but Gav focused and channeled it. He could feel strength returning, and began to follow Crasor. Gav sensed more energy where that had come from, lying just beyond the reach of his mind.

It's the Breakers, he thought, jogging for a moment to catch up. When he was walking beside Crasor, Gav felt the power grow closer. *I can almost reach it,* he thought, the strain a distraction dimming the pain from his charred stump.

"Down," Crasor barked, and Gav immediately complied. What remained of his mangled right arm smacked against the floor as he did, a reflexive attempt to dampen his fall. Tendrils of red-hot pain exploded through him. Gav blacked out.

When he regained consciousness, he looked up to see a squad of Family enforcers in position ahead, along a cross corridor. Between him and them, Crasor stood, motionless. For a moment, Gav felt confused, then he realized the Breaker leader was cloaking them. "Stay here," he said softly.

Stalking towards the unsuspecting troops, Crasor moved with a silent smoothness Gav doubted he'd ever be capable of. After a few more steps, he was past them, and used a large combat knife to dispatch a single troop. The others turned to look, but didn't fire their odd looking rifles. Their movements were lethargic and abnormal, and Gav guessed Crasor was impairing them somehow. He tried to understand what the Breaker was doing, but every time Gav began to see it, it slipped out of his grasp.

Crasor stabbed the pointy fingers of his right hand into each of the enforcers in turn, and they collapsed, convulsing. "Let's keep moving," Crasor yelled back, picking up one of the enforcer's ungainly looking weapons. "This will cause some beneficial chaos."

As Gav ran by the still twitching forms, they began to rise to their feet. *Is that how I looked after my conversion?* he thought, trying not to trip. Things were happening so quickly since the Breakers arrived. *This is only the beginning.*

When they finally reached the door to the Council chamber, Crasor stopped. Gav halted as well. They'd descended four levels to reach this place, but the Families had unleashed every weapon and guard under their control. Pain still coursed from Gav's stump, but as time had gone on, he'd been able to compartmentalize it and focus on fighting.

Gav had expected things to get easier as they penetrated deeper and deeper into the building, but the Families isolated each security and weapons system, preventing a complete takeover. This had caused tense situations, especially when they'd encountered devious traps. Gav had thought he knew this building and it's capabilities fairly well, but obviously the Council kept him ignorant. The thought made him snarl.

"These are your betrayers," Crasor said, motioning Gav towards the heavy doors. "It is only fitting you get your revenge. But remember, you may only kill those bound for blackness, as I said before. The rest have secrets and knowledge that will be an asset to the Breakers. Feel free to inflict as much pain as you would like, however."

Gav nodded. As he stepped forward, a suspicion Crasor might place some Family Council higher than him in the Breakers sparked in his mind. *No,* he thought, reaching out to touch the control for the heavy doors. *None of them will rise higher than I.*

The doors retracted. Flechette needles began whistling into the wall behind them. Gav stayed out of the line of fire, waiting. He was glad those in the room weren't equipped with energy beam weapons. There had been enough of those on the way down here, and it was the only thing he actually feared.

Gav found the well of power within himself. It was still a difficult task, but considering just an hour or two ago he'd been unable to touch it at all, he didn't mind. He used the strength to reach out and grab space-time, folding it around him as Crasor had demonstrated. His grip threatened to fail, but Gav bore down, exerting his will. The folds stabilized and he knew the cloak was solid. Flechette darts continued to streak through the doorway, but they were growing less frequent. Still, he didn't want to risk additional injury, so he dropped down to his single hand and knees. It was awkward trying to crawl this way, but Gav made it work. He knew it had to look silly, but Crasor said nothing, and his desire for revenge overrode thoughts of shame.

Once he was inside the expansive room, he moved off to the side before rising to his feet. His strength was solid and the cloak still in place. Gav took a second to enjoy the moment. The heads of the Families had clustered themselves on the other side of the room, barricaded behind some metal furniture. He could see the fear in their eyes. It had been a long time since any of these people had been in real danger. *They are out of practice,* Gav thought, casually strolling towards them.

The only one who did not seem terrified was Salla Markond. The look of grim determination in her eyes chilled Gav. *What is she planning?* he wondered, trying to think of a strategy of his own.

As he neared the group, Gav kept his steps slow and silent. The crack and boom of the flechette pistols was frequent enough to make this unnecessary, but he wasn't going to risk anything spoiling his revenge. A strange sensation flooded through his mind, making him stop. *None? Not a single one?* Crasor had marked all the Council members bound for the Seed. *All protected,* he seethed, *but perhaps pain is more fitting than death anyway.*

Gav resumed stalking towards them, carefully keeping the edge of his cloak out of range. He tried to draw it closer to his body, but the strain threatened to collapse it altogether, so he relented.

Sliding in behind the group, Gav stopped. He savored the moment, having them all at his mercy. *And they don't even know I'm here.* He smiled, taking a step towards Salla. *First or last?* He thought about it for a moment. *Last.* After holstering his flechette pistol, Gav drew one of his synth-diamond combat knives. Usually he wielded one in each hand, but with his right hand a charred stump, he'd have to settle for just the one. Holding the knife in a reverse grip, edge out, he relished the situation for a moment longer. *Blood will flow.*

Darting forward, Gav raked the transparent blade across the back of one of the council members. The old man screamed in pain even as crimson stained his elegant clothes. Gav moved sideways, punching the knife through the thigh of a second, prone enemy. He then leapt backwards, getting himself outside their visual range.

Confusion and chaos overtook the Council as they frantically looked for the invisible attacker. Gav watched Salla intently, needing to see terror on her face. But she stayed calm, her only reaction a narrowing of the eyes. *Perhaps she thinks we will spare her because of her status,* Gav thought, gritting his teeth. He slipped over to the other side of the group, now completely distracted by the bleeding men.

Pret Alenthos was one of them. Gav moved in, deftly flipping the knife in his hand to a traditional grip. Keeping his footfalls silent, he stalked to within a meter of the old bugger. Pulling the knife back, he stepped forward, slamming it into his kidneys. "You may not die," Gav whispered in the hateful man's ear, using his diminished right arm to cover the scream, "but I'll make you suffer."

Gav tried to drag Pret backwards, to get out of the Council's sight before they realized what was happening, but the old man was stronger than he realized. Without a hand, Gav's arm slipped away from Pret's mouth and the old man shrieked.

The remaining Council members turned, and those inside his cloak radius raised their weapons. Thankfully, Pret was a meat shield between them, and none were willing to risk firing. Salla smiled, her deep blue eyes sparkling viciously. Gav noticed she kept both hands beneath her jacket.

"So, Gav," she said, stepping away from the group, "you've returned." She was being too confident, too in control. Her whole world was falling down, and she was talking casually. "It's hard for me to imagine that decrypting our files gave you the power to overthrow the entirety of Exis-7." She paused for a moment, the intensity of her stare boring into him. Pret whimpered, and Gav twisted the knife a little farther, causing him to scream. "Obviously you have an alliance with an outside party. May I inquire who it is?"

Gav felt thrown off balance by her composure, and his mind raced for an answer. As words formed on his tongue, he heard Crasor enter on the other side of the room.

"We are the Breakers," Crasor announced. Everyone turned to look, and Gav used the opportunity to shove Pret away from him and back out of visible range. Only at the last moment did he realize Salla was still staring at him, but it didn't matter. She didn't have a weapon trained on him anyway. Gav moved silently towards the side of the room, knowing she couldn't see through his cloak, but still feeling exposed.

"And what is a Breaker?" Salla asked, turning to face Crasor.

"That requires much explanation," Crasor shrugged. "It is something best experienced firsthand."

"I would rather not."

"I don't think you understand the situation," Crasor said, his voice deepening to a growl. "You don't have a choice."

"There is always a choice," Salla replied, pulling her hands out from beneath her large jacket. Clasped in one of them was a small device. "This is what I believe was historically called a dead man's switch," she continued, holding it up. "Gav should recognize it. Injure or kill me and my hand opens, the switch triggers, and a fusion weapon in the sub-levels reduces the building to particles. You didn't see it, since you came in through the roof, but I assure you it's there."

Gav wondered if he could dart in and grab the device before she saw him, but he felt a command in his mind to stay still, emanating from Crasor. "A wise precaution indeed," Crasor replied, his voice losing its aggression. "It appears we are under your control. Gav, let them see you so there aren't any unfortunate accidents." Gritting his teeth in anger, Gav complied, trying to keep a calm look on his face. "Now," Crasor continued, "perhaps we can discuss this."

"Indeed," Salla said, a smile tainting the corners of her severe look. "Give me a position in your organization. You are obviously quite powerful, but so am I. The Families are growing quite dull anyway."

"What?" one of the uninjured Council members snarled. "You can't do that to us." The rest of them began yelling, their lack of control showing Gav how weak they really were. *I used to look up to them, used to want to be one of them.* Now he just felt disgusted.

"I can, I will, and I am," Salla replied, her words cutting through the chaos. "Your lack of forethought or intelligence proves you don't deserve anything, not even life." Despite his desire for revenge, Gav felt some of his respect for Salla return.

Crasor laughed, a loud, cruel sound that filled the silence following Salla's declaration. "I admire your lack of compunction for your fellow Council members," he said, walking towards her. "And yes, I will make you a Breaker, although I'm sure you don't understand what that means."

Salla stepped back, holding the device up between them. "No tricks," she said, eyes narrowing.

"No tricks," Crasor replied. "But one thing you must know, is that all these friends will be coming with you."

"That's unacceptable," Salla answered, looking confused. "I will never be able to trust them again. I'll be dead as soon as I sleep."

"Oh, give them time. In fact, it won't take much at all."

"No," Salla said, gritting her teeth. "It is my way, or we are all cleansed in stellar fire."

Crasor sighed. "I thought for once I might be able to get by with reason, especially with someone of your intelligence, but I have too much hope for humans." The group of Councilors went slack faced. Gav sensed Crasor was using the same compulsion he'd implemented several times as they'd fought their way to this room.

Looking back at Salla, Gav saw her face twisted in a snarl. It twitched and shuddered before finally going slack as well. As Crasor stepped forward, she flipped a small toggle on her device.

The Breaker leader took it from her and stepped back. "There," he said, "now we can proceed without any nuclear interruptions."

After a moment, Salla shook her head and blinked, as if clearing her mind. The rest of the group stayed complacent, and Gav barely noticed them.

Salla stared into Crasor's eyes, a look of wonder coming over her. "Teach me," she said, sounding desperate. "Show me how to do that. I will give you whatever you want, do whatever you require. I will serve you completely."

"I accept," Crasor said, a smile twisting his face, "and you shall." He stepped forward and plunged the fingers of his right hand into her abdomen. A look of ecstasy formed on Salla's face as she collapsed to the floor, convulsing.

Competition, Gav thought, feeling his previous joy and elation evaporate.

42 – CAZZ-AK-TAK

As Cazz-ak and Lothis made their way around the edge of the cavern, Cazz-ak mentally reached out to the surrounding space. He sensed Tremmilly, the Queen, and the shattered bodies of his troops. The corruption of the Breakers told him there were more below in addition to those in the city. These dark splotches felt similar to Aeron, the Breaker that had nearly killed him back on Malesis' ship.

"These Breakers," he told Lothis over the raging battle, "they're abnormal, different from the ones we dealt with on the Justice."

"What do you mean?"

"They have more power, abilities their predecessors did not." Cazz-ak wished he could explain further, but his feelings were too jumbled. He didn't have time to focus and refine his observations. Lothis fell silent, looking determined.

When they reached the back of the main cavern, Cazz-ak felt a new fear creep up inside him. He'd only been in the sub-levels a few times, as part of an exploration team when the Entho-la-ah-mines had first arrived on world. After that, no one had ventured down, leaving only a faint and bewildering mental map.

Cazz-ak turned to look at Lothis. He could see, both in physical and mental aspects, the boy was struggling. The stories he'd told of his experience on Haak-ah-tar, of his confinement, the darkness and the monstrosities, made Cazz-ak wonder if he'd be able to go forward. "We need light," he said, trying to ignore the cloud hanging over them. Walking over to a small hollow in a nearby wall, he picked up an organic cylinder of bioluminescent algae and handed it to Lothis. He took one for himself, carrying it with his front left leg. It made him less agile, but he could still walk.

As they started down the ever-narrowing passage way, Cazz-ak continued trying to strengthen his connection to the Great Thought. It was difficult, and he gained no progress. Something was blocking him, a static or interference, making it hard to immerse himself. The link to his Elrahi mind was clear, so it seemed most likely the Breakers were dampening the Great Thought.

They went deeper and deeper as the corridors branched, merged, and expanded quicker than Cazz-ak could keep track of. "How will we find our way back?" Lothis asked, and Cazz-ak guessed even with his exceptional mental abilities, the boy too had lost track.

"We keep heading up, following our essence." Their passage would create a mental trail, but it wouldn't be strong enough to last long. Cazz-ak didn't tell Lothis, not wanting to create additional pressure.

More time passed. Tremmilly and the Queen's energy wavered. It felt similar to the current feeling of the Great Thought, and Cazz-ak guessed the two phenomena shared a connection. As they descended deeper into Lith-elo-hi-rosh, he felt the locations of Tremmilly and the Queen resolve and separate. "They aren't together," Cazz-ak said, unable to think of a reason why that would be a good thing.

"Who do we go after first?" Lothis asked, a question Cazz-ak was avoiding in his own mind.

"I don't know," he answered. The blue light of the algae illuminated a huge branch in their tunnel, and Cazz-ak knew he would have to decide.

"Tremmilly would want us to help Na-ah-co first. She came down here to do just that."

Cazz-ak knew Lothis was right, but he felt torn in two. His Elrahi self said to assist the Empress. Tremmilly was the most important of them all. He'd also spent the last 400 years of consciousness as an Entho-la-ah-mine, had struggled and sacrificed to bring a new queen into existence, going to great lengths to protect her.

"I don't think we should split up," Lothis continued. "If these Breakers are more powerful, we need to concentrate our strength as much as possible. Crasor and Aeron have been the strongest we've faced so far. We defeated them by working as a team."

Cazz-ak had to agree, but it didn't make the decision easier. He stalled for a moment longer, knowing their chances of saving either of them diminished by the second. "The Queen," he said finally.

"Let's move." Lothis led them down the right most corridor, moving as quickly as the rough floor and dim illumination allowed. Cazz-ak tried to push thoughts of self-condemnation out of his mind, knowing he had to focus. It felt impossible, images of the Empress dying threatening to overwhelm him.

"We need to turn around," Lothis said as the shaft they'd chosen bent away from the Queen. Cazz-ak was about to agree when a laugh startled him.

"Divide and destroy," a female voice said. Cazz-ak brought up a shield of mental energy as a lance darker than the surrounding blackness streaked towards him. The point of darkness slammed into his barrier, but Cazz-ak held strong. As he watched, the dark energy began inexorably boring through. Lothis created a barrier of his own, meshing their strength. Although it wasn't as thick as Cazz-ak's, its additional power stopped the Breaker weapon. The lance disappeared, but Cazz-ak and Lothis kept their shield in place.

"Crasor said we wouldn't be powerful enough to take you on as a united group, especially with your bug hive backing you up, but then you did us the favor of separating." The female voice laughed again. A tall figure emerged from the darkness. Her skin was black, glinting faintly in the blue light of the algae. "Did you believe we wouldn't find you and your precious planet?"

Two more darkly glinting figures strode out of the blackness behind the tall Breaker, one male, one female. "It took some time to find this place. We had to move quickly to arrive while you were fighting your pathetic war, but here we are."

Cazz-ak tried to think of a counter-attack or at least a response, but he felt stunned. His mind churned. In the next instant, despite his bewilderment, he felt both the Queen and Tremmilly's energy vanish. The startled look on Lothis' face told him he'd lost them as well.

The tall Breaker smiled sadistically. *She knows,* Cazz-ak thought, feeling his Harbinger power growing. *They did something to them.* Dropping the shield, Cazz-ak summoned his dull red cubes, three of them filling up the space between them and the Breakers.

"Your weak Elrahi weaponry may have worked at one point," the Breaker said, snorting, "but now you face Descended." A solid block of something Cazz-ak had never seen before engulfed his cubes and he felt it absorb his energy. He tried to pull back, to disengage, but it trapped his mind, even as the cubes shrank.

"It's like a singularity," Lothis said. Cazz-ak felt himself draining away, a coldness filling him.

A moment later, a light as bright as any star came into being inside the Descended's weapon. A sudden burst of energy filled Cazz-ak.

"Can't hold it much longer," Lothis said, strain creasing his face.

"I'm out," Cazz-ak said.

"We need to flee," Lothis replied, his bright ball of stellar energy still burning between them and the Descended.

"We can't run," Cazz-ak replied, drawing on every scrap of power he could. "Not this time. Our friends are relying on us."

Lothis said nothing, only nodded. A grim determination settled over him, even as his energy ball winked out.

Cazz-ak was ready. Before his eyes adjusted to the dark, he acted. He formed the cubes once again, only this time they were smaller, a more energetic red. In the next instant, he spun and launched them towards the trio of Descended. They shattered the energy drain, obliterating it. When the blur of whirling cubes reached the figures, they deflected off a shield, and went careening through the stone ceiling. A grinding sound accompanied a blast of rock and gravel. Cazz-ak let the cubes dissipate, knowing that changing their trajectory would take more energy than summoning new ones.

Lothis flared with energy as a narrow beam of particles shot from him. It was thinner and more densely concentrated than a standard lance. It also moved faster. The beam slammed into the Descended's shield, heading straight for the leader's head. Unfortunately, breaking the barrier deflected it, sending it into the male's torso instead. A mist of black particles filled the air as the Breaker collapsed to the floor. The leader bared her teeth, a snarl that made her human features look monstrous and unrecognizable.

"I grow tired of this play," she growled. "You aren't as fun as I'd hoped." As Cazz-ak watched, the two remaining Descended each sent tendrils of dark power out, combining and intertwining them. A sense of dread welled up in Cazz-ak. He knew Lothis had been right to suggest flight. Looking down at the boy, he saw his own emotions mirrored on his face.

Before they could retreat, a flaring arc of dark power surged towards them, filling the entire tunnel. Blackness swallowed up Cazz-ak's vision as the energy slammed into him.

43 – TREMMILLY

You have to keep going, Tremmilly thought, worried she'd somehow attract the Breakers' attention. *The Queen needs you.* Earlier, when she stepped from the underground city into the tunnel, she felt the claustrophobic weight of all the stone and dirt above her. That feeling still lingered, a nagging sensation refusing to go away. Thankfully, she'd grabbed two bioluminescent lights. This pushed the darkness away, allowing Tremmilly to keep her emotions under control. She checked to make sure Beowulf was at her side. His presence brought additional comfort. Tremmilly wished Maxar was here with her in human form, but having part of him present as the wolf-dog was amazing.

They'd already passed numerous junctions. Each forced Tremmilly to focus hard on the Queen. All she had was a vague direction and sense of proximity. That wasn't good enough to find her, not quickly anyway.

Using her Elrahi strength, Tremmilly touched the surrounding space. *The Queen's path,* she thought excitedly, seeing a faint, yet distinctive line through the darkness. Cazz-ak had told them the Entho-la-ah-mines navigated in this fashion, following the trails of those who'd gone before. Excitement bubbled up in Tremmilly as she opened the top of her second bioluminescent light. She took a small bit of the blue algae and smeared it on the floor, creating an arrow that was barely noticeable. *The way out,* she thought, feeling a bit of relief. Each arrow she drew gave her confidence to venture deeper into the maze of tunnels.

With her mind squarely locked on the path of the Queen, Tremmilly moved more confidently. At each junction, she continued marking with arrows. Early on, she'd also tried to memorize the sequence of turns, but it quickly became too much to remember.

Tremmilly lost track of time, continuing to follow the Queen's trail. The path grew stronger, which led her to believe she was getting close. Several times, Tremmilly heard the Breakers prowling elsewhere in the tunnel system. Once, she even saw white light reflect around a bend. She darted down a side path, throwing her jacket over the bio lights until she was sure the Breakers weren't coming after her.

After several additional junctions, the trail led into a low, narrow passage. Tremmilly knew she would have to crawl. The idea of entering an even more confined space was revolting, but it led towards the Queen. Getting down on all fours, Tremmilly crawled inside, pushing her lights ahead. She could hear Beowulf behind her, so she shut the fear out of her mind.

A few seconds later, Tremmilly saw Na-ah-co's exoskeleton shimmering in the blue light. "Greetings, Tremmilly," the Queen said in her mind, turning to face her. Their eyes met, and despite the anatomical difference between their species, Tremmilly could see she was in pain. "How did you find me?"

"I followed the path of your energy."

"How is that possible?"

"Using my Elrahi abilities. We have to get out of the caves. The Breakers are everywhere, but I think if we can leave the sub-tunnels, we can escape them."

"So many have died," Na-ah-co said, not seeming to hear Tremmilly. "There are more cities on Lith-elo-hi-rosh, and a few other Entho-la-ah-mine worlds remain, but we are close to extinction."

"I know," Tremmilly replied, feeling her heart break. She'd gotten to know the Entho-la-ah-mine queen somewhat after Wake had brought them aboard Jaydon's ship. Since the Harbingers had come to Lith-elo, there'd been little additional contact. The Queen was busy doing her job, and although Tremmilly had been an empress, she didn't understand the intricacies of the Entho-la-ah-mines. "We must get out of here, or else more will die. Your people need you."

"Yes," the Queen said, and Tremmilly could hear her strength returning. "I'm ashamed to admit I lost my way. My path will have faded away between here and the exit. I don't know how to get out."

"That's OK," Tremmilly smiled. "I made marks on the way in. We should be able to follow them instead."

"That was a smart—" Na-ah-co cut off mid-sentence. Tremmilly could hear it too. A scuffling of boots on stone. She scrunched herself up and turned around in the small space, trying not to make any noise. Over Beowulf's shoulder, she could see a white light shining outside the mouth of their tunnel, less than ten meters away. Tremmilly shoved the bio light under herself. She barely noticed the cylinder poking her in the ribs. Darkness swallowed them up, and Tremmilly felt tense. *They won't know we are here. Didn't find me before, and they were almost as close.*

The light intensified, and the faint scuffing grew louder, until a pair of boots stopped just outside the low tunnel. *Don't look in,* Tremmilly pleaded. *Just keep going.*

"How are we ever supposed to find a blighthearted bug down in this buggering maze?" A gruff male voice asked.

"Do you feel that?" a female responded.

"What? All I can sense is Detri and Yuith. I could feel Jaras a moment before, but now he is gone."

"No, no. Not them. This is different. It feels human. Might be the bug. Feels like both combined."

"A Harbinger?"

"Don't know, but it's close."

The pair of boots disappeared. Tremmilly breathed easier. Despite the danger, she felt a sensation stir the back of her mind. *Lothis and Cazz-ak,* she thought. They were above her, getting closer every second. *Help is coming!* She wondered how long she'd sensed them, but was distracted by the situation. *Maybe they are almost here!*

Tremmilly briefly wondered what had happened to Felar, but a moment later, the boots returned and she forgot about everything else.

"It's strongest here," the female said.

"But we've checked all the tunnels."

"That doesn't change that it's close to this spot."

Seconds passed, and Tremmilly held her breath. The light outside the small tunnel flared and dimmed erratically.

"What's that?"

An angular female face filled the tunnel exit just before a blinding flash of light stunned Tremmilly.

"I told you," the female voice growled. "They're in this little tube. Let's go in and pull them out."

Tremmilly bumped her head in her haste to turn around. As her eyes adjusted, she saw the Queen doing the same thing, although more fluidly. They began crawling as fast as they could.

"I don't know how much farther this goes," Na-ah-co said. She was in control of her fear, but it was still evident in her voice. "It might be a dead end."

"We will face it as it comes," Tremmilly replied, a statement she'd heard Maxar use before. She glanced over her shoulder, checking to make sure Beowulf was behind her. The shaggy wolf-dog was at her heels. Behind him, she caught a hurried glance of jittering white light.

As they progressed, the top of the tunnel began to drop, forcing Tremmilly lower and lower. Just when she thought she wouldn't be able to go any farther, the passageway opened up into a large chamber. Tremmilly turned and pulled Beowulf through the last claustrophobic meter.

Several large rocks lay in range of her light, and they gave Tremmilly an idea. Grabbing the heaviest one she could move quickly, she pushed it into the tunnel's exit. She caught a brief glimpse of light as she bent down, and part of her wanted to run. *No. Finish this and you won't have to.* Tremmilly picked up a second large rock and shoved it behind the first. As she grabbed another, she saw Na-ah-co rolling a stone of her own towards the entrance. When they stacked them inside the tunnel, Tremmilly could hear muffled cursing as the Breakers reached the blockage.

Looking around for more rocks, Tremmilly realized there were none. *It isn't enough,* she thought, hearing scraping inside the tunnel as the Breakers began moving the obstruction.

"Why are we waiting?" Na-ah-co asked, voice sounding desperate. "We must go."

"Wait," Tremmilly replied, shutting out the distraction of their impeding capture. *I may not be able to form weapons, but I'm not totally powerless.* She reached out, meshing her mind with space-time. The Breakers were a dark, snarling splotch of energy, reaching out to grab her. She shielded herself, careful to stay outside the radius of their strength. Tracing the elemental matrix of the rock, Tremmilly found a system of weaknesses between the grains.

Perfect, she thought, feeding power into the void spaces. They expanded, slowly at first, but then more quickly. The desperate yells of the Breakers were drowned by a huge crack and subsequent rumbling. Dust and debris shot out of the tunnel, then all was silent.

Tremmilly smiled, feeling relieved.

"Can they survive that?" Na-ah-co asked.

"I don't know, but at least we bought time."

"Unfortunately, even if we killed both, I think we now face new problems."

"What do you mean?"

"They can track us. They know how to find our energy. We can no longer hide."

Tremmilly's heart sank. "But don't they need to be close?"

"Perhaps. But now that they know what to look for, I don't think we can rely on distance. And without your marks, we have no idea how to get out. If we can figure out how to pull our minds back, to cloak our energy, then I believe we can solve the first of those problems."

"I don't know how."

"We will discover it together. I think I understand what I need to do." The Queen paused for a moment. "I will disconnect myself from the Great Thought."

"Won't that hurt you?"

"Maybe, but death or capture is far worse than pain." The Queen fell silent for several moments, and Tremmilly sensed it was important to be quiet.

"It is done," Na-ah-co said finally, voice strained.

"How can I still hear you in my mind?"

"Our communication is not a result of my connection to the Great Thought. I don't understand the exact science, but it is near-field and low power. The Breakers shouldn't sense it, not without being within meters of us."

My Elrahi strength, Tremmilly realized, understanding how the Breakers could track her. *But how do I sever that? Is it even possible?*

"I think I need to disconnect from my Elrahi being," Tremmilly said, not quite understanding what she meant. Na-ah-co didn't reply, and Tremmilly set to work. For a moment she didn't know what to do, but then finally inspiration struck. Do the opposite of how you increase your connection.

Normally, she reached out to the surrounding space-time and all the particles and atoms it contained. Now, she focused on creating distance, separating herself from that existence. Her core protested, not wanting to give up the beautiful thing she had so recently rediscovered.

Atom by atom and strand by strand, Tremmilly severed the connection. Pain rose, threatening to crescendo in an annihilating swell. *Can't stop,* she thought, knowing if she couldn't shield herself, the Breakers would find and kill them anyway.

Finally, something broke, and Tremmilly felt her link to Felar, Lothis, and Cazz-ak disappear. She couldn't sense them anymore, and she guessed they wouldn't feel her either. *They won't find us now.* She reached to scratch Beowulf behind the ear, once again taking comfort in his presence.

"We are alone," Na-ah-co said, echoing Tremmilly's fear, "but we still have each other."

Tremmilly nodded, smiling. "Let's go find my blaze trail before the Breakers find us again."

As they moved on, Tremmilly wondered what had created the tunnel system. She'd read several geology books back on Eishon-2, but nothing she'd learned would explain the process that created this. Her mind drifted, as the monotony of the search took over.

Initially, Tremmilly expected prolonged disconnection from her Elrahi being would be painful, much like how it felt for the Entho-la-ah-mines to separate from the Great Thought, but that wasn't the case. *You lived this way for 21 years,* she thought. *If anything, it feels more natural.*

As they reached a junction, Tremmilly concealed their single remaining bio light. She'd lost the other in the haste of their escape. She looked around for any faint blue arrows, but there was nothing. Tremmilly sighed, removing the cylinder from under her jacket and continuing onward. Na-ah-co and Beowulf's quiet foot falls told her they still followed.

More time passed and Tremmilly wondered how Felar, Lothis, and Cazz-ak were faring against the Breakers. *They will destroy them,* she thought, remembering Cazz-ak as her Elrahi Protector and Felar as a Sentry. *And Lothis is your brother.* The idea still seemed strange, but it was beginning to sit better as time passed. *We were close as Elrahi, and we will be close again.* The thought brought a smile to her face.

At the next junction, Tremmilly repeated the procedure. "There!" Na-ah-co said excitedly. Tremmilly found it, a wave of relief flooding through her. The arrow was small, but clearly visible, pointing towards one of the three twisting passages leading from this spot. Tremmilly followed it. It felt so good to find the way back towards the surface.

The next way point took slightly longer to find, as she'd draw the arrow on rock that faced away, but eventually they were on track again. *We're doing it!* Tremmilly thought exultantly, proud her plan was working.

At the next junction, she immediately spotted the glowing blue arrow. When Tremmilly started in that direction, a pair of Breakers came around a corner just ahead of her. She tried to dive out of sight, but shouts told her it was already too late. "This way," she whispered, running down the nearest side corridor. After a moment, she turned back to see if the Breakers were following. Their yells echoed and faded in the distance. *They went down a different tunnel,* she thought, calming her breathing.

"We got away," Tremmilly whispered, looking around. Only Beowulf was with her. Queen Na-ah-co was nowhere to be seen.

44 – LOTHIS

In the instant before the black energy smashed into him, Lothis cast a small shield around himself. It was weak, barely extending beyond his skin. The arc collided with his barrier. The resulting interaction sent him flying backwards. A flash of light and a thunderous boom overwhelmed his senses as his shield evaporated. For a moment, he couldn't tell where he was or what was happening. Then he careened from one rough stone wall to another. When he finally bounced to a stop on the floor, agony hit him. Lothis had never broken a bone before, but based on the pain in his ribs, arms, and legs, that had changed. Every gouge, scrape, and laceration burned.

Lothis' head spun. He tried to find Cazz-ak. All around him was darkness. He'd lost his bioluminescent light. Casting his mind out, he looked for Cazz-ak's energy. *You're assuming he is alive,* Lothis thought, desperately hoping they hadn't obliterated his friend.

Several frantic seconds passed before he finally found Cazz-ak. His energy wasn't strong, but it was still there. Lothis tried to stand, but the movement almost made him pass out. So he began crawling instead, meter by painful meter.

As his eyes began to adjust, he realized there was a tiny bit of light. The blast had smeared algae across the wall, the streak terminating in a broken light on the floor. Lothis could finally see Cazz-ak, a few meters back towards the Descended. He wasn't moving.

Lothis heard the enemy approaching, voices loud and jeering with promises of what was to come. He shut the Breakers out of his mind, focusing instead on Cazz-ak. *Can't let him die alone,* Lothis thought, knowing even as a pair they'd been unable to stand against this trio of Descended. *I have no chance alone,* he despaired.

When he reached Cazz-ak's side, he had to bite his lip hard to keep from bursting into tears. The dark energy had mangled his friend, and

Lothis briefly recalled the memory of standing over Cazz-ak when he'd been an Elrahi Protector, broken and battered from his fight with See'dek. He'd recovered then. Lothis wasn't sure he would now.

Two of his legs were missing on the right side, now just bloody stumps. Cracks split his exoskeleton. The blast had bent one of the legs on his left side to an unnatural angle. He looked dead, but when Lothis checked, life still moved within.

He briefly considered trying to pull Cazz-ak with him to safety, but he didn't think he could even flee by himself.

The Descended were close now. They had activated an illumination device, concealing their bodies behind the harsh light. *This is how you die,* Lothis thought, embracing Cazz-ak.

"You are strong, Harbinger," the Descended leader said, "stronger than your friend. It is a shame you have bound yourself for darkness instead of the Seed." Lothis looked up to see the tall female looming over him. Her metallic skin reflected the light where it wasn't concealed under her dark combat suit. He felt a flare of energy, and a black mind dagger materialized in her hand. "You tried. You failed. Your end has come, just as we knew it would. Once we subjugate the Entho queen, we'll add the strength of the Great Thought to the power of the One. The remnants of humanity will be a trivial foe."

Lothis lost track of the Breaker's gloating as he thought about the lance and ball of stellar energy he'd created. Both were new. He'd never seen either done before. He'd flipped his singularity to create the stellar ball and energized and confined the lance to make it more effective. *But those things won't help you now,* he thought, feeling drained. *And besides, their defense is too strong.*

He felt the draw of space-time around him, the desire to flee his coming death. If my body dies, what happens to my consciousness?

With a start, Lothis realized the Descended had raised her dagger. "May darkness take all who oppose us."

No time, he thought, grabbing both space-time and the spark of Cazz-ak's life. He acted instinctively, not understanding how he could take hold of the unconscious Harbinger's energy. Despite the pain and diminished energy, Lothis felt united with the flow of the universe, his intuition more powerful than ever.

Growling, the Descended brought her dagger down. Lothis had a brief sensation of intense pain as black energy entered his eye. Then, he was gone.

45 – MAXAR

"Two minutes till the surface," Dras said calmly.

"Affirm," Maxar replied, trying not to look at the rapidly growing Lith-elo.

"No way we will slow down in time," Jaydon said under his breath.

Maxar trusted the sentient machine, despite his own unease. They would be stuck on Traynos-6 otherwise, captured or killed by the Ashamine. Dras had gotten them here faster than any of them thought possible. *He's nothing like the Breakers, and that means the nanites inside me are nothing like them either.*

Thinking about the tiny machines coursing in his blood recalled the feeling of hyper-awareness and strength he'd experienced. In the short time they'd spent traveling back to Lith-elo, he and Dras had done their best to exchange information. Maxar had a better understanding of his nano-tech augmentation. Now he was excited to put it to use.

The view surrounding the ship shifted rapidly, pulling Maxar out of his reverie. He looked to Dras.

"A ship just lifted off the surface," Dras explained. "I maneuvered us to an intercept course. The energy signatures of those on board are muddled. I cannot say for certain what the ship contains, but I do know it is a gunship, Ashamine in origin."

With each word Dras said, Maxar felt terror build within him. Thoughts bombarded his mind, questions of Tremmilly's safety, of the condition of the Entho-la-ah-mines and the rest of his friends. *Who is on the ship? Did the Breakers capture someone or are they fleeing in defeat? Is Crasor on board?*

Maxar knew Felar and Cazz-ak could fight, but what if the Breakers had ambushed them? *And Tremmilly,* he thought, heart clenching, *she learned how to use human weapons, but if the Breakers cloak or shield themselves? She's defenseless.*

Reconnecting to the Heltasoth ship, Maxar shut out the cascade of information that had previously overwhelmed him. He'd practiced this a few times during the journey, and now was able to reach out and find the Breaker vessel. With his human mind, he couldn't analyze the data with nearly the resolution Dras could, but Maxar still wanted to try. *Perhaps I can sense if Tremmilly is on board,* he thought, feeling desperate. Moments passed, and Maxar felt nothing more than Dras had already told them.

After disconnecting from the ship, he tried using his Elrahi connection. *Nothing,* he thought, wondering if this was a good or bad sign. *You're still learning. What if you blighthearted it up? What if the Breakers have them shielded?*

"Can you shoot them down?" Wake asked.

"They could all be on the ship," Maxar said, biting his lip, "the Harbingers, the Queen, our friends. We don't know. If we shoot them down, we could kill everyone."

"Wake, the weapons on this vessel are capable of what you ask," Dras replied. "While I wish I could just disable their maneuvering thrusters or main propulsion, I don't believe I can be that precise. As Maxar said, if I strike, it will likely result in the death of everyone on board, friend and enemy alike."

"If any Harbingers or Entho-la-ah-mines are on that ship," Jaydon said, voice grim, "do you want to let the Breakers have them? Besides, we might not be able to take them out. It's a small, maneuverable gunship and we don't know what modifications or abilities the Breakers might have."

"What if we wait till they leave atmosphere?" Wake said. "Then, if we disable them, they won't crash back to the surface. We can board them and rescue any prisoners."

As Wake finished speaking, Dras took them in behind the fleeing gunship. Ion tracers immediately began streaming towards them. The Heltasoth ship maneuvered to avoid the cannon rounds, but Maxar could feel it was only a matter of time till one hit. *And what then?* Dras hadn't said how much armor his ship had, if any.

"The longer we wait," Jaydon said, "the more opportunity they have to get away or hit us. If we let them out into space, we risk Breaker backup or some other surprise. We have to take them out now."

"Jaydon's right," Maxar said, feeling a cold determination overcome him. "Dras, do the best you can to disable them without destroying the vessel."

"As you wish," he replied, a bright lance of violet light streaking out from the Heltasoth ship. As it neared the fleeing vessel, the Breaker ship disappeared.

"What happened?" Jaydon asked. "Did the beam do that?"

"No," Dras said, sounding puzzled. "It is the weakest weapon I have, meant to destroy small sections of hull, not dissolve an entire vessel. Could they have generated a worm? I don't detect a signature. Is it the cloaking you told me of?"

"Possibly," Maxar replied.

"With the Breakers," Wake interjected, "anything is possible."

Maxar reached out again, using his mind's connection to space-time to find the fleeing vessel. *If they wormed away, all hope is lost, especially if Dras can't find a signature to follow.* Seconds dragged by. Maxar felt nothing. Then, he sensed it.

"It's a cloak or a warp," Maxar blurted. "I can feel it. Space-time is bent around an object the size of the Breaker ship."

"If I can't see them," Dras replied, "I can't hit them. I'm sorry."

Maxar desperately tried to think of a way to stop the fleeing ship. *If our weapons are useless...*

"So, what," Jaydon said, "we can't stop them?"

Dras shrugged, his mannerisms so human it made sense he'd blended in with the Brotherhood of Azak-so. *He's a good observer and mimic,* Maxar thought, distracted for a moment.

"Maybe they won't be able to cloak indefinitely?" Wake asked. "The power requirement has to be huge."

"We can't take the risk," Maxar said, focusing. Something shifted inside him, instinct taking hold. He knew what to do. "I have a plan. Wake, bond with me." The saying evoked a sense of power within Maxar. It was old, connected to his Elrahi memories.

The engineer looked puzzled for a moment, then his eyes widened. "OK, you got it."

Maxar felt Wake embrace his Elrahi strength, and he did the same. He filled himself up, drawing on as much of it as he could before taking Wake's as well. Power flowed through him, and he felt ready to begin.

Reaching out with his mind, Maxar took hold of the Breaker's warp and pulled. Immediately, he felt resistance, but kept tugging.

"I saw the ship for a moment," Dras said. "Keep trying."

Maxar gave a massive heave. The warp unraveled, smoothing out and dissipating.

Violet light shone as Dras energized the beam weapon again. In the next instant, Maxar saw a massive lance of dark energy streaking towards him from the Breaker ship. His eyes went wide. Raising his hand defensively, Maxar summoned all the Elrahi energy available to him. Instinct took over, and the nanites within him connected to the Heltasoth ship, supplying further power.

Blightheart you buggers to the fires of the dark star, Maxar raged, his collected power bursting out into a concentrated shield. The dark lance struck. Light exploded in Maxar's mind, blinding him.

"Direct hit," Dras said. Maxar felt himself waver for a second, then collapse to the floor.

"What happened?" Jaydon asked. Maxar felt a hand on his arm. "You OK? Maxar? Blightheart. Why is he always passing out?"

Slowly, Maxar felt vision and bodily control return to him. He sat up. "What happened?

"We disabled the enemy ship," Dras answered. "It's falling back to the surface. I will follow it and land nearby, in the event of survivors. I caution you not to become optimistic. I sense a spike in energy consistent with a power core breach. The erratic movement and small size of the ship made such a strike likely. Even if the impact with the ground doesn't kill everyone, the heat will."

Maxar regained his feet and stood next to everyone as they watched the Breaker ship tumble towards the surface of Lith-elo. He wanted to talk about what had just happened, how he'd deflected or absorbed the Breaker weapon, but thoughts of Tremmilly and his friends quickly overrode it. A sick feeling grew inside him. *We killed them all,* he thought, as the atmosphere ripped away pieces of armor plate and heat shielding. The wreck began to glow, tumbling.

"Can a Breaker survive that?" Wake asked. Maxar had no answer, but he hoped so. He needed something to take his growing anger out on.

Several minutes passed in silence as they watched for ejecting escape vehicles. None came. Finally, the glowing carcass of the gunship slammed into the ground.

"I'll set down and let you off," Dras said, voice somber. "I feel it best for me to provide overwatch. The Breakers may have cloaked vessels nearby. If I am not in the ship, we will be defenseless."

Without a word, Maxar made his way to the spot Dras pointed at. He didn't look to see if Wake or Jaydon were following.

When he stepped on the circle in the floor, Maxar pulled out his flechette pistol, checking the ammo and energy reserve. Everything was as it should be.

"I'm going with you," Wake said, joining him. "We're doing this together."

Jaydon stepped in the circle as well, saying nothing.

Maxar simply nodded, knowing if he spoke he would break down, that all his resolve to face the consequences of their actions would vanish. The ship slammed down onto the surface, and the next moment, they slid down a chute and onto Lith-elo.

As Maxar rolled to his feet, the smell of hot metal, burning grass, and churned earth filled his lungs. A huge crater stretched out before him, the wreckage of the Breaker gunship at its center. It was glowing, reminding Maxar of a fallen meteor. *Is Tremmilly inside that?* Without further thought, Maxar jumped, sliding down the crater's wall.

The heat of the ship's remains were intense, forcing Maxar to stop. There seemed more energy here than what friction with the atmosphere could account for. *Dras was right about the power core,* he thought, trying to see into the glow.

"I don't think anything could survive that," Wake said, startling him. Brightwing was radiant in the bright light, the color of fresh blood.

Maxar looked up to see Jaydon standing on the edge of the crater, hands shielding his face. "We have to be sure," Maxar replied. He didn't know what he wanted to find, or if anything organic would still be intact. He pushed forward, feeling his skin begin to burn. Maxar fought through the pain, protecting his eyes with one arm as he searched the mangled wreckage. Peripherally, he was aware of Wake's presence, but the other man said nothing.

Finally, his skin began to blister. The intensity of the pain helped him fight off his despair, but Maxar had to admit he could go no farther. A growing pain in his hand reminded him of the flechette pistol. When he looked down, it was glowing dull red. *Probably worthless now,* Maxar thought, tossing the weapon away.

As it bounced across the twisted decking, Maxar saw something deep in the fiery heart of the ship. It looked like a shell of some sort, or a cocoon. The spot was darker than its surroundings, indicating it hadn't absorbed as much radiation.

Maxar took a step forward, knowing it was important. He tried to think of what it could be. *Do the Ashamine have survival pods?* He'd not seen anything like it on the Watch, but his knowledge of military ships was limited.

"You can't go in there," Wake said, his hand clasping Maxar's shoulder. "Let me." The crimson suited figure stepped past. As Wake ventured farther, Brightwing began to shimmer. The crimson paint cracked, shriveled, and fell off. "I can't make it," Wake said, stopping five or six meters from the shape. "Brightwing can't handle this much energy. The ship's core is leaking. Any farther, and its basically a star."

Closing his eyes, Maxar felt the energy surrounding him, the heat of glowing metal, the burning of his skin, the nanites coursing through his blood. *I need you,* he thought, focusing on everything he'd learned in his short time with Dras. *Do your job.* When he opened his eyes, Wake was almost back.

"I have to get her," he said, not sure how he knew it was female, or even who she was.

"Maxar," Wake yelled, "you're going to kill yourself."

"No," was all he replied, taking one step, then another, towards the dark shape.

"Fine," Wake growled in reply, "if you are going into the fires of the dark star, I'll be right there with you."

Maxar took another step forward, feeling the heat increase exponentially. Pain washed over him, and he knew his skin was burning. He focused on the dark shape, and took two more. Thick sweat began to flood from his pores. Without another thought, Maxar darted forward.

When he reached the dark mass, he tried to pick it up, but a beam of hot metal had it pinned down. A second later, Wake was there, Brightwing glowing with absorbed energy. He grabbed the beam, set his feet, and pulled. The metal moaned, bending slightly, but when Maxar tried to pull the cocoon out, it was still stuck. Wake reset himself and heaved. This time, the metal moved substantially and Maxar freed the bundle.

Wake helped him carry the object out of the crater and back towards the Heltasoth ship. When they finally set it down, Maxar realized the skin of his hands and arms was a shiny black. Then he looked down and saw the energy had burned away all his clothes. *It charred my skin,* he thought, wondering that the pain was no worse than a horrible sunburn. *Must have obliterated my nerve endings.* But then, he felt a sensation similar to sweating, and as he watched, the blackness began to dissipate, revealing bright red skin.

"The nanites," he said, looking at Wake.

"I don't know how you're alive."

A cracking sound drew their attention back to the object. Maxar could see the heat shimmering off it, and when he looked closer, he discovered a split had formed in the side. Jaydon inched closer, trying to get a view, but the energy radiating from Brightwing and the object was still high. The surrounding grass began to smolder.

More cracking sounds emanated from within. Something about the exterior material looked familiar to Maxar, but he couldn't think of where he'd seen it before. It wasn't metal, or plasti-glass. *It looks organic,* he thought, reaching down to pry at the crack.

"Are you sure you should do that?" Jaydon asked, stepping farther back.

"It's OK," Maxar said, pulling off the outer covering of material. Before him was another layer, which he also removed. Each additional covering he took off made his heart sink lower, until it became apparent the remaining space would be too small for a human woman. Finally, he pulled off the last shell, shimmering an emerald green that looked like Cazz-ak's exoskeleton. Inside the cocoon, Na-ah-co, Queen of the Entho-la-ah-mines, had curled herself into a small ball.

A bittersweet tide of emotions flooded Maxar as Wake pulled the Queen out of the remains of her protective shell. *Where are you, Tremmilly?* Maxar thought, gazing back into the glowing crater, tears streaking down burned cheeks.

46 – CRASOR

Crasor drummed his fingers on the chair arm, staring at the terminal screen. It displayed the status of the Justice's systems. He barely noticed. *If all is going according to plan, the Descended are attacking the Enthos and Harbingers at this moment.*

Now that everything was in motion, Crasor was beginning to have doubts. You should have gone with them, he scolded, thinking back to when Detri, the Descended squad leader, had reported their discovery of the hidden planet.

Just after he and Gav had taken the Family Council building, Detri's priority transmission pinged on his terminal. "We've found the Entho world, as well as at least four of the Harbingers."

Crasor could barely contain his excitement. "How?"

"With the limitation of time and forces for a physical search, we've been experimenting with a new technique. We listened for abnormalities in the folds of space-time, guessing the Harbingers might be using that technique to observe us. We found one, in deep space. It developed into a system of several folds, a trail. Following back to its source, we discovered a world with humans and bugs."

"And you're sure it is the Harbingers?"

"Not completely, but we know of no beings other than Breakers and Harbingers who manipulate space-time in this way. We are sure, however, that the Entho queen is there."

Crasor smiled, feeling a weight lift from him. "Go, before they realize we've discovered their location and have a chance to escape again. Take the entire squad and capture the Queen." He thought for a moment, considering. "Kill the Harbingers, if they aren't too powerful for you, but don't wage war. Capture the Queen and get out. We can always send troops after I've ended the Exis resistance." If the Descended involved themselves in a prolonged battle, especially with the Entho hive mind nearby, the Harbingers might overpower them. But if they brought the Queen back to Crasor, he could corrupt her, and by extension, the entire species. *The Harbingers would have no allies,* Crasor thought, *and I will wield the power of the hive.*

"Understood," Detri replied, a smile also on her face. "We will do as you command."

Crasor snapped out of his reverie, realizing he was staring uncomprehendingly at the terminal screen. He wished he could check in with Detri, but with no Ashamine relay to hash in that system, direct communication was impossible.

They are too far away to get a real sense of their status. Crasor could feel their existence, but nothing more. He thought about using the dimensional folds to send his consciousness to observe, but whenever he left his body, he was less powerful. *And being close to the Harbingers or hive mind in that state would be dangerous.*

He decided to trust Detri's leadership, knowing she would bring back the Queen. He pulled up a report from Gav, and one from Salla, side by side on his terminal. They both stated Exis-7 was almost entirely under Breaker control. With the Council subjugated, all Family knowledge and technology was at his disposal.

Crasor had tasked Gav to root out the pockets of resistance, and in his report, the promising Breaker said he was almost done. Since all his Descended were gone, Crasor would need to return to the surface to seed the captured humans. *At the rate Gav is developing, he'll soon be able to do that task on his own.*

Salla, with the help of Breaker troops, had dismantled the fusion missile system and was transferring it up to the orbital shipyards. Crasor had toured the facilities, looking for ships in the right stage of production. The Exis yards weren't large enough to produce Tarton class ships, but that was fine. He didn't need anything that big. If he could outfit just one of them with fusion missiles, he would be satisfied.

A chime announced a visitor, and Crasor authorized entry. Karoth strode through the doorway. "I finished preparing the tactical assessment you requested," the squat-framed man announced, saluting even though Crasor told him several times it was unnecessary.

Some human traits persist, Crasor thought, beckoning him to sit down. A prick of pain stabbed Crasor's mind, then disappeared. *What was that?* Blinking hard, he returned his focus to Karoth. "Thank you. Please, continue."

"With the domination of Exis, we now control six systems, although the border worlds of Eishon, Qi, and Taggardt are small and barely worth counting. Exis, Noor, and Psinar are valuable assets, both for resources and personnel." Karoth paused, weighing his words. "In my opinion, even with the additional ships we captured in the Exis campaign, I do not believe we are strong enough to go against either Ashamine-2 or 4. The Founder kept a large home fleet, and despite the chaos and apathy we're witnessing on the Ashamine Network, the commanders of those ships will not easily capitulate."

Crasor nodded, Karoth's thoughts confirming his opinion. Another burst of pain crackled across his mind, making him wince.

Karoth continued, brow furrowing. "We also have the Founder's Light to contend with. It is the last of the Ashamine's surviving Tarton class ships. I couldn't find its location in any record. Based on what little I could discover about its capabilities, it would be a match for our entire fleet."

"It's more powerful than the Justice?"

"By orders of magnitude," Karoth said.

Crasor felt his stomach sink. He'd been so proud of the Justice, of controlling the most dominant ship in the entire Akked. *Blighthearted Founder kept the Light's capabilities secret from me,* he seethed. After abandoning his role as Facilitator, Crasor realized his relationship to the most powerful man in the Akked was not as deep as he thought. *At least I got to feel his heart's last beat when I killed him.*

Focusing back on the present, Crasor shifted to a more productive line of thought. "How should we proceed?" Another wave of pain coursed through his mind, lasting several seconds. Crasor gritted his teeth, hoping this was related to his continued development as a Breaker.

"Sir, are you OK?" Karoth asked, half rising from his seat.

"Yes, yes. I'm fine. Continue."

"With the destruction of Haak-ah-tar and the exclusion of the governing worlds, there are seven primary Ashamine planets remaining. I believe we should capture each of them in turn, from weakest to greatest. If any of the small colony worlds have resources we require, we can invade them on an as-needed basis, but I do not think they are worth the diversion otherwise. Time is of the utmost importance. Perhaps, the government will continue in the stupor that has lingered since you assassinated the Founder. If we keep carving away at their resources, the Ashamine won't have the reserves or ships to resist if they do recover."

"And what about the Light?"

Karoth shrugged. "A large variable indeed. Our best hope is the Forces have it stationed near the Ashamine Primary system, and we can face it when we've built our greatest strength. If we run across it at one of the other Ashamine systems, or they send it after us, there will be extensive casualties."

"Would it be able to withstand fusion weaponry?"

"Unknown. I think it unlikely, but the Founder kept almost

everything about the Light a secret. Even its weaponry is unknown. They may have point defenses that would render the missile cloaking ineffective. The armor may be too strong for us to penetrate. It would take big advances to make those things possible, but as you know, the Founder kept the branches of his government compartmentalized. We won't know until we find the Light, or it finds us."

Silence filled the room as Crasor considered his options. Everything within him wanted to push for the Ashamine governing system, to crush the last vestiges of human authority. *The risk is far too great,* he thought. Karoth's assessment of the Light worried him. *Just when I was beginning to feel our invasion was on stable footing.* The knowledge the Light could worm in system at any moment, obliterating everything he'd built, created a deep terror within him.

"We must work as quickly as possible to capture the seven main worlds," Crasor said finally, fighting not to groan as another stab of pain assaulted his mind. "I leave it to you to decide the order, tactics, and forces required. I will accompany as needed. Otherwise, I'll divide my time between dealing with the surviving Harbingers and developing new weapon platforms based on the Families' knowledge. Some of the earliest converts are developing the ability to seed. If you do not require my presence specifically, you can use them to convert the new planets." It felt odd giving so much control to another Breaker, but he had to do it. *We are growing large and have too many things to accomplish. If I continue to be a part of every invasion, I will be micromanaging and wasting time.*

Another spark of pain shot through his head, but was weaker than the previous ones. He easily ignored it. *Perhaps the phenomenon is subsiding.*

Karoth stood and saluted once again. "As you command," he said, leaving the room.

Settling back into his chair, Crasor thought about the future. *Spreading our forces will also provide redundancy, preventing the Light from devastating us.* Fear still welled up within him when he thought of a ship more powerful than the Justice.

And what does this new pain signal? An ability or a weakness? He sat with his eyes closed, waiting for another wave. *Perhaps I can trace it to its source.* As he thought more, Crasor began wondering if the pains were a sign of an aneurysm or stroke. *The nanites would protect me from that,* he decided, shaking his head.

Crasor's vision blurred. He grasped the arms of his chair. His head begin to implode. Waves of nausea rose within Crasor as the force mounted, grinding and inexorable. *Hold on,* he thought, *it will pass.*

When the pain vanished, Crasor began searching through his mind, trying to find what was wrong. It felt unrelated to the Breaker mind. He scanned his body and consciousness, finding them free of blemish. Looking outside himself, he sensed no space-time intruders. *Not the Harbingers,* he decided, relief overcoming him despite the lingering ache.

What if the Ashamine is attacking somewhere and I'm sensing it through my troops? Crasor slowly searched the mass of the Breaker network, trying to find anything out of place. He spiraled further and further out, losing track of time in the enormity of the task.

Crasor finally realized what might have happened, and a sense of dread overwhelmed him. *Stupid,* he thought. *Should have checked them first.* He looked for the connections to the Descended, but they felt faint and far away. Just as he enhanced the link, agony blasted through it. Crasor's mind nearly shattered, the force of pain a roaring inferno. He felt as if he was plunged into the fires of the dark star, his skin charring. When the experience finally subsided, Crasor discovered the links to the Descended had disappeared.

47 – AZA

"Why don't you believe me?" Aza yelled, the frustration of the last two days boiling over. "You've never taken my side."

"Why do you persist in lying?" her father asked.

"First my brother," her mother said under her breath, "now my daughter." Tears began running down her face.

"If you would have just told the truth at the hearing, perhaps they would have been lenient," her father said, emotionless. "They would have prescribed a penance or an atonement. But no, you had to hold to the wild tale of underworld cannibals." Aza gritted her teeth to keep from screaming. "They have severed you from the Holy Order. What will you do with your life?"

The question hung in the air. Aza realized not too long ago, this situation would have destroyed her. Now, she believed there were much bigger problems she had to face. She almost answered by telling him once again of her fears and suspicions, of the dreadful Miss Shinn and the Sunless Ones, but it was useless, so she remained silent.

"She will have to join the common workforce," her mother said finally, her own words making her burst into a fit of sobbing. Aza wanted to comfort her mother, but knew she wouldn't accept it.

"Go to your room," her father said, pointing angrily. "Meditate on how you've broken the trust of your family, the Holy Order, and the entire Ashamine."

Aza turned and strode to her room, head held high. She closed the door, sat on the bed, but quickly got up, too energetic to sit still.

How can they be so naive? Aza raged, mind churning. *Why do they blind themselves to the truth?* A darker, more painful thought crushed her: *How can they side with the Order against their own daughter?* She couldn't believe it was happening. A pit formed in Aza's stomach as the full weight of the situation settled over her, outrage resolving into anxiety and sadness.

When she'd returned to the Holy Order school, far past the assigned time, they'd questioned Aza. On her way back from the horrible sub-levels, she'd considered lying, of telling them she'd lost track of time ministering to the needy. They would almost certainly believe the story. It worked every time the older students used it as a cover to go to sub-level parties. In the end though, Aza resolved to tell the truth, or at least most of it. *And look what it got you.*

The head of ministrations had scoffed at her warnings about what was happening under the Founder's City. When Aza persisted, the woman had called a disciplinary hearing. Each step of the way, they'd told her that even if what she said was true—which they didn't believe—it was not the place of the Holy Order to involve itself in those affairs. Her parents begged her to tell the truth. Then, as they got increasingly angry, they too had started yelling. When the disciplinary hearing convened, she'd told them about Miss Shinn, repeating the ominous things the horrible woman had said. They'd asked why Aza had been down there in the first place. She'd gotten creative and told them how one of the women in the sub-levels had asked for help in locating her missing son. This easily transitioned into recounting the hasher and his payment requirement.

None of it had mattered though. They hadn't even bothered sending an investigator down to the junction room. "You acted in a manner unfit for a sister of the Holy Order," the head of the hearing had said. "At this age, many acolytes participate in untoward behavior; it is simply the nature of youth. However, when caught in their indiscretions, they speak the truth. This council then sees fit to forgive them. You, Aza Kissawai, have persisted in lies, which reveals an impermissible character flaw. We are removing you from the Order and stripping you of your name. If you cannot speak truth, we will not permit you the honor of a name beginning with A. This council believes it best if your parents cut you off from support, so they do not waste additional resources on a flawed individual. If they choose to keep you in their household, however, that is their right. You will go to a standard Ashamine school, and it will assign you work like the common of your age. We strip you of all titles and rank associated with the Holy Order. We have made note of your behavior in your Ashamine file."

The memory of the hearing threatened to bring tears to her eyes again, not of sadness, but of frustration. *They are all willingly blind! They only see the world as they wish it to be, not for what it is.*

Aza ground her teeth, feeling helpless. *They will not break me. I will not quit.* Aza began packing a small bag, selecting the least conspicuous of her clothes. *And I will not let them take my name!* She knew her parents wouldn't throw her out, but things had irrevocably changed. She couldn't stay here any longer.

But where will you go? The thought made her stop, as despair threatened to take over. Aza imagined Ash, his warm smile. *He'll help me.* Her heart lightened. Then she remembered how he'd said never to contact him again. *But the situation changed. What if he still won't help?* The remembrance of the sub-levels, of the people who lived on little or nothing, flooded through her mind. *I will make a way,* she thought, going into her closet. She pulled out a drawer to retrieve the hidden data square.

Returning to the main area of her room, Aza looked around, realizing this was probably the last time she'd see it. The white walls seemed to mock her, repeating the council member's words about her impurity, about her unfitness to be a priestess. *None of that matters anymore,* she thought. Each time she learned new information about what was happening, she felt additional confirmation about her suspicion of impending doom.

Aza closed the top of her packed bag, grabbed her portable terminal, and cautiously opened her door. Her parents were nowhere to be seen, so she headed down the hall, walking as quietly as possible. She could hear her mother wailing. This made Aza want to go comfort her again, but she knew of nothing she could do. Her mother was mourning for a lost dream, a vanished hope that her daughter would follow her path. Aza was mourning the same thing.

The Ashamine, the Holy Order, my parents: they've all changed, she thought, stepping through the main entrance and out into the Founder's City. *No,* Aza realized, feeling like she had opened her eyes for the first time. *Now I'm just seeing the world for how it really is.* The thought was simultaneously devastating and exciting. *No matter what happens, I can never go back. I will find the truth, will show them I was right.*

***

Sliding into the grimy seat, Aza entered her temporary pass code on the public terminal's prompt. She tried not to think of what people did in these chairs, what she was potentially sitting in, nor that the seat itself was still warm from the one-legged woman who'd left it moments before.

The screen froze for a moment, analyzing her code, before finally giving a list of options. With no Ashcreds, Aza was unable to secure a private room. *This will work,* she thought, happy to have this space. She'd strategically picked a time of day when the terminal plaza was only half full. Most of the other patrons were spread evenly, making privacy difficult, but this particular terminal had a wall on one side and a terminal listing "Error code 00033 – Technician req'd – Queued 597," on the other. *They won't be here to fix it any time soon.*

A timer in the upper right of the display showed she had 29 standard minutes left. Trying to look inconspicuous, Aza removed the data square and its reader from her bag. After plugging the device in, she nonchalantly covered it with the rest of her belongings. Aza waited, feeling time drag by. *What if it doesn't work?* she wondered. *What if he doesn't answer?* She tried to look around and see if anyone was paying attention to her, but so far, they all seemed consumed in their own screens. *I wonder how long I'll have to stay down here.*

Aza had returned to the sub-levels with trepidation, but she knew it was the only place she could pass without scrutiny. After dirtying her clothes, no one took a second look at her, for which she was grateful. Now that she had terminal access, things were beginning to brighten.

Ash's face finally came up on the terminal. "Aza?" he asked, and she quickly lowered the terminal's volume. "I told you, you can't contact me unless it's an emergency." He didn't look angry, but did seem upset.

"I know," she replied quickly, "but this is an emergency."

Ash's lined face stiffened. "What happened?"

Aza told him the whole story, complete with the real reason she'd gone to see the hasher. When she finished, she expected Ash to scold or yell at her, but he said nothing. He just stared into the screen, brow furrowed in thought.

"So the Breakers have made it to Ashamine-2," he said finally.

"You're not mad at me?"

"No," Ash said, his mouth turning up in a tight smile. "I'm furious at Ammi and Amar for not believing you. They are sacrificing your best interests for the Order, but I'm not surprised. Your parents have always been blinded by the Ashamine and its doctrines. I never thought it would go this far, however."

Even though she knew he was right, Aza felt uncomfortable with the negative feelings he was directing at her parents. She changed the subject. "What are Breakers?"

"We don't have time, Aza. If the Ashamine knew you were speaking to me, they'd do more than just expel you from school. I can tell you everything later, but for now, you need to maintain a low profile. No more running around the sub-levels."

Aza felt herself blush. "I'm already there."

"Why?"

"I can't go home, and I have no access to the higher levels."

"Did your parents throw you out?" Ash's voice was tight. "I can believe them siding with the Order's ruling, but that's damnable to the fires of the dark star."

"No," Aza replied, anxiety rising.

"OK, good," Ash said, relaxing. "Well, then you can stay there until I get some things in order."

"No, I can't—and won't—go home. It's too uncomfortable. The way they look at me..." Memories of her parents' disappointment flooded back through her, and Aza fought hard not to cry.

"You'd rather be in danger in the sub-levels?"

"Yes."

Ash chuckled, shaking his head. "I think I understand. OK, well then, I will be initiating an anonymous Ashcred transfer to an account I'll give you access to. It won't be a lot—we can't transfer large sums and stay off the Ashamine's sensors—but it should be enough to get you through a couple days."

"Who is the 'we' you are talking about?"

"Aza, I can't say more. This connection might not be secure, and we don't have time." A list of letters and numbers appeared on the screen. "Here are the codes for the account. Keep them secure."

She quickly transferred them to her personal terminal and erased the larger screen. "Got it."

"Parick," a voice off-screen said, and Ash turned to look. "We've found another ship that fits the profile of a Breaker scout. We need you on the command deck."

"Acknowledged," Ash replied, turning back to Aza. "I have to go. Do as instructed and try not to get into any further trouble, at least not until I get there. Contact me from a different terminal in exactly three standard days from now. I'll let you know what to do next."

Aza felt bewildered. She wanted to ask why the person had called him Parick, of what he was doing and where he was, but she had no time. "I'll do it," she replied. "Love you, Uncle Ash."

"I love you too, Aza. Stay strong, stay safe, and may the wisdom of Azak-so guide you."

48 – CAZZ-AK-TAK

Pain and confusion filled Cazz-ak. He tried to look around, but everything was cloudy. His back felt like someone had raked it with fire. Several of his legs pulsed with agony. Dimly, he heard someone talking. The words made no sense, far away and muffled.

Breakers, he thought, the memory of arcing dark energy shifting back into place. Cazz-ak tried to focus, to fight through the pain, but nothing happened. Even the realization the Breakers were about to kill him and Lothis wasn't enough to lift him out of the haze.

Then, Cazz-ak felt something take hold of his mind. The grip was strong and easily overcame his resistance. Slowly, it tore his consciousness from his body, a rending that added to his myriad of pains. The agony built to a crescendo, then disappeared.

Am I dead? Cazz-ak wondered, trying to understand where he was. *No, I have dimensions. This place is still space-time, but it feels different somehow. Is this a Breaker trap?* He readied himself, trying to summon power despite his exhaustion.

Energy appeared before him, forming into Lothis. Cazz-ak momentarily felt relief flood through him, then he saw the fear and pain on the boy's face. "What's happening? Are you OK?"

"They killed us," Lothis replied. Cazz-ak knew he was speaking mentally, but the boy's voice still carried inflections of anguish.

"Then how are we talking? Perhaps our bodies still live."

"No. I wish that were true. I grabbed your consciousness and fled just as they executed us. Try to find your physical form."

Cazz-ak did so, using the familiar technique he'd learned as a young Entho-la-ah-mine. *Nothing.* This frightened him more than taking on the Breakers had. *My body is gone.* He'd learned to live without the connection to the Great Thought for short periods of time, but now, it too had vanished.

After a moment, Cazz-ak realized the implications of what had happened. He was grateful the boy had rescued him, but with their physical forms obliterated, he wondered what their lives would be like. *Can we even exist in this place long-term?* He'd never heard of such a thing, at least amongst the Entho-la-ah-mines. Death was death, and now he was somewhere in between. *There is nothing to anchor us,* he thought, anxiety growing within him.

They stood silently, waiting for something neither knew. Cazz-ak still expected the Breakers to come after them, but as time passed and nothing happened, the possibility seemed more remote.

"What do we do now?" Lothis asked, still looking frightened. Cazz-ak had to remind himself he was still a child. As Lothis had regained more of his Elrahi self, Cazz-ak had watched him show greater wisdom and understanding.

"As long as we can still function," Cazz-ak said, "we assist the Harbingers and fight the Breakers." Lothis nodded, standing up straighter. "The Queen needs us. We should find her and do whatever we can." Cazz-ak could see his words positively impacting Lothis, for which he was glad, but inwardly he wondered what they could do. *We weren't able to stand against the Breakers with physical forms. What makes you think we can do anything now?*

Shutting doubts out of his mind, Cazz-ak searched for the Queen. It was difficult work. He'd left his body countless times before and ventured to this strange dimension, but things were different now. *Why does it feel so alien?* With no connection to the Great Thought, he lacked a way to reference Na-ah-co's location, had no easy way to find her.

As he looked around, Cazz-ak realized this dimension mirrored the physical world dimly. This was the way it always had been, but he felt his connection was less substantial than before. The real world was farther away, fuzzier, more vague.

"I think we should stay together," Cazz-ak said. "If we get separated, I don't know how we will locate each other. I don't have the spatial referencing I always used before. I feel..." he trailed off, thinking. "I feel untethered."

Lothis nodded.

"We will work through this," Cazz-ak said, trying to comfort the boy. He had no idea how, but he wouldn't let uncertainty crush them.

Taking the lead, Cazz-ak began manually searching for the Queen. They quickly moved through the faint corridors and tunnels, trying to find her energy signature. Cazz-ak had little sense of the passage of time, and he wondered how it was moving in the physical dimension. *Is it already too late? Have the Breakers found her?*

Thinking of the enemy brought up more questions for Cazz-ak. *Can we strike at them from here? Can they attack us?*

"There she is," Cazz-ak said finally, spotting the ball of energy connecting Na-ah-co to this dimension. He checked the surrounding area, but if the Breakers were nearby, their energy did not show up.

"Tremmilly!" Lothis said excitedly. The two were conversing, wisps of energy flowing between them. Just as Cazz-ak was about to add his own love and support, they began moving.

Cazz-ak and Lothis followed, easily keeping up. Just as Cazz-ak had thought of a way to help direct them towards the surface, a dark splotch caught his attention. "Two Breakers," he said, sensing the energy they drained from space-time. *Should have guessed that was the form they'd take.*

"They are heading right for them," Lothis replied, sounding desperate.

Thinking rapidly, Cazz-ak tried to form a shield around the two females. While the barrier materialized correctly, he found it nearly impossible to move it in position around them. Lothis added his power. The barrier slid farther into place, but it was already too late. The Breakers closed in, Tremmilly ran one way, the Queen another.

"Go with Tremmilly," Cazz-ak said, feeling torn between the two females he had committed to protect. Without a word, Lothis obeyed and Cazz-ak could see him repositioning his shield. In the next few seconds, it became evident the Breakers were focusing on the Queen. *Either Lothis' barrier is working, or they didn't come here for Tremmilly.*

Cazz-ak tried to strike at the two female Breakers, to distract or prevent them from seeing Na-ah-co, but his efforts were ineffective. Everything materialized properly, but didn't affect things physically in the way it used to. *What is it about lacking a body that causes this?* Cazz-ak wondered, trying everything he could think of. The feeling of being untethered grew stronger as time passed.

Finally, the Breakers caught up to the Queen. Instead of killing her, they began dragging Na-ah-co towards the Entho-la-ah-mine city. *They are taking her to Crasor,* he thought, cold dread washing through him. *He'll use her to corrupt the Great Thought.*

As they moved through the complex system of tunnels, Cazz-ak desperately tried to think of a way to help. He felt powerless to stop the Breakers. The Queen would rather die at his hand than let Crasor subjugate her, but Cazz-ak couldn't find a way to kill her. *I'm useless.*

When they passed through the city, Cazz-ak watched survivors from the previous battle try to rescue the Queen. The Breakers slaughtered those who got in the way. *Why isn't Felar leading them?* Cazz-ak thought, fearing her body lay amongst the carnage.

After a quick search, Cazz-ak found her, noting she was unconscious, but still breathing. He hoped she would recover from her injury, but Cazz-ak had no time to help or check further. *Thankfully, the departing Breakers didn't see her,* he thought, moving quickly to catch up.

Reaching the canyon, Cazz-ak saw the Breakers levitate themselves up to the rim. Some of their methods of manipulating space-time reminded Cazz-ak of how Entho-la-ah-mines did it, but there was a corruption, a brute forcing, that felt totally foreign to him.

When the Breakers boarded their ship, despair took hold of him. *Can I move fast enough to stay with them? Does it even matter?* Cazz-ak didn't want to leave Na-ah-co alone, so he settled in next to her. *I am with you,* he thought, trying to lend her whatever support he could as they powered up the ship. *We will face this together.*

A small variance in the space-time between Cazz-ak and the Queen caught his attention. It felt thinner somehow, less fuzzy than anything he'd seen so far. As the Breakers took off, he clung to the variance, using it to stay with Na-ah-co. *It is the special bond we share,* he thought, dimly feeling her terror, pain, and grim determination.

I am with you. We will face this together, he repeated, hoping she would hear him. He wondered how long his strength would last.

A huge jolt rocked the ship as a beam of violet energy shot through it. Bulk heads disintegrated, sending debris and shrapnel flying through the air. Bits of white-hot metal lacerated and burned the Breaker guarding Na-ah-co. Cazz-ak didn't understand what was happening, but he could feel the ship falling back towards the surface. *Crashing,* he thought, knowing the Queen would never survive. Energy began radiating from the interior.

You have to protect her, he thought, desperation increasing as the meters between them and the ground decreased. He'd tried everything he could think of. None of it worked. As he attempted to connect more strongly with the physical dimension, he saw Na-ah-co glow with mental energy. The floor surrounding her warped, metal alloy tearing. It bent around the Queen, creating a protective cocoon.

The energy radiating from deep inside the Breaker ship rose, creating a dazzling display of hot metal and emanating particles. She needs more insulation, Cazz-ak thought. The impact will be severe.

Cazz-ak poured what remained of his strength into his link with the Queen. After a moment of intense struggle, he felt the connection widen, allowing him to bond more deeply with her. It wasn't like the Great Thought, or the Elrahi link, but with his diminished strength, it was enough.

While the Breaker ship fell out of the sky, Na-ah-co continued crafting layer upon layer of alloy shielding, adding in thin shells of energy to act as reflective insulation. Cazz-ak sent every scrap of power he had left through their bond, uncaring of the effect on himself. A spark of hope and positivity bloomed within him, the first he'd experienced since death.

49 – WAKE

"Na-ah-co is exhausted, but otherwise, seems OK," Wake said over the comm. He, Maxar, and Jaydon carried the Entho-la-ah-mine queen to the Heltasoth ship's strange entrance and into the vessel.

"What about other Harbingers?" Dras replied.

"No sign of Felar, Lothis, or Cazz-ak," Maxar replied. "I checked the wreckage as best I could. Before the Queen passed out, she said she was with Tremmilly under their city. They got separated just before the Descended captured Na-ah-co. She doesn't know what happened after that."

Wake felt the heaviness of uncertainty weighing on him. *They could all be safe,* he thought, carefully settling the Queen on the transparent bridge, *or they could all be dead.*

"Where should we go?" Dras asked as they arrived on the bridge.

"Take us back into orbit and I'll direct where to land," Jaydon said.

"I can show him, using the nanite connection," Maxar interjected.

"Good," Jaydon replied, "Saves time."

As Dras piloted the ship towards the Harbinger settlement, Wake began thinking about the next step. "We have to find a way down into the canyon. I don't think it likely we will get Entho-la-ah-mine help."

"I could use the phase drive to get through the narrow spots," Dras said, "but based on what I sense from Maxar's experience, there is no place large enough to land."

"Yeah, I don't think we'd fit," Maxar said, biting his lip.

With the Queen settled in, Wake stood. *How did she and Maxar survive that much heat?* He looked from one to the other. Maxar looked like he had the worst sunburn Wake had ever seen, but was otherwise unharmed. *His nano-machines are so powerful,* Wake thought, remembering how they'd covered him like a black skin. Maxar's abilities reminded him of things Crasor was capable of. *Good thing Maxar is on our side.*

Wake still felt stunned they'd gone into the inferno of the downed Breaker ship and survived. Looking down at the gauntlet of Brightwing, he realized the formerly crimson suit was now a burnished golden color. *At least that is closer to its name.*

"Huh?" Wake said, realizing Maxar had been speaking to him.

"Can you think of a way to get down to the Entho-la-ah-mine city?"

Wake thought for a moment. "At first I theorized Brightwing could fly, but that was just hopeful dreaming." He paused. "With the density of Lith-elo's atmosphere, I think we might craft a parachute."

"Where will we get the materials?"

"I can do it with what is available in our village."

"We set down there first, get the materials on board, and hop over to the canyon. There is no time to waste. We don't know what trouble the rest of the Harbingers might be in."

***

"Burn the Breakers in the fires of the dark star," Maxar uttered. The Entho-la-ah-mine bodies stretched out before them. Wake fought hard against nausea. He wanted to turn around, to leave this horrible scene, but Maxar pressed on. He knew they had to find their friends. *But if all these died, why would any Harbingers be alive?* Four Breaker corpses stood out amongst the hundreds of shattered Entho-la-ah-mine carapaces.

As they passed through the main cavern, Wake saw a bit of movement in the edge of his vision.

"Survivors," Maxar said, heading in that direction. When they arrived, a small group of Entho-la-ah-mines approached, coming out of smaller sub-caves.

"Have you seen the Queen?" one of them asked, voice sounding surprisingly strong in Wake's mind.

"We have your friend here," another said.

"Yes," Wake answered.

"Where?" Maxar asked simultaneously.

"The Queen is OK," Wake continued, as one of the Entho-la-ah-mines led Maxar inside a small cave. "We rescued her from the Breakers. She is asleep on our ship, unharmed."

"Get in here," Maxar ordered. Wake did so. When he entered the small space, he found Maxar and a group of Entho-la-ah-mines surrounding Felar. She wasn't moving.

"What's wrong with her?" Wake asked, feeling his heart beat harder. He'd known this was a possibility, but hadn't believed any of his friends could be dead. *Not her,* Wake thought, feeling a sadness deeper than he could explain.

"She led us to victory," one of the Entho-la-ah-mines said reverently, "but then, just after the battle, she collapsed. We believe the leader Haltro is under the effect of the calath plant."

"Will she be OK?" Wake replied, realizing she was still breathing.

"We do not know. She has been here for some time. We bandaged her wound and watched over her, but there is nothing more we can do. The Great Thought does not understand human biology enough to stop what the calath is doing to her."

"We need to keep searching," Maxar said. "Will you continue to protect her?"

"Yes," the Entho-la-ah-mine replied. "As the battle raged, some of us saw Tremmilly, and then later, Cazz-ak-tak and Lothis, descend into the caverns below the city. None of them have returned. Only two Breakers and the Queen came out. We tried to stop them, but there weren't enough of us left."

"Thank you," Maxar said, ducking out of the small cavern. "We appreciate your help."

"Wait," Wake said, torn between following him and staying. He didn't want to leave Felar's side. "We can't just abandon her."

"Do you want to carry her? There is nothing we can do. The Entho-la-ah-mines are watching over her. She won't be alone. Stay here if you want, but I have to keep looking for Tremmilly." Wake couldn't think of a response, so he kept his mouth shut and followed Maxar.

When they had crossed the rest of the expansive cavern city, they found the small tunnel heading downwards. It was dark, allowing Wake's mind to conjure up horrible images of his friends, disemboweled, eyes staring into infinity.

Forcing the thoughts away, Wake activated Brightwing's illumination points. Maxar did the same in his own suit, casting off the darkness. As they wound deeper and deeper into the maze, Wake was glad for Brightwing's terrain mapping feature. *No wonder none of them have come out,* he thought, the monotonous tunnels blending together.

"We could cover more ground if we split up," Maxar said, "but I don't think I could keep track of where I've been, or how to get out." Wake nodded his agreement, glad that despite his anxiety, Maxar was staying calm.

As time passed, Wake lost himself in the search. They descended deeper and deeper. Occasionally, he'd pull up the HUD map to make sure they weren't in a tunnel they'd already searched.

"How are we ever going to find them?" Maxar finally asked, breaking the silence. "This could go down klick after klick. It could take days." Before Wake could reply, he felt a flare of energy burst in his mind.

"Tremmilly!" Maxar exclaimed.

Wake didn't quite understand how he could sense her, but there she was, above and to the magnetic north of them. "We're too deep."

"Can you find the fastest way back up?"

"Yeah," Wake replied, quickly highlighting a path in his HUD. When he was sure of the route, he began running along it.

Even with the energy leading them, it still took quite some time to locate Tremmilly. The tunnels twisted and turned so erratically it made heading directly towards her impossible.

"She's still alive. She's still alive. She's still alive," Maxar kept repeating to himself. Wake hoped there was a positive explanation for why they hadn't sensed Cazz-ak and Lothis, but he couldn't think of one.

"We are so close," Maxar said, hurrying ahead of Wake. "Tremmilly?" he yelled. "Tremmilly!"

"I'm here," Tremmilly replied, entering their illumination from a side corridor. Her cheeks were red and blotchy, streaked with tears. She ran forward, directly into Maxar's arms. "I tried," she sobbed, "but they took her. They took the Queen. And they killed them. What are we going to do?"

"It's OK," Maxar said, hugging her tightly. Wake felt he was invading a private moment, but he didn't know what else to do, so he brought up Brightwing's HUD and began plotting the way out. "We rescued the Queen. The Breakers are dead. We shot down their ship."

"Really?" Tremmilly said. "She's OK?"

"Yeah, Na-ah-co is exhausted, but fine. She created a mental field and wrapped metal around her like a cocoon. Between her energy and lots and lots of thin layers, she insulated herself from the crash."

"I'm glad to hear it, but that isn't everything, Maxar."

"What do you mean?"

"Lothis and Cazz-ak," she trailed off, looking down.

Wake felt his heart drop, and Tremmilly's renewed sobs seemed a fitting soundtrack for the news.

"How do you know?" Maxar asked.

"They're just around the corner. I can't... I can't go back."

Without a word, Wake went in the direction she pointed. He had to know for himself, even though he didn't doubt her. The Breakers had evolved, were now more powerful than ever before.

When he turned the corner, Wake confirmed all his worst images. Cazz-ak and Lothis lay sprawled across the tunnel. They'd broken the Entho-la-ah-mine, two legs missing and another obviously fractured. His exoskeleton was shattered, exposing internal organs. Lothis appeared in better shape, but his stillness indicated something was wrong. They were both dirty, covered in rock dust, burnt and lacerated from some terrible weapon. When Wake looked into Lothis' face, he saw the cause of death. The Breakers had destroyed his eye, and by the look of the wound, driven a blade into his brain. Farther down, a Breaker corpse lay crumpled on the uneven floor, a wide hole passing through his torso.

Wake felt numb. "Need to sit down," he breathed to himself, collapsing in a heap as he attempted to do so. He felt tears coming to his eyes and did nothing to stop them. Sobs wracked Wake's body, grief pouring out uncontrollably. *What will we do now?*

50 – FELAR

"Get in here," Felar heard an unknown, yet familiar voice say.

"What's wrong with her?" another voice asked. It too was recognizable, but she couldn't remember its owner's name.

Who are they talking about, I wonder?

"She led us to victory, but then, just after the battle, she collapsed. We believe the leader Haltro is under the effect of the calath plant."

Felar felt overwhelmed. There was too much happening, too much stimulation. She tried to force the voices away, but doing so made them draw closer. They boomed and echoed in her mind, causing swirls of color and sensation to course through her body.

"Wait. We can't just abandon her." This voice was close, and it brought comfort.

Without warning, a giant void of darkness swallowed Felar. *Alone,* she wailed, fear and anxiety flooding her. The ever present burning in her chest faded, as did all other bodily sensations. Her negative feelings evaporated as she drifted away. A small part of her mind tried to assert itself, to be an observer, but that too vanished.

Before Felar, a ball of energy materialized. It was dazzling, emitting a radiant intensity that threatened to overwhelm her vision. The ball unfolded, growing larger and larger. She wanted to move forward, to join with it, but something held her in place. It spoke no words, gave no commands, but Felar knew it was not time yet.

The unfolding light took shape, its form hard to see because of the intensity. *A flower,* Felar thought, her heart aching from its beauty.

"We did the best we could." Felar turned to see the speaker, surprised someone else was here.

"Lothis?" she asked. "How did you find me?" He was as she remembered from the Elrahi memories, older than his human form and with blue eyes. He wavered, edges fuzzy, energy dissipating.

"I'm sorry," he said.

"What do you mean?" Felar found it hard to concentrate on his words, even harder to form responses.

"The Breakers killed us."

A stab of fear shot through Felar. The flower of energy began retreating, and with it, the rest of her good feelings. "No, no, no," she said, feeling herself accelerate backwards.

"They destroyed our bodies," Lothis yelled. "We don't have a way back."

Felar began to sob, not understanding what was happening. She just wanted to stay with her son.

"I could surrender to the Dawn," Lothis said, now just a tiny speck, "but I don't think Cazz-ak is strong enough to get here. I won't abandon him!"

The flower disappeared in the distance, and with it, her son. In next instant, she was back inside the facility under Haak-ah-tar, the one she'd rescued Lothis from. *No, impossible,* she thought, *this was destroyed by the supernova.*

"Met! Met! Met!" Director Kasol chanted, blood smearing his cheeks. Behind him, the monstrosities danced, maws drooling in anticipation. The group advanced on Felar, and she sprinted away. When she looked back, they were still right behind her. *I'm not moving,* she thought desperately. Kasol grabbed her arm, dragging it towards his gaping mouth. She pulled as hard as she could, but his grip was inexorable.

Just as his teeth were about to break her flesh, Felar felt the scene shift. She was laughing, gathered with the rest of the Harbingers on the filthy deck of the A'tal's Revenge. Happiness coursed through her, a feeling like warm sunlight on a beautiful day. She smiled.

A knife descended towards her face, and Felar brought up a forearm to block. Searing pain exploded near her elbow, but she shut it out, bringing up a knee to strike her attacker. The air was humid and close. Her view was obscured by huge ferns, trees, and vines. *Taggardt-6,* she thought, even as her strike landed in her opponent's midsection. Before he could recover, Felar aimed a kick at his knife hand, sending the synthdiamond blade flying off into the undergrowth. After tackling the man, she put him in full body restraints.

"En-3 subbed," she said over her comm, even as her perspective shifted.

Blackness swallowed her again and the burning returned. Felar screamed in agony, feeling the horrible sensation over her entire body.

"She isn't metabolizing the plant's chemical compound," a voice said through her haze of pain.

"Can you help her?"

"My knowledge of human anatomy and medicine is lacking."

"You said you thought you might help."

"Indeed. But you must remember, despite my appearance, I am inorganic. My solution uses nano-machines. I must introduce them into her blood. I will try to reverse the procedure afterwards, but there may be complications. Is this permissible?"

There was a pause, and for a moment, Felar wondered if she was leaving her body once again.

"Yes," a lighter, female voice said finally. "Do it. We have no other option."

The pain in her leg soared. Felar screamed. But then, through the agony, a coolness developed. It spread. Slowly, her pain subsided. Her screams turned to whimpers. Felar calmed. The surrounding voices faded into deeper blackness.

***

Felar's eyes fluttered open, and daylight dazzled her.

"I think she's waking up," Tremmilly said, voice close. When Felar looked around, she could see her friend sitting less than a meter away, hovering in midair.

The battle, my troops, the Harbingers, she thought, trying to sit up.

"Relax," Tremmilly said, placing a hand on Felar's shoulder. "You've been through a lot. Dras says he got the poison out, but we don't know how it impacted you." Felar tried to remember what had happened, but her mind was a hazy mess of jumbled memories and sensations.

Wake approached, looking fatigued. He smiled at her as he strode above the top of the grass. A weight she didn't fully understand lifted from her mind. "Glad to see you're awake."

Felar ignored the oddities of the situation, hoping she wasn't still in a dream. "You look like you've been buggered and blighthearted in the fires of the dark star," she replied, trying to grin.

Chuckling, he sprawled out in the air next to her bed. "I think that's exactly what happened to me, to all of us in fact."

"Where are Lothis, Cazz-ak, and Maxar? And the Queen? Did we save her? And Jaydon?" Felar sat up with the hazy intention of going to find them all. The motion made the room spin. Tremmilly reached out to steady her. Felar closed her eyes, but the memory of darkness was intolerable, so she opened them again and gritted her teeth through the vertigo.

When it finally subsided, Felar realized Maxar, Jaydon, and another, unknown man had appeared, standing above the grass. The new person was plain and bald, with a medium build. When she saw his eyes, Felar knew she was still in a dream. *Black?* she wondered, unable to look away.

"Felar," Tremmilly said, "this is Dras. He extracted the poison from you."

"Thanks," she said.

"You are welcome," the robed man replied. "I believe you won't suffer any lingering effects from either the poison or the nano-tech I utilized to get it out, but I want to monitor you closely."

Felar felt a stab of fear. *Nano-machines? Inside me?* Both her Elrahi memories and the stories the Ashamine told had always made them sound destructive and harmful. *But Maxar's had them inside him for months. He is healthy and strong.*

A new thought occurred to Felar, and she forgot about the nano-tech. "Why aren't Lothis and Cazz-ak here?"

Silence met her question. Everyone looked uneasy. Tremmilly's face scrunched up. Tears began to run down her face. "They're gone," she sobbed.

Numbness settled over Felar. Logically, she knew she should be crying, that she had lost her son in addition to a good friend and powerful ally. A memory tickled the back of her mind, but it was too vague to make sense. "What happened to them?" she asked.

"We don't know for sure," Wake said, sitting up, "but it looks like they were battling a couple Breakers, down in the tunnels under the Entho-la-ah-mine city."

"They put up a good fight," Maxar added, not meeting her eyes. "We saw indications both sides utilized powerful weapons."

"Where are their bodies?" Felar asked, feeling her wall of numbness threaten to collapse.

"You don't want to see them, not as they are now," Jaydon said. "Won't be good for you. Let us put them in the ground."

"No," Felar said, anger flaring. "Just tell me where in the blightheart they are!" She started to rise from the bed, the effort renewing her dizziness and nausea.

"They're outside," Tremmilly replied, helping her up, "we put them by the village ruins."

"Can't be real," Felar whispered as Tremmilly and Wake helped her rise. "Just another dream." As they walked, she saw her feet hover a meter above the grass, just like everyone else. A circle appeared in the air and they stood on it. Felar's perspective shifted, her stomach protesting violently. After the world stabilized, she saw they were standing in the grass. A dark mass above drew Felar's attention. With a sudden realization, Felar understood they had been on a ship. *Not a dream. All real...*

As they crossed the plain, Felar had to stop every ten meters or so, her body wracked with dry heaves. Tremmilly stayed at her side the whole time, holding her steady and speaking words of comfort. After a particularly hard retching fit, Wake returned and added his support. Felar was grateful. She didn't think she could make it any other way.

Then Felar saw them, two Ashamine body transport capsules. *Forgot we unloaded those off the Watch,* she thought, trying fruitlessly to steady her legs. Tremmilly and Wake set her down before the black containers. She wanted to ask who was in which, but her throat hurt and she didn't trust her voice. Besides, Felar couldn't decide which she wanted to see first anyway. *Doesn't matter.* Both had been special to her, for their own reasons. *Lothis,* she thought, hand hovering over the latch of the left capsule, *I loved you so much. You were the son I never had, unexpected, yet treasured.*

Her other hand hovered over the right container, and thoughts of Cazz-ak rushed to her. *You were a strong ally, a close friend, a treasured teammate.* She'd grown close to him as they'd trained the Entho-la-ah-mine troops, developing a relationship Felar found deep and rewarding. *I failed you,* she thought, *I failed you both.*

She hit the latches simultaneously. The lids slid back to reveal mangled bodies. Felar's breath caught, but she held back the tears that threatened to destroy her composure. Their injuries were obvious. Felar couldn't help but assess them like the soldier she was. *Blast damage,* she thought, seeing Cazz-ak's missing limbs. *Direct brain trauma,* Felar told herself, noting the hole through Lothis' eye. The ingrained assessment routine helped disconnect her from the situation, but when it was over, all the pain and agony rushed back in.

Despite everything, she felt the earlier tickle of memory growing. Something about seeing the bodies triggered a powerful recollection, dragging her back into one of the calath experiences.

"They're not dead," Felar announced.

"Felar," Tremmilly replied, taking her hand. "I thought the same thing about Psidonnis, but you just have to—"

"I'm not saying their bodies aren't dead," Felar replied, feeling exasperated, but understanding why Tremmilly had misunderstood. *You'd think you were crazy too.* "I saw them, while I was dreaming or whatever the calath poison did to me. We were all around a flower, made of energy."

"You saw the Dawn?" Tremmilly said, eyes wide.

"Yes, but I knew I shouldn't join it. Lothis was there." More of the memory came flooding back as she spoke of it. "He told me the Breakers had killed them, destroyed their bodies. Lothis said he could join the Dawn, but that he wouldn't because Cazz-ak wasn't strong enough to do the same. He didn't want to abandon him."

"That's too coincidental to be a dream," Wake said, looking thoughtful.

"What if they—I mean their consciousness—left their bodies before they died?" Felar felt hope surge within her as an idea sparked.

"I've never considered that," Tremmilly said, "but it seems possible."

"They might exist between the dimensional folds or something," Felar said, looking towards Dras. The odds of her plan succeeding were small, and they relied almost completely on this unknown person. *Bad odds are better than impossible ones,* she thought.

51 – GAV

Gav shoved the pointy fingers of his left hand into the diplomat's gut. The woman let out a guttural *oof* as she fell to the floor, convulsing. A smile tugged at the corners of Gav's mouth as he moved on to the next person. He'd discovered this bunker after gaining complete control of the Ashamine Network on Exis-7. From what he could tell, it contained the last humans on the planet. He stabbed two more of the Ashamine cowards, relishing their conversion, then realized he'd finished his task. *Over too soon.*

Looking down at his bloody fingers, Gav marveled at the rapid changes occurring over the past few days. The Families declared him a traitor. He'd become a fugitive and stopped a nuclear bombardment. Then, an alien species promoted him to leadership. *And now you've evolved the power to spread their seed and make converts of your own.*

Exiting the bunker, Gav got on the lift to take him up to the surface of the remote, artificial island. He could hardly believe such a thing existed. Gav had learned many secrets, both Ashamine and Family, which had astounded him.

His squad of troops boarded the lift behind him. The door shut and they shot towards the surface. Those who remained would take charge of the new converts and make sure they got back to the Exis-7 mainland safely.

As the lift settled to a stop, Gav braced himself for the inevitable storm. *Blighthearted ocean,* he thought, wishing he was back in the city. *Rainy there, but at least the weather is a little better.* When the door opened, a gust of wind knocked Gav and the rest of his squad off their feet, sending them sprawling inside the lift.

The bad weather had intensified by orders of magnitude. For a moment, he considered riding back down and waiting for better conditions, but he could see his ship anchored to the deck just thirty meters away. *Any delay will look bad,* Gav thought, getting to his hands and knees. *Salla will hold Crasor's attention, and she'll advance more quickly.*

Squinting his eyes against the driving wind, Gav stood and stepped out of the lift. The wind screamed a fury greater than he'd ever experienced, but this time he was ready. Gav leaned into the gale, trying to ignore the sting of driving rain. He had to keep his head down, eyes slitted.

Glancing back quickly, he saw his squad following. They were imitating his technique, shuffling through the storm, trying to maintain balance.

Finally, Gav reached the airlock of his starship. Thankfully, despite the intensifying storm, the wind had not changed direction and the airlock was still leeward of it.

Gav was leaning into the wind as he ducked behind the ship, nearly falling over as its bulk shielded him from the gale. After recovering his balance, he looked back at his struggling troops. They were still fighting the wind, although it blew a few down in the short time he watched. He waited the additional minute it took them to reach the airlock.

"Tell those still down in the bunker to wait until the storm subsides," he commanded as he headed for the flight deck. *I don't want to think about how those uncoordinated new converts would do out in the storm.* "Get the ship powered and take me to the fleet as quickly as possible."

Gav went to his stateroom and changed his wet clothes. As he did so, he marveled at the dark metallic hand that had replaced the one shot off during the Family Council assault. It was stronger, quicker, and more sensitive than the original appendage. Small splotches of black metallic skin were appearing on other parts of his body as well. *Just like Crasor,* he thought, smiling.

As he dressed, Gav considered what he would say for his report. With Crasor placing both him and Salla over important tasks, Gav felt it was a competition. He'd pushed hard to subdue the planet, hoping to finish before Salla could dismantle the missile system and send it up to the orbital yards. *I have to be first,* he thought, sitting at his terminal.

He selected the icons to contact Crasor and then waited. A few moments later, the Breaker leader appeared on his screen. Gav clenched his jaw when he saw Salla standing next to him.

"The subjugation of Exis-7 is complete," Gav said, trying to keep his face neutral. Salla's knowing smile brought forth rage, lust, and envy within him. "I'm on my way to the fleet."

"Good," Crasor replied. "Send me the location of those bound for seed, and I will go when it's convenient."

"I just seeded the last human holdouts. You need not trouble yourself." Gav wanted to smile, but Salla would see his pleasure as weakness. He kept his face placid instead.

"Really?" Crasor said, eyebrows raised. "You and Salla are evolving almost as fast as I did." The horrible woman brought her right hand out from behind her back, revealing pointy fingers. Gav's jaw tightened. "Well then," Crasor continued, "I suppose we are ready to resume our advance across the Akked. With the destruction of my Descended at the hands of the Harbingers, I will be relying on you two to take their place. I want to keep you close, to guide your development. Already, you are almost as strong as any of the Descended. With more time and proper training, perhaps you will be ready to face the Harbingers."

Crasor's words made Gav feel both excitement and dread. He was elated to work directly with the Breaker leader, but having to do so alongside Salla would present challenges. *Just kill her when you get the first opportunity.*

You can't, the logical side of him protested. *It would anger Crasor.* A tightening in his crotch signaled there was more to it than that. Gav fought hard to keep the turmoil from showing on his face, but evidently, he didn't do a good job.

"Something wrong?" Crasor asked.

"No, not at all."

"Alright. As I've told Salla, I've sent Karoth off with the main fleet, including the Justice. He will capture what remains of the smaller Ashamine worlds while we focus on the Harbingers, Enthos, and weapon development."

Gav felt disappointed. He wished he was attacking the Ashamine core, rather than chasing individuals or managing shipbuilding. *Do as he tells you. Your time will come.* Salla was doing just that. Gav's stomach churned as he thought about competing with her.

"Understood," he replied, nodding.

"Come to the primary orbital dock," Crasor said. "We have much work yet to break the Dawn."

52 – CAZZ-AK-TAK

Cazz-ak felt exhausted. His connection to reality was fading. At first, it had just been the link to physical space-time, but now it extended to this dimension. *I'm untethered, lost in the universe,* he thought. *Nothing is binding my energy together.*

After the Breaker ship crashed, he'd watched a strange vessel land next to it, black hull wavering between solid and liquid. His heart had broken, thinking it a Breaker transport. When Maxar, Wake, and Jaydon jumped out, he'd felt rejuvenated. They'd pulled the Queen from the wreckage, moments before the inferno would have killed her.

The strange ship shuttled the Queen back to the edge of the canyon, taking her to the Entho-la-ah-mines. Cazz-ak wanted to follow them down, to stay by her side, but he couldn't go fast enough. The exhaustion had only deepened from there.

Eventually, he and Lothis had reunited, discovering Felar's consciousness in the process. She flitted from dream, to reality, to dimensional travel, confusing them both as to what was wrong with her. Cazz-ak was too exhausted to keep up. Lothis, concerned for her, pushed himself, following through a dimensional fold.

"I don't know how, but she found the Dawn," he said when he'd returned.

Excitement bloomed in Cazz-ak. "You could go back, join with it. It is salvation."

"We will go together," Lothis said. "Can you make a fold? I will lead you there."

Cazz-ak tried, but it kept slipping away. He gathered what was left of his energy and tried one last time. Cazz-ak couldn't even crease space-time, let alone fold it.

"Blightheart," Lothis said, lips in a tight frown.

"It's OK," Cazz-ak replied. "Go without me."

"No," the boy said flatly, "I won't leave you."

"We will both die if you don't."

"I'm not going to abandon you."

After that conversation, they'd become silent. Cazz-ak used the last of his waning energy to follow his friends inside the strange ship. *If I can't go to the Dawn, at least I can be with them.* They'd left and returned once, making him panic. Now, they surrounded him once again, bringing comfort that helped stave off despair. He watched as their conversations moved energy back and forth, although he couldn't understand what they were saying. *I love you all,* he thought.

Cazz-ak tried to find Lothis, but his vision had become too blurry. Everything was vague and hazy, growing darker by the moment. He tried to speak, tried to reach out to find the boy, but he was too weak to do either. *Hopefully, Lothis goes to the Dawn before it's too late.*

More time passed, and soon, Cazz-ak couldn't sense anything outside himself. *Not much longer,* he thought, knowing just a fragment of his energy remained. *Will the Dawn greet me? Or blackness?*

53 – LOTHIS

Lothis felt himself dissolving, evaporating into a dark abyss. *So tired,* he thought, trying to find Cazz-ak. The Entho-la-ah-mine had vanished into the black haze along with everything else.

I should have listened to Cazz-ak, he thought, knowing he was now too weak fold his way to the Dawn. Still, it had been worth it to stand by his friend, to not let Cazz-ak face the blackness alone. Now, Lothis had to do just that.

Why am I still struggling? It would be simple just to let go, to disappear into the universe, to let his energy feed entropy.

Not yet, Lothis thought, holding on tight despite the overwhelming pull.

So much easier to surrender. Moments passed, how long Lothis couldn't sense exactly.

The time is not right, he thought, trying in vain to catch one last glimpse of Tremmilly, Felar, Cazz-ak, Wake, or even Maxar. *Nothing.* The inexorable tug of the abyss intensified, and Lothis knew he could resist no longer. *Perhaps we will meet again, in yet another life,* he thought.

Just as he was about to give himself to darkness, Lothis saw a bright flare. It cut through the gloom like a synth-diamond sword, breathing energy and connectivity into him. *My body,* he thought, seeing it lying in the grass outside a strange ship.

There was a moment when the pull between the abyss and his body equalized, and Lothis felt his consciousness splitting in two. Then, the blackness let go. He rushed towards his prone form, feeling the joy and elation of life fill him.

Lothis opened his eyes with a start, a myriad of sensations exploding in him. There was much pain, in his head, right eye, and to a lesser extent, the rest of his body. He sat up, bright light dazzling him.

"Easy," Felar's voice said, and he felt hands steadying him. Once

Lothis' vision adjusted, he saw Tremmilly kneeling next to him. His field of view seemed strange, so he turned his head to the right and saw Felar. He felt ecstatic to have them close again, one special to his Elrahi life, the other to his human.

The realization he'd lost sight in his right eye hit him, but the fact he'd returned after being dead mitigated the sadness. *I'm alive,* he thought, hugging first Felar, then Tremmilly.

They both helped him stand, his legs wobbly and unsure. When he was finally on his feet, he felt dizzy. Tremmilly and Felar stayed by his side. Beowulf stood before him, facing away. He looked like he was on watch, body stiff and ready to attack.

Each movement Lothis made felt foreign, like his body was a familiar place, but someone had changed the decorations or lighting. He didn't know what to make of it. *There are more important things to think about.*

Lothis looked eagerly for Cazz-ak, excited that they'd somehow survived such a traumatic experience. He saw Maxar, Jaydon, Wake, and an unknown person standing around something on the ground, but the Entho-la-ah-mine was nowhere to be seen. Lothis had noticed the unknown man through the blackness, but given the state of his cognition, he'd thought perhaps he'd been hallucinating.

"Who is that?" Lothis asked.

"His name is Dras," Tremmilly said, her voice upbeat, but containing an edge Lothis felt unaccustomed to. "He brought Jaydon, Wake, and Maxar back from Traynos-6."

As Lothis studied the figure more, he could sense unusual, dense energy emanating from him. With Dras standing next to Maxar, everything made sense. "He is a machine," Lothis said.

"Yes. How did you know?" Felar replied.

"His energy is identical to Maxar's in several aspects, although it is stronger." Lothis looked down at his own lacerated and bruised arms. "And now it radiates from me."

"It was the only way to fix you," Felar said, the look on her face ambiguous. Lothis could usually read her, but the combination of fear, excitement, joy, and trepidation made it difficult to know how she really felt.

"Are the nanites permanent?"

"Dras said the damage was too extensive to ever remove them. They've created systems inside your brain to replace the damaged structures."

Lothis could see why Felar felt so many emotions. "Am I corrupted now? Is this the perversion of the Dawn we've seen in Elrahi memories? Am I now just like the Breakers?"

"No, I don't think so," Tremmilly said, biting her lip. "As you've said,

Maxar has similar technology inside him, and he is still a Harbinger." Lothis wasn't sure if he believed her, but there was no way to know at this point, so he put the thought out of his mind and refocused.

"I need to see Cazz-ak," he said, a feeling of dread creeping through him. He began taking jerky steps towards the other group. Tremmilly and Felar were silent, adding to his feeling of unease.

Jaydon saw his approach and stepped aside, a weak smile on his face. "Glad to see you're back." Lothis nodded his reply, afraid to speak. His throat felt tight and gritty.

When Lothis entered the circle, he saw Cazz-ak, as expected. He was still maimed, missing two legs, but the cracks in his exoskeleton were now just scars. "I've done all I can," Dras said, his voice deep and rich.

"He should be back by now," Lothis said, his dread turning to panic. "I'm back. I found my way to my body. Why hasn't he?"

Silence answered, and Lothis pulled away from Tremmilly and Felar, falling onto his friend's body. "You're right here," he yelled, feeling tears course down his cheeks. "Come back!"

Time passed. Cazz-ak remained motionless. "I don't think he's coming," Maxar said, voice cracking.

"His body is whole, at least enough to support life," Dras said, "so that is not the problem. I do not understand the dimensional space you explained to me, but perhaps something went wrong there."

"He gave everything to protect the Queen," Lothis said, breath coming in short, ragged gasps. "We split up, he with Na-ah-co, and I with Tremmilly." He paused, futilely trying to regain control of his emotions. "Once we rejoined, Cazz-ak told me of his tiredness. I felt it too, but I think he'd used up so much of himself. I only had to shield Tremmilly for short bits before the Breakers left. He had to strengthen the Queen through the entire crash." Lothis kept hoping his friend would move, that at any moment Cazz-ak would return to his body, but as time passed, his hope turned rancid. *You were on the edge of death,* Lothis thought, tears falling onto Cazz-ak's emerald green back. *But you held out for so long.*

Finally, he had to admit Cazz-ak really wasn't coming, that the abyss had swallowed him. Lothis closed his eyes, released his emotions, and let himself sob. *Goodbye Protector,* he thought. *Goodbye teacher. Goodbye friend.*

54 – MAXAR

"For the Heltasoth, integration with their nanites is as seamless as a human and their blood," Dras said. "We do not provide conscious thought to make them function. I believe that is a skill you need to continue developing."

Maxar looked out across the plain, fixating on the mountains momentarily before turning back to Dras. "Are their any weaknesses I should know about?"

"As you mentioned earlier, strong magnetic fields, but they have a much greater impact on you than I, so my best advice is just to avoid them. It must be something with how the nanites integrate with your body."

"And there is nothing else you can think of to help me utilize their power better?"

"I think I explained everything I could on our way here. With the stories you've told me and what I experienced during the battle, it seems you have implemented it well and are making discoveries of your own. You protected yourself from both a rail round and overwhelming radiation. You've given yourself strength in times of need. Perhaps, with Lothis' addition, we'll all learn faster." Dras paused, looking thoughtful. "Before we came to this system, the Heltasoth had never heard of humans. Now, our technologies augment two of the species. I will continue to work with you and Lothis, if he wishes. But as I said before, it is a partnership, rather than a mentorship."

"Yeah," Maxar said, "let's just hope we all live long enough to keep learning." He felt grim and negative. *Body removal will do that to you,* Maxar thought, remembering the past few days. Entombing thousands and thousands of Entho-la-ah-mines had taken a toll on him, both mentally and physically. It had on all the remaining Harbingers. The Queen had officiated numerous ceremonies. Entho-la-ah-mines from other settlements across Lith-elo had traveled in to help. They'd filled up numerous sub-caverns with bodies and unidentifiable parts, sealing off the entrances in the Entho-la-ah-mine custom.

Just one more left, Maxar considered, thinking of Cazz-ak. They'd all been in shock, Lothis most of all. A lot had happened to the boy: fighting Breakers, almost dying, resurrection by alien technology, and losing his best friend and mentor. *He'll survive. He's strong.*

"What will you do now?" Maxar asked.

"I have asked myself the same thing each day as we moved deceased Entho-la-ah-mines. Historically, the Heltasoth have only been observers. That is the reason I originally stayed in the Akked. Now, I'm not so sure. The Breakers are irrational, like a virus. They are growing, seeking to infect the entire galaxy. I'm sure they won't stop once they dominate the Akked. Given enough time, they will find Heltasoth worlds. With each individual, planet, and species they dominate, our chances of stopping them diminish. The Ashamine have some power left, but their people are apathetic and unwilling to stand. Perhaps that will change before it's too late.

"I want to learn more about you Harbingers. I offer my assistance in whatever actions you take against the Breakers, if you feel I would be helpful."

"You've already been an asset," Maxar replied. "I would love for you to join us. I'm sure everyone else will feel the same as well."

"Very good," Dras replied. "Then may I ask what our plan is?" Maxar had been thinking about the future as he'd collected and moved bodies, his mind trying to insulate itself from the horrible task.

"The Breakers have our location. They found Lith-elo-hi-rosh and know where the Queen is. I think we have to evacuate, get Na-ah-co to one of the other hidden Entho-la-ah-mine worlds. Then we cannot go near her. It's just too dangerous. You heard Tremmilly's story about how the Breakers found this place. We can't risk that again. Cazz-ak thought if the Queen was ever corrupted, their hive mind would fall, becoming part of Crasor's power." Maxar shook his head, thinking of how close the Breakers had been to capturing Na-ah-co. "You saw their cloaking technology. I got lucky in overcoming it. Next time it might not go so well."

Dras nodded, the bluish light of Lith-elo primary shining off his bald head.

"After we help with the evacuation," Maxar continued, "I think we need to develop a plan to offensively strike at Crasor and the Breakers. We've been defensive the whole time, running away."

"Understandable, given the odds you've faced."

"Agreed, but it is no way to win a war. Even though we face superior numbers, we can create a strategy utilizing that fact." Maxar's gaze once again turned to the mountains. "It's going to take a while for us to recover."

Dras said nothing, simply nodding.

"Cazz-ak was one of the strongest. His death will leave a wound in the Harbingers."

"I'm sorry I didn't repair his body in time."

"You are not to blame for that. No one is. Cazz-ak sacrificed himself to protect the Queen. That was the kind of individual he was. And if he hadn't, the entire race would have fallen, and the Akked with it. It was a worthy sacrifice."

***

"Blightheart," Felar cursed, pacing back and forth across the trampled grass. "We shouldn't have split up. It was a buggering mistake. Now we've lost vital personnel and equipment. Cazz-ak is dead and the Death Watch is gone. We have no way to replace either."

They were all gathered under the rudimentary shelter Wake had constructed. He'd been able to salvage enough building materials from the wreck of their village to create a temporary structure. Maxar appreciated having the shade, but he hoped it wouldn't fall on them. Every time the breeze shifted, the roof creaked ominously.

"It's easy to look back and say what we should've done," Maxar interjected, "but we did the best we could with the available intel." They'd already talked about a myriad of subjects, debriefing and covering everything that had happened since the Death Watch left Lith-elo. Felar was growing increasingly angry, and while he understood she was grieving and scared, her mood wasn't helpful. *Uncharacteristic for Felar.*

"I know that," she fired back. "I've been in battles and war before, Maxar. You're not the only one who sees the tactical situation."

Maxar raised his hands, deciding he wasn't the right person to calm her down. He glanced at Tremmilly, eyebrows raised.

"Felar," she said after a moment, voice calm, "going to Traynos and splitting up obviously weakened us, but it was a calculated risk. It paid off and now we have a powerful ally." She paused, and Felar remained silent. "When we went after the Arche, it was a similar situation. They attacked us on several occasions and it was just a matter of time before they found a weakness and exploited it. You believed we should strike back when we did, to protect Maxar and Wake while they were gone. You did a fantastic job leading the offensive and we now have one less enemy. Our entire effort can now be focused on the Breakers, our true foe."

Felar opened her mouth, but Tremmilly kept speaking. "I grieve for

Cazz-ak, as we all do. I shudder at the thought of how close we came to losing Lothis and the Queen. Lothis is my brother, and Cazz-ak a friend since birth. But this is war, and as you know more than any of us, Felar, people die in war.

"Cazz-ak's sacrifice was not in vain. We eliminated the Arche and an entire squad of Descended. I believe Crasor sent his strongest troops, and we killed all nine of them. Yes, we had losses, but as you mentioned, we split up. Now, we better understand how our strength works. His tactic will not surprise us again. We will stick together and focus our energy."

Looking down at the ground, Felar nodded slowly. "I'm sorry," she said. "You are both right. I've lost people before, but never someone so close."

Wake moved next to Felar and put his arm around her. Lothis did the same.

"Your anger is understandable," Tremmilly continued, "but direct it at the enemy, not at us, and certainly not at yourself. As Maxar said, we made good decisions with the information we had. Now, we have more knowledge and will change tactics accordingly."

"Since Crasor knows our location," Jaydon interjected, looking at each of them in turn, "we need to get off Lith-elo. He could be sending ships here at this moment."

"Agreed," Tremmilly replied, nodding. "Any plan we make must involve the Entho-la-ah-mines, however. The Queen will meet with us once she has recovered sufficiently. I would like to have a tentative plan ready when we do. The time for hiding has passed. Now, we must go on the offensive."

Tremmilly's tone and bearing made Maxar feel proud. She'd regained her strength as Empress, leading them confidently.

"Fade needs our help," Lothis said quietly. He'd barely said a word since coming back from the dead. His right eye was cloudy and sightless, a constant reminder of the boy's loss, both physical and emotional.

Maxar wished there was something he could do to help him, but didn't know how. *He has Felar and Tremmilly,* he thought. Jaydon was also trying to help, sometimes just sitting silently with him as he stared into space.

"He's stuck in the same dimension Cazz-ak and I were in," Lothis continued. "After helping us defeat the Arche, he folded his way back to Exis-7, looking for his body. He couldn't get close to the planet though. The Breakers are there."

"Blightheart," Maxar said, stiffening. "Exis-7 is a Family controlled planet. Has he ever mentioned his last name?"

"Yes," Lothis answered. "It is Alenthos. Why would that matter? Who or what is the Family?"

"It's what the organized crime calls itself. The Families are who I worked for back on Noor-5. It's been a long time since I've been a part of that world, but I think I remember Alenthos was one of the smaller groups."

"Oh," Lothis replied. "Well," he continued, barely audible, "if we don't help him, I think he will completely vanish."

Maxar felt bad he'd crushed the boy's hopes. "Even if he was one of them, that doesn't mean he's evil. Some people were born into that world and just had to survive. Some do it because they are sadistic blighthearts. Many are in between. We just need to be careful until we know his motives."

"Has he told you anything about himself?" Dras said, head cocked in the perfect imitation of human inquiry. "What happened to him? How was he separated from his body?"

"Fade said he doesn't know exactly, but that someone trapped him inside a computer. They made him work for them, tortured him when he didn't. The Arche got him out, although with what we overheard, it sounds like they were trying to enslave him as well."

"Somebody actually created a quantum human," Maxar said, remembering the hologram he'd encountered during the Nex-Delta job. "It's technology the Families have wanted for years. When they sent me in to destroy a competitor's quantum project, I ran into a hologram claiming it was human." Maxar thought for a moment, putting things together. "Nex-Delta released its QC years ago, and there has been no talk of quantum humans since. Either they gave up after I destroyed it, or the hologram was a manipulative AI. Since Fade is Family, that means one of them figured out how to put human consciousness inside a computer."

"Just like how the Arche downloaded themselves," Tremmilly said, scratching behind Beowulf's ear. For a brief moment, Maxar thought he could feel her touch behind his own ear, but then it was gone.

"So what do we do?" Wake asked. "It seems like we owe him for helping us with the Arche, although I suppose it benefited him as well."

"He needs a storage system," Lothis said, brightening, "a way to contain his energy. I think his quantum existence on Exis-7 was similar to our experience in the Arche's dimension. That gave me an idea. I told him he could go back to the Arche's computer and live there, but he is too afraid they might return and capture him. He is not diminishing as fast as Cazz-ak and I were, but he says if we can't help him, he'll be forced to try."

"Yeah," Felar said, "I have to agree with him. It doesn't seem like the best idea. Who knows what kind of backups or traps he might trigger."

"I know," Lothis continued, "but neither of us can think of another option. We do not have access to any quantum computers. Originally, I hoped the Great Thought might accept him, but with his criminal status, that seems foolish. Besides, I'm not even sure it would work."

"Perhaps I might help," Dras interjected. "Heltasoth systems function on a quantum level. Based on what I have learned in my interactions with you, Felar, and Maxar, I think my ship might be compatible. I would need to implement proper firewalls, but Fade could occupy a portion of what you think of as my ship's computer."

"Really?" Lothis replied, the excitement on his face at odds with his dead eye and scarred arms.

Despite his earlier encouragement, Maxar wondered if this was a smart idea. They were allowing a big unknown into their midst. *Trust Dras,* he thought, *he's proven himself enough already. If he says he can securely keep Fade, then there's nothing to worry about.*

"Of course. It is another opportunity to study humans, as well as a unique phenomenon. The space I create for him will feel like a prison. Since I have no reason to keep him captive, Fade will be free to leave at any time."

"You're sure he won't be able to take over the ship or lock us out?" Felar asked, some of her earlier intensity returning. "If he does, we're all stuck here."

"I appreciate your concern," Dras said calmly, "and it is warranted. Fade was enslaved by a human. The only way he escaped was through the Arche's help. I don't feel he would be powerful enough to overcome my security measures. While it certainly is possible, it is unlikely in the extreme."

"Perhaps," Felar replied, "since the Breakers have conquered his world, he might be persuaded to join the war. I don't know how a quantum human could help, but the Arche had a similar existence and still caused plenty of problems."

"I'm sorry to interrupt," Tremmilly said, rising to her feet, "and I know this is an important conversation, but it's almost time for Cazz-ak's ceremony. I propose we meditate and prepare before it begins."

Everyone agreed and the group split. Maxar embraced Tremmilly in a long hug. When he released, there were tears in her eyes. "I will be strong," she whispered. "I have to be."

"You are," he told her, wishing she could see herself the way he did.

"Thank you," Tremmilly replied. She hesitated for a moment "I would like to be by myself before the ceremony. I need time to meditate." Maxar nodded, giving her another hug.

He watched the group disperse, glad for some alone time. His mind needed a break from the constant strain, both from within and without. Maxar gazed at the faraway mountains, trying not to let his mind summon images of mangled Entho-la-ah-mine bodies. He traced the ridges and saddles, the snow-covered gullies and plateaus. Finally, he relaxed, although a deep part of him still brooded.

When they reconvened near the canyon's edge, Maxar could see the same weight he felt hanging on everyone else. The beautiful day and gorgeous setting did little to lighten it.

Maxar studied each of those gathered: his friends, a vast group of Entho-la-ah-mines, the Queen. While planning the ceremony, they'd explained Cazz-ak's position as a Protector to her. Elrahi custom was to travel the universe after death, but since he was also Entho-la-ah-mine, they hoped she would compromise the two. Tremmilly suggested they bury and memorialize him on the surface of the planet. The Queen agreed.

"I owe my life and existence to Cazz-ak," Na-ah-co began. "Several times he protected me. In the end, he gave his life to save me from corruption and servitude. I can never repay him, never reciprocate the gift he bestowed upon me. We will forever remember him as the greatest warrior and savior of the Entho-la-ah-mines. The Great Thought will always honor him, even after a million generations pass."

Silence fell over the group, as her words finished echoing in Maxar's mind. Wake stepped forward from the circle and bowed his head. "He was my friend, my ally, and stronger than I can ever hope to be, both in wisdom and in action. May the Dawn harbor and protect him." Looking embarrassed, Wake returned to the circle.

Felar and Lothis moved inward, the boy clinging to her arm. He looked gaunt, like the child Maxar had met when they'd rescued him and Felar from the Hammer's escape pod. All strength and confidence he'd gained since then seemed drained from him.

"Cazz-ak..." Lothis said, trailing off. He began to cry, unable to continue. Lothis looked down at his feet, still clinging to Felar.

"Cazz-ak," she said, "had the best qualities of us all, without any of the negatives. May the Dawn harbor and protect him. May the light of a million stars illuminate his soul. May his energy always be a part of the universe." Felar stepped back, wrapping Lothis in a tight hug.

Tremmilly joined their embrace for a full minute, before finally stepping away. She walked into the midst of the circle, kneeling before the monument Wake had created over Cazz-ak's tomb. It was a bright cube crafted of metal and palos tree wood, a fitting blend of Elrahi and Entho-la-ah-mine cultures.

Leaning her head down to touch the surface, Tremmilly spoke. "You were the greatest of Protectors, both of the Entho-la-ah-mine and the Elrahi. Thank you for following me into this strange existence, for giving everything. You could have gone to the Dawn, but you chose instead to watch over me, just as you have since I was a child."

Maxar couldn't look away from Tremmilly. She was so beautiful, her mannerisms and speech the same as when she'd been Empress of the Accord. He'd fallen in love with her as an Elrahi, and once again as a human. *I would give everything to protect her.* He felt a connection to the rest of the Harbingers, and thought of them as friends, but none would ever mean as much to him as Tremmilly.

"I give you honor in death, as I did in life, Cazz-ak-tak, Tha'sis, Protector," Tremmilly continued. "May you find the Dawn. May you find peace. May you unite with the energy and power of the universe." She stood, returning to embrace both Felar and Lothis. Silence once again descended. Maxar thought about speaking, but they'd said all the words, and in a better way than he could say them, so he just stood. After a minute of silence, the ceremony ended as informally as it had begun. The humans and Entho-la-ah-mines dispersed.

Tremmilly walked over to him, tears in her beautiful green eyes. "Grove?" she asked.

Maxar took her hand, nodding.

55 – TREMMILLY

As they entered the palos grove, Tremmilly felt relief flood through her. Her mind had been racing for the past few days, unable to find any rest as they dealt with the aftermath of the Descended attack. Cazz-ak's memorial had been the final event. It was over. *But really, it's all just begun.* Tremmilly's mood stayed elevated, despite the realization.

"Your words were a fitting honor for Cazz-ak," Maxar said as they walked to their spot. Beowulf followed behind, his gait easy, but still alert.

"Thank you," she replied. Her grief for their fallen friend was still strong, but he had died protecting the Queen. He would have given up his life just as easily for her, if it had been required. It was his nature, his path in life, both as an Elrahi and an Entho-la-ah-mine. Tremmilly would always have a place in her heart for him, remembering Cazz-ak with honor, gratitude, and joy.

"There is something I wanted to ask you." Maxar sounded on edge, but Tremmilly didn't understand why.

"Of course."

He paused as they settled into the embrace of their tree, spongy moss making the massive root structure comfortable. "About the Elrahi memories," he said, hesitating. Tremmilly let out her breath, realizing what he was about to say. "You still want to be with me, even though you are an empress and I'm a criminal convicted of a planet wide massacre?"

Tremmilly bit her lip, trying not to laugh. Despite everything that had happened, or perhaps because of it, she felt happy to be back with Maxar, in a familiar, safe place. "Of course I do," she replied, smiling. "I believed your story and pardoned you then. That still stands in my mind. I accept you for what you are, as both human and Elrahi."

"But you're an empress. You directed a government leading a million worlds."

"And that means I can't love you?"

"No, but—"

"I don't know how people saw me when I was Empress," Tremmilly said, trying to recall fuzzy memories of the Accord, "but I was not a slave or figurehead. I made choices and the councils respected them. They didn't always agree, but I had the freedom to be myself. It's part of the reason they selected me as Empress. If I wanted to pardon you and take you as a lover, that was acceptable, although I'm sure they didn't agree. In this life—well, it doesn't really matter what anyone else thinks."

She leaned into Maxar and kissed him, feeling her body relax as he embraced her.

"Everything about you is so beautiful," Maxar said, his skin warm against hers. "How could you love someone like me? How could you want to bond with me for life?"

"Because, despite the trouble you've gotten into in two different lives, you're still an amazing individual. You're talented and smart. And," she said, pausing, "you love me."

"That I do." He leaned back, and they settled into a comfortable position cradled amongst the roots. Tremmilly looked up at the canopy, sky barely visible between interlocked leaves. Her mind wandered, trying to make shapes out of the pattern of gaps.

"There is no place in the entire Akked I'd rather be right now," she said finally. Maxar didn't reply. When Tremmilly turned to look at him, she realized he'd fallen asleep.

Returning to enjoying the world around her, Tremmilly rested her head on Maxar's shoulder. The weight of what lay ahead of them hovered on the edge of her mind, but Tremmilly didn't let it bother her. There would be time to handle it later. For now, she just wanted to enjoy the peace of this grove and the warmth of her lover. She breathed in deeply, feeling her own eyelids grow heavy.

Tremmilly slid into the twilight between wakefulness and sleep. Just as she was about to drift away completely, a distant flare of energy startled her. Before she could resist, her consciousness was drawn towards the object. The shape blossomed and grew, its radiation dazzling her. As seconds passed, it resolved into a familiar shape that brought Tremmilly immense joy. *The Dawn,* she thought, drawing as close as she could to the expanding flower.

As Tremmilly watched, though, a feeling of dread rose within her. Several of the normally majestic petals were dark and wilted. What's wrong? She'd never seen corruption blemish the cosmic entity, not even during the height of See'dek's rebellion.

The stain brought back all her feelings of helplessness and fragility. *I've led my friends to destruction,* she thought, knowing if she was still in her body, she'd be sobbing. *The Breakers killed our most powerful*

Harbinger. Crasor and his forces are stronger than ever. Nothing I've done has even slowed them down. I've failed! I've ruined everything!

The cosmic flower flared once again, bathing Tremmilly in energy. It felt like her people were there, a quadrillion Elrah all supporting her. She knew it was only a metaphor, her mind's way of explaining how the Dawn functioned, but she still felt empowered.

Tremmilly's anxiety and fear faded, replaced by grim determination. *Nothing will stop me,* she thought, *not even death. I will protect you all. I will do whatever it takes. No matter what, we will succeed.*

###

Want a free, exclusive Dawn Saga short story?

Subscribe to my newsletter, and I'll send you *Jaydon*. I'll also keep you updated on new Dawn Saga releases and short stories:

http://zachariahwahrer.com/jaydon

Dear Reader,

Thank you for investing your time in my fiction! If you enjoyed this book, I'd really appreciate it if you would share the experience with your friends and leave a review online at your favorite retailer.

If you'd like to get in contact with me, you can email:
zachariah@wahreroftheworlds.com.
My website, **www.zachariahwahrer.com** is a great way to find more of my writing. If you are more of a social media person, I'm on:
Facebook: www.facebook.com/ZachariahWahrer
Twitter: www.twitter.com/ZachariahWahrer
and Instagram: www.instagram.com/ZachariahWahrer

May the fires of the black star be quenched in your life,
Zachariah Wahrer

***

ABOUT THE AUTHOR

Zachariah Wahrer spent the first twelve years of his adult life doing various jobs around the United States, such as eBay salesman, punk rock musician, horse halter craftsman, and rock climbing gym route-setter.

Near the end of 2014, Zachariah moved into a Honda Odyssey with his wife, Sarah, and began traveling the United States and Canada, seeking inspiration and adventure while writing and rock climbing full-time. His first novel, Breakers of the Dawn: Book 1 of the Dawn Saga, was electronically published in December of 2014.

When not deeply immersed in imaginary worlds, Zachariah loves to experience the outdoors as well as read about science, futurology, and trans-humanism. He also enjoys home-brewing and creating digital art to accompany his writing.

While writing this novel, Zachariah lived in Bozeman, MT.